NERO

ALLIANCE BOOK ONE

S. J. TILLY

To all my ladies who see those walking Red Flags as a pretty shade of pink... repeat after me, only when the men are fictional.

Dear Reader

This is an adult dark mafia romance. There is graphic on page violence, death, and kidnapping. There is on page past emotional trauma and physical abuse. There are instances of dubious consent and extreme stalker tendencies. As well as a man who is basically a walking red flag. Please proceed well-informed and with caution.

CHAPTER 1

Payton

A RED AND GOLD LEAF FLOATS ACROSS THE ROOM, seemingly weightless, before settling onto the carpet between my spot on the couch and the TV.

I glance at my open patio door where another gust of wind brings the scent of promised rain, but instead of getting up, I tuck my legs underneath me and pull my fleece blanket up to my chin, careful not to tip the bowl of popcorn resting on the cushion next to me.

A storm is coming.

You spoiled brat, I'm gonna teach you...

I snuggle further into the corner of my couch. *That was so long ago,* I remind myself, inhaling deeply through my nose, willing new memories to replace the old.

This is my home.

I'm safe here.

The low rumble of distant thunder calms me further.

No matter how much they tried to beat it out of me, I never lost my love of violent weather.

I never understood why I was supposed to be scared of storms. Didn't understand why it made me different, or wrong, or stupid--like they claimed.

It wasn't the violence I craved, it was the change. The washing away. The cleansing. That smallest sliver of hope that a wave might crash through, dragging away the old, leaving something new.

And maybe that's why I still like them. There's still that spot in my chest, deep inside of me, that wants to be sucked up into the sky, whisked away from it all, and dropped into Oz.

As if summoned by the wind, the woman on screen opens her front door and the world around her morphs from black and white to color, and I let the familiar sense of nostalgia wash over me.

The sounds of the nearing storm keep filtering in and out of my awareness, even as I sway my head to the familiar songs.

My hand is halfway to my mouth, popcorn between my fingers, when the dull noise of groaning metal drags my gaze to the patio, the sliding glass door open wide.

The gauzy curtains I installed last year are flowing eerily with the breeze, but the streetlamp outside is burnt out, so I can't see beyond my tiny balcony.

I've never really trusted that balcony, it's as shabby as the rest of this building. But I figured it'd take more than a little inclement weather to knock it down.

I give myself a mental gold star for never bothering with furniture out there as I lick the salt off my fingers.

Another roll of thunder, closer this time, draws my attention back to the balcony.

And the man standing in my open door.

CHAPTER 2

Payton

A SCREAM CATCHES IN MY THROAT, TOO STRANGLED TO be heard.

I'm dreaming.

My eyes squeeze shut, and I force myself to breathe.

I must be dreaming.

But when I open them again, the man is still there. And coming closer.

The man crosses half of my apartment in two long strides, putting him only feet away.

Adrenaline courses through my body, yet I don't move.

To my own humiliation, I don't do anything.

There's a man in my home.

Aside from the television, the lamp in the corner is the only light on. And it does little to illuminate the man in front of me.

He's tall. I'm sitting but I can tell he's tall. And... he's wearing a suit.

Why is he wearing a suit?

Does that make this worse?

"Evening." His voice is deep. But gentle. Soft even. And my brain doesn't know how to react.

My heart is racing.

My hands are shaking.

But the rest of me doesn't move.

"You know," he says, as he takes a few slow steps, crossing in front of the TV. "You really shouldn't leave your door open like that."

My lips part, but my words get jumbled on my tongue and I have to swallow before trying again.

"I'm on the second floor," I whisper, still trying to understand what's happening.

He tilts his head, and it feels like he's humoring my response, but I can't focus on that. Because the angle allows the light to fall across his features. And...

Dark eyes. Dark brows. Nearly black hair tousled yet styled back, and sharp cheekbones outlined with a trimmed beard in the same shade.

I swallow again.

He looks like he came from a photoshoot. Or a boardroom. Or a photoshoot of a boardroom. And an inner voice is shouting at me that that should make this even scarier.

Should.

I also notice that his clothes aren't wet, which means the rain hasn't started. And for some reason, that saddens me. Like that detail alone seals my ruin.

This is why I've always been such a victim.

My instincts are broken. My mind always steers away from the important parts. Zeroing in on ridiculous details, and not on a game plan.

Keeping his body facing me, the man glances around my apartment.

I don't know a lot about men's suits, but I'm guessing his clothes cost more than all my belongings put together.

My stuff isn't fancy, and it looks just as cheap as it is. A second hand couch and scuffed coffee table. The small TV on a cheap stand I had to assemble myself with an Allen wrench. My round table with one chair, tucked in the corner. And a thin stretch of island designating the divide between the living room and kitchen. A kitchen that's more of a kitchenette, complete with laminate counters that are peeling at the edges.

I resist the urge to sigh at the sight of my phone sitting on said kitchen counter. Mocking me with the idea of calling the police, knowing I'll never get the chance.

Not that they've ever helped me in the past.

My single bedroom and bathroom are on the other side of the kitchen, but darkness swallows them.

The man makes a noise in the back of his throat as he takes it all in. I have no idea what he's thinking. Or why I should be so anxious for his approval. Like there's anything in this sad setting to approve of. Or any benefit if one's murderer likes their apartment.

A police siren wails outside.

Then another.

And a moment later, I watch the flash of red and blue lights bounce down through the night as cop cars speed past my building.

Slowly, I turn my gaze back to the man facing me.

He lifts a shoulder, and the edge of his mouth pulls up into a smirk.

This man is running from the cops.

He's running from the cops and he's standing in my living room. Like nothing is amiss. Like he just decided to take a different route home.

His body shifts and I think that maybe that's all this will be. The police have passed by, now he can leave.

But he lifts a foot and steps closer.

Panic starts to flare brighter inside me, hitting its flash point, when another gust of wind lifts the edge of his suit jacket.

Oh god, he has a gun.

He doesn't reach for it though. He just... lowers himself onto the couch.

My couch.

Beside me.

Once again, my mouth opens with nothing coming out.

What is he doing?

What is happening?

"I love this movie," he says, almost to himself.

What. In. The. Hell. Is happening?

His large body fills up too much space on the couch. All my furniture is small. Small because my apartment is small. Small because it's only ever me here.

I sit frozen, wondering if I should say something, but he keeps his focus on the tv.

Is he... is he just gonna stay here?

I start to shift, wondering if I can just get up and slip away.

"I'd rather you didn't get up." He doesn't turn his head when he says it, his tone casual. But there's no hiding the fact that it's not a request.

My breathing picks up, as I remain facing forward. Prickles running up and down my arms.

Great, now *my animal reaction decides to catch up to the situation.*

There's no question that this man is dangerous.

And he's too close.

I never let men get this close.

My entire body starts to tremble. "Please don't—" I cut off my plea, not wanting to put my specific fears into words.

I can hear the rustle of fabric as he starts to turn toward me, and I squeeze my eyes shut.

This can't be happening.

This can't be real.

"Relax."

A large hand settles on my thigh, and I stiffen even more.

The weight of his palm is alarming, the heat of his touch searing me through the blanket.

His hand presses down with a little more force. "Relax."

His tone is even gentler this time, and I try to take a steady breath.

A dark scent fills my nostrils. It's leather and fire and cologne.

Jesus, is that him?

My eyes slip open.

He's leaning toward me, invading my space further, and the stance should feel dominating. But there's something in his body language, or maybe it's something in his eyes, that makes my body obey. Makes me relax, just a little.

His gaze travels over my face, and this close, I can see a tinge of green in his eyes. They're stunning.

His eyes move back to mine. "I'm not going to hurt you."

When I don't reply, he tips his head down, a command implied with the movement.

"Okay." I mostly mouth the word, my voice too quiet to hear, but he nods anyway, a pleased look crossing his features.

Pleased that I believe him?

Do I believe him?

His hand slides off my thigh, taking the heat with him. "May I?"

May you what?!

Before I have time to start spiraling, he lifts the bowl of popcorn from the spot between us.

Oh.

Without waiting for an answer, he settles back, props his feet up on the coffee table and sets the bowl on his lap. Then, casual as ever, he drapes one arm across the back of the couch, fingers nearly touching my shoulder, like he's here for a date and not a home invasion.

I watch as he starts to eat the popcorn, whole handfuls at a time, never dropping a single piece on himself.

I should do something.

There must be something I should do.

His jaw works as he chews, the muscles in the side of his neck flexing.

I mean I know I should leave. Or make him leave. But how?

With my eyes still on his profile, waiting for whatever's going to happen next, I hear the character on the screen talk about courage. And I wish more than anything I had some.

"What's your name?"

I jump when he speaks, then bite my lip. "Um... I don't think I should tell you that."

I see his eyes flick over in my direction. "Clever girl."

Those two syllables bounce across my skin.

My fingers tighten around the blanket, pulling it even higher.

I can't find this man attractive.

I really can not.

My stomach clenches and my stupid brain takes this moment to remind me that I probably look like a disheveled mess.

Not that it matters. I don't need this intruder to think I'm sexy. In fact it's probably better that he doesn't. It's probably better that I have popcorn breath and a ponytail that needs adjusting. And bangs that are going every which way since they got damp when I washed the makeup off my face before sitting down to watch my favorite movie for the four-hundredth time.

The fingers near my shoulder tap against the backrest, keeping in time with the characters on TV as they skip down the road.

This has got to be the weirdest thing that's ever happened to me.

A hot as hell man walks in through my second story balcony. Strolls through my apartment with a confidence I can only dream of having. Flashes me a glimpse of his gun. Then settles in to eat my popcorn.

And... is he humming?

Sweet Mother Mary, he's humming.

With careful, small movements, I push myself further into the corner. Trying to add any amount of distance I can between us.

I want to ask his name. Ask him what he's running from. But I feel like the less knowledge I have, the better.

Except you've seen his face, my inner voice unhelpfully reminds me.

Not knowing what else to do, I stare at his profile. Watching the way the light dances off his eyes. The way his mouth opens and closes around handfuls of popcorn. The way his shoulders seem relaxed.

He seems so at ease. So... comfortable.

My lids lower in a slow blink and I force them wide.

I can't make out the clock on the microwave from here, but I know it's past my bedtime. I didn't intend on staying up for the entire film because waking up at five a.m. every weekday means I go to bed early. And I haven't been sleeping well this week. Hell, I haven't been sleeping well the past twenty-seven years.

He chews another mouthful, and I watch the movement of his Adam's apple as he swallows.

Maybe this really is all a dream.

Maybe I'm already in bed, sound asleep.

CHAPTER 3

Nero

I CAN SENSE HER EYES CLOSING.

Sense her muscles loosening as sleep pulls her consciousness away from me and the situation I've put her in.

And it makes me furious.

This soft creature shouldn't let her guard down. Not around a stranger.

Not around me.

My fists start to clench, but I stop the urge. I'm in control.

I'm always in fucking control.

My fingers curl around another handful of popcorn and I shove it into my mouth.

I know my anger is misplaced. I told her to relax. Told her I wouldn't hurt her. She's done nothing wrong. Except trust me.

She should absolutely not trust me.

Her body finally gives up the fight, and her head lulls to the side. Her lips nearly brushing the backs of my fingers. Her breath a warm caress on my skin.

For too long I watch her.

Stare at her.

Observe her.

Her lashes flutter in her sleep, dreams affecting her although her body remains unmoving.

She's a temptation; even with her body hidden under the blanket, I can tell I'll like the rest of her. The softness of her cheeks surely continues down her frame.

The women I'm often seen with, the ones I'm expected to be with, don't look like her. Don't look innocent. Or sweet. *Or fed.* They usually look exactly like the vipers they are. That they need to be. Because my world isn't a place for sweet innocence. My world is the dark pit that sucks all the light and goodness out of everything it touches.

A small sound crawls out of her dream. One that's too close to distress. Before I can stop myself, I'm reaching out.

The pad of my thumb ghosts over her bottom lip. The flesh feeling as delicate as it looks.

Get a fucking grip.

Snatching my hand away, I stand. My movements silent.

I need to leave.

I should've left the second the cop cars drove past.

Popcorn bowl in hand, I walk to the small kitchen.

The counters are clean. Everything is in its rightful place, just like the living room.

Setting the bowl down, I unplug her phone and pick it up. Tapping on the screen, it scans my face, before displaying a number pad.

Figures she keeps this *locked.*

"Who are you, Sweet Girl?"

I trail the fingers of my free hand across the fronts of her cupboards. I know better than to leave fingerprints, but can't fight the compulsion to leave a mark. To leave some sort of trace behind. Even if she can't see it.

Then my eyes snag on a small stack of mail tucked between an unplugged toaster and the wall.

"Got you."

I pick the envelopes up, reading the name and address on the unopened ones.

Hello, Payton Vawdrey.

Pretty name, for a pretty girl.

Carrying on with my inspection, I step up to a tiny table hosting an ancient laptop, and—I reach out and touch the leaves —a fake plant.

I grit my teeth.

Why does her fake plant make me so goddamn angry?

Because I've lost my fucking mind.

It's time to leave.

My feet turn away from the table, and I walk deeper into the apartment.

The dark hallway—you can barely call it that—is only long enough to have one doorway on either side.

Stepping into the bathroom, I flip on the light.

It's small and clean, as expected, the visible dinginess inherent to the age of the building and not to her cleaning skills.

The room is filled with the same lingering scent I thought I smelled earlier.

What is that? Flowers?

I open the medicine cabinet, finding a few items. It's mostly makeup and some over-the-counter medications, but no perfume. Nothing to tie the smell to.

The shower curtain is pulled closed. It's a vibrant yellow, matching the floor mat in front of the sink. An attempt at cheeriness in a windowless room.

I drag the curtain back, revealing a variety of bottles lining the edge of the tub. My eyes catch on a clear bottle with a black top, half full of a dark pink liquid.

I press the back of the lid, popping it open, and inhale the rich scent of roses.

It's her.

Exiting the bathroom, I cross into the one and only bedroom. More yellow. More clean sparseness.

I'm not surprised by the fact that her bed is made. There's something about this woman that compels her to keep everything in its place. Something I respect.

The closed closet door beckons me. And I'm not one to deny myself, so I pull it open.

This is not like the wardrobes I'm used to seeing. I'm used to walk-in closets, clothes worn once, some never worn. Abundance.

This is not abundance.

That place long-dead inside of me gives a beat.

I haven't forgotten what it's like to live without.

I'll never forget.

Just like I'll never go back.

Leaving everything as I found it, I make my way back to the living room.

Years of practice lets me get close to her without making a sound.

She looks so calm.

I should walk out now, leave her be.

Leaning in closer, I hold out her phone and wait for the facial ID software to allow me in.

CHAPTER 4

Payton

A RAINDROP ROLLS DOWN THE BACK OF MY HAND, *beading on my fingertip before falling to the carpet.*

"Such a stupid girl."

"I'm not stupid!" The shout is out of me before I realize what I've done.

A large, weathered hand shoots out, gripping my throat. Cutting off my air.

Stop.

I think the word, but I can't say it.

I can't speak.

My fingers claw at the hand, nails scratching at flesh, catching on that damn gold pinky ring he wears. But it's useless, I'm not strong enough to break his hold on me.

"Not stupid, huh?" the man sneers.

Darkness starts to spot my vision, my eyes rolling wildly, looking for help. But the only other person here is my mother. And even the small unbroken parts of me aren't naive enough to think she'll step in.

The hand tightens. His sneered words blurring in my mind as my brain begs for oxygen.

Tears streak from my eyes.

Maybe I am stupid.

Worthless like he always says.

Finally, weakness softens my limbs, and my knees give out.

His fingers release my neck as I collapse to the floor.

"Fat and stupid." He wipes his hand on his jeans like he's trying to wipe away the disgust of touching me.

My impact with the thin carpet knocked the last breath out of me, so I can't reply. Not that I would. I learned my lesson.

Fighting for breath, I watch as he turns his back and walks away, like nothing happened.

My body jolts as I gasp for air.

"Sweet Girl."

The murmur doesn't sound like the voice that haunts my nightmares. But I can still hear it. I can still feel his hand on me, fingers around my neck.

Blinking back the dream, my hands blindly reach up to push him away even though I know he's not here. It's just a memory. No one is touching—

My fingers collide with warm flesh.

Panic flares back to life and I try to scramble away, but I can't. I'm in the corner of the couch.

My couch.

I'm an adult. It's not him.

My brain adjusts to the sight in front of me. To the man from the balcony.

Oh my god, did I seriously fall asleep with this stranger in my home?!

"Breathe." The hand that I thought was trying to choke me presses against my breastbone. The warmth from his palm seeps into my chest, causing my lungs to stop seizing. "Just breathe, Sweet Girl."

I'm going to blame exhaustion and confusion for the tears that fill my eyes, not the kindness in his voice. Not hearing him call me *sweet* after the vivid and vicious memories of being called *stupid*.

"Hush." His hand slides a fraction lower, his standing body bent over my reclined form. "You're fine now."

My lungs fill with another shaky inhale, and I nod.

Fabric shifts underneath my fingers, and I glance down to see I'm gripping his forearm with both my hands.

I let go as quickly as I can, moving my hands back to my blanket. But his palm prevents me from being able to lift the blanket back to my chin.

Our gazes are locked together, and I startle when he speaks again.

"What's his name?" His voice is still quiet, but it's also different. A little menacing.

"Wh-whose name?"

His head tilts, and it reminds me of the nature channel when they show a wild animal stalking its prey. "The man who laid his hands on you. Tell me his name."

I suck in more air. My heart continues racing, but the reason for it is shifting. Morphing from fear to... something else.

"Why do you want to know?" I ask.

The tip of his tongue swipes at the corner of his mouth like he's thinking; then his lips tip up, the smallest amount. "Call it morbid curiosity."

When I don't reply, he leans closer, applying a little more pressure where his hand is touching me.

"I bet you've never told anyone. I bet you did as you were told." I can feel his exhale against my lips. "Break the rules for me, Sweet Girl. Put yourself first and give me a name."

There's a part of me that knows I should stay silent, but I ignore it. "Arthur."

He makes a humming sound before slowly straightening, his thumb drawing a line between my collarbones, before leaving me completely when he stands.

"Now, let's make a deal." He breaks eye contact with me when he looks down to fasten his suit coat.

I swallow, but don't say anything as I wait for him to

continue.

"I won't tell Arthur you're the one that sent me, and you don't tell anyone about tonight."

I blink up at him.

Did he...? Did he just say what I think he did?

"Tell me you agree, Payton." His voice is firmer now and hearing him say my name sends a burst of electricity down my spine.

He knows my name.

How does he know my name?

Looking into his beautifully haunting eyes, I whisper, "I agree."

He takes a step backwards. "Good."

I steel myself, knowing I'll hate myself later if I don't ask. "What's your name?"

He pauses, and for a moment I think he's going to tell me. But then he turns away from me and heads toward my front door. "It's safer if you don't know."

"Safer for who?" I ask.

"Both of us."

He's reaching for the handle when he pauses, and I follow his gaze down to the basket of laundry I left by the door.

I sit up and watch, eyes wide, as he bends down and picks up a pair of my underwear from the top of the pile.

"Those are dirty," I choke out.

The man smirks at me over his shoulder, as he shoves them into his pocket.

My mouth pops open, as is becoming my habit. I don't know what to say.

He unlocks the deadbolt and pulls the door open, the light from the hallway spilling in, lighting up his features as he turns just enough to look at me.

"Keep your doors closed, Payton. Leaving them open could be seen as an invitation."

Then, just as silently as he arrived, he leaves.

CHAPTER 5

Payton

THE CLICK OF THE DOOR CLOSING SNAPS ME OUT OF the trance I've been stuck in since he showed up in my living room.

Scrambling off the couch, I stumble my way to the door. My legs rubber beneath me.

I press my hands against the cheap wood, steadying myself.

My whole body is trembling, like the adrenaline that should've been coursing through me all night finally hit, all at once.

Breathe.

He's gone, just breathe.

Slowly, I lift my head until my eye is lined up with the peephole.

Taking another breath, I lean closer and look through.

A startled gasp clogs my throat.

Standing in the hallway, the man is staring back at me. Like he knew I'd look out.

He lifts a hand and points to the door handle.

Jerking my head away, I have to try twice before I flip the deadbolt into place.

My chest hurts from how frantic my heart is beating.

It's locked.

He can't get in now.

A voice in the corner of my mind whispers that something as simple as a lock wouldn't be able to keep that man out.

That man. Whoever he is.

Knowing I won't be able to walk away without checking, I put my eye back to the peephole, just in time to see him stride out of view.

I stay like that, watching the hallway, for too long. The sight of him pointing at my door burned into my memory.

I already thought he was dangerously handsome, but seeing him in the light confirms that he's so much more handsome than I thought.

His sharp features and firm body make me think he might be in his thirties, maybe late thirties. And his eyes...

I'm all too familiar with the look of someone who's experienced too much trauma. I see it every day when I look in the mirror. His eyes shine with a history I'm all too aware of.

A door bangs shut somewhere on my floor, reminding me that I'm not alone in this building.

I wonder if anyone else saw my mystery man as he left.

The thought has me finally pulling my eye away from the door and turning back toward the living room.

My limbs are still trembling, but I'm now able to stand upright on my own.

I'm halfway to the patio doors when I see that they're already closed. I cross the rest of the distance and see that the latch has been flipped and the loose length of board has been laid back in the track. My poor man's barricade.

It's as secure as it's ever gonna get, and yet...

My arms wrap around my body, fighting off a shiver.

I'd let the blanket drop when I climbed off the couch, and now a chill has seeped into the center of my body.

Payton.

The memory of him saying my name sends another shiver skittering across my skin.

The power of a name. It's something so simple, but it can make you feel so exposed. He held the power the moment he walked through my patio door. Not knowing his name puts us on even more uneven ground. Because I have nothing to call him. Nothing to shout. Nothing to tell anyone.

Staring at the limp curtains, I wonder if maybe I made it all up. Maybe my mind has finally cracked. Maybe I was asleep the whole time. Dreamed him.

My hand reaches up to rub over the spot where his hand had been, on my exposed skin.

He can't be fake. His touch was real. It has to be. Because the way my body reacted--that was real.

My nipples are tight against the thin fabric of my sleep shirt, making me all too aware of the fact that I'm not wearing a bra.

Jesus, who cares, Payton?

Plus I had the blanket pulled up, hiding my body from his view.

Except when I woke up, when his hand was against the base of my throat, his palm against my chest, the blanket wasn't pulled up then.

Did he pull it away, or did I drop it?

I shake my head at that thought because I would've woken up if he'd pulled the blanket away.

But I didn't.

I shake my head harder.

He didn't touch me. Not like *that*. I'd know. *I'd know.*

And why would he?

He's so handsome. So large and masculine and pure male perfection. Someone like him would have no time for someone like me--soft and scared--who only runs when they're running from the past.

I hug myself tighter.

Not now. I don't have time for a mental breakdown now.

Glancing at the clock, I curse. It's after midnight already. Puffing out my cheeks, I decide I'll catch an Uber to work, rather than take the bus. It will blow half a day's pay, but give me an extra twenty minutes of sleeping, so it'll be worth it.

Which is good in theory, but I already know that I won't get any rest.

Unplugging my phone from its spot on the counter, I notice one of my pieces of mail is askew.

Pinching the edge of the envelope, I pull it free from the stack.

Like a shiny beacon, my name is printed right there for me, and my intruder, to see.

"Great."

Not able to walk away with the mail not in place, I quickly straighten the pile.

I hate when things are out of place. Hate it so much. The sight of clutter sends me down a dark spiral. I've lived in a filthy home before. Never again.

Leaving the light on--like it will stop any more monsters from entering my home--I head into my bedroom, happy to see that this room looks untouched.

CHAPTER 6
Nero

I tip my head back, inhaling the stormy air as the phone rings.

By the fourth ring, I'm clenching my jaw.

Another two rings and I'm thoroughly annoyed when he finally picks up.

"Yeah?" King's voice is surly. No surprise there.

"I need a favor." Then I think about it. "Two, actually."

He scoffs, "What makes you think I'd give you one fucking favor, let alone two?"

"Fuck you," I tell him without heat. "Come pick me up."

"Seriously? Now?" Another sound floats through the line, a woman's voice.

"Yeah, now. Tell your girlfriend it's time to go."

"She's not my fucking girlfriend," he snaps.

"She know that?" I shouldn't goad him when I need something. I just can't help it, he's fun to fuck with.

"She knows." His tone is dark but I don't feel bad about pushing him.

There's some muffled talking then the sound of a door slamming.

"God, you're a prick," he sighs.

I smile into the dark. "You're one to talk."

He lets out a snort before he groans, and I hear furniture creaking.

"Noises like that," I tsk. "Maybe it's time for you to retire."

"I'm not that much older than you," King grunts.

"Not much?" I question, thinking that four years in this life is quite a bit.

"Like I said. A fucking prick. No wonder you have no one else to call for favors. Wait——" I can picture him tossing his hands up. "Why you callin' me to pick your ass up when you have a literal legion of men under your command?"

Honestly, I'm surprised it's taken him this long to ask. "Because I don't want my men anywhere near here."

"Huh." There's a beat of silence. "Consider me curious enough to put up with your shit for another night. Where are you?"

I think of an intersection a few blocks away that'll be a good place for a quick pick-up, and give him the directions.

"Got it," King replies and hangs up.

He's the only one that can get away with talking to me the way he does, but that's because we're equals. He runs the money. I run the men. And the things the men do.

FIFTEEN MINUTES LATER I'M CLIMBING INTO THE passenger side of King's blacked-out SUV. The ultra-dark tinted windows and windshield keeping any eyes or cameras from catching us together.

It's no secret that King and I know each other. Though as far as common knowledge goes, that's all that's between us. A passing acquaintance. We move in the same upper circles of society, so it's expected.

In actuality, we go back. Way back. To a fucked up youth and an even more fucked up adulthood. It started in a bloodbath, and ended with us forming The Alliance.

"Favor one complete," King says, pulling away from the curb and into the sparse traffic. "What's favor two?"

I type out a quick message then hit send. "Favor two was just texted to you."

With one hand on the wheel, King lifts his phone and glances at the text.

"Who is she?" He looks back down. "And who's Arthur?"

"She's no one." I turn my attention out the window. "But he's a dead man."

CHAPTER 7

Payton

My body aches in protest as I roll out of bed, my phone alarm blaring from the other side of the room.

I suck in a breath when my bare feet connect with the cold floor, but I fight through the temptation to jump back into bed. The whole purpose of not leaving my phone in its usual spot on the nightstand was so I'd have to get up to turn it off. I already set it for the latest time possible which means I don't even have the option to hit snooze.

It's not until I have my phone silenced in my hand that I realize how stupid that plan probably was. A man was literally in my apartment last night, and I couldn't call for help because my phone was across the room. And I just did it again, on purpose.

"Idiot," I chastise myself out loud.

My grogginess is bone deep, so as dumb as my plan may have been, it was probably the right choice. I doubt I'd get fired for sleeping through the beginning of my shift, but it's not worth the risk.

If I could afford to take a day off, I would. But I can't. And even though I don't hate my job, it doesn't exactly come with PTO.

My steps drag as I cross the hall and enter the bathroom. I

preemptively squint my eyes as I turn on the light, blocking out the brightness that still manages to sear straight into my brain.

Blindly, I reach into the shower and turn on the water, letting it heat up while I strip and use the toilet.

Coffee would go a long way to making me feel more human. Unfortunately, I didn't give myself any extra time to brew some, meaning I'll have to wait until I'm at work to have my caffeine boost. One perk of working at a café, free coffee all day.

Slipping into the shower, I stand under the hot water and let the warmth wake me. Only for a minute though, knowing I'm limited on time. When that minute is over, I pick up my shampoo bottle and do my routine in fast forward.

Done with my hair, I reach for my body wash, but my fingers brush against the tiled wall.

I open one eye and tip my head away from the spray.

"What...?"

I wipe at my eyes, clearing the water from my lashes and stare at the soggy hundred-dollar bill on the tub ledge, where my body wash should be.

"What the hell?"

I pick it up, the real currency not disintegrating under my wet grip.

Did he...

Did he really take my body wash?

A new sort of warmth starts at my hips and works its way up to my chest.

This shouldn't make me feel...

I shouldn't like that he did that.

But my body does.

My heart rate speeds up and a different type of dampness gathers between my thighs.

Stop it!

I clench my eyes shut.

Just stop it, Payton!

Reaching up, I drop the bill over the top of the curtain and it falls to the bathmat on the other side.

The stranger that climbed in through my second-story patio door, sat on my couch, watched my favorite movie and ate my popcorn––the man who went through my mail and learned my name, and apparently walked through my whole apartment while I slept; also, the same man who woke me up from a nightmare with his hand on my bare skin, shushing me, which should've terrified me, instead calming me–– stole my body wash. Or rather, he paid one hundred dollars in exchange for taking my half-used miniature bottle of body wash. A bottle I splurged on because I loved the dusky rose scent, but could only afford the smallest size.

I bite my lip.

I can buy the bigger bottle now.

My lips pull into a smile.

I should probably call the police.

My smile falters.

Filling my palm, I lather up my hands with the store-brand face wash I use. If it cleans my face, it should clean my body.

Scrubbing, then rinsing, I turn off the water and pointedly ignore the part of my brain that tells me to report the *crime*.

Gingerly, I set the money on my bathroom counter before I quickly swipe some concealer under my eyes.

I pretend my hands aren't shaking as I put my hair in a quick braid, and roughly scrub a towel over my bangs so they'll air dry somewhat straight.

Convincing myself this is just another day, I race around my room throwing on clothes, trying not to think about the fact that he was probably in this room too. He had to be. If he went through the stuff in my shower, there's no way he didn't go into my bedroom.

What did he look at?

What did he touch?

But I don't see anything out of order. And I don't find any

more money in place of missing items, so I don't think he took anything else.

Tension prickles the back of my neck as I hurry out of my apartment and down the stairs to the first floor. Rushing out of my building, I find the Uber I requested waiting for me.

Only when my butt hits the seat, and I've pulled the car door shut, do I glance around the street.

Like maybe he's still out here.

Watching.

Waiting.

For me.

CHAPTER 8

Payton

My ride to work is short and uneventful, and the driver is thankfully quiet as he navigates the empty streets of Minneapolis.

It's nice being so close to everything, but I'd love to live in a house again someday. One that's clean. In a safe neighborhood. Somewhere with a yard big enough for a garden, and a couple of chairs. Maybe a fenced-in yard so I could get a dog.

I bet if I had a dog, he would've barked his head off when that guy walked into my apartment last night. I bet my dog would've been so protective the guy would've turned around and left the way he came.

The fantasy is nice, but I can't get a dog. No matter how much I might want one.

I work too much. I have a tiny apartment. I don't actually know how to take care of one. And none of that even matters because mostly, I can't afford a dog. I mean maybe if it was small, and only ate a little bit, and never ever got sick...

An ache starts to form in my chest at the thought of that sort of companionship, but I shove the feeling down just as the driver pulls to a stop right in front of Twin's Cafe. I thank him before stepping out onto the sidewalk.

Just in time.

My cheeks puff out with a sigh as I use my key to enter through the front door and walk into the brightly lit establishment.

I stuff my purse into the cupboard under the register, and I almost laugh as thoughts wander back to the dog idea.

I may only have a high school diploma, but I'm smart enough to know it's naïve to hope. I mean in general, it's a bad idea. Especially about this. If my past luck is any indication, I'd wind up getting a pet with a never-ending appetite who gets sick with every change of season.

"Morning," Jean, one of the owners, greets me distractedly as she carries a tray of scones up to the bakery display.

"Morning," I reply, shrugging my jacket off and swapping it for a plain white apron.

"Miss the bus?"

Her question surprises me since I didn't think she noticed me through the windows.

"Yeah." I nod.

It's easier to just say I missed the bus rather than saying I spent the money on an Uber on purpose. And there's no way I'm telling her, or anyone, about what happened last night. At least not yet.

Jean makes a sound that might be construed as understanding, then goes back to straightening the items in the display case.

On autopilot, I go through the motions with her——brewing coffee, counting the till, and removing the cling wrap covering the deli salads in the cooler case.

Twin's Café is a small, but consistently busy, breakfast and brunch spot. We open at six a.m. and close at four p.m., serving coffee, deli salads, soup, and sandwiches. There's a kitchen in the back where Tamara, Jean's twin sister, does most of the cooking, along with Tommy. He's an older guy that doesn't talk much. But he's never been mean, or grabby, so he's basically my best friend.

"First customer!" Jean calls out loud enough to make me jump.

She does this every morning, like we all need some sort of heads up to prepare ourselves. But today I was so in my own head that I didn't even notice her unlock the front door.

"Okay!" Tamara's cigarette-scratched voice shouts from the back.

As always, Tommy stays silent.

When I ring up my first cup of to-go coffee, I let the normalcy pull me in. And by the time 10:00 rolls around, I've almost tricked myself into forgetting about last night.

"Howdy, Payton!"

I smile as I turn toward the door to watch one of our regulars walk in, his usual swagger and charm in place.

"Hey, Carlton," I greet him.

"How's my favorite barista?" He grins as he approaches the counter, stopping when he's across from me.

I just roll my eyes; I'm no barista. My talents are hardly worthy of the title. But no matter how many times I correct him, he keeps calling me that.

"You want the usual?"

Carlton dips his chin. "You know I do. Gotta keep this figure." He runs a hand down his flat stomach.

I smile. "Uh-huh."

I type his order in––a large, iced coffee with four sugars and cream and a chicken salad sandwich on a croissant with extra mayo.

Carlton is tall and lanky, and one of those people gifted with a high metabolism. Because no matter how often he comes in, no matter how many of these oversized sandwiches he consumes, he's always thin as a stick.

Taking his card, I swipe it through the reader. "How's the band doing?"

His grin widens. "Great! I don't want to jinx it yet, but we might have a good gig coming up."

"Oh, yeah?"

Carlton nods. "You'll still come if we book it?" When I hesitate, my shoulders stiffening with nerves, he sticks his lower lip out in a pout. "You said you would."

I force myself to relax a little at his teasing tone. He's just being nice. "As long as the tickets aren't like three hundred dollars, I'll come."

My attempt at making a joke flops as my mouth forms the word *hundred*. Reminding me of the damp hundred-dollar bill sogging up my wallet.

Call me paranoid, but I didn't trust leaving it at home, even if letting it sit out to dry would've been the smarter idea.

Carlton laughs. "Deal." Holding his hand out, like he wants to shake on it, causes my tenseness to reappear tenfold.

We've never touched before. That's the safety of our friendship. That's the safety of this job. I stay on my side of the counter, everyone else stays over there.

I don't like to be touched.

It's never gone well for me.

You didn't mind when that man touched you last night.

My heart jumps a beat.

Because it's true.

I didn't mind it.

Carlton's smile doesn't waver, not seeming to read my hesitation.

Tentatively, I reach out. If I can let a stranger touch my body after breaking into my apartment, I can let a friend shake my hand.

His long fingers close around mine. And nothing bad happens.

I haven't had much need for handshakes in my life, so I've never mastered them. In TV and movies, they always make it look so easy. Just take a hand and shake it.

But how hard do you hold on? How many shakes do you do? How big is the movement supposed to be?

Carlton doesn't say anything about my loose grip, giving my hand two big shakes before he lets go.

Okay, that wasn't so bad. I can be normal about this.

"I'll keep you posted."

I tuck my hands into my apron pocket. "I'm looking forward to it."

That sounds like the right thing to say, even though I'm not sure if it's a lie or the truth.

Movement just outside the cafe catches my attention. And when my eyes follow the distraction, my lungs clench.

It couldn't be.

Carlton, following my gaze, turns to look back through the large windows onto the street. "Something wrong?"

He's unintentionally blocked my view, so I have to shuffle to look around him, but the sidewalk is empty now.

Or was it always?

"Payton?" There's concern in his voice as he shifts his attention back to me.

My attempt at a smile is brittle. "Oh no, it's fine. I just thought I saw..." I trail off. Because what I thought I saw, I can't vocalize.

I thought I saw a man in a suit. Staring at me. And Carlton. Jaw tight, fists clenched.

"Earth to Payton." A hand waves in front of my face, and I jump.

"Sorry." I press a hand to my chest. "I thought I saw a, um, dog." My cheeks flush at my lie, so I follow it up with a truth. "I really want a dog."

I'm saved from further awkwardness when Jean calls out Carlton's name, signaling that his sandwich is ready at the other end of the counter. Gathering his lunch, Carlton holds the wrapped sandwich to his forehead in a salute goodbye, while backing out the door.

When he steps out of view, my eyes scan the street again.

Sill finding it empty, I wonder if maybe *this* is how I'll die. Slowly losing my sanity, until even the nicest of customers stops talking to me.

CHAPTER 9

Nero

"Take care of it," I snap.

"I just wasn't sure—"

When my second-in-command, Rocco, starts to make an excuse, I lose my patience. "I said, take care of it. Have the men get the money from him *now*. Or take limbs as payment. I don't give a fuck which."

I hang up before I become more pissed off.

My men are loyal. They have to be. Sometimes I want to slit their throats. But King and I can't do it all on our own––we've tried, right after we destroyed the previous regime––it's just simply too much work to run a criminal empire without cannon fodder.

Striding into my bedroom, I kick the door shut behind me.

I don't lock it. I don't need to. No one would dare walk in.

Leaving a trail of clothes as I go, I strip my way into the bathroom.

Peeling off my socks, the black marble floors are cool on my bare feet.

The black-on-black design in my suite of rooms is cliché. The classic mobster aesthetic. But black is fitting, as it matches my cold dead heart.

I keep the lights dimmed in here. Not needing a bright reflection of all my scars, I stand in front of the mirror, and I take them in. The slashes of raised skin up and down my ribs, the circular rise of flesh low on my abdomen, and the matching round marks on the front and back of my thigh are still visible even now.

They tell my story. One of torment, survival and violence.

My tale is not a pretty one. But it is mine. And so far, the plot has sided in my favor. I've lived when so many others haven't.

Still, my luck won't last forever.

It never does for men like me.

And that's exactly why I need to forget Payton. Why I need to pretend she doesn't exist. Why I need to delete every shred of information I've collected on her and let her live out her own differently-miserable existence.

Turning from the mirror, I don't bother looking over my shoulder at the canvas of memories etched onto my back, as I stride into the shower.

With my face tilted back, I turn the handle and the cold spray pours over me, shocking me back into the present.

My muscles start to unclench as the water slowly warms.

I need to focus on what's important. And that's the same thing it's always been. Surviving.

When King and I made our move all those years ago, we knew exactly what it meant.

It meant freedom from the shackles of servitude. It meant retribution against those who stole our futures away from us.

But we aren't good men. Not King, and especially not me. Because more than anything, it meant vengeance. And we took our pound of flesh.

A dark sort of glee fills my chest.

We took more than a pound.

We took it all.

The sewers ran red that night.

The night we cut down the Russians and the Irish, we had an option. For the first time in so many years, we actually had an option. We could leave this life and walk away. Try to find some sense of normalcy. Or we could take control of the territory and build our own legacy.

A quiet life was a nice daydream. But the first time I killed a man, I knew there'd be no going back. So, we climbed the mountain of bodies, their slit throats making the path slick and treacherous; and we formed our own destinies.

We formed The Alliance.

Heavy with memories, my head tips forward.

Steaming water cascades through my hair. The warm after the cold making me appreciate it even more.

It's easy to get used to luxury. Easier yet to get swept up in the feeling of invincibility.

As if to remind myself that I'm human, my hand reaches down to trace the gunshot scar on my stomach. It's the closest I've ever come. Even with the beatings, the cold nights, the starved days, that little piece of metal was the closest I ever came to death.

There've been times I wish it would've taken me. Done me in. But I still have moments I'm glad I'm alive.

Like last night.

My eyes slowly open, locking on the small, stolen bottle on the shelf in my shower.

I shouldn't have taken it. But *shouldn't have* never stopped me before. And, I blow out a breath, it's not gonna stop me now.

Bending, I scoop up the bottle, pop the lid open and inhale the scent of roses.

It's floral, but it's not light. Not girly or carefree. It's... dark.

I breathe it in again, and my mind is filled with her.

Payton.

Her pale skin. Her scared eyes.

My breathing picks up.

The fear in her eyes shouldn't excite me.

I want to protect her.

I want to walk away so she doesn't get hurt.

But her eyes... those goddamn eyes. The flecks of midnight in those blue orbs.

When I woke her from that nightmare, she stared up at me like I might save her. Like I was something other than the boogeyman lurking in the shadows. Like maybe I could be more.

And the moment her fingers curled around my forearm...

I groan, and my dick reacts the same way it did in that moment, hardening to its full length.

"Fuck." I bite out the word even as I tip the bottle over and fill my palm with her body wash. The red liquid glistening in the dim light.

Setting the bottle down, I brace my free hand on the marble wall and lower the other.

You're a sick fuck.

But even my inner hatred can't stop me now.

My palm connects with my cock, and I let the rose scent engulf my senses.

"Jesus," I hiss, as I tighten my grip. The body wash making my cock slippery.

Squeezing my eyes shut, I tighten my grip on my dick and begin to stroke. Only instead of *my* hand, I imagine it's Payton's sweet hot cunt hugging my dick. Her slickness, her need for me, removing the friction.

Pumping my hips, I fuck my fist and I pretend I'm hovering over her.

Pretend it's her eyes blinking up at me. A mix of fear and hero-worship looking back at me, tightening my balls.

I think about the way her tits would bounce as I slammed into her. Our hips connecting, jolting her body.

Her soft curves writhing underneath me. Trying to get away, yet trying to pull me in deeper.

She'd probably cry out.

My fingers squeeze harder.

She'd probably scream. Her previous lovers not as endowed as me. Not as ruthless. Not as cruel.

My hips thrust faster.

I bet she'd suck me so good.

Those pouty lips. Those full cheeks.

That Sweet Girl could take me.

She could swallow my cock.

A groan rolls up my throat.

Or she'd do her best and gag trying.

My balls tighten.

Her throat would constrict around me. Her eyes would stare up at me. Tears rolling down her cheeks, fear in her expression, wondering if I'll let her breathe.

If I'll give her a break or if I'll shove my dick all the way down––

My cock jumps, my orgasm tearing through me, as I splash my release across the wall.

CHAPTER 10

Payton

"Hey, beautiful! We've got some samples set up in the center for you to try." The employee gestures with a head nod, his hands filled with product. "And let me know if you need any help finding something."

"Thanks." I can't bring myself to call out across the store as loud as he did, but he must read my lips because he smiles before turning back to stock the shelf in front of him.

It's been nearly a week since the Mystery Man walked into my apartment, and after much internal debate, I decided to come to the mall after work today to replace the body wash he took.

Having only been in this store once before, it takes me a moment to find the scent I'm looking for.

Part of me is tempted to get a different kind. Change it up. The other part of me, the part buried deeper inside of me, where I safekeep my secrets, won't let me do that. He, *that man*, took my body wash for a reason. And I might be inexperienced, but I have a feeling he took it because he liked it. Because it smelled like me.

Maybe it's sick and twisted, and it's definitely fucked up, but I like the idea of him in his shower, sniffing my soap, while I'm in my shower, lathering the same scent all over my body.

My cheeks flush pink. I shouldn't be thinking about this here.

"Oh, good choice!" The employee's voice startles a gasp out of me, and I clutch the bottle to my chest. "Sorry––" He laughs. "Didn't mean to sneak up on you."

"It's okay." I try to act like a normal human and brush it off.

"Have you tried the matching lotion?" he asks, reaching past me to pick up a little black container with a screw-on lid.

"I didn't know there was one," I murmur, bending to sniff after he removes the top and holds it up for me.

As I take another inhale, the employee lists off all the attributes, the hydration, the softening, the environmental story... but all I can focus on is the rose scent. It smells like the soap in my hands, only this would stay with me longer.

My eyes close, and I can picture it now––getting out of the shower, the steamy air filled with the scent. Toweling off and reaching for this jar of lotion. Dipping my fingers in, scooping out the soft substance, then warming it between my palms before running it up and down my limbs. Coating my body in the essence of roses. Using it as a shield and a lure. Feeling brave for putting it on, hoping it might be enough to bring the man back through my door. Back into my life.

"Good, right?"

My eyes fly open to see a conspiratorial expression on his face, and I feel my own heat with embarrassment.

Pressing my lips together, I nod.

With the lid secure he hands me the little jar asking if I need anything else.

I eye the piles of bath bombs, considering if it's worth the expense, but decide against it.

Following the worker to the register, I try to keep my hands steady as I pull the hundred-dollar bill out of my wallet and pass it across the counter.

It feels like some sort of giant secret, as if someone like me shouldn't have this sort of cash on them. And usually, I wouldn't. Honestly, it's been causing me anxiety all week. Like someone might spot it through my purse and just *know* that it came into my possession through nefarious means.

Even though the cost of the body wash plus the lotion is insanely expensive, I'm happy to put the twenty-seven dollars and change back into my wallet. It's still technically *his* money, but it's a much more reasonable amount to justify.

With the bag in my hands, I check the time on my phone and decide I can treat myself to the food court before catching the bus home.

Because really, what's one more indulgence?

CHAPTER 11

Nero

I can feel King's gaze on the side of my face when I tell him to take a right at the next light.

He knows this isn't the way back to my car. I know this isn't the way back to my car. But it's been over two weeks since I've seen her. And I *need to* see her.

King takes the turn at a snail's pace. He's fucking with me, and I decide to not give him the satisfaction of reacting.

We drive the next few blocks in silence, and when I open my mouth to tell him where to go next, he flips the blinker, indicating a left turn.

This time, I glance at him. And I instantly want to punch the look off his face.

Without me saying another word, he takes all the correct turns, finally slowing to a stop against the curb, across the street from a little café that's getting ready to open.

King shifts the vehicle into park before slowly shifting to face me. "This is where you wanted to go, right?"

My teeth grind.

Even though this piece of shit is my best friend, I'm not in the mood to be fucked with. Which is why I tracked his ass down in the first place. Taking a few hours to skin a man who was trying to sell human fucking beings in my city is one thing, but having to ride in a car with my men when they're all keyed up after a fresh kill--now that's torture.

"Have you been here before?" My voice is level, but I'm not fooling him with my placid tone.

He holds his hand up. "I swear on your grave, I haven't been here before."

I roll my eyes. "You're such a prick."

King shrugs a massive shoulder. "Says the stalker to the madman."

"I'm not her fucking stalker."

"No? My bad then. I just figured since I picked you up near her apartment, in the middle of the night. And you had me do a background check, run her financials, and track down her surviving family members..." he trails off, then tips his head toward Twin's Café. "And now you have me stopping here"—he glances at the clock—"one minute before her shift starts."

His eyes move back to meet mine, but I hold his gaze. "I'm not stalking her."

"Alright, cool." We both look toward the movement behind the front door of the café, as an older woman walks up and unlocks the door. King unbuckles his seat belt. "Then you won't mind me grabbing a coffee."

"What?" My brain is distracted because I finally catch sight of her. It's just the back of her head, but it's her. I know it is.

The sound of King's door opening jerks my attention back. "The fuck are you doing?" I lunge across the center counsel to grab him, but he slides out of my reach.

King arches his back in a stretch. "You want something?"

"I want you to get your stupid ass back in the fucking car," I growl.

Making a tsking sound, King shakes his head. "So much anger for so early in the morning."

"I swear to god--" My threat is cut off when King grins and slams his door shut.

My fingers twitch at my side, unsure if I want to grab my own door handle and follow him, or grab my gun to shoot him in the back of the head. I don't do either of those things because I can't let her see me. And I can't kill King. So, I stay exactly where I am as King enters the café.

The second Payton turns, and I finally get to see her face again, my hand closes around the door handle.

I'm too far away to see the details of her face, but I can picture the blue of those big innocent eyes, as she looks up to see who entered. Her bangs are brushing low over her brows, and I pretend I can see her dark lashes fluttering under the veil.

My fingers tighten their grip.

I want to see her.

Stay put, idiot. It's bad enough that King is in there.

Then she smiles at King, I shove my door open.

Those smiles are mine.

I have one leg out of the vehicle before I stop myself.

Get your shit together, man!

Cursing aloud, I pull my leg back and shut the door.

CHAPTER 12

Payton

"FIRST CUSTOMER!"

I dust the coffee grounds off my palms. "Starting early this morning," I say to Jean as she walks past me toward the back, having just unlocked the door a moment ago.

She grunts in reply, and I sigh. Guess today will be like every other day.

Turning to the door, I pull in a breath to greet the customer, but my lungs catch. Because, for a flicker of a moment, I thought the man striding through the doorway was the same man from my apartment.

Tall, broad, and in a suit, it's easy to see why I thought that. Despite his hair being slightly lighter, his handsome face still stops me, but I realize it's not the one that's starred in my dreams. This isn't my man.

My man.

That absurd thought is enough to get my mouth to pull into a smile.

"Good morning!" I say brightly to the stranger.

His grin is immediate. "Mornin'."

The closer he gets, the more unsure I become about him.

At first, he looked like a normal guy. I mean, he's good-looking. And his posture, haircut, suit... it's all *normal*. But there's an energy around him. Like maybe he's dangerous. Just like my Mystery Man.

I'm probably just projecting.

"How're you doing today?" he asks.

The question throws me off. Most people just order. "Uh, can't complain. You?"

The man's grin widens. "Day's getting better by the moment."

"Oh, um..." I don't know what to say to that. It feels like he's maybe flirting with me. Which I'm sure he isn't, but just the idea of it is making me feel guilty.

Which is stupid. I don't have a boyfriend.

My brain flashes back to that night, when there was a man sharing my couch, and it makes me want to bang my head on the counter because that intruder certainly isn't my boyfriend. He was probably a criminal. And he certainly hasn't spared me a thought since that day.

When the man continues to stare at me, I give an awkward smile and gesture to the sign with the daily specials. "What can I get for you?"

He glances at the list but doesn't read it, just leans to the side to look at the pastries displayed behind the glass.

"I'll take two black coffees and two of the..." His eyes trail across the shelves. "Cranberry lime muffins."

"Good choice," I reply as I type his order into the register.

He holds up a finger. "What's your favorite drink here?"

I feel my eyebrows lift. "Me?"

He nods and smirks. "You."

"Like a coffee drink?"

He nods again. "It's for a friend."

"Uh, I guess..." I bite my lip. "I really like our coconut and honey latte." My voice goes up at the end, like I'm asking a question.

The man barks out a laugh, startling me back a step.

"Sorry, sorry." He shakes his head. "I'll do one of those."

"So, two black coffees or one coffee and one latte?"

"The second option."

Typing in the new order, I tell him the total.

I'm not sure what's so funny about a coconut honey latte, but I'm not here to question people's choices.

He takes his wallet out of his back pocket. "Here you go."

I glance up, and for the second time since this man has walked in, I freeze. His hand is extended between us, a crisp hundred-dollar bill between his fingers.

He gives it a little shake. "Do you not do cash here?"

"Oh, no, we do. Sorry." It's my turn to apologize.

I take the bill and make change while internally chastising myself. *Way to act like a poor girl, getting all flustered about a little cash.*

I quickly hand the change back, without making eye contact, and spin around to gather his order.

I should've told him that I like black coffee, too. Then I could've had his order sorted in under a minute. But black coffee isn't my favorite, coconut honey is. And no one has ever asked me what my favorite anything is, so I didn't even consider lying.

My hands hesitate when I reach for the whipped cream.

Usually, I'd ask the customer if they'd like some on top, but since the man asked what I like, I decide to make it how I like it.

When the cup is filled to the brim with fresh whipped cream, I drizzle honey over the top, before finally securing the lid.

"Here you go." I slide the bag with the two muffins across the counter before setting down the to-go cups. "Do you need a drink carrier?"

"Nah, I'm good." He picks up his items before nodding to a stack of cash on the counter. "That's for you, Payton."

He's striding toward the exit before I catch on to what he said.

He called me Payton.

My fingers tremble as I reach for the bills.

How does he know my name? We don't wear name tags.

There's a five on top, with thirty-seven cents on top of that.

Okay so he left some of his change.

I trap the corner of the top bill between my fingers and tug it away from the others, revealing a stack of twenties.

He left all of his change. The rest of that hundred.

It's a coincidence.

It's all a coincidence.

Jean must've said my name after he came in. It doesn't mean anything.

My eyes move to the front windows, just in time to see the customer climbing into a big SUV parked across the street. There's no overhead light on in the vehicle, but as he's pulling his door shut, I swear I see movement.

Is there someone else out there?

CHAPTER 13

Nero

My gaze stays focused past King, on Payton's shaken look, as he climbs into the driver's seat.

It's the same look she had on her face when he paid.

Just as King pulls his door shut, Payton looks up, and I swear we lock eyes. But then the car door is slammed shut, and the heavily tinted glass blocks any view Payton might've had of me.

"Here," King grunts, handing me a coffee.

"What did you say to her?" I snap.

"I ordered us breakfast. What the hell do you think I said?"

I roll my shoulders and sit back in my seat, breaking my sightline of Payton.

King drops a paper bag in my lap. "One of those is for me."

"What is it?"

"Muffins," King replies as he shifts the vehicle into drive and pulls away from the corner.

I'd make an effort to pay King back, but he's already rich as royalty so I don't even bother asking how much it was.

With my free hand, I open the bag, allowing the scent of citrus and sugar to waft out.

"Smells good," I grumble.

I wish I could've seen her up close. I want to see the flecks of midnight that shine in her eyes. I miss her face.

"Did you take a picture?" The second the words are out of my mouth I realize how dumb it sounds.

The car crawls to a stop, and out of the corner of my eye I can see King slowly turn his face toward me. "I'm sorry, I must be losing my fucking mind because it sounded like you just asked me if I took her picture." He waits a beat for me to answer, but I don't. "What? You figured I'd just casually take out my phone and snap a pic of her fucking face? As if she wouldn't immediately call the cops on me for that? Are you insane? Seriously, that's fucking creepy. Even for us."

"Okay!" I snap. "I get it."

"Do you?" King's tone is incredulous. "What is up with this girl anyway? She got a magic snatch or something?"

"Don't--" I cut myself off, grinding my teeth. "It's not like that."

"*It's not like that.*" He repeats the words back to me slowly. "Sounds like something some idiot would say, right before we put a bullet in his forehead."

"Can we drop it?"

"Oh, hell no. I'm not dropping this."

"She's just a girl," I grit out.

I'm beginning to question how much I really need him because, right now silence might be better than having a best friend.

Wanting to delay an explanation, I lift the coffee cup to my mouth and take a sip. What hits my tongue is not the bitter, plain coffee I was expecting.

My body lurches forward in a bend and I have to force myself not to spit the liquid out all over King's dashboard. King's booming laughter fills the car, and the urge to end him increases tenfold.

"What the fuck is that?!" I snap when I finally swallow.

But chuckle-face is too busy laughing to reply.

I lift his drink out of the cupholder and sniff it. Plain coffee.

"Seriously?" I sniff at the small opening in my lid. "What the fuck did you get me?"

I'm swapping our drinks, putting the sweet shit he got me in his cupholder when he catches his breath to reply. "Man, I've been waiting for your reaction to that, and you did not disappoint."

"Glad you found it so funny. Because now it's yours." I take a deliberate drink of his plain coffee.

"Suit yourself." He lifts a shoulder. "I just figured you'd like to try your girl's favorite drink."

My eyes move back to the original cup. "It's her favorite?"

"That's what she said. Took the time to make it herself. Even added some fancy shit on top. But if you don't want it..."

King starts to reach for it, but I snatch it back, shoving the plain coffee into his hand.

He sighs. "You want to slobber around the rest of the rim first? Since you've put your filthy mouth on both of these now."

"Deal with it." My tone doesn't hold the bite I mean it to, I'm too busy sniffing Payton's favorite drink again. Unreasonably disappointed that it doesn't smell like roses. "What is it?"

"Coconut and honey, I think she said." I must pull a face because King snorts. "Yeah, sounded nasty to me too."

"It's not nasty," I admit. "I just wasn't expecting it."

Turning the cup in my hands I see *C&H Latte* scrawled in sharpie.

It's her handwriting.

Then I remember what King said about her making it herself.

I wonder...?

I lift the cup to my face and press my nose to the side opposite the writing, where her palm would've been, and inhale.

Still no roses.

Damnit.

"Dude." King sounds exasperated. "Seriously, man, this woman has got you unhinged."

I tune out King's words. I don't have time for his judgment.

He doesn't understand.

I need her.

Need to consume her.

Prying the lid off, I put the rim of the cup to my lips and drink down the entire thing in a few large gulps. Relishing the way the hot liquid scorches my throat. Feeding the fire of obsession roaring through my bloodstream.

CHAPTER 14
Payton

"I said decaf," a woman snaps.

"Huh?" I glance up at the suddenly angry woman across the counter from me.

"I. Said. Decaf." She says it slowly like she's talking to an idiot.

I look down at the cup I'm holding out to her. "Oh, um, I'm sorry."

"I watched you walk right past the decaf pot. If it's empty, I'll wait for you to brew more. I'm not drinking *that*."

My shoulders slide higher with each sentence she speaks.

She saw me doing the wrong thing and didn't stop me. Just let me fail.

"I'm sorry," I repeat. "We have decaf made, I just... forgot."

She scoffs, crossing her arms over her chest.

My face is hot when I turn away from the woman. She's acting like I tried to force-feed her something she's allergic to. Though now I'm sorely tempted to.

Like you'd ever retaliate.

I keep my eyes turned down as I set aside the cup of offending *caffeinated* coffee and reach for an empty one.

I'm not a kid, but when I get yelled at like this, it makes me feel like one. Like another powerless victim. Again.

When my fingers close around the bright orange lever on the correct pot, the woman comments a condescending, "Good job." And I've never wanted to quit on the spot more than I do right now.

It's been a long day.

A long week.

It's been a long life. Why can't I ever just catch a freaking break?!

And a good break. Not a bad break--like when my oven started making a rattling noise last week. Or three days ago when someone apparently used bleach in the washing machine right before I put my clothes in, ruining the only pair of decent jeans that I owned.

"I'd love to get that sometime today." The woman's voice slithers up my neck.

Without looking at her, I secure the lid on her *decaf* and set the cup on the counter.

I can sense her hesitating before she takes the cup and strides out of the café.

Good riddance. I don't know what she was waiting for. I think my body language should be enough to let someone know I'm not interested in fighting.

I'd love to keep my shoulders back and head up when someone's mean to me. But it's hard. And that woman was old enough to be my mother, which triggered a whole other set of emotions. And too many memories that I've tried my best to repress.

I've never wanted to fight.

I don't like it. I do everything I can to avoid it.

The few times I couldn't help it and snapped back never ended well for me.

Just behave yourself and it won't be a problem.

My mother's voice, brought on by that awful customer, rings around in my head.

Mom was always shoveling the blame for Arthur's behavior onto my shoulders. Always telling me *"if only you'd* this*"*, or *"if* *you'd act like* that"... But I was a kid. An innocent kid with no way to defend myself from his bullying. And we both knew that no matter how perfectly I behaved, it wouldn't make a difference. When he was in one of his moods, he'd hit me whether I did something to bother him or not.

Unconsciously, one of my hands moves up to gently rub the front of my neck.

I've had stitches. Broke my arm that one time. All things that *physically* hurt more than the times he put his hands around my throat. But somehow that one was the worst.

Because when he choked me, it wasn't about the pain. It was about the fear. The fear that maybe he'd go too far. Squeeze a little too hard.

My lips press together, and I force myself to breathe through the memories.

The worst part was the fear I felt when I saw *that* look in his eyes. The one that said he knew just how close he was to silencing me, once and for all. And that he was considering it.

I can almost feel the cold press of his god-awful ring against my neck.

I try not to think about it, any of it, but I'm almost certain he would've killed me if we hadn't been so poor. Arthur always seemed to find a way out of trouble, but he didn't have the sort of money a person would need to bribe the police to look the other way over a murder.

On my darkest days, there's a part of me that wishes he would've. To end my misery, and add to his. Of course, I wouldn't be around to enjoy his punishment, but I'd've died happy knowing he'd rot in prison.

It's my biggest regret, that he gets to live a normal life. He might not be a happy person, but he's free. He has control over his days. And he doesn't deserve that. He doesn't deserve to breathe after what he said––what caused me to finally run away, two days before my eighteenth birthday.

"WAIT! PLEASE!" I HIKE MY PURSE HIGHER ON MY shoulder. "This is my stop!"

The bus is overly crowded today, a by-product of the shitty weather, and I was on the verge of nodding off when the person next to me jabbed their elbow into my ribs, jolting me awake. It's a good thing they did, because this terrible day would've been made even worse if I missed my stop entirely.

"Sorry. Excuse me." I mutter my apologies as I shuffle sideways up the aisle.

I've come to terms with my size long ago. It's just who I am. Wide hips, thick thighs... it is what it is. It's fine. And I usually don't care. But right now, when the bus driver is already glaring at me through the overhead mirror, I wish I could just sprint out of here. But narrow aisles, full of elbows, and wide hips don't mix.

"Sorry," I apologize one last time as I reach the front.

The driver doesn't reply, only makes a show of opening the door.

A gust of damp wind flies up the steps, sending the sides of my coat flapping, like some sort of dumpy Marilyn Monroe skit.

God, I'm so over this day.

I grip the handrail tightly as I take the final step off the bus and onto the sidewalk. And I'm glad I did, because I nearly lose my balance when my sneaker makes contact with the thin slippery layer of slush covering the curb.

My hand has barely passed the threshold when the door snaps shut behind me and the bus speeds away.

"Jerk," I grumble, pulling the sides of my coat together.

I should've zipped up before I left Twin's, but I was rushing. Which I'll blame on that bitchy customer, because it was her left-over caffeinated cup of coffee that I accidentally bumped over when I was putting on said coat. But now, with half a block left between me and home, I'm not pausing for anything. Cold wind be damned.

Another gust of wind has me tucking my chin to my chest and squinting my eyes. This wintery mix of snow and rain is early, even for Minnesota. The weight of the precipitation is going to knock more leaves off of the trees and that makes me sad. Because fall is my favorite season and a premature end to it will surely bring on a bout of seasonal depression.

With my head down, I don't notice the small branch on the sidewalk until the toe of my right shoe catches on it.

I try to stop myself from falling. I really do. But I'm too slow.

A cry of alarm leaves my lips as I tip forward.

I try to shift my weight to my left leg, but that knee buckles.

There's just enough time for me to let go of my jacket and stretch my hands out in front of me, bracing for the fall.

My left knee hits first, then both of my palms, then my other knee.

Pain ricochets up through my limbs.

The sharp sting is immediate, and I hold still, afraid to move just yet. Everything hurts––my body, my pride––but I don't think I broke any skin.

I wait until the pain morphs into a throb before I shift my weight to look.

A piece of gravel grates against my palm, like the preverbal salt in the wound. "Shit!" I try to shout the word, in a sad attempt to dispel the emotion clawing against the back of my eyes. But it comes out as a croak.

"Shit," I repeat, this time with a voice barely louder than a whisper.

Carefully, I get myself back up to standing. Glad that no one else seems to be around to witness my clumsiness. And extra glad that, unlike my jacket, I'd managed to zip my purse shut. The bag is dirty from the fall, but all the contents remain inside.

I blink down at the state of myself. My pant leg isn't torn, which is a miracle in itself; and my wet palms are tinged gray from the sidewalk dirt, but not freely bleeding.

It's nothing.

This is nothing.

You're tougher than this.

You'll get through this too.

It's just a bad day.

I sniff. My throat constricting as that familiar hopelessness digs deeper into my chest.

This is nothing, I tell myself.

"You're nothing!" An old but vivid voice shouts back.

My eyes squeeze closed. I hate that his voice still echoes in my head. Hate that he has any effect on me at all.

I'm not nothing.

My chest shakes as I pull in a lungful of air.

I'm not nothing.

I force my eyes open.

Today may have put me on the edge of a mental breakdown, but I'm not letting Arthur get one more tear out of me. He ruined my home. Ruined whatever relationship I may have had with my mom. He tried to...

I breathe through the horror of that last memory and remind myself that I got away.

But hasn't he been controlling your life ever since?

Anger rolls through me.

I want to snap at my inner voice that they're wrong. That all of my choices are my own. But deep down, I know that's a lie. One simple word is all it takes to remind me how deep my trauma goes.

Virginity.

It's a constant reminder of what I've been too afraid to let go of.

But, I held onto it with both my hands, even when I was the only one who believed it was worth protecting. The only one who saw it as mine to give.

I gently brush my palms off on my thighs, then begin limping the last few steps to my building.

I systematically avoided men when I ran away from home. They were terrifying. Stronger than me. Crueler than me.

It wasn't my intention to hold on to my virginity forever. I just wanted to wait until I was ready. The years just sorta slipped away.

I don't still go out of my way to avoid men. I no longer tremble, or sweat, when a man makes eye contact with me. I also don't do anything to seek out their attention either. With how much I work, I don't really give myself the opportunity to meet new people. The men I see come into the café are pretty much it for me. And as the poorly dressed, overworked, sleep-deprived woman who serves them their breakfast, I don't really scream *ask me out.*

Even before *everything*, I can't really say if any of the boys at school were interested in me or not. I kept my head down in class. Worked every day after school.

It's nearly impossible to make close friends, let alone a boyfriend, if you can never invite anyone to your house. And I *never* invited anyone to my house.

Arthur wasn't predictable. And no matter how much I wanted to have a friend, I wasn't willing to subject anyone else to his torment. His attention on me was bad enough; I wouldn't have been able to live with myself if I was the reason he directed that torment on someone else.

But for all the times he terrorized me--hit me, choked me... Arthur never crossed *that* line.

There were times I'd wonder--worry--if that was going to change. Like when I got a little older, and he started to look at me like he *truly* hated me, rather than the annoyed indifference he'd treated me with for years. Other times, his eyes would linger for too long on my chest, or on my hips. And I knew something bad would eventually happen. Knew it was inevitable. But I didn't know *what.*

I wasn't supposed to be home that day, but my shift ended early, and I had nowhere else to go. Every day since, I've thanked a god I'm not sure I believe in, for the fact that I got home when I did. That I heard what I did.

Because if I hadn't...

My feet stop at the front door of my building, and my hands are shaking so bad, it takes me three tries to unlock the latch.

Stepping out of the cold, and into the lobby, I stomp the slush off my shoes.

I want to go straight to my apartment and straight into the shower, but since I'm already in the lobby, I limp over to the wall of mailboxes.

Whatever might've happened way back then... didn't. And it's not going to. Because if they haven't tracked me down by now, ten years later, then they aren't going to.

And yet, still a virgin.

Using the small, tarnished gold key, I yank the little mailbox door open with more force than necessary. There are only a few items, but the one on the top catches my attention. It's the same pale green paper that all the building notices come on.

My heart rate picks up as I pull the letter out, confirming it's from the landlord.

My hands are dirty. I need to change. And shower. And eat something. But the bad feeling in my gut grows with every passing second I stare down at the folded-in-half piece of paper. Tucking the other letters into my purse, I rip through the little piece of tape holding the ends of the page together and flatten the note out.

Dear Renter...

My breath catches, each line sending me closer and closer to full panic mode.

...improvements that have been made to the building...

... starting January, 1st...

The words begin to blur in my vision.

...monthly increase of $250...

It can't be.

They can't do that.

Not by that much.

Dread settles across my shoulders like an old friend.

There you go, proof you don't have control over anything in your life.

How am I going to save for a better life if I can barely pay for the shitty one I already have?

My next inhale is choppy. I have until January, a couple of months to figure it out.

And do what? You'll never find another place around here for cheaper.

The paper in my hands trembles in the air.

You'll never be able to afford that dog.

And with it, fat ugly tears start to roll down my cheeks.

CHAPTER 15

Nero

I DON'T LIKE THE LOOK ON HER FACE.

It's full of defeat. Sadness.

"What's wrong, Sweet Girl?" My words are loud in the empty room.

Payton has been sitting on her couch for the last hour--possibly longer, but that's how long I've been observing--and she hasn't moved. She's just staring off into space with an utterly dejected look on her face.

I want to ask her what's wrong. Ask who I need to bury for making her look that way.

But I can't do that.

Because she can't know that I'm here. Watching.

If King could see me now, huddled up in an unoccupied apartment across the street from Payton's place, using binoculars to soak in every detail of her life, he'd laugh his fucking ass off.

But there's just something about this woman that I can't shake.

I know it's insane. Certifiably psychotic. But considering I've probably killed more people than I've fucked, I'm not really concerned about the state of my mental health anymore.

She moves, and I focus my gaze to watch as she brushes the backs of her hands over her cheeks.

My fingers tighten around the binoculars. "Who made you cry?"

It's her air of innocence. That's what gets me. What draws me to her.

It doesn't even make sense. Not after what King pulled up about her past. About all the ER visits. The stitches. The fractured bones. With everything she's been through, she shouldn't feel so... precious.

The plastic pops with a crack under my grip.

You need to leave her alone. Knowing you will only cause her more pain.

I've told myself this same thing, time and time again.

I can only offer her danger and heartache. There's nothing safe about knowing me. No matter how much I wish it were different.

Slowly, I lower my hands. The magnified view of my obsession slipping away.

My eyes stay on her, but I've lost her features. Her sorrowful eyes now hidden by distance.

Leave.

Leave now and never come back.

But as I start to stand, so does Payton.

I freeze.

She's walking across her small living room, toward me, and my heart beats harder with each step.

Payton stops with her hand resting on the handle of the sliding glass door, the one I walked through a few weeks ago. She blinks, then heaves the door open.

A gust of wind, that I know is cold, blows through the opening, sending her hair flying around her tear-splotched face.

But she doesn't move out onto the little balcony.

"What are you doing, Payton?"

I step closer to the window.

She takes a step back. And then another, causing her hand to fall away from the door.

"Payton," I growl her name into the dark room.

Her shoulders rise with one final deep breath, then she turns away and walks out of view.

Leaving the door open... for me.

CHAPTER 16

Payton

I WAKE WITH A GASP, SOMETHING INVISIBLE PULLING me out of sleep.

"Shit," I whisper toward the ceiling, as I roll onto my back, my chest rising and falling with quick inhales.

My bladder makes itself known and, with a groan, I roll the rest of the way out of bed.

It's only a matter of steps to cross the hall and enter the dark bathroom. And I don't bother with the light, dropping my sleep shorts and sitting on the toilet.

Looking down at the shadowy outline of my shorts, I shake my head. I never wear these pajamas. I bought them last year in an after-Christmas sale in a fit of impulse shopping. The silk shorts are a bright red, clashing with my pale thighs; and the top is a cream-colored silk with short sleeves, red buttons, and a red collar. And I don't need the lights on to tell me they aren't the sexy pjs I thought they were. They're basic. Cheap. Another failed attempt at being something I'm not.

Yanking my shorts up, I wash my hands and am grateful I can't see my reflection.

This whole outfit was for *him*.

Leaving my hair down when I went to bed was for *him*.

Stupid, Payton.

Seriously, what was I thinking? I left my patio door open, in the ridiculous hope that my Mystery Man would see it, take it for the invitation that it was, and come ravish me.

So stupid.

And on top of being dumb, now my apartment is freezing.

I feel around on the vanity until I find a hair binder and quickly pull my hair up.

I haven't seen *that man* since he walked out my front door.

There's been a few times that I could've sworn I'd seen him outside the café, but every time I've turned my head to look, the street has always been empty.

He's not watching over me. I'm not on his radar.

I cross my arms against the chill, and trudge to the living room. I need to close that door before I get myself sick.

My footsteps slow on the carpet. The apartment is quiet.

Too quiet.

My heart clenches, and I stop walking.

The door is closed.

CHAPTER 17

Nero

I DROP THE BINOCULARS IN A GARBAGE CAN OUTSIDE the building before I cross the street. I won't be needing those anymore. Payton made the decision, and we're switching this to an up-close and personal relationship.

My long strides bring me to the edge of Payton's balcony in seconds.

I sat in that empty apartment for an hour after she walked away from the open door. Waiting for her to change her mind and close the door. To lock me out.

But she didn't.

And I'm not a good enough man to stay away.

It's barely midnight, but it's a weekday and this is a relatively quiet part of town, so no one is around to see me climb up onto the patio railing of the first-floor apartment. Stretching up, I grab the crossbar at the bottom of Payton's railing. The metal creaks under my weight, but like last time, it holds as I brace my feet against the brick façade of the building and walk my hands up to the top banister.

It makes me mad all over again, how easy it is to just get into Payton's home.

She shouldn't live here. She's completely unprotected.

I lower myself onto the floor of her balcony slowly.

This isn't breaking and entering, since she left the door wide open *for me*, but even if it was, it wouldn't be my first time. And I'm sure it won't be my last. Because as the saying goes, if you want it done right...

The damp, cold air flows past me and into the apartment, the curtains billowing the same way they did the first time I walked through this door.

If she makes herself sick with this little stunt, I'm gonna drag her over my knee and use my palms to teach her a lesson she won't forget.

Not that you'll see her again after this.

One time.

That's all this is going to be.

One time. One fuck. One taste. Then I'll demand she lock this door every night. Hell, I'll nail it shut if I have to.

Taking a slow inhale, I fill my lungs with the fall air. Then I cross the threshold.

Standing in her home, I slide the door closed and flip the lock.

No turning back now.

CHAPTER 18
Payton

MY GAZE DARTS ALL AROUND THE LIVING ROOM AND kitchen, but there's no one here. And nowhere to hide.

But I can feel the energy. It's different.

He's here.

My legs are trembling as I turn back toward my bedroom.

He has to be here.

Closing the last few steps to my doorway, I pointedly ignore the bathroom and the fact I left the door open when I went in there to pee.

I didn't know.

How could I have known?

Tremors race up and down my limbs.

This is what I wanted.

What I asked for.

And now it's time.

CHAPTER 19

Nero

SHE'S SO FUCKING BEAUTIFUL.

Her soft breaths fanning the hair that's fallen across her cheek.

The blankets are pulled up over her shoulders, and even though the bed looks small and uncomfortable, the blanket is thick, so I know she's warm.

Perfectly warm.

Fuck, I want to touch her. That soft *soft* skin, the heat of sleep relaxing all her muscles. Leaving her limber. Ready.

My cock starts to harden.

Okay, arguably, this is the creepiest thing I've ever done. Standing in the corner of a sleeping woman's room, watching her when she doesn't know I'm here. Soaking in the scent of *her*. The colors and textures and expressions of *her*.

But she wants me here.

And I can't shake this feeling that she needs me.

I can't offer her what she's really seeking, can't give her a future or happiness, but I can give her *this*. I can give her tonight. Give her pleasure.

Payton makes a soft sound, and my body goes taut. She shifts, her eyes squeezing closed, another murmur working its way out of her chest.

My left foot lifts, readying myself to reach out and comfort her. But before I can step my leg forward, Payton's eyes pop open on a gasp.

I carefully lower my foot back to the carpet, holding my body completely still.

"Shit." Her whisper might as well be a shout with the way it hits me and reverberates around in my skull.

She lays there for a moment, looking at the ceiling, and I wonder the best way to announce my presence. I'm certain that open door was an invitation. Still, there's no way for me to let her know I'm standing here, in the dark, without scaring her.

Payton lets out a small groan, and I watch with rapt attention as she shoves the blanket off her body and climbs out of the bed. Even with the curtains closed, there's enough streetlight filtering in around the edges of the window to highlight the bare skin of her thighs.

I've never seen her like this. Not up close.

The last time I was here, she had a blanket pulled up to her chin most of the time. And then later --I clench my teeth so I don't groan as my cock grows even harder--when I pulled that blanket down a few inches, put my hands on her, actually felt her skin under my palms... it was fucking addicting. One hit of that sweetness was all it took to hook me.

And now. Well fuck, now she's barely dressed.

It's a good thing I know that she put those shorts on for me. Because if another man sees her like this, I'll rip their eyeballs out with my bare fingers.

Payton rolls her shoulders when she stands up from the bed, and it stretches her cute little shirt tight across her tits. And, *Jesus Christ,* her nipples are pebbled and pressing against the shiny fabric like little beacons, leading me home.

When she walks away, I nearly moan. Her ass has the perfect amount of jiggle. The cheeks bouncing beneath the thin material every time her foot strikes the carpet. I want to grab my dick. Squeeze it to calm it the fuck down. But where I am right now,

I'm in her peripheral vision, and I don't want her to see me yet. Not until I'm ready.

She pads across the hallway, and a small smirk pulls across my lips when I hear her in the bathroom.

It's nothing. Everyone pees. But I bet that'll stress her out more than finding me here, sitting on her bed.

When I hear her steps move toward the living room, I push away from the wall.

And when her steps stop, and I hear her sharp intake of breath above the silence of the apartment. I smile.

She knows.

And when her steps head back toward the bedroom, back toward me, I take a seat.

CHAPTER 20

Payton

I'M HOLDING MY BREATH WHEN I TURN INTO MY bedroom. And even though I knew he'd be here, I still startle.

Sitting on my bed, just feet away, is the man from my patio.

The only hint of light is coming from behind him, so he's a silhouette. But there's no mistaking that it's him.

The broad shoulders. The air of menace.

And just like last time, he's in a suit. Only this time, his tie is loose around his neck and several buttons on his shirt are open.

I wish I could see more. I want to run my eyes over every inch of him.

His shoulders rise as he takes a deep breath. "Closer."

My feet comply. Sliding forward, coming another foot nearer.

The hands resting on his knees clench into fists before slowly releasing again.

I know he can't see me any better than I can see him, but I have to fight the urge to cross my arms over my body. There's no use hiding now.

"This is your one chance, Payton." His voice is rougher than I remember. The deepness of it filling the room. "Your one chance to make the right choice. The only time I'll let you tell me no."

It feels like my heart is going to beat straight through my ribs.

73

I should tell him to leave. I should put an end to this madness while I still can. But that's not what I *want*. And for the first time in my life, I'm going to throw *safe* out the window and give in to my wants.

I want to take control of my body.

To be touched.

I want this man.

I step closer, trembling all over. But not a single doubt crosses my mind, because this is what I want.

Taking a breath, I answer him with a question. "What do I call you?"

A low sound rumbles from his chest. "I'll tell you when I'm inside of you. Now strip."

"St— W-what?"

Did he really just say that?

His shoulders roll back, like he's fighting himself to not move. "Yeah, Sweet Girl, strip for me. Show me all of you."

Every word out of his mouth hits me in the chest before gliding down, straight to my core.

This is what I want.

My fingers are unsteady, but the top button on my shirt finally pushes through, coming undone.

I've never let anyone see me naked. And I've certainly never stripped for an audience. I don't know if he's expecting me to move around while I do it because I don't have the skills it takes to be a stripper, so the rest of me stays perfectly still until the final button slips free.

The material parts an inch, but remains clinging to me.

"Off, Payton. Show me those fucking tits."

He sounds almost angry. Yet I don't think anger is the emotion he's feeling.

He's turned on.

Somehow this handsome, intimidating man is attracted to me. Pining for me.

With a confidence I only partially feel, I pull the front of my shirt open before shrugging it off my shoulders. The material floats to the floor, pooling at my feet.

I've been too overwhelmed to even think about sucking my stomach in, and it's too late now.

"The rest." His voice is so scratchy, it sounds like it hurts. "Take off the rest."

This is it.

I'm taking control.

With one quick motion, I shove my shorts down my hips and they drop down my legs. I kick the bunched material away from my feet. I don't wear underwear to bed, so I'm bared to him. Completely.

Standing there, unsure what to do, I just let him look.

The man's breathing is audible in the still room. And I can almost see the tension crackling in the space between us.

His knees widen, making room for me. "Closer."

Trembling from nerves, or the cold, or excitement, I move forward until I'm standing between his spread legs.

My bed isn't high off the ground, but his height puts us nearly face to face.

He raises his hands, ghosting them over the flesh at my hips... my sides... his thumbs brushing ever-so-softly along the underside of my breasts.

"This isn't going to be gentle." His sentence is punctuated by his hands closing around my breasts.

The heat startles me. It all startles me. The feeling of someone else's hands on my bare skin is all new.

His fingers squeeze as he groans, pushing my breasts together. "I'm not going to make love to you, Sweet Girl." He drops his hands to my hips, allowing my breasts to bounce free, and he jerks me forward, my body colliding with his. "I'm going to fuck you."

He closes his mouth around one of my nipples.

A startled sound leaves me, and my hands fly out to grab at his shoulders. "Oh my god! What are—"

Teeth scrape against my pebbled flesh before he sucks. Hard.

Sensations rolls through my body. And when he moans against my skin, I feel the answering call between my legs.

His mouth pulls free, dragging a wet kiss across to the other breast.

"Fucking divine," he growls as his mouth closes around my other peak. His tongue swirls around my nipple before he devours it. Every flick of his tongue echoed in my clit. The pulsing growing stronger with each second.

This feels so good.

Who knew it would feel so damn good?

Every part of me is throbbing. Needing more.

"Please?"

His hands flex around my hips just before sliding around to my backside. His palms smooth over my ass. Then lower.

He pulls me even closer, and then I feel his fingers push at the junction of my thighs from behind. His fingers running along my seam, easily slipping over my entrance.

We both groan at the same time, the man releasing my nipple. "You're soaking wet for me."

"I am," I agree, even though it wasn't a question.

Without warning, he stands.

I start to stumble back, but he catches me by the upper arms.

"You should've kept your door shut," he growls.

Before I can respond, he spins us and shoves me backward.

I yelp as I fall, landing with a bounce on the mattress.

His gaze doesn't leave me as he strips. Moving just as quickly and efficiently as I had. The suit jacket drops, the tie, then his shirt is gone.

He's all sculpted muscles and flexing forearms and my mouth is watering before he even starts working on his belt.

With our positions switched, him facing the bed, the light illuminates his face, I can finally see him. And he's perfect.

Even better than perfect.

He shoves the rest of his clothes off all at once and... And, *holy shit.* That's his cock.

I've never seen a cock in person before.

I shuffle backwards on the bed.

Maybe this was a bad idea.

Maybe I should lose it to an average guy. A smaller guy. Because surely that's not normal.

He steps out of his pants and closes the distance to the bed.

I try to scoot further away but he catches my ankle in one hand, holding me in place, as he crawls up the mattress.

"The time to run is over, Baby. Now it's time to give."

I'm so turned on and overstimulated that I can't formulate a reply. And so when he presses my legs open, I let him.

"That's my girl," he praises me, rubbing a hand up the inside of my thigh as I keep my legs open for him.

His tongue swipes across his lower lip and he shuffles closer.

He lifts my foot out of the way, then does the same to the other, allowing room for his knees to frame my hips. My legs are left spread wide, feet in the air.

From his kneeling position, he's looking straight down at my exposed sex.

"So wet, I can see it." He swipes two fingers across my pussy, making me jump. And my eyes widen when I watch him rub those same two fingers up and down his length.

Is that... do people do that?

I want to ask if I can touch him. I want to know what a dick feels like in my hand. But there's no way for me to ask without giving away just how little I know about this. And I don't want to give him the chance to change his mind.

He strokes his fist up and down his cock a few more times, keeping his eyes between my legs. With his other hand he reaches down and spreads me open.

I shift on the sheets, not knowing what I'm supposed to be doing. What I should do with my hands. If I should be quiet.

"Such a pretty pussy." He slides a finger up and down my slit but doesn't push in. "I bet it's gonna be tight. Bet you're gonna squeeze the cum right out of me."

His words make me squirm as much as his touch does.

I keep alternating between watching what's happening and letting my eyes close in ecstasy.

I've spent a lot of time imagining what sex would be like, but it was never like this. Even in my dreams, I couldn't have imagined a man like this.

Something bigger presses against my entrance, and my eyes fly open. The head of his cock is there. *Right there.*

It's about to happen.

My hands reach out for him, but he's too far away, kneeling just out of reach.

He can't push in like this, can he? I thought he had to be more on top of me?

Without warning, he shifts his hips forward a few inches, and I feel myself spreading around him. My body slick, begging for his entry.

"Nero." His voice is low as he slides his hands up to grip my waist. "This is when you call me Nero."

The two syllables flutter over my skin. It's exactly right. The perfect name.

"Nero," I whisper his name and watch his eyes fall shut.

Bliss crosses his features and I open my mouth to say his name again, but what comes out next is a scream.

CHAPTER 21

Nero

HEARING MY NAME ON HER LIPS UNLOCKS SOMETHING warm inside of me. I give it a second to envelop me, then I ram my hips forward.

The head of my cock meets a slight resistance, but I'm already pushing, breaking through, burying my entire length in her sweet, hot cunt.

Her pussy is clamped around me so tightly I can hardly think. But I swear...

I swear I felt...

Her scream is still ringing in my ears. And it wasn't a sound made purely of pleasure.

"What?" I pant the question, holding my body as steady as possible.

Opening my eyes, I look down at Payton, seeing her features pinched in pain. And even though her eyes are squeezed shut, I can see tears escaping. Trailing down the sides of her face.

"How...?" I can't formulate my questions.

Is my Sweet Girl seriously a virgin?

How is this fucking possible?

I pull my hips back, needing to see the evidence.

She whimpers at the movement, but even in the unlit room, I

can see the dark streak of blood running up the length of my dick. And the sight of it has my balls tightening, nearly bursting.

"Payton." Her name comes out strangled.

I can't believe it.

Why? Why would she give such an honor to me?

To me?!

Her eyes fly open, and she reaches out for me once again. "D-don't go."

I almost chuckle.

Go? She thinks I'm gonna fucking leave?

Not a chance in hell.

I can't laugh because my focus is back down between us, on the innocence staining my length.

I ask the question, even as I swipe my finger up my cock, collecting the proof. "You're a virgin?"

Her head gives the smallest shake, the side of her mouth pulling up into a strained smile. "Not anymore."

I eye the blood on my fingertip, before shoving it into my mouth.

The moan that leaves me is bone deep. The coppery taste that floods my senses is my new addiction, and I don't think, I just shove back inside her. All the way to the hilt.

Payton cries out at the intrusion and the sound is a song to my soul.

I drop my weight forward, one hand on either side of her head, so her little hands can finally reach me. And when they do, they clutch at my sides.

Her legs spread further to accommodate me, and her feet press into my hips, pulling me closer one second, then trying to push me away the next. Like she can't decide if she wants me off, or if she wants more.

But she's only going to get one of those options.

I roll my hips, lodging myself even deeper. "Say my name, Payton. Tell me who owns this pussy now."

"Y-You do, Nero," she cries.

I can hardly hear her over my roaring pulse, but I feel it. I feel it everywhere. Her lightness settling into my rotten soul.

"Again," I grit out.

"Nero!" She's panting, writhing beneath me. "Nero owns it." Her hands drag me closer. "Please!"

Dropping onto my elbows, I slide one hand under the back of her head and into her hair, gripping it at the roots.

"That's right, Baby. This belongs to me." I thrust in again. "All of you belongs to me now."

Tightening my hold, her neck arches back and I use the angle to fuse my lips to hers.

CHAPTER 22

Payton

MY ENTIRE BODY IS ON FIRE. WITH PAIN AND PLEASURE and an intensity I don't know what to do with.

But now he's kissing me.

Nero is kissing me.

His lips are warm and demanding. And maybe it's because I've never been kissed, but it feels like he's claiming me.

This kiss is just as ferocious as everything else about him. His grip in my hair. His hips slamming between my thighs. It feels like ownership.

And I let it all happen. I follow his movements, kissing him back.

I've finally let go of my control, only to give it to someone else. And it feels amazing. Wonderful.

When his tongue swipes into my mouth, I taste... oh god, I can taste it. Taste what he's taken, what I've given him. And it makes me feel feral.

"Nero," I gasp, opening my mouth for him.

The tug on my hair intensifies and the burn on my skull makes my core clench around him.

"Payton." His hips slam against me. "My Sweet fucking Girl." He withdraws his cock as he licks into my mouth. "You're mine now." He thrusts back into me. "That sweet cherry juice all over my cock made you mine." His head tilts and he deepens our kiss even more, our teeth clicking together, tongues tangling. "Gonna stay buried in this pussy forever."

I whimper. My unpracticed hips rolling to meet his. My hands clinging to his broad muscled shoulders.

When my tongue darts out to enter his mouth, he slams into me even harder.

"Let me in," he growls against my lips.

He's in, so far in, but I don't know how to let him in more.

"Come on." The hand not holding my hair reaches down and grips my leg, yanking it up until my knee is hooked over his forearm, opening me even wider.

"Let me fucking in!" he snaps.

I'm not fighting him. I'm not stopping him. And before I can reply he's thrusting up, and he's hitting inside me, deeper than he was before.

The hand in my hair lets go, and his fingers start to massage my scalp. "That's it. That's my Sweet Girl. Letting me in so good. So deep."

"Nero," I moan.

My body is on fire. Flames filling my veins. Setting me close to combustion.

His hips don't stop moving, and the arm holding my leg lifts even higher, stretching me wider. The fingers massaging through my hair are a stark contrast, soft and soothing. And it's all too much.

My breath hiccups, and before I can stop myself, I start crying in earnest. It's not from pain. And I definitely don't want him to stop. It's just the feeling of overwhelming freedom I've been craving for so long finally taking over.

"That's it, Payton." His words are hot against my ear. "Take me. Feel me."

"I am." I choke. "I do."

His tongue traces across my temple, and I know he's licking my tears away.

Nero's thrusts slow, just a little, but his strength is still punishing. Our bodies connect with a brutal collision each time.

"I need you to do one more thing for me, Baby. Give me one more thing."

"Anything." I nod my head. "I'll do anything."

I can feel his breath against my cheek. "I need to feel this virgin pussy come all over my cock."

"I—"

He cuts off my rebuttal by pressing his mouth back to mine. The kiss is slower this time. And I focus on the feeling of his lips against mine, the deliberate movements, and I move with him. Opening up for him. Tasting him. And then I feel it, his fingers on my clit.

I didn't notice him letting go of my leg, but now his hand is between us and it's...

We groan into each other's mouths as I clench around him. I'm so close.

"You're so close," he moans.

"Y-yes."

He catches my bottom lip in his teeth, biting down hard enough that I feel it in my nipples.

"Oh god! Nero, I'm almost—"

The hand tangled in my hair flattens against the back of my head and he pulls me to him, supporting his full weight on his elbow.

Wrapping my arms and legs around him, I curl around his body, shoving my face into his neck as his fingers dance over my clit. Strumming me toward a crescendo.

"Say it again," he growls. "Say my name while you come."

He thrusts up into me, his cock bottoming out as his fingers pinch my clit, and I explode.

CHAPTER 23

Nero

"NERO!" HER CRY IS HOARSE. AND IT'S A SOUND I'LL never forget.

Payton convulses around my dick and I don't hold back. Instead, I piston my hips faster.

"That's it, Baby," I pant. "Come for me. Squeeze my cock until it's pumping you full of my seed."

More tears stream from her eyes, the glittering trails searing themselves into my memory, putting me that much closer to the edge. And when her legs tighten around my back, tugging me in just a fraction of an inch deeper, I'm done.

Bellowing into her hair, I shove myself as deep as I can go, cock pulsing as I empty my balls into her channel.

CHAPTER 24

Payton

My breathing stays ragged for long moments. Minutes? It may as well be an eternity.

I feel boneless. Drained, in every possible way. But I also feel so at peace.

It's messed up. My brain is fuzzy, but I'm aware enough to know that this is all so messed up.

I don't know anything about the man whose body is still draped over me, still inside of me, except his name. *Nero*.

That's not entirely true. I know that he was here when I needed him most. I know he took the reins I handed him. And, oh boy, did he do a good job.

I toiled over the decision all evening, but I opened that door because I wanted him to walk through it. Just like he did before. And when he did, he gave me even more than I'd dared to dream for.

I let my hands flatten on his bare back, feeling it rise and fall, his skin hot under my palms.

Nero makes a sound I can only describe as contentment, as he burrows his face into that spot between my neck and shoulder, causing me to smile.

He's not so intimidating now. Not so scary.

But the situation is surreal all the same.

It's hard to breathe with his weight on top of me, but I work to take short inhales, so he won't move. I'm not ready to break this spell. And I don't want to deal with the consequences of my actions just yet. I'm enjoying the feel of his skin under my palms.

Then his teeth sink into my neck, causing me to jolt in response, making all of my muscles contract.

"Payton, you keep squeezing my cock like that and I'm gonna fuck you again." His lips brush against my skin with each word, and I can't stop my core from clenching around him, again.

He groans, and I brace for him to roll off me.

That's what the men always do in movies, and the books I read. Instead, he pushes back until he's kneeling between my legs, just like he was when we started. And he's still inside me.

Nero's fingers dig into the soft flesh on my inner thighs, holding me open.

Now that we're done, and the intensity of the passion has subsided, my cheeks start to burn with embarrassment. The room isn't any less dark, but our eyes have adjusted; and laying, spread eagle, completely naked in front of a wonderfully fit man, is not a comfortable situation for me.

A rumble rolls through Nero's chest, his fingers flexing against my legs as he shifts his hips back, his cock finally slipping free.

I try to close my legs, but the grip he has on me prevents it.

"Nero?" I don't know how to voice my discomfort, but it doesn't matter. He's not giving any notice to my words. His full attention is focused between my legs.

Shifting under his gaze, I feel it. His... *release*, leaking out of me.

I try to close my legs, but he only tightens his grip.

"Just wait," he grits out.

Giving up, I let my knees drop open, my legs relaxing as much as possible. But when he swipes a finger up my entrance, my knees automatically try to snap closed.

"Nero!" His name is a squeak. And when he lifts his glistening fingers, I slap my hands over my eyes.

A second later he lets out a deep moan, and I'd swear his finger is in his mouth again, but I don't lower my hands to watch. It's all just too overwhelming.

The hand on my thigh squeezes once more. "Don't move."

I nod my head at his command, noncomplying with my compliance.

The mattress shifts and I finally peek through my fingers when I sense the room is empty. I'm tempted to close my legs, but I know there's no point. Plus, I can feel the cooling mess slipping down to the mattress, to pool between my thighs.

The bathroom faucet turns on, and a few seconds later Nero is striding back into my room. There's not a shred of concern on his face over the fact that he's walking around fully nude. And if he's not going to hide, then I'm going to look.

I almost ask him to turn on a light, just so I can see him in detail, but that would mean he could do the same with me; and even though he seems *very* happy with my body, I'm not ready for that level of scrutiny.

Nero climbs back onto the bed, reclaiming his spot between my legs.

I'm about to ask him what he's doing, when he presses the cold damp washcloth against my pussy, dragging it through my folds.

I jerk away with a startled cry.

"Stay still."

That's what he says--*stay still*--before proceeding to use one hand to hold me open, while the other, wielding the cloth, cleans me. *Intimately.*

"It's cold," I hiss.

He gently passes the cloth over me once more. "I know, Baby."

"You could've used warm water," I grumble, apparently accepting the whole weird situation.

"You're gonna be sore enough the way it is, the cold might

help." He says it matter-of-factly while climbing out of the bed once more.

"Oh."

The water runs again for a minute, and when he reappears in the doorway, I realize I can finally close my legs.

And he's right about one thing at least. As I flatten my legs to the mattress, I'm already aching, inside and out.

Nero stands there, watching me for another moment, before clipping out, "I'm not staying."

And just like that, it feels like my whole body has been covered by a cold towel.

"Alright," I whisper my reply and reach for the blankets, pulling them up over my nakedness.

There's a wet spot on the sheet underneath me, but I'm going to ignore that until he leaves.

I watch in silence as Nero picks up his articles of clothing, pulling them on one by one.

I don't know why his actions now are making me sad. This is what I expected him to do. Truly, I didn't think this would suddenly become some sort of loving relationship. I've never been foolish enough to hope for that. From anyone.

When he turns to grab his pants, the small bits of light reflect off his back, and I can see discolored marks of scars.

I felt them when I had my limbs wrapped around him, thinking nothing of the raised texture in the moment. Seeing them now, even just in bits and pieces, it's jarring. There are several.

The urge to ask him about them, to touch them again, dances across my tongue. But I stay quiet.

Nero shrugs his shirt on. "I'm not staying."

It's a repeat of what he already said. And its meaning is clear. *I'm not staying* is different than *I can't stay.*

He's choosing to leave. Choosing to walk away.

And since he didn't acknowledge my reply before, I don't bother saying anything.

And it's fine. It really is. Hell, I basically tricked him into taking my virginity. He's probably dis--I nearly shake my head at that thought. He's clearly *not* disgusted. In fact, he was the exact opposite of disgusted.

Nero pulls his suit coat on last, and I watch him stuff his tie into the pocket, rather than put it back on.

He's larger than life standing there at the foot of my bed. Looking dangerous. Like a twisted mix of savior and executioner, wound together to create one confusing and sinful package.

Well, that's it then.

Opening my mouth, I say the only thing I can think of. "Thank you, Nero."

And I mean it. I mean it so much.

Nero stares at me, releasing a sigh so long and loud, that it has me tugging the blankets up all the way to my nose.

His cheeks flex as he clenches his jaw. Then he tips his head back and lets out another sigh toward the ceiling. "Goddammit, Payton."

My lips pinch together. I don't know what's happening.

I didn't think thanking him would be such a misstep, but it's not like I can take the words back.

Then he's ripping his suit coat back off and striding to the side of the bed.

Automatically, I start to scoot away, my body's natural reaction to being stalked.

"Stop," Nero snaps, and I do. I swear my eyes widen comically when he yanks the blankets back and climbs into bed next to me.

"What, um..." I trail off.

"I'm not staying," he mutters it this time.

He sounds so resigned, even as he does the opposite of what he just said, and I almost laugh.

Nero drops onto his back, shifting the pillow, lifting his head and smacking it back down against the lumpy cotton, trying to get comfortable. With one final sigh, he stretches his arm out in my direction. "Come fucking cuddle with me."

CHAPTER 25
Nero

I'm not staying.
I stare at the dark ceiling.
I'm seriously not staying.
My eyes start to close.
Maybe just for a minute.

CHAPTER 26

Nero

PAYTON'S WHIMPERS VIBRATE AGAINST MY EAR.

Her soft body is writhing under mine.

I can feel her pleasure pooling between us.

She's perfection. The light in my dark room.

I run my fingers through her sweet pussy and trail them up over her belly.

But then her breaths stop. And her chest stills.

"Payton." My voice is so garbled, I can hardly understand myself.

She doesn't reply.

"Payton!"

Slowly, so slowly, my eyes move up her naked form.

Her pretty pink pussy.

The red splash of her virginity.

Beads of sweat.

The flow of blood over her breasts.

Deep slash across her throat.

I lurch toward her, hands outstretched to stop the bleeding,

I gasp awake, into the present.

It's been so long since I've dreamed, I'm not used to the jarring feeling of being stuck between realities. When the dream is so fresh it feels like a memory. Feels so damn real. Hell, it looked so damn real.

Breathing through my nose, I drag myself back to the crappy apartment on Fifth Street and the living woman pressed against my side.

Another lungful--roses, clean laundry and sex.

Payton.

I rub my thumb against her bare shoulder.

A fucking virgin.

I was not expecting that. Never even crossed my mind as a possibility. Payton's young, probably too young for me, but she's plenty old to have popped her cherry. Old enough to have slept with multiple men.

My inner beast growls at the idea.

It's a good fucking thing she was a virgin. Just thinking of some dude walking around that's had his cock anywhere near Payton's pussy fills me with a boiling, murderous rage.

And if anyone else ever touches her...

If anyone else ever hurts her...

A crushing sensation presses into my chest.

Somebody did hurt her.

My fingers slowly fold into a fist.

Somebody hurt her a lot.

And it's time someone hurt him back.

CHAPTER 27

Nero

"FUCK MAN, DO YOU KNOW WHAT TIME IT IS?"

I ignore King's grumble and jump right into it. "Want to go with me to Fargo?"

"Why would anyone––" he breaks off, and I hear the rustling of him sitting up in bed. "You're gonna go fuck that old guy up, aren't you?"

I flip on my blinker. "Yep."

"Well hot diggity damn, count me in." He sounds wide awake now. "The usual hangar?"

"Yeah. Wheels up in forty."

Ending the call, I pull onto the freeway and head to the small private airport in silence.

I already called Sloan to get the flight plan filed and the plane readied. He bitched about it the whole time, but he'll do it, because it's his job. And I don't pay for him to live next to the airfield for nothing.

I hate leaving a trail of my comings and goings with flight plans, but I'd hate getting shot out of the sky more. And I don't have the time to drive my ass across the *nothing* that exists between here and there. Plus, I have a warehouse in Fargo, so I have a ready excuse to be there. Which is precisely the reason why

I have warehouses in every nearby state. Even if they're empty, they're my property, so I always have a valid reason for a flight.

The drive is uneventful, and I'm pulling up to the guard house at just before three in the morning.

This isn't the first time I've left in the middle of the night, so the security guard waves me through with a nod of his head and nothing more. I've thought about replacing him with one of my own, but the need hasn't arisen yet.

Driving slowly, I make my way to the back of my hangar and pull into one of the parking spots.

I hesitate for just a moment before deciding to leave my gun in the glove box. Based on the information King found, I'm certain he'll be alone. Just like I'm certain I'll be able to handle him with my bare hands.

The overhead door is already open when I walk around to the front of the building. Sloan is already inside, getting my Cessna ready for flight.

Private jets are overrated. They're ostentatious. And they require too many people. My plane is perfect for flying under the radar, figuratively speaking.

Sloan nods at me through the windshield, and I nod back.

I'll double check his work, but he's been around planes longer than I've been alive and has yet to mess up.

Exactly forty minutes after we hung up, King climbs the steps and boards the plane.

I wait until we're rolling onto the runway before I look over at him in the co-pilot seat. "You know we're going there to kill a guy, right?"

He snorts, running a hand down the front of his perfectly cut suit. "Giving the man a good view before he dies seems like a kindness."

I might also be in a suit, but this is the one I've been wearing all day. He woke up and *chose* to get dressed this way.

I shake my head. "You're an idiot."

King shifts in his seat, trying to get comfortable. "If you must know, *mother*, I have to go to brunch with Aspen and her husband after this. And I figured there's a chance I won't have time to go home between *killing a guy* and French Toast."

"Hmm." He has a point. "I thought you hated your sister's husband?" I ask, pushing down the throttle.

"I do," King grunts. "But my hatred for him is overshadowed by my fear of her. And she'll make my life hell if I don't show."

"God, you're such a pussy."

"Fine, whatever. Now shut up and pay attention to what you're doing."

"You suddenly afraid of flying?" I taunt. "I'm a good pilot and you know it."

"Uh-huh." He tightens his seat belt. "I also know what grades you got in physics, so don't get all fucking cocky."

An honest laugh rolls out of me as I pull back the yoke, the aircraft smoothly rising off the ground.

THE SKY IS STILL DARK WITH NIGHT WHEN WE CLIMB off the plane and onto the Fargo tarmac.

King makes a scene of stretching out his back when he unfolds from the plane, as he always does. Usually, it's accompanied with a comment about how the aircraft is too small, or how I need to upgrade to a *real plane*. He knows I'm not in the mood for jokes right now though, as I use this time to prepare myself for what's to come.

Reacting to aggression is one thing. But premeditated violence, that's something else entirely.

I'm good at both.

King strides ahead to get a set of car keys from one of our local men. Sloan took care of everything we'd need on this end too.

I glance over, hearing snippets of their conversation, and notice the man standing in front of King keeps his eyes down.

There's a good chance that man has no idea who King is, but he's smart enough to know that anyone traveling with me, in the middle of the night, is someone to be scared of.

King and I have separate lives, run separate careers, but in the underground, we rule together.

We *are* The Alliance.

To the public, King is just another rich-as-hell businessman, busy fucking his way through high society and making millions through clever investments.

I'm a little different. To the public, I'm basically a nobody. A rich nobody, just some guy who owns a security company, and moves in the right circles because of the money I have. But not someone to concern yourself with.

That same public has never heard of The Alliance. And if they do, if they hear the whispers, they figure it's just a bunch of campfire stories. Something from Gotham City, but not here. The bad guys never live *here*.

And that's exactly how we want it.

We don't want everyday people knowing who we really are. That we're the ones that go bump in the night.

I flex my fingers, breathing in the cold North Dakota air.

But The Alliance is real. And the people in our world know to be scared of us.

To fear me.

To them, the name Nero is synonymous with Hades.

I hear King say one last thing before dismissing the man and heading my way.

There are a couple of reasons we try to avoid being seen together. First, and most obvious, is that we never want to present ourselves as an easy target for our enemies. One well-placed bomb could rip the entire organization apart if it took both of us out.

But the second, more complicated reason, is that we don't want King's face associated with the organization. He's an equal partner to me, although very few people know that, including those in the organization.

Unlike me, King comes from money. And he has family members. Which means collateral. Liabilities. And being associated with The Alliance means constantly looking over your shoulder. He didn't want that for his sisters. So, he weighed the options and decided to distance himself from me––publicly.

But there are always two sides to a coin. Sure, as an unknown player, he doesn't have every crime family breathing down his neck, trying to kill him at every turn. But on the flip side, since the men of The Alliance don't know they work for him, like they work for me, King doesn't readily have the protection of our army. He'll only get it if I command it. And if I die before I can reveal our connection to our men, well, then he's fucked.

Because that's the thing about slaughtering dozens during a hostile takeover. Almost everybody who knew about King's connection to the previous mafia families, and therefore me, is dead. And dead men don't talk.

King stops at my side. "Just confirmed the woman is working. And someone drove by ten minutes ago saying the house looks quiet."

I dip my chin.

Arthur still lives with Payton's mother, but she works overnights at a gas station on the edge of town. I wouldn't be opposed to wiping her off the face of the earth too, but it's better that she's out of the house and Arthur is alone.

"Alright." I roll out my shoulders. "Let's go."

King nods at me before circling around to the driver's side of the borrowed SUV.

Less than twenty minutes later, we're pulling to a stop in front of a run down, piece of shit, two-story house.

The neighborhood is lower class, a little rough around the edges, but it doesn't look dangerous. It's quiet. A gunshot here would definitely get the cops called. Good thing we don't need guns.

Climbing out of the vehicle, I take a second to look closely at the houses across the street, confirming that the folks around here aren't spending their money on those fucking doorbells with cameras. Good.

Our footsteps eat up the sidewalk, and when we reach the house, I lift a hand, signaling King to wait.

The front porch looks half-rotted. It'll be a miracle if it doesn't collapse under my weight, so I'm sure as shit not walking next to King on those boards.

People always think the back door is better, but it's not. Seeing someone standing at your neighbor's door, even at night, is not that weird. Seeing someone jump the fence into your neighbor's backyard is always suspicious.

The stairs creak as I climb them, but they hold.

A curtain is pulled shut across the front window, but the corner of it is caught on a lamp, showing a pie slice view of the room.

I reach into my pocket, going for my lock-picking tools, but pause.

I wonder...

Abandoning the tools, I close my hand around the door handle and... it clicks open.

"Hillbilly," King mutters behind me.

I don't disagree, but the small-town mentality of leaving your doors unlocked just saved us half a minute.

Moving with the door, I step into the house.

To my right, there's a coat closet with the door missing, and on the left, there's a half wall extending a few feet out into the room, separating the worn linoleum of the entryway from the matted gray carpet in the living room.

And in the center of the living room is Arthur. Asleep in a shit-brown recliner, facing an obnoxiously large TV playing an old football game just a few notches too loud.

It's annoying, but I leave it on.

I take in the details of the room as I walk toward the man, flipping the corner of the curtain closed on my way.

Empty beer bottles. Empty whiskey bottles. Cigarettes piled on glass trays, the old tobacco smell thick and cloying.

It's all too much like some of the houses I was passed between when I was without a real home.

My eyes pass over the small kitchen in the far corner of the space, with its empty fast-food wrappers on the counter and small dining table covered in junk.

The anger that's been simmering inside my veins starts to bubble.

I look toward the stairs––the hard wooden stairs, with the dented banister––and I think of Payton. I think of my sweet girl growing up in this house. Being terrorized in this house.

A vision of her medical records flashes into my mind. The X-ray of her arm when she was 14. The accompanying statement by her parents, claiming she fell down the stairs.

Fell. I don't think so.

I let my eyes close, settling into the darkness, allowing my true self to take over.

And when my eyes open, all I feel is rage.

My steps are measured when I circle around the front of the chair, brushing against Arthur's extended feet.

Moving next to the recliner, I stop close enough to see the crumbs stuck in his scraggly beard.

He's not as big as me, but he's not a small man. A little soft with age and booze, but ten years ago... Ten years ago he would've been a formidable figure. No match at all for a teenage girl.

I bend down, inches from his face, and shout his name. "Arthur!"

And when his eyes fly open, I slam my fist into the center of his chest, hard enough to send the chair tipping backward.

Arthur lets out a grunt when the back of the chair hits the ground, his head bouncing against the padded headrest. The hit to his sternum seized his lungs. And he's struggling to catch his breath when he should be struggling to get away.

He's not scared enough.

Not yet.

Before he can roll out of his current splayed position, I step across to straddle him, then drop down—sitting heavily on his stomach, with my knees pinning his shoulders to the chair beneath him.

"What--" He finally chokes a word out.

And I slap him. Hard.

King snorts.

Arthur blinks against the sting in his cheek, then starts to struggle.

I easily bat his hands away. And when one of his knees thuds into my spine, I throw my elbow back into his thigh, causing him to cry out. Before he can try to nail me again, King grips Arthur's ankles, jerking them away from me, forcing Arthur to look like he's sitting properly in the chair. Only this chair is laying on its back, and I'm sitting on the occupant.

"Okay! Okay!" Arthur frantically pleads, assuming we're here for something we're not. "I just need a little more time!"

He shakily holds his hands up in surrender, and it almost makes me smile.

I don't need his surrender. I'm here to take without permission.

I lean more of my weight onto my knees, feeling his shoulders grind beneath me.

"T-Tell him! I'll have the money soon!"

I ignore Arthur's words, distracted by a flash of gold on one of his wavering hands.

A pinky ring. *Typical.*

And when the lamp light reflects off it again, a memory pops into my head.

Payton on the couch. Crying in her sleep. Clawing at her neck. Fighting an invisible monster.

Giving me a name.

"Have you always worn that?" The sound of my voice makes Arthur stop struggling.

"What?" He tries to look down at his stained and holey t-shirt.

"The ring." I gesture toward his hand. "Have you always worn it?"

He's nodding as he closes his hand into a loose fist, allowing us to both see the top. As I expected, it's a gaudy class ring. A wide gold band, covered in engravings that circle a large, obviously fake, red stone.

"I see."

I can feel Arthur's confusion as I stare at that fucking ring. Imagining the distress that would've covered a young Payton's face, as she tried to push that hand away. Imagining the tears streaking down her face while *that ring* pressed into her flesh.

The viciousness that lives inside me slithers up my spine, and in my mind I smell the scent of roses.

Without another word, I dart my left hand out and grip his wrist.

My weight shifts further forward, until I'm looming over him, his hand trapped between us.

Arthur's struggling now. His eyes are wide, his animal instincts kicking in.

She would've looked the same way.

With my right hand, I grab his pinky. The ring warm where it meets my skin.

Arthur really starts to fight now. And I hear King grunt behind me, as he puts more weight against Arthur's legs.

Arthur tries to hit me with his free hand, so I widen my stance, my left knee jamming hard into his right bicep.

"Just take it!" Arthur's shout is garbled. "Take the ring!"

My lips curl into a grin. "Okay."

But instead of sliding the ring off, I tighten my grip around his pinky finger, squeezing it, as tight as I can.

I jerk my hands apart. A crackling sound fills the room.

And Arthur starts to scream.

The finger is broken, in a couple of places, but it's still attached.

Huh.

I give the finger another sharp pull. This time the bone breaks through the skin, causing my grip to become slick with blood.

This is tougher than I thought.

A howl escapes Arthur, so I let go long enough to punch him once in the face.

He doesn't even have the decency to take it like a man.

I need a better grip.

Spotting a hole at the collar of his shirt, I drop his hand completely and rip a strip of fabric off. Using the piece of Arthur's own shirt--much to his dislike--I wrap his pinky in the rough cotton, giving me the friction I need.

Arthur's howls of pain, never subsiding.

Exhaling, I channel my fury into my grip, and with one final yank, I rip Arthur's finger off.

Finally.

Holding onto one end of the strip of cloth, I let it unwind. The loose finger dropping onto Arthur's chest.

"Gross," King mutters.

I let go of Arthur's hand, shifting my knees back to his chest, and he immediately clutches his four-digit hand in his five-digit hand.

His sobs make his words incoherent. But it wouldn't matter if I could understand him anyway. His fate was sealed the night I walked through Payton's patio door.

I pick up the finger and slide the ring off the bloody end.

"This is mine now." I wipe the ring clean on his shirt then slide it into my pocket.

Arthur finally catches his breath enough to form words. "Who are you?"

"Ah, finally the right question." I lean down, invading his space. "I'm Payton's wrath. And you're about to die."

When he opens his mouth to respond, I jam the balled-up piece of bloody cloth between his molars, keeping his mouth open, then I shove his newly unattached appendage into his mouth.

King makes a gagging noise behind me, but I don't stop shoving until the finger is wedged into his throat.

Yanking the cloth free, I close my hand over his mouth. And use my other hand to pinch his nose shut.

Arthur's eyes are bulging up at me.

Frantic.

Begging.

Terrified.

His hands are ineffectively scratching at my shirt, and when his eyes are on the verge of rolling back, I remove my hands, giving him the briefest glimpse of hope before I throw my fist into the front of his throat. Collapsing his trachea.

He blinks––soundlessly––up at me. His mind doesn't seem to understand that he's already dead.

CHAPTER 28

Nero

THE CHAIR ROCKS SLIGHTLY AS KING USES IT TO SHOVE himself up. "Man, that was an uncomfortable way to hold someone down. I think I pulled a muscle."

I ignore King.

Some killings leave me feeling riled. Or restless. But not this one. Right now... Right now, I feel content.

Until I notice a warmth seeping into my pants, and I jump up.

"The fuck?!" I spin around, looking at the dead man on the floor and the large wet spot where he pissed all over himself. And how I was fucking sitting in it.

"Are you kidding me?!" I swing a foot out and kick Arthur's body in the side.

"What?" King stops, trying to stretch out his neck.

"This motherfucker peed on me!"

King barks out a laugh.

"You fucking fuck!" I kick Arthur again, before undoing my belt.

"What are you doing?" King asks between laughs.

"Go find what we need," I snap, as I step into the small bathroom I spied sitting opposite the kitchen.

Cursing the whole time, I take my pants and boxer briefs off. Both of them soaked through with that asshole's piss.

The towel on the edge of the sink looks as dirty as the fucking floor. But I find a roll of paper towels under the sink and I rip off a handful, lathering them up with some water and hand soap before scrubbing at my ass.

I want to scrub my whole body clean but stepping out of my pants in my socks was bad enough. You couldn't pay me enough to shower in this house.

Payton had to.

Payton had to live in this hellhole.

Leaving the water running, I pull the ring out of my pocket and scrub it clean.

I wasn't planning on taking it. I didn't even know about it. But looking at it now, I know I'll find a way to give it to Payton. Hopefully giving her the closure she deserves.

The scent of alcohol and chemicals fill my nostrils when I step back into the living room.

I drop my pants and underwear onto Arthur, before picking up a half-full bottle of whiskey and emptying it over them.

"Uh, you forgetting something?" King raises his brows, like maybe I didn't know I was standing in just socks and shoes with my dick out.

"Yeah, give me your pants."

All the humor leaves his face. "You're joking."

"Even if this prick had clean clothes, they wouldn't fit me." I gesture to his lower half. "So, give me your pants. Unless you'd prefer to stare at my junk, for the next several hours, until we land back in Minneapolis."

I watch King's fists clench as he strides toward Arthur's body and administers his own set of kicks. "You stupid bastard."

King unzips his fly, then steps up and kicks the corpse one more time. "Fuck you, man."

Grumbling, King braces a shoulder against the wall as he steps in and out of his shoes, pulling his pant legs off, then putting his feet back into his shoes, without ever touching his socks to the floor.

Finished, King throws the pants at me, and I make sure not to say anything about his red silk boxers. Because as much as I want to laugh, there's a good chance King would get pissy enough to take his pants back and make me fly home with my balls stuck to the pilot's seat.

"I get to light the match," King snaps when I've threaded my belt through my new pants.

"Fine by me."

We step over the trail of whiskey and junk mail that King laid out between the chair and the front door. The paper won't do much, but the more to burn, the better.

It's gonna look like murder. Arthur's not worth the effort of disposing properly. But the fire will obscure traces of DNA we may have left behind. And there's nothing about this scene, or this man, that ties back to me.

Except, of course, Payton.

CHAPTER 29
Payton

M<small>Y</small> BLARING ALARM SLOWLY SEEPS INTO MY consciousness, and I crack my eyes open.

Groaning, I try to reach for it, but I'm on the wrong side of the mattress.

My eyes snap all the way open.

He was here. In my bed. And we-

The volume of the alarm increases, and I force myself to roll toward it. Every single muscle screams in protest as I move, and I let out the most pitiful moan.

Finally silencing the obnoxious blaring, I lay flat on my back and take stock of my body.

Even though yesterday--before Nero--was the worst day I've had in a long time, I feel as though I slept deeper than I ever have.

Part of that could be exhaustion, but I've fallen asleep crying more times than I care to admit, and I've never woken up feeling like this.

With effort, I wiggle my fingers and toes.

My limbs are heavy, muscles exhausted. And, without prompting, I picture myself with my arms and legs wrapped around Nero's solid body.

Nero.

I mouth his name. Not daring to say it out loud again, not just yet.

I bend one knee, putting my foot flat on the bed, and the motion tugs at my stomach muscles. Apparently, I need to try doing a few crunches, since holding my legs around his hips was more of a core workout than I'm used to.

Or I could just start having sex on a regular basis. That's an exercise I might actually do.

Except that would require seeing Nero again. And as much as I want to, I'm not sure that'll happen. He didn't exactly ask for my number.

He does like to cuddle.

But then it's only five in the morning, and he's not here.

Lifting my head off the mattress, I look around at the dark corners of the room, confirming he's gone, and a small shiver works its way across my skin.

He must've been in here last night, when I woke up.

I was half-asleep, but I would've noticed him walking past the open bathroom door. And he certainly didn't pass me in my tiny hallway when I went into the living room to shut the patio door.

My throat works on a swallow.

The fact that I feel that tendril of fear *now* is rather ridiculous. Instead, I choose to get up. Moving to my tiny closet, I pull open the door and make sure there's not a man lurking in the shadows. And I tell myself that I'm leaving the door open so it's easier to get dressed for work. Not because I'm sure I'll feel compelled to check again.

The soreness between my legs flares to life with each step I take. I feel a foreign dampness, reminding me that I let him clean me last night, but I never got up to use the bathroom.

What I did was foolish. Dangerous. Reckless. Nonetheless, it doesn't stop me from smiling.

Not a virgin.

My smile pulls into a grimace as I wince my way to the bathroom. I don't know if this is a normal amount of pain after your first time, or if it has more to do with the vigor that Nero used to... fuck me.

My stomach clenches.

I really hope we can do that again.

Not wanting to ruin my current good mood by seeing my naked disheveled state, I ignore the vanity mirror and head right to the shower, turning the water on to warm.

But before I drop onto the toilet, I spin back around, and, keeping my eyes averted, tug the mirror, exposing the small medicine cabinet hidden behind it.

Snagging my little holder, I pop one of the tiny pills out of the packet, courtesy of the local clinic and their discounted birth control.

I really *really* hope he isn't carrying some sort of communicable disease, because I hadn't even thought about protection last night. Not that I even own condoms. Why would I? It's lucky I have the pill. But my periods were horrendous, and I remember reading somewhere that a contraceptive might help. And it did.

Silently thanking my past self, I use the small cup I keep by the sink and take my daily pill. Paying for antibiotics would be hardship enough so paying for an abortion is definitely not in the budget. And I'd have to, because if I can't afford a dog, I certainly can't afford a kid.

I snap the pill case closed, then return it to its shelf and head into the shower.

My routine takes longer than normal, with my achy muscles, so I'm running behind when I hustle back across the hall into my bedroom.

Because I was so distracted when I woke up, I didn't even think to make my coffee earlier.

I'll celebrate with a coconut honey latte when I get to work.

I snort, feeling like a complete loser for wanting to celebrate losing my virginity. But I've been guarding it for so long, it's honestly a relief to be done with it. And I did it on my own terms, with a man that affects me in ways I couldn't have even imagined.

So it's with thoughts of Nero on my brain, that I pull open my underwear drawer and freeze. Sitting on top of my little pile of panties, is a crisp hundred-dollar bill.

CHAPTER 30

Nero

"Well, if you hadn't missed our appointment yesterday morning"—Abdul adjusts one of the many stacks of papers on his desk—"we wouldn't need to do these all today."

I pinch the bridge of my nose. "I was busy," I growl.

My realtor sighs. "Fine, fine, I'll drop it."

"Appreciate that," I say flatly.

"Well, the good news is, I've rescheduled the showings for this afternoon. I have the three properties you said you were interested in, plus another two that I think fit your needs. And they're all in the districts you requested."

"Good." I push out of the extremely uncomfortable chair across from Abdul's desk.

He may be the best in town, but my patience is thinner than usual today. I consider telling him why I was late this morning, that choking a man to death with his own finger altered my schedule for the week, then decide against it.

"I'll see you in a couple of hours," he calls after me, as I stride out the door.

But I'm no longer listening, because now I have a little time to spare, and it's been too long since I've laid eyes on my Sweet Girl.

Flipping my blinker on, I turn down the block
Payton works on, and remind myself that I'm not going in.

It's mid-morning, and the early rush should be over, though it
seems like there's almost always a couple of customers in the shop.

My foot depresses on the brake as I come even with Twin's
Café, but the afternoon sun is glinting off the glass of the large
windows at just the wrong angle, messing with my view of the
interior.

I tighten my grip around the steering wheel.

I should leave. I didn't make any promises to her. Never said
I'd call.

And I can go back to that empty apartment across the street
from hers tonight and see her that way.

I don't need to go in.

A car pulls out of a metered parking spot just ahead of me,
and my foot lifts itself off the brake.

CHAPTER 31
Payton

EVERY TIME I LOOK OUT AT THE STREET, I THINK I SEE Nero. Every man in a suit. Every man who fills the doorway. Even when there's no one there, I swear I see the shadows move, and I swear it's him.

But it never is.

My cheeks round as I blow out a breath.

All the customers are settled. I'm sure someone will need something soon, but I should have a quick second to steal a drink from the coffee I have sitting in back.

The cup has just touched my lips when I hear the front door open.

"Of course," I huff, before setting it back down. I get that they don't want customers to see us eating or drinking, but it'll be a miracle if I ever finish this latte.

Dusting my hands off, I hurry back toward my spot behind the counter.

I'm halfway to the register, when my gaze falls on the man striding in from the entrance. And the sight of him pulls all the breath from my body.

He's so handsome.

So goddamn handsome.

His dark beard is trimmed and neat, his hair is styled perfectly back from his serious face. His shoulders are set, and his chest is broad under another perfectly tailored suit.

His eyes lock on mine and even though he's several paces away, I know the exact shade of green that's looking back at me. Because they're the eyes I see when I dream.

Only this isn't a dream. This is real life. And the first time I've seen him in the daylight.

Him.

Nero.

Memories of his body over mine flicker behind my eyes, and my mouth lifts into a shy smile.

"Nero!" A new voice booms from inside the cafe, startling me.

But my gaze doesn't tear away from the man who was inside me less than forty-eight hours ago. And because I'm watching, staring, I witness the shift in his features. Witness him transforming into someone I don't recognize at all. Something shutters closed inside of him, dimming the energy he exudes, and blocking the wildness I usually see in his eyes.

Unlike me, Nero doesn't ignore the voice. Instead, he ignores me. Turning away from me, not acknowledging me in any way.

A pang of hurt sears into my chest, sinking deep.

You're a nobody.

I bat the voice away as soon as it tries to take root.

It would be rude of Nero to not go say hello to whoever called out. He can go, greet his friend, then he can come back and talk to me.

Talk to me.

In my place of work.

The magnitude of him being *here* finally hits me. Nero is here, in Twin's Café.

He didn't look surprised to see me. I mean, maybe it's a coincidence. Maybe he works around here? Or was walking past and wanted a coffee.

Unlikely, but possible.

Except the way he was walking right to me... The way he was staring at me... It felt intentional.

"Nero, my boy!" The voice comes again, and I turn my head to follow Nero as he stops across from an older overweight man in a blue suit.

How does he know—

"Mr. Mayor," Nero greets him, taking the extended hand of the Mayor of Minneapolis.

"What an unexpected visitor to my little slice of heaven." The mayor spreads his arms wide. "Have you eaten here before?"

Nero glances at the glass displays next to me. "I have not."

"Of course not. Twin's opens about the time you're going to bed, I'd imagine." The other man laughs. "And they close long before your night starts."

"Indeed." Nero's tone is bland.

What does that mean?

Does Nero work some sort of night shift? In a suit?

The mayor gestures toward the empty seat at his table. "Come, come. Go order some lunch, then sit with me. I insist."

Not wanting to get caught eavesdropping, I quickly avert my eyes. Though it's hardly a private conversation, given how loud the mayor talks and the fact that the dining room is rather small.

"Alright." Nero's voice is followed by his footsteps, and I busy my hands, straightening a stack of napkins.

When I can no longer pretend I don't hear him approaching, I look up.

My mouth is suddenly so dry, I have to wet my lips before I can speak.

I'm not sure what to say. He's acting like we don't know each other.

Do we know each other?

"I'll take the turkey and bacon panini." He holds my gaze while he says it, but that's it. There's no hello. No recognition or acting like I'm anything other than some girl taking his lunch order.

A lump builds in my throat, and I try so hard to keep the pain off my face.

I let my gaze drop and focus all my attention on typing his order onto the small screen in front of me.

When he doesn't ask for more, I force myself to speak. "Would you like something to drink?"

There's a beat before he replies. "Coconut honey latte."

Hearing him repeat my favorite drink almost shocks me into looking up, but I force my eyes to stay lowered.

That can't really be what he likes. Ordering it must be just another way to mess with me.

But... there's no way for him to know that.

Maybe I really am losing my mind. Maybe our night together never even happened and I imagined it all.

Dread fuses with the hurt feelings building inside my chest.

Oh my god... What if none of it happened?

A man walking through my patio door, sitting on my couch, eating my popcorn... It's crazy.

Leaving my patio door open for that same man to miraculously climb back through... to take my virginity... That's insanity.

One long finger taps the counter, causing me to blink.

My hand lifts. "Are you real?" I whisper the question. Not meaning to, but not able to stop myself.

But he doesn't answer me, and I don't dare reach across the counter to see if he's really there.

With shaky fingers, I type in the drink order. Hoping that there really is a man in front of me. That I didn't make it all up.

The little display shows the total and instead of saying it out loud, I swivel the screen around so he can see it too.

A twenty gets set down on the counter, and I quickly make

change, sliding the small stack of bills and coins across the counter.

I watch the hand that picks up the money, putting it back in his wallet. But before he closes the black leather, he pulls out a hundred-dollar bill, setting it down between us.

"I'm real, Sweet Girl."

CHAPTER 32
Nero

WHEN PAYTON FINALLY LOOKS UP AT ME, THE STRICKEN expression feels like a punch to the ribcage.

And I get it. Two nights ago, I took her innocence, and today, I'm acting like I've never even seen her before.

I want to grip her chin and tell her that I'm doing this for her. To keep her safe. That no one can know that I-

I grit my teeth.

I what? *Care* for her?

I don't even know her.

Turning my back on Payton, and the hurt in her eyes, I hold in my sigh as I take a seat across from Mayor Devon.

Thankfully, he doesn't question why I came into this specific café, he just starts in on some new hotel he's invested in. He's acting like he found it through some clever investigating, but I know for a fact he heard about it from King, because so did I. But it's clear that Mayor Devon doesn't realize The Alliance owns the parent company. I'm tempted to thank him for his investment in my money laundering front, but as satisfying as that would be, I know better than to utter a word because the mayor is the biggest fucking gossip I've ever met.

And he's careless.

He thinks we have some sort of partnership. But that's because he's a fucking idiot. He's in my pocket, indebted to *me*.

As he prattles on, I nod my head. It's all good information to know, but honestly, I've learned more about his dealings from the hookers he uses than I have from the man himself. Which is both a perk and a downside of using the same escort service.

Not that I'll have the need for a whore again anytime soon.

My attention slides over to Payton, who's still busy behind the counter making my drink.

You're the only man who's ever been inside of her.

Lust courses down my spine.

And I'm the only man that ever will.

CHAPTER 33

Payton

PRESSING THE LID ONTO NERO'S DRINK I TRY TO DECIDE what would be worse, having to call his name across the dining room or trying to catch his attention silently, but having to look at him.

Truly, it's a lose-lose situation.

The decision is made for me when I glance up and find Nero staring right at me.

Freaking hell.

I can feel his gaze like a weight draped around my shoulders. It's heavy and uncomfortable. And it makes me hate how good looking he is. It makes it all so much worse.

Here I am, barely-there makeup, plain gray shirt, hair in a not-so-cute messy bun, and an apron. Not exactly looking my best.

Nero says something to the other man at his table. The mayor. Because whatever it is that Nero does for a living, he knows the mayor. And the mayor knows him well enough to call him by name and make a comment about Nero being out late.

Considering how we met, I don't really doubt him.

My internal thoughts distracted me, so I'm still holding the cup when Nero stops opposite me at the counter. It'd probably be weird now to set it down rather than hand it to him. So, reluctantly, I hold out the latte. One hand flat under the bottom of the cup, the other holding near the top, giving him plenty of space to take it from me without our hands touching.

He uses both of his hands to take the drink from me. His fingertips brushing against the backs of my hands as he does.

My teeth clamp down on my lower lip, biting back the pathetic sound that wants to crawl out of my throat. Refusing to let it free.

I want to feel his touch again, so badly. And I feel so weak for desiring something he clearly doesn't want to give.

"Payton." His voice is quiet, lowered so no one can hear him call me by name. "I--"

Whatever he's about to say gets cut off when the front door is pushed open. Nero closes his mouth and takes a step back, distancing himself from me. Again.

I swallow. "Your food will be ready in a minute."

He nods and goes back to his table.

When Jean shouts his name for his sandwich, I block out his movements as he rises to get it.

I pretend he's not a dozen steps away while I help the next customer.

I tell myself that I'll get over it, him, soon.

I'm busying myself by wiping down the coffee station when my phone vibrates from inside my apron pocket.

Mostly, I use my phone for entertainment. I don't really have anyone, that isn't working in this very café, who would call or text me.

With my brow scrunched together, I pull out my phone, seeing a text from an unknown number.

> Unknown: Eyes up, Baby.

My eyes snap up. Nero is sitting at the table, with his phone in his hand. The Mayor busy on a phone call.

My phone vibrates in my hand.

> Unknown: Keep acting like we don't know each other.

> Unknown: I'll explain later.

The hurt coiled through my body starts to vibrate with anger, and I have to focus on the letters as I type out my reply.

> Me: We don't know each other.

I shove my phone back into my pocket.

You know what, this is good. I'd much rather be mad than sad.

My phone vibrates once more. And I manage to ignore it for a whole ten seconds before I take it out again.

> Unknown: I know what your virgin blood tastes like when it's painted across my cock. We know each other.

Heat flares across my cheeks and I shove the phone back into my pocket.

I cannot believe he just said that.

And I refuse to admit that my thighs clenched when I read it.

Good news--I didn't make it all up in my head, Nero is a real man, and we really did have sex.

Bad news--he's a dick.

The front door opens again, giving me a distraction.

"Hey, Pay!" Carlton lifts one wiry arm as he walks the short distance to the register.

My heart does a quick succession of double beats. This feels bad.

"Hi, Carlton." I try to greet him as normally as possible, even though my smile feels fake.

I don't know why having him in the same room as Nero fills me with this sense of anxiety, but it does. It's like watching one of those nature videos where the unsuspecting gazelle stands grazing in the field, unaware of the lion prowling in the grass behind him.

Carlton isn't even a gazelle with super speed on his side though, he's just a nice guy. The type of nice guy that would get chewed up and spit out by a man like Nero.

Unbidden, my mind conjures up an image of what it would've been like to give my virginity to Carlton.

It would've been sweet. And slow. A night probably filled with flowers and maybe a nice dinner. Probably wouldn't have been messy and hard.

He wouldn't have sat in the dark corner of my room while I slept.

He wouldn't have *tasted* me like Nero did.

It would've been so different. And not at all what I wanted.

"Everything okay?" Carlton asks, breaking my daydream.

I nod. "Yeah, it's just, uh, been a day."

"I hear that. But..." He pauses, raising his brows conspiratorially. "I have something that might make your day better."

"Oh yeah?" I try to stay focused on Carlton. Trying so hard not to look past his shoulder, but my eyes are drawn over, to see if Nero notices that someone is talking to me.

Nero definitely notices, because he's glaring at the back of Carlton's head.

"Yeah!" Carlton replies. "Because..." He uses his two pointer fingers to do a little drumroll on the countertop. "We got a gig opening for a band tonight! Like a real band! In a real venue!"

My mouth pulls into the first genuine smile of the day. "Really? That's so cool!"

"Right!?" Carlton pulls his phone out of his back pocket. "So I need your number, then I can send you a ticket."

"A ticket?"

"Don't tell me you already forgot." He shakes his head playfully. "You said you'd come watch us play. Remember?"

"Oh. Right." I think about the hundred-dollar bill that Nero just gave me. I never thought I'd shy away from the sight of money, but now that he's pretending like I don't exist, it feels dirty to keep it. "I have some cash," I offer, deciding that spending it on a concert ticket right now would be an easy way to get rid of it.

"Pssh." Carlton waves his hand like he's shooing a fly away. "You don't have to pay. I was given a couple of freebies. But I gotta text you the ticket so you have it."

I worry my lip.

A part of me feels like I shouldn't take him up on it. But I did tell him I'd go. And I've never been to a concert before. And it's not like Nero and I are dating, we're too busy pretending like we don't know each other.

Screw it.

I force my eyes to stay on the man in front of me and recite my number to Carlton as he types it into his phone.

I've barely finished saying the last digit when I feel my own phone vibrate.

He's still tapping at something, but I pull my phone out, expecting to find the ticket.

> Unknown: Did you seriously just give that man your phone number?

I swallow, my mouth feeling suddenly dry.
Not a ticket.

> Unknown: Who the fuck is he?

I set my phone face down on the counter, feeling it vibrate as I do.

I don't owe Nero an explanation. This is none of his business.

"Okay." Carlton tips his phone toward mine on the counter. "Click on the link I sent you and it will open to your ticket. Then just show it at the main doors, and voila!"

My phone vibrates again, the sound amplified since it's sitting on the hard surface, but I don't look down. This time I'm sure it's the ticket.

"Who--" I start, but the screech of a chair scraping across the floor makes me fumble the question. "Um, who're you opening for?"

Carlton launches into a detailed background on the other band, but I'm not really listening. All my energy is focused on *not* watching Nero's approach.

Nero is holding his phone in his hand when he stops uncomfortably close to Carlton. But Carlton is so deep in his story, he doesn't even notice the unhappy man inches behind him. "--which is how we even heard about it," he continues.

Nero's fingers work swiftly across his phone screen.

My phone vibrates.

"--so Dan sent them a message on Insta—"

And vibrates again.

"--should be pretty killer. But we need to get there--"

And again.

"Do you need to get that?" Carlton gestures toward my phone.

I shake my head. "It's nothing."

Then, cutting a look to Nero, I pick up my phone and slide it into my apron without looking at the screen. The muscle in his neck twitches a second before I feel my pocket vibrate with yet another text.

Luckily, Carlton takes me at my word, going back to telling me about their soundcheck, oblivious to Nero's looming presence.

How did Nero get my number?

When did he get it?

Why did he never reach out before?

Why is he texting me now?

My pocket starts a new vibration pattern and I glance over to see Nero, with his phone pressed to his ear, eyes narrowed on me.

Is this man seriously calling me right now, while standing four feet away?

My fingers grope around in my pocket before I'm able to click the side button, effectively sending the call to voice mail.

I feel a small surge of victory. Which is swiftly crushed.

"Hey." Nero's voice directly behind Carlton, causes the smaller man to startle and look behind him. But all he sees is some guy in a suit talking loudly into a phone.

Leaving me a voice mail.

Nero's eyes are on me. "I'll be done with work early tonight. I'll see you at home."

Without adding more, Nero hangs up, then he turns his full focus to Carlton. "You done here?"

I feel myself holding my breath.

"Oh, yeah. Sorry, man." Carlton steps back and holds an arm out. "We're just chatting, you can go ahead and order."

Nero holds his stare. "I'll wait."

CHAPTER 34

Nero

THIS FUCKING PUNK BLINKS AT ME, LIKE I MIGHT BE joking, but I'm not. I'm not going to walk away while this bitch stands here talking to Payton.

"Yeah, okay." He holds his hands up as he turns back to face my girl.

Yeah, okay.

God, I want to punch him in the face. Or pull my gun out and pistol whip him. Then he'd be too busy crying to flirt with Payton.

"Want your usual?" Her voice glides over my skin.

Or maybe I should just kill him.

"You know it, babe."

I'm reaching for the Ruger at the small of my back before I even realize what I'm doing.

I pause, but I don't drop my hand, debating how much trouble I'd be in for murdering this tool in broad daylight.

Payton wouldn't like it.

My hand drops back to my side. Tapping my fingers against my thigh as this asshole pays for his *usual.*

"Let me grab your coffee." Payton darts her eyes toward me, shifting on her feet. "I'll bring it to the end of the counter."

"Alright." The guy slides a ratty-looking wallet into his pocket.

What the fuck is he even thinking talking to a girl like Payton? She's way too good for him. Completely out of his league.

She's stunning. Feminine. Kind and sweet. He would never be able to provide her with the kind of life that I could. The kind of life she deserves.

A life full of armored cars and bullets.

My teeth grind, annoyed with my own internal voice. But it's the reminder I need to keep my mouth shut.

I watch Payton's ass while she moves around, making the guy's drink, positive she's taking longer than usual. But I said I'd wait, so I cross my arms and lean my hip against the counter.

I feel like I'm doing a pretty good job of being epically patient, until the punk says, "See you tonight" as he takes the drink from Payton, and an audible growl rolls up my throat.

No. No, you will not see her tonight.

The man has to walk past me to leave, and I turn my head with his movement, tracking every step he takes. He looks up and makes eye contact, then weaves out between the tables so he doesn't have to pass near me.

What a pussy.

"Is there something else I can get for you, *sir*?"

Payton's tart voice goes straight to my balls, and I slowly turn back to face her. "Watch your tone, Baby."

"Or what?" she hisses, before slamming her lips shut. Her eyes widen, clearly surprised at herself for asking the question.

"You'll find out tonight, Sweet Girl." Only she can hear me. And I watch with hungry fascination as her throat works on a swallow. She's as affected as I am. "Now give me that cherry tart."

"What!?"

I nod toward the pastry display. "The cherry tart. To go."

She turns her head to follow my gaze, and her lips part, but she closes them again before speaking.

Using a loose piece of paper to pick up the tart from under

the glass, she slides it into a small paper bag, hesitating before handing it over. "How long have you had my number?"

"Payton," I grit out her name. "Not here."

Her pretty eyes sparkle under the bright lights, and I take the moment to just look at her. Really look at her.

Payton is uncommonly pretty. Her navy eyes, half hidden under thick lashes, and casually messy hair highlight her beauty. She has freckles on her full cheeks that I haven't had the time to appreciate yet. I want to pin her below me and trace the pattern they make with my tongue. And those lips. Fuck--those lips. *I'll have them on me soon enough.*

Her clothes don't flaunt her shape, but even with the loose fit, there's no hiding her curves. And when she turns around, her gorgeous ass is framed by the edges of that damn white apron. It makes me want to drape her in silk. Or put her in a slutty dress, only to wear around the house.

The corner of my mouth pulls into a smirk.

She could dress up just for me.

Her eyes narrow at my expression and she drops the package with the tart onto the counter.

"What do I owe you?" When it's clear she's not going to tell me the total, I sigh and pull a twenty out of my wallet, swapping it for the tart. Then tell her, "Tonight."

Turning back around I find the mayor's attention focused on me, and I know I showed too much of my hand.

So I secure the mask of indifference over my features, as I walk back to his table.

"Pretty girl." The mayor tips his head toward Payton. "I've had my eye on her for a while, but maybe you beat me to it?"

He leaves it open, waiting for me to confirm his statement. And even though I want to peel the skin off his body for daring to call her *pretty* in front of me, I keep a bland expression on my face. "Not my type. I'm just here for the food." He doesn't look entirely convinced but saying anything more would be out of character for me.

I make a point to look at my watch. "I gotta run. Abdul is showing me some new properties."

As planned, that draws his attention. "Oh? You'll have to let me know if you decide to pass on anything that I might like."

Dipping my chin, I turn away and leave.

Never looking back in Payton's direction.

CHAPTER 35

Payton

FOR THE THIRTIETH TIME, I STRAIGHTEN THE SAME stack of cups before the mayor finally gets up from his table. And I stay focused on the cups until I hear the front door open and close.

His presence has never bothered me before. I didn't even know who he was the first few times that he came in while I was working, but eventually I heard someone call him by his title and I put it together.

He always came off as friendly and nice, but that was before today, before I knew he knew Nero. And before I overheard him say he's had his eye on me.

I suppress a shudder. I've googled him. I know he's married. And I doubt his wife would appreciate his comments, because it sure didn't sound like he was kidding.

And him knowing Nero...

A band wraps around my ribs, tightening until it's hard to inhale.

I'm not a total idiot. I know Nero has to be... into some stuff. You don't dodge the cops by climbing in through someone's balcony if you're not causing some sort of trouble. But even knowing that, I've always felt a sort of safeness with him. And I know it should be extra messed up that the night I left my door open for him, he magically appeared. Because that means he must've been watching. But it also means he didn't cross that threshold again until I invited him. He came because I asked him to. And he took what I offered because I wanted him to.

None of that felt as wrong as him walking in here today and acting like I was a nobody.

Heat builds behind my eyes, and I catch myself sniffing against a tingling sensation in my nose.

I get that Nero wasn't expecting the mayor to be here. It was obvious that they weren't planning to meet. But he didn't have to act how he did.

Not my type.

I'm just here for the food.

I blink rapidly, tipping my gaze up toward the ceiling.

Don't you dare cry over him.

Needing to distract myself, I make my way around the table to clear off the dishes the two men left behind.

Jean approaches with a rag when I pick up the last item, and I move out of her way so she can spray down the table when I hear her grumble, "Damn mobster."

A smile starts to form on my mouth, her usual cynical attitude about politicians amusing me.

That smile slips when I stop and think--

What if she was talking about Nero?

CHAPTER 36

Nero

"The last two," I snap at Abdul, opening my car door.

His brows shoot up. "Both of them?"

"That's what I said."

Before he can ask more questions, I climb into the driver's seat and slam the door.

I'm not mad at him, per se, I'm just pissed that these site visits took so long.

A glance at the clock tells me that it's already after six p.m.

"Fuck!" I stomp on the gas as I pull out of the parking lot.

My fingers twitch to call Payton's phone, to make sure that she's staying put tonight. But I don't.

Mostly because I'm pretty sure she wouldn't answer. And a small part of me is actually hoping for her disobedience. Or rather, the consequences of those actions.

Swerving through traffic, a sweet fruity scent finally permeates my senses. *The tart.*

Using my knee to hold the steering wheel steady, I pick up the small white bag and carefully slide the tart into my palm.

My nostrils expand as I bring the pastry to my nose and inhale.

If I think on it, *really hard*, I imagine that I can smell Payton's rose warmth, from where her hand was wrapped around the paper.

Opening wide, I shove half the tart into my mouth and bite down.

Flavor bursts across my tongue. Sweetness mixed with the tang of the cherries.

My lids lower and I need to remind myself that I'm driving so I don't close my eyes all the way.

It's so good.

It tastes like her.

I lick across the surface of the cherries on the uneaten half, noticing that my dick is now completely hard.

"Jesus."

Still steering with my knee, I press my other hand down on my length.

My gaze darts back and forth between the baked good in my hand and the road ahead of me, and for more than a moment, I consider the logistics of jerking off while I fill my mouth with the rest of Payton's cherries.

I press down harder on my cock as it throbs. And before I can do something truly ridiculous, I shove the rest of the tart into my mouth, groaning as I chew, leaving my dick in my pants.

When I finally make it to Payton's neighborhood, I slow, stopping against the curb at the end of her block.

I hate this shit. I want to drive right up to her front door.

Well, what I really want to do is drag her out of that building by her hair and move her in with me. My big empty house has felt even emptier than ever since that night I first laid eyes on her. And the reasons for staying away from her are getting harder and harder to listen to.

I am Nero.

Feared by the underworld.

Yet here I am, sneaking around outside my girlfriend's house like a teenage boy breaking curfew.

Girlfriend?

Jesus Christ. I've completely lost it.

I haven't had a girlfriend since... Tipping my head back against the headrest, I think. Have I ever? Maybe that one girl in high school? And then there was that chick I fucked for the better part of a year in my twenties...

Doesn't matter. It's irrelevant. Because Payton isn't my fucking girlfriend.

My fingers reach out and turn off the ignition.

It's hard to tell at this angle and distance, but Payton's patio door looks closed. Not a surprise, considering the death glare she was trying to perfect on me earlier at the café. A light shining out from her windows catches my attention. She must be home.

I'm half tempted to break back into that empty apartment across the street from hers, so I can watch and take in her attitude. But there's a chance she'll try to go to that fucking concert tonight.

Gripping my door handle tighter than necessary, I wrench it open.

The nerve of that fucking guy. Asking for her number right in front of me. And her giving it to him.

Bad Payton.

Just as I swing a foot out onto the street, a car flies past my open door, with inches to spare, and for the second time today I'm tempted to pull my gun.

When the car's brake lights illuminate the street, I notice it has one of those glowing neon lights on the dashboard signifying it as a rideshare vehicle. And something inside of me pauses.

While I stand there, half-in and half-out of my vehicle, the door to Payton's building swings open; and the woman herself darts down the concrete steps, and across the sidewalk, before she practically dives into the back seat of the car.

The back seat of a car driven by a stranger.

By a motherfucking stranger.

I'm back inside my own car, turning it on, and shoving the shifter into drive before Payton's car even starts to move.

My foot twitches toward the gas, but before I can roll forward more than a foot, I hit the brake.

I can't just ram the car off the road and kidnap Payton.

I mean, I'd like to.

I want to.

But I won't.

Easing out into the street, I keep a few car lengths between us.

Being that it's a weeknight, there's enough traffic heading downtown to hide myself in. The dark making me one of many headlights in their rearview mirror. But as we pull away from the main streets and move toward the edge of town, next to the quiet baseball stadium, I realize the error in my plan. And sure enough, the car ahead of me takes one more turn, then slows as it approaches a venue I'm not familiar with.

A venue with a line out the door and down the block. And nowhere to fucking park.

The car Payton's in stops, and the second she stretches a leg out of the back seat, a jealous and possessive anger squeezes my ribs.

She's in a fucking dress. Or a skirt. Whatever it is, is short enough that her skirt rides up when she bends to climb out, showing a flash of pale skin above thigh-high stockings.

Thigh. High. Stockings.

My cock is rock hard as I slowly roll past her.

I want to put an end to this bullshit right now. Jump out of my car, snatch her off the sidewalk, and throw her in my trunk. But I can see four cops outside the building helping with security and I'm pretty sure my actions wouldn't go unnoticed.

Even though I'm sure I'd get away with it, it's the exact sort of attention I'm trying to avoid with Payton.

Gripping the steering wheel so tight it creaks, I circle around the next block until I find a parking spot.

My anger grows when I jog up to the building and find that Payton's already made it through the line. Then I eye up the nearly hundred people and decide there's no way. Which means that little prick got her some sort of side entrance ticket.

Seething, I go to the back of the line and wait like the rest of these fucking mouth breathers. This is one of those times I wish regular people knew who I was, so I could intimidate them into letting me through.

Should've canceled on Abdul the second Payton agreed to share her number.

But I've already been absent enough because of this little siren. I'm delegating more. Which has people talking. Of course the assumption everyone is making is *it's a woman*. And in this case, they're right. Only, instead of spending my nights in her bed, I spend them across the street from her, waiting for glimpses, like a goddamn creep.

It's fully dark and the temperature has plummeted by the time I finally make it up to security.

"Belt, sir." The deep voice of a bouncer stops me before I walk through the metal detectors, and I'm glad I decided to disarm in the car.

Gritting my teeth as I take my belt off and pull my phone and wallet out of my pocket, setting it all in a little tray.

My patience is wearing extremely thin and being corralled through here like fucking cattle is getting real old, real quick.

"You're good," the bouncer nods at me to collect my items.

I pick up the belt. Then quickly realize it's not my belt. It's black, non-leather and covered in square silver studs. Setting it down I grab my belt, also black but real leather, and no tacky studs. While I slide it through my pants' loops, I take notice of the crowd around me. Lots of black. Lots of leather. Lots of long hair. On everyone.

What the hell sort of concert is this?

I shuffle ahead, my suit and loafers standing out in this sea of... what even is this?

"Phone?" a woman asks me. She's about Payton's age, hair cut short, and wearing a red polo signaling that she works here. When I don't answer quick enough, she holds up a handheld scanner. "You got your ticket?"

Fuck. Me.

My jaw tics. "I don't."

She lifts a brow, then gives me a once over, as if to say *you lost?* Her weight shifts, one hip jutting out. "You here for the show? Or for that new owner's thing?"

"The show," I answer before I can think better of it. I don't know who the owner is, but I should've winged it.

"Alright." Her tone says she doesn't believe me, but she points off to the side. "Head over there and get yourself a ticket, then come back to me and I won't make you go through the line again."

"Thanks." My voice is gruffer than she deserves, but I'm one delay away from losing my shit.

The line to buy tickets is thankfully short and I'm sliding my credit card through the opening below the glass before the guy can even greet me. "One ticket."

He picks up my card. "Regular or balcony?"

I wasn't expecting options. "What's the difference?"

"General will get you anywhere on the main floor. Balcony gets you access to the upper levels too."

"Balcony," I tell him. I don't know where Payton's going to be, and I'm not taking any chances.

Since it's apparently 1994, the guy hands me a paper ticket and I turn around to stride back to the woman at the entrance.

"Nice." She makes an impressed face when she reads the ticket. "Give me your left hand."

"Why?"

The woman rolls her eyes at me. In public. At me.

What is happening to my life?

She picks up a neon green wristband. "So people know you can go upstairs."

"Can't they just look at my ticket?"

It's a reasonable question, but the woman just blinks at me.

With an audible exhale, I hold my left arm up and I swear it's on purpose when she catches one of my arm hairs in the adhesive.

"Enjoy the show!" she calls after me as I stride away.

Finally entering the building, I move through a plain entryway before stepping into a decent-sized concert space. The main floor is standing room only and it's packed with bodies. And like the ticket guy said, there's a balcony circling the back half of the venue, giving the spectators up there unobstructed views.

An emcee is announcing that the main act is about to start, meaning I spent the entire time the opening band was playing stuck in line.

Still trying to figure out what we'll be listening to, I look past the sea of people to the large banner strung up behind the band.

Söta Kakor.

What the fuck is a Söta Kakor?

Then the lights drop and the heavy metal starts.

CHAPTER 37

Payton

THE MUSIC IS SO LOUD I CAN FEEL EVERY BEAT OF THE drum, and strum of guitar, as they vibrate through my bones.

I've never been to a concert, but when I pictured it, it wasn't like this. And it wasn't *this* type of music.

Turns out I like it. I like it a lot.

I missed some of Carlton's performance, but he is actually really good. I never would have figured him for having a good singing voice, but he does. And he looked at home with a shiny red guitar slung across his chest.

When a round of flashing strobe lights go off, I close my eyes. The laser lights and changing color spotlights on the musicians are one thing, but the strobe lights are just too much for me.

Absorbing the music, I pretend there isn't a sea of humanity around me. If I think too much about all the people that are in here with me, I'll slip into a panic. Not that anyone has been mean, or looked at me in any sort of bad way, it's just more people than I'm used to. And it's mostly men. Big, hairy, dressed head-to-toe in black men. One more reason why I found a place to stand by the back wall.

I don't need to be close to the stage, and I don't want to be anywhere near the people jumping wildly into each other. Plus, I prefer to not have strangers behind me. And with the balcony jutting out above me, this spot feels almost private.

Crossing my arms over my chest, I let my head bob with the beat. And even with the fast beat overwhelming my senses, as always when I close my eyes, my mind wanders to Nero.

Only today, thoughts of him make my heart ache.

I really don't know what to think about everything that happened in the café.

And when he left that ridiculous voice mail—*I'll be done with work early tonight. I'll see you at home.*—I knew I couldn't just go home after work. And that only became more clear when I read through the texts he sent to me while I was talking to Carlton.

> Unknown: Answer me.
>
> Unknown: Payton.
>
> Unknown: I swear to god, if you smile at him...
>
> Unknown: You are not going to his fucking concert.
>
> Unknown: End this conversation.
>
> Unknown: This is not good for his long-term health.

I eventually added Nero's contact to my phone. Not because I plan to use it but seeing *unknown* made the messages scarier.

So, in order to avoid some sort of confrontation at my apartment, I found myself once again taking the bus to the mall, to spend Nero's hundred dollars. Only instead of buying body wash, I went to Marshall's and spent three hours pawing through all the racks looking for an outfit to wear tonight.

On the bus ride, I did some googling and found photos of Söta Kakor in concert so I could zoom in on the people in the crowd and see what they were wearing. The photos were blurry, but I got enough of an idea. And being here in person, I feel pretty good about my purchases.

When I was climbing into that Uber, I started to worry that maybe my outfit was too... showy. Now I see my choices have nothing on some of the things I've seen the few women wearing. Don't get me wrong, they look amazing. Sexy as hell. But it makes my mid-thigh skater skirt seem like a nun's habit.

The skirt was a lucky find, since it was in my exact size. Same with the thick-knit dark gray sweater. The scoop neckline isn't super low, but it does help draw attention to my cleavage and away from my not-so-snatched waist.

The crowning glory of my outfit––the detail that makes me feel sexy, something I'm not used to feeling––are the thigh-high black stockings.

I've seen them in movies, and on models in magazines, but I never thought they were something that a girl like me could wear. I figured they'd be too tight and cause a weird roll in the middle of my thigh, but these ones are soft and stretchy, and there's something along the inside of the top that makes them stick in place. Plus the thick bands act as a buffer between my legs, so I'm not suffering from having my thighs rubbing together with every step.

A body bumps into me and my eyes fly open.

"Sorry!" the dude shouts above the music, then keeps moving past me, on a mission to get somewhere.

I shuffle back a step in my not-new black ankle boots, putting my back just an arm's length away from the back wall.

I'm thinking maybe I should just take another step so I'm leaning against the wall when a hand presses gently on my side.

Assuming the person is just trying to alert me that they're attempting to pass behind me, I try to step forward. Except the pressure slides across my ribs to the front of my body, until the hand splays across my belly, holding me in place.

Panic surges inside me, and I'm reaching down to shove the hand away, when a body presses against my back. And a fiery masculine scent I'm all too familiar with swirls around me.

Nero.

Warm breath fans across my cheek as he lowers his mouth to my ear. "You've been a bad girl, Payton."

Heat pools in my core at the feel of him. At the sound of him.

Then I remember I'm angry with him.

"Go away," I hiss, keeping my eyes forward.

"No." His lips brush against my ear, sending a shiver across my scalp.

"No?" I try to snap at him, but my traitorous body sinks back into his warmth.

"No, Baby. You wanted to talk. So, now, we'll talk."

"It's a little loud," I say, facing forward.

"What was that?"

I sigh since he's proving my point. "I said"—I turn my head to look back at him—"it's--"

His lips seal over mine.

CHAPTER 38
Payton

THE SHOCK OF HIS KISS CAUSES ME TO TRY AND PULL away, but his other hand spans across my neck and chin, holding me in place.

And, because I'm weak, I let myself melt into his heat.

Just for a moment, I soak in the feeling of his warm lips pressed against mine.

But just for a moment, because I can't let myself forget how he treated me today, so I strain away, my hands shoving at the grip he has on my face.

"What are you doing?" I ask when his hand drops away, even though his firm grip around my waist keeps my body against his.

"I'm reminding you who you belong to."

His words send a wave of emotion through my soul.

If only.

Sadness settles on my shoulders, and I turn my head back toward the stage, away from Nero.

His free arm circles around my chest, resting his forearm along the top of my breasts. "You shouldn't turn your back on me, Sweet Girl." Nero's cheek presses against the side of my head, his voice ruffling my hair.

"Why are you even talking to me? I thought I was supposed to be your secret." My voice cracks over the last few words, and I hope that the volume of the concert is enough to keep Nero from hearing it.

He tips his head down until his lips are against my ear. "You are my secret."

Those four words pierce through the warmth his body is giving me.

His arms tighten like he knows I'm going to try to jerk away. "You're my secret because being mine puts you in danger."

What?

Nero's fingers curl into my sides as he hugs me from behind. "I have enemies that would love to hurt me by hurting you."

"Enemies?" I repeat the word like I've never heard it before because normal people don't have enemies.

I suppose I'm not normal either, because Arthur... my mom... they're as much of an enemy as anyone could ever be to me.

"I'm not a good man, Payton. Don't ever forget that. I'm trying to keep my distance *for you*. Because I don't want to be the one to ruin you." The hand on my stomach slides lower, and I'm startled by the sudden touch of skin on skin.

I automatically reach up and grab hold of his forearm to stop him. But the feel of his fingers sliding beneath the waistband of my skirt is divine. So, I don't try to stop him, I just cling to him.

"If what you're saying is true, why are you even here?" My words are quiet, but Nero wraps himself around me even more, lowering his ear.

"Because dangerous doesn't stop me." His fingers travel lower, slipping into my underwear. "And you've earned a punishment."

Every nerve in my body is on fire. "Punishment?"

"Yeah, Baby, punishment." Nero's fingertips brush against the curls between my legs.

"Is it not punishment enough that you keep stealing my panties?"

He huffs out a breath, the hand around my chest dropping

away. "You mean these?" His hand reappears in front of me, a pair of my crumpled-up panties in his palm.

I try to ignore his fingers, sliding ever closer to where I want them. "Give those back."

"I'll give you them back if you give me the ones you have on now."

My mouth drops open. "You can't be serious."

His teeth scrape against the side of my neck. "Deadly."

"I'm not taking my underwear off in public."

"Yeah, Baby, you are." He slides his hand higher, away from my center. "And hurry up, before I'm forced to remove them for you. Which would draw a lot more attention."

My cheeks are flaming hot. But my core is throbbing.

None of this should turn me on. His shitty attitude. His threatening to punish me for something he has no say over. But I can't help how my body responds to Nero. And, if I'm being honest with myself, I don't want to. I want to hand him control.

"Take them off, Payton. Now."

Instead of forcing me, Nero unwinds his body from mine. Cool air rushing in to fill the space where he just was, and I feel his loss on an even deeper level.

Stress swamps me as I worry that he might just turn and walk away.

But when I look back, I find him shrugging out of his suit coat.

Of course, he's wearing a suit coat.

I finally take a second to look at him, and just like earlier today, he's breathtakingly handsome.

And totally out of place with this crowd.

Nero steps forward again, pressing against my back.

"Here." Before I can react, Nero's draping his suit coat over my shoulder, the other side of the coat draped over his shoulder, creating a makeshift barrier between us and the crowd to our right. "It's not perfect, so try to stay still."

A flood of desire passes through me.

I hate him. I shouldn't be letting him anywhere near me, let alone... this.

I know I should just walk forward, disappear into the sea of people, but I don't. And I almost convince myself that I'm only doing this for the pleasure he's about to give me. Nothing more.

I'm such a liar.

Checking to make sure no one is looking directly at us, I inch my hands up the sides of my thighs until I can hook my fingers around the top of my panties. Then I slowly drag them down.

And down.

Until they drop, catching on the top of my ankle boots, so they aren't touching the floor.

I drop into a crouch and struggle for a moment to step out of them.

The moment I stand, Nero has the suit coat back over my shoulder.

"That's my girl." I can feel the rumble of his chest against my back. And the hardness of his cock against my ass.

"What now?" I arch into him, keeping my gaze forward.

"Now." The hand, under the cover of the jacket, glides over my stomach. "You pay."

The entire crowd shouts as one, fists in the air, chanting with the beat; and that's when Nero slides his hand down the front of my skirt, his fingers not stopping until they're pressing against my swollen clit.

I cry out in surprise, but the sound disappears under all the other noise.

"Jesus, Baby. You're so fucking slick." His fingers brush back then forth before he plunges one inside me. "So fucking ready for me." I moan at the intrusion. "One fuck and you're already horny for more. Turned you into the perfect little slut, didn't I?"

CHAPTER 39

Nero

Her pussy clenches around my finger and I need more.

I shove another finger inside her, wedging it in next to the first. And with my other hand, I undo my zipper.

The plan was to steal her underwear, touch her until she got wet, then leave her wanting more. But that plan was out the window long before I felt just how soaked her pussy was for me. Now that I have her juices running down my fingers...

Payton leans her weight back into me.

I pull my hips back, giving myself space to wedge my dick out of my pants without undoing my belt.

With my jacket blocking my actions to one side, and her skirt blocking my actions from the front, I only have to worry about anyone passing by on our exposed left side. Because if anyone looks too closely, and sees any part of Payton's ass, I'll have to end them.

I push my fingers deeper and press my palm against her clit as I start to stroke my cock. The feel of her slippery slit under my fingers making me painfully hard.

"Is that it, Baby? Just one time with my dick and now you need more?"

She writhes under my touch. "Who said I haven't had another dick since you?"

Red tinges the edge of my vision. "I said." I curl my fingers and press my palm harder against her, getting a literal grip on her pussy. "If someone even thinks about putting their cock in you, I'll slice their head off and put their skull on a pike outside your balcony." I jerk my cock rougher. "So keep that in mind, my pretty little thing."

Payton's breath hitches, but she doesn't tense at my threat. No, she trembles. From the inside out.

"You like that?" I rasp, my strokes getting longer.

Still curling my fingers inside her, I jiggle my hand, the fast back and forth movement rubbing my palm against her bud.

"Nero!"

"That's right, say my name, Baby. But not too loud, remember?" I bend my knees enough that I can use the tip of my dick to catch the bottom hem of her skirt. When I rise, I let my dick slap up between her thighs, making Payton clench in surprise, squeezing the shit out of my fingers once again.

I wish she was naked, so I could see every inch of her, but this... fuck. Having her at my mercy, surrounded by strangers, one poorly timed glance away from disaster, makes precum seep from my tip.

I thrust forward, my cock sliding between her slick thighs, her hot pussy searing the top of my length.

"Holy shit," Payton gasps.

I slide my hips back, then forward, two more times, and I'm nearly ready to blow.

Payton stands so still, it's like she's not affected. But her lips are parted, her eyes are unfocused, and her chest is rising and falling with frantic breaths.

"So wet for me." I slide my cock out from between her thighs and grip my length again. Only this time, I keep the head pressed against her. "Are you close? Do you want to come, Payton?"

She nods, her hair slipping from behind her ear to cover the side of her face I can see.

My hand inside her stills, even as I continue to jack off against her ass.

I use her slickness coating me to slide the head of my cock between her ass cheeks. "I told you not to come here tonight. But you didn't listen." I slide my cock up and down, the tip rubbing against her unused hole. "So, you don't get to come." Her muscles clench, her cheeks working to grip my dick. "Not without my dick inside you." I let go of my cock and reach down to slide two fingers through her heat. "I don't have time to get you ready." I drag my fingers up, rubbing her slickness against her hole. "I'll give you one finger." I press my fingertip forward, and between her wetness, and what I already rubbed against her, I get inside. "That's it." I work her muscles and feel her relax. "Maybe two." I slide the first finger out, then join it with a second, my other palm not moving, just pressing against her clit. "Fuck, Baby. You want it so bad."

"Please." Payton shifts on her feet.

"Please what?" I can barely grit out the words.

"Please, Nero." The hands that had balled into fists at her sides reach up and claw at my arm. "I need you."

Fuuuuck.

There's nothing she could say that would affect me more.

She needs me.

And I need her.

My hand tightens around my cock and I jerk my dick faster.

"Please!" she cries, her little fingertips digging into my arm.

And that tiny pinch of pain is all it takes before the first rope of cum shoots out of me. "That's my Baby." I grind my palm over her clit. "Take it." My hips push forward and another burst of cum lubes my way. "Take it and you can come."

I can hardly speak, my entire focus on the head of my dick as it pushes through her tight ring of resistance.

And it's too much.

I drop my forehead to her shoulder and my cock pulses two times, three times more, filling her with my release.

And with the tip of my dick inside her ass, and my fingers buried in her pussy, she explodes.

Her entire body trembles and my balls squeeze painfully.

I tip my head up in time to catch the look on her face.

With her eyes closed, lips parted, and cheeks flushed, she looks like passion personified.

My lips seal against the side of her neck, and even though she's lost in bliss, her body relaxes against me. And my cock slides just a little bit deeper.

Christ.

Movement at the edge of my vision, near our uncovered side, pulls my attention, and I look up to lock eyes with a familiar face.

The man from the café.

The guy who gave Payton the ticket to this event, is standing just a few feet away. The colored lights from the show flashing over his shocked features.

So, with him watching, I slowly slide my hand up and out of Payton's skirt, drawing an invisible line of wetness up her stomach on the way. When my fingers, covered in her shine, are visible over the top of her waistband, I splay my hand across her stomach, holding her against me.

Affronted anger rolls off him, but he just keeps impotently standing there.

Grinning against her neck, I shift my foot to the inside of Payton's, nudging it until she spreads her legs a little more. Her muscles relax their grip on my dick, and I gently slip free from her ass.

Payton lets out a delicious moan, that only I can hear, but my eyes stay on the man as my release starts dripping out of her.

The music is too loud for anyone to hear the splatter when it hits the ground, but I watch the punk's eyes flick down.

Only then does he turn and leave.

CHAPTER 40
Payton

THE MUSIC CONTINUES TO BOMBARD MY EARDRUMS, but I can hardly hear it over the pounding of my own pulse and Nero's heavy breathing against my ear.

I can't believe...

My eyes squeeze shut even tighter, as if to block out the reality of what I just did. And how much I enjoyed it.

Nero's hand slides up and away from my overly sensitive clit, and I can feel the dampness on my skin as he slides his hand all the way out of my skirt.

My body continues to quiver from the mind-shattering orgasm Nero just gave me, and if it weren't for his arm around me, I'd crumple to the ground right here.

The feeling of Nero's cock sliding out of... *oh god*, out of my ass, is so foreign. So dirty. I take a deep breath, the sensation of him dripping out of me heats my cheeks even more.

I almost hate how sexy it makes me feel. But something that makes me feel this good, this desired, can't possibly be all bad.

Maybe what Nero said, about one *fuck* turning me into a slut, is true.

It's another thing I'm sure I should be upset about, him

calling me that. But he said it so approvingly. Like the way that my body readied itself for him made him proud.

Nero's forehead drops back down to my shoulder, and his hands slip away. I can feel the jostling behind me, and I assume he's... putting himself back in order.

Half afraid of what I'll see, I force my eyes to crack open.

I have to squint against the flashing lights, but when my eyes adjust, I note that no one seems to be looking at us. *Thank god.*

Nero groans, then stands to his full height, taking his suit coat with him. Once he has it back on, he wraps both arms around my shoulders, hugging me to his chest, and rests his chin on the top of my head.

I sink back into his hold.

"I'm driving you home." His words are echoed in a rumble against my back.

"Okay," I murmur back. "In a minute."

"In a minute," he repeats, showing he heard me, and presses a kiss to the top of my head.

I shouldn't let him drive me home. Or touch me. But clearly, I don't do the things that I should.

And if I have him alone in my apartment, maybe I can get him to expand on what he said earlier. About enemies, and not being a good man.

So we stand together, watching a band I've never heard of before, blending into the crowd.

After a while, I tilt my head back. "Nero?"

His chin slides against my hair, and he looks down into my eyes. "Yeah, Baby?"

"Can I have my underwear back?"

The second his lips start to pull up into a smile, I know what answer he's gonna give me. "No."

Even though it's the response I expected, I narrow my eyes. "No?"

"No, Payton, you can't have your *underwear* back."

He says underwear like it's the wrong term. But calling them my *panties* out loud, to his face, is not something I'm ready for.

"You said you'd give me that other pair back," I argue.

He clicks his tongue. "Clearly you're not listening."

"You said--"

He cuts me off. "I told you I wasn't a good man, Payton. That includes lying. Because you're not ever getting them back. And I'm keeping the ones you just gave me, too."

I narrow my eyes. "How do I know you're not lying about that too?"

He shrugs.

My lips purse. "Are you saying I shouldn't trust you?"

His arms tighten around me. "You *shouldn't* trust me. But I'm asking you to anyway." Nero presses his nose to my hair and inhales. "I'll lie, and cheat, and steal, and kill, and do whatever I need to do to protect you. But I'll never lie to you about who I am. Okay?"

"Okay," I sigh, ignoring all the red flags in that statement. "But can I at least wear them home?"

He huffs out a laugh. "No. Now are you ready to go?"

I nod, straightening from his hold. And when I tentatively flex my leg and butt muscles, I feel the ache *there*.

One step... One step is all it takes before I feel more of *him* drip down my thighs.

"Nero," I whine, and the look on his face tells me he knows exactly what my issue is.

But he doesn't stop, he just twines his fingers with mine and pulls me along behind him.

My only saving grace is the darkness, both inside and outside the club, that should hide the state I'm in.

As we circle around the back of the crowd, the current song ends and instead of jumping right into the next one, the lead singer addresses the crowd.

"I love you, Minneapolis!" A cheer roars through the crowd at the mention of our city. "This next one we're going to do a little differently. We're gonna sing it in Swedish."

Another loud cheer goes up, distracting me, so I don't notice Nero's steps have slowed until I'm bumping into his back.

Before I can apologize, he squeezes my hand and continues walking at his previous pace.

We make it through the lobby, and out the front doors, before Nero stops again.

This time, I manage to put my free hand up, pressing my palm to his back to keep from crashing into him.

"You okay?" I question.

He grunts, then looks both ways before tugging me toward a pair of security guards standing off to the side, clearly waiting for the concert to end.

"Hey, Mr. Suit. Enjoy the show?" the woman asks him, with a knowing smirk on her face.

She's young, pretty, has an edgy haircut, and I don't like the way she's looking at him.

I step up so Nero and I are side-by-side, then I let go of his hand and run my hand up the inside of his forearm until I've hooked my arm through his.

The movement doesn't go unnoticed, and I watch the woman's smirk grow even wider.

Okay, so she's amused by me, not intimidated. And I'm not sure how to feel about that.

But then Nero presses his arm to his side, trapping mine where it is. And I know exactly how to feel about that.

"It was quite the experience."

I have to take a moment to remember the woman's question after Nero responds, and when I do, I feel my cheeks heat. I fervently hope she keeps her gaze on Nero's handsome face and away from anything that might be going on below the hem of my skirt.

"Glad to hear it." Her eyes flick back to me. "Was there something you needed?"

"Just wondering if Hans was here tonight?" Nero asks.

I know I don't know him that well, but something about his tone feels off.

The woman straightens from her spot leaning against a pillar, as she glances at her colleague. "I thought you said you weren't here for the owner's meeting?"

"I'm not." His faux friendliness evaporates with those two words.

The worker glances back to me, but I'm just as confused as she is.

"Have a good night." Nero dips his chin, then drags me away.

"What was that about?" I ask when we've put some distance between us and the security guards.

"Nothing."

"Who's Hans?"

He's quiet for a few strides, then heaves out a breath. "No one you want to know."

I press my lips together but decide to take him at his word.

The walk to Nero's car goes by in a swirl of dancing thoughts while I pretend the cold air isn't licking at my bare butt.

Nero turns into a small surface lot and walks me up to the passenger side door of a low, probably expensive, sports car.

He lets go of my hand to pull the door open, then stands off to the side so I can get in. But I don't.

"If you didn't want me to drive you home, you shouldn't have walked all the way over here."

I roll my eyes. "As if you'd let me do anything else."

Nero grins. "Smart girl. Now get in."

"Nero..." I press my thighs together, then whisper. "I'm going to get your seats dirty."

His eyes slowly drop and I feel like he can see straight through my skirt. "Are you messy, Payton?" He steps forward, closing the distance between us. "Is my cum still dripping out of your ass?"

I tip my head down, letting my hair fall around my face, as I admit, "Yes."

Nero groans, gripping me on my hips. "If you think that bothers me, you need to think again."

I shift my weight. "Nero."

He lets out the biggest sigh. "Fine." He pulls his suit coat off, then leans into the car and spreads it out on the seat.

"I can't sit on that!"

His eyes are narrowed when he stands back upright. "Why not?"

I gesture to the jacket. "It's... expensive," I say lamely.

"Payton, get your ass in the fucking car."

"But––"

"Get in." He points to the car. "Squeeze out every drop of spunk onto the seat. Hell, run your fingers through it and draw hearts on my dashboard. I don't give a shit."

My face scrunches up at the visual. "That's––"

He grips my chin. "I know we have a lot to talk about, but I'll tell you one thing about me right now. One thing that you need to just believe, okay?"

"Okay..."

"I'm rich."

I almost snort. His delivery is just so... blasé.

But then he keeps going, not letting me look away. "I'm very, very rich. I have millions in the bank. Millions more in less *official* locations. And five times that in property." I swallow. "You could set this car on fire, roll it into the Mississippi, and it wouldn't cause so much as a ripple in my finances. You could tear my custom suit to shreds and twist them into pretty silk tampons, and I wouldn't give two shits. You could––"

"Okay!" I half-shout the word, just to get him to stop talking.

But he doesn't let go. "You will never worry about money." I open my mouth, but he shuts it with his grip. "Not for me. And not for you."

I keep my lips pressed together as I stare up at him.

What an actual dream it would be to not worry about money. What I wouldn't give.

But as much as he's acting obsessed with me now––for whatever reason––when that fades, I'll be back to my regularly scheduled poorness.

"Get in the car, Payton." Nero punctuates his command by pressing his lips to mine in a brief but harsh kiss. And more than anything he said, the kiss shuts me up.

CHAPTER 41

Nero

THE RIDE TO PAYTON'S APARTMENT PASSES QUICKLY, IN silence.

I'm not sure if she's quiet because of what I said, or from the discomfort of sitting with our combined cum clinging to her skin.

I shift in my seat, wishing that I hadn't put my jacket on the seat, craving the mark of her when she's not with me.

But I suppose if I'd let her leak all over my seat, I'd never let anyone else sit in my car ever again.

"Um." Payton raises her hand, finger pointing toward her building's front door as I drive past it.

"I know where you live, Baby."

"Yeah, but..." she doesn't finish the sentence, the implication obvious as we pass several empty parking spots.

"I'm not parking right in front of where you live. That'd be like painting a bullseye." I can feel her gaze on me, more questions hovering in the air between us. "Inside," I tell her.

Payton doesn't say more, and I find a parking spot two blocks down.

If I were a gentleman, I'd've dropped her off at the door, but I'm not letting her out of my sight. Not giving her a chance to run.

Not that she'd get far.

"Wait for me," I say, turning the car off.

She waits as I circle around the car and open her door for her. There's no one around, as far as I can tell, but I haven't forgotten the flash of thigh I saw when she climbed out of that Uber earlier, and I'll be damned if I chance anyone getting a peek when she's bare under that skirt.

Payton places her soft hand in mine and lets me help her out.

Leaving the suit coat behind, I twine our fingers together again, and we walk the empty sidewalk back to her place.

"Almost feels like I should make you climb in through the balcony," she teases as we pass her unit, heading to the front steps.

"Cute."

Payton tips her head up to me and I nearly stumble.

The smile on her face is the most genuine one I've ever seen on her. And there's something so heartbreaking about that.

Probably because I've spent hours looking at her face, while she's at home or work, and this is the first time she's ever looked truly happy. And it makes me crave more.

More of her.

More of her smiles.

More of her happiness.

More of her everything.

I want to be the one to make her feel that way.

Whatever expression I'm making causes the smile to slip off her face. "What is it?"

"Nothing." My voice is husky, but I act like it isn't.

Her fingers tighten around mine like she's trying to comfort me.

And for the second time in a matter of heartbeats, she tilts me off my axis.

Is she trying to comfort me?

Uneasiness rolls across my shoulders. And it's not from the fact that she seems to be able to read me, I'm uneasy because it almost feels like she cares about me.

Could that even be possible?

I've been with women. Felt desire and being desired. I've had women that want to be with me, stay with me. But it wasn't because of *me*. It was always about my bank account, or my position of power, or even the rebellion of being with a bad guy. It was always about what I could give them, nothing more.

It's been... It's been a long fucking time since anyone cared.

Distracted by thoughts of affection, I pull a key out of my pocket and use it to unlock the door to Payton's building.

"Umm, Nero?"

I hold the door open and guide Payton though, with a hand on her back. "Yeah?"

"How'd you get a key to my building?"

My eyes drop to the key I just used.

Oh. Right.

I hadn't meant to reveal that I had this, but deciding the cat's out of the bag, I lift a shoulder in a shrug. "I have a security company."

Payton's eyebrows rise, disappearing behind her bangs. "You do?"

She somehow seems more impressed by that, then when I told her how much money I have. "I do." I nod. "Elevator or stairs."

The question deflates her shoulders. "Stairs." She sighs the word. "I don't trust the elevator in this building."

A sound of distaste rolls around in my chest. I hate that she lives here. There's so much room in my house, she should be there. Not here.

We step into the narrow stairwell, and the scent of poorly made pasta hangs thick in the air.

I need to get her out of here.

Payton starts up the steps ahead of me. "So, what does your security company do?"

"Everything," I answer. But my attention is focused on the small streaks visible on the inside of her legs.

When she glances over her shoulder at me, I acquiesce. "We do everything from door locks to full security systems, to software development, to hired manpower."

"That's pretty cool." She waits at the top step. "What's it called."

My lips tip up on one side, and I place my hand on her back to keep her moving. "Nero's."

She tries to stop but I keep pushing her to her door.

"Seriously?" She sounds annoyed.

I wait, pretending like I don't have the key to her apartment, as Payton opens her door and steps inside.

"You don't like the name?" I lock the door behind me.

Payton tries to shrug. "It's obviously a good name. But you made me wait weeks to learn it, and now I find out there's a whole freaking company with your name." She bends down to unzip the sides of her little boots, and I don't miss the slight wince on her face. "And I mean, it's really neat that you have that. I guess I'm just feeling a little jealous that so many people already know who you are." *Jealous?* Payton kicks her second shoe off. "Like the mayor," she grumbles, before turning to face me. "I'm still mad at you, by the way."

"Because I know the mayor?"

She crosses her arms over her chest. "Because you acted like I was nothing."

The sentence wraps around my ribs. "You're not nothing."

The sadness stays in her eyes, that smile nowhere to be found.

I step closer and frame her pretty face with my large hands. "You are not nothing, Payton."

She blinks. Then she blinks some more.

"Okay." Her whisper is hardly convincing.

"Go take a shower." I press a gentle kiss on her forehead. "We'll talk after."

I can see her doubt, and I don't know if it's because she doesn't believe me, or if she thinks I won't be here when she gets out of the shower. But I plan to prove her wrong on both accounts.

CHAPTER 42

Payton

I HESITATE FOR A SECOND BEFORE DEPRESSING THE button in the center of the doorknob, locking the bathroom door.

Living alone means I rarely ever close this door, let alone lock it, but I feel raw. Inside and out.

It's been such a long day and if I didn't feel so filthy, literally, I'd just drop face first onto my bed. Thankfully, I don't have to work tomorrow. I plan to sleep for twelve hours. At least.

Peeling off my clothes, I drop them into a pile on the floor in front of the sink, purposefully not looking at my new, stained thigh highs.

Letting the water warm up, I brush through my hair and twist it into a bun on the top of my head. I don't want to deal with a full head of wet hair if we're going to be talking when I get out.

Talking.

My teeth clamp down on my lower lip and I hurry to step over the tub ledge.

Hold it together, Payton.

I don't.

Tears start filling my eyes.

Moving into the stream, I let the water wash over my roiling emotions.

I'm still hurt by Nero ignoring me at the café.

And I'm confused by the reaction he had to Carlton when we were simply talking.

Ashamed of how much I loved him showing up at the concert.

Nero found me. He came after me. He touched me, let me feel how much he wanted me.

But, when you put it all together, it doesn't make sense. Or it does, but it means that Nero wants to have sex with me, but he doesn't want anyone to know about it.

I turn away from the water, resting my forehead against the wall and letting the stream flow over my side and back.

I'm trying to keep the intrusive thoughts out. Trying to push them away as they tell me this is what I deserve. That it's all I deserve. That I'll never be more than someone's dirty little secret.

At least I got to choose the who.

Cool air swirls around me, a breeze flowing past the pulled back curtain, and I turn my head to find Nero stepping into my small shower.

The sight of his naked body in the light forces me to pause and take him in. No matter how confused I might be about this situation, there's no question that he's something to behold.

He's built like a... well, like a warrior. Or maybe a soldier of old. Hard muscles and scarred flesh. Strength and violence twisted together into a formidable adversary.

He's hard where I'm soft. Tough where I'm not. And if I could ever afford to go to therapy, I'm sure I'd be able to unpack these feelings of insecurity. But since that's not in the cards, I'll just have to trust the look in his eyes, and believe he finds me as attractive as I find him.

Nero pulls the curtain closed behind him, and my body automatically turns to face him.

Even though my brain is shouting at me that I don't actually know this man, my heart is telling me to cling to him with both hands.

His eyes flick across my body, cataloging all my parts, but not lingering. He meets my gaze again.

There's not much room in here, so even standing on opposite ends of the tub, there's barely a foot of space between us.

Silently, Nero reaches up and starts to pull my hair loose from its bun. His fingers are gentle, and he manages to get it out without tearing any strands of hair out.

"What are you doing?" I finally ask when he slips the black elastic around his wrist.

With his fingertips at my temples, he tips my head back, wetting my hair in the stream of water. "I'm washing your hair."

I squint my eyes against the spray. "Why?"

"Because I want to."

He tips my head back upright and I guess we're both going to pretend that his dick isn't hard right now.

Nero picks up my bottle of shampoo, filling his palm.

He moves back just a bit. "Come here."

I step toward him, so the hair hanging down my back is no longer in the water. And then, for the first time that I can remember, someone washes my hair.

His fingers scrub my locks, scraping lightly across my scalp, sending tingles up and down my spine.

He runs his hands down the length, before moving his attention back to my roots. The touch is so tender, and I have to take deep inhales through my nose, hoping to keep the rest of my tears at bay.

I don't know how to handle this, the hot and cold, the rough and sweet, with him. But a part of me knows that I'm just broken enough to accept it. To take what he's willing to give, because what he gives feels so damn close to love.

"Back."

Keeping my eyes closed, I let him guide me back under the spray, where he continues his soft touches, rinsing the shampoo out of my hair.

His hands on my shoulders let me know it's time to step

forward again.

And this time I watch him, I watch his face, and the tender look in his eyes, as he runs conditioner through my hair; taking the time to separate the sections and run his fingers through the strands to make sure nothing is tangled.

Again, he moves me back under the spray and rinses the product out of my hair.

But he doesn't stop there.

Nero reaches down, picking up my facewash next.

I expect him to hand me the bottle. But, of course, he doesn't.

Squeezing a small amount out, he rubs his fingertips together. "Close your eyes, Baby."

My body complies and I tip my head back as I do so, giving him a better view of my face from his taller height. And when his touch glides over my cheeks, I feel another traitorous tear roll down from my eye to meet his touch.

"Shh." His thumb brushes the tear away. "I've got you."

Instead of calming my nerves, his words fray them even more.

I want to ask him why, but instead, I murmur, "I thought I locked the door."

He wipes away another tear. "You did. And I'm going to let that go. This time."

It's a controlling douchebag thing to say, but it still causes the edges of my mouth to turn up into a smile.

Warm lips press against mine, but before I can kiss them back, they pull away. "Rinse your face off, Payton."

Wanting the moment for myself, I give Nero my back and do as I'm told.

His body presses against my back, and an arm circles around my waist, holding me in place. Tipping my head out of the direct spray, I open my eyes to see Nero's other hand reaching around me for the loofa that I have hanging from the faucet handle.

He drags his hand across my stomach before I lose his touch, then the click of my body wash being opened fills the shower.

When I look back over my shoulder, I see Nero squeeze way

too much out of the bottle.

"Don't use so much," I chastise lightly.

He clicks it shut. "I'll get you more."

Shaking my head, because there's no point in arguing, I melt into the sensation of Nero running the soapy loofa up the backs of my arms, across my back, down my spine. He takes time rubbing soft circles on each butt cheek. And I'm so absorbed in the moment, I don't have time to be embarrassed when he slides a soapy hand down my crack.

Nero continues to clean every inch of my legs, lowering himself behind me. Again my embarrassment doesn't flare. Not even when he tells me to turn and face him so he can work his way up from my toes.

I feel like I should feel so much more self-conscious about this. I know I'm not built like, well, like the type of girl a guy like him would normally go out with. Something I feel bad for thinking, because I know our bodies don't tell anything about the type of people we are. But there's knowing something, and then there's believing something.

Somehow, I feel nothing but cherished when I'm with Nero.

I feel safe.

Unbidden, I think of this afternoon and my stomach drops.

"Why did you pretend not to know me?" I whisper the question.

Nero rinses out the loofa, then hands it to me. "I'll tell you."

Taking it, I turn off the water and hang the loofa back in its spot.

We stay quiet as Nero uses one of the towels to dry me off, as he stands damp in the cool air, apparently unaffected.

When he's done with me, I slip into a pair of my plain cotton pajamas and climb into bed.

Nero turns the lights off, one-by-one, as he makes his way into the bedroom. The final lamp going dark a moment before the mattress dips beside me.

"Roll onto your side." The box spring creaks under our

combined weight. "Your bed is too fucking small."

I almost ask about the size of his bed, because I bet it's bigger than my Full, but I don't, rolling onto my side instead.

There's more shuffling, then Nero, clad in only a pair of boxer briefs, pulls me into his body. His whole front, covering my whole back. His skin a simmering heat against mine.

"I'll tell you something." Nero's words brush against the top of my head. "But then I want you to tell me something."

"Okay," I agree, blinking into the dark.

The arm around my waist adjusts until his fingers are tucked between my side and the mattress.

"I have my security company. It's real. And I make good money from that." His chest expands on a slow inhale. "But it's not what I really do."

"What do you really do?"

"Bad things."

"Do you hurt people?"

I can feel his head nodding on the pillow. "Sometimes."

"Are they bad people?"

He sighs. "Usually, but that doesn't make what I do good."

I think about what Jean said this morning and wet my lips.

"Are you a mobster?"

The arm around my waist tightens. "You could say that."

"And that's why you don't want us to be together?"

"Payton," his voice rumbles through me. "I *want* to be together. That's not the problem."

"It's your enemies," I repeat what he'd said earlier.

"That's right. It's not safe to be associated with me."

"What does that mean for me?" I hate how meek I sound. But I need to know where I stand.

"I'm trying to figure that out."

"Will you tell me more about what you do?"

"Not yet," he answers truthfully.

"I don't really know what mobster means," I admit.

"Hmm," he hums. "Why'd you use it?"

I chew on the inside of my cheek, not waiting to snitch on my boss, but if she knows enough about Nero to use it, then maybe it's not some big secret.

Or maybe she's in that world too?

His thumb strokes against my stomach.

"My boss said something after you and the mayor left today. But I didn't know which of you she was referring to."

Nero huffs out a laugh. "I didn't recognize anyone else in there, but if she said that, I recommend staying on her good side."

I shudder. "She's scary enough already, I don't need extra reasons to fear her."

Nero nuzzles against my hair. "I'll protect you."

I make a doubtful sound. "How are you supposed to protect me if you have to pretend like you don't know me?"

There's a beat of silence. "Like I said, I'm figuring that out."

Obviously, I want to know more. I want to know everything. But this might be one of those *ignorance is bliss* moments that I should take advantage of.

"My turn," Nero's voice is like a lullaby, causing me to sink further into his embrace. "Tell me why you were still a virgin."

The question rips apart the wall of calm I was starting to build.

"It just... never happened."

"There's more." He says it confidently. "You didn't hold onto it all this time for no reason. And I want to know what that reason is."

"You're right," I whisper.

My eyes close.

And I let myself remember.

THE NEWSPAPER CRINKLES UNDER MY GRIP WHILE I *read and walk.*

If they're gonna keep cutting my hours, I'm going to need to find a new job.

Running my finger across a help wanted ad for one of the big bakeries in town, I remind myself that I have my diploma in my bedroom nightstand, and in two days I'll be eighteen. Meaning I'll be able to start working full-time.

And with the cash I've hidden away in my old textbooks it won't be long before I can move out. And hopefully far, far away.

I don't bother pulling my keys out of my purse as I walk up the short driveway and past Arthur's car. He never locks the door. Which I hate. But I always hold out hope that someone will break in some day, and they'll kill Arthur before stealing the tv that he's no doubt sprawled in front of.

Tipping my head down to avoid confrontation, I open the front door and step inside. But there's no one in the living room.

Crossing my fingers that I can make it to my room without being seen, I sneak toward the stairs leading to the second floor.

I'm halfway up the flight when I hear the voices.

"Can I do it in here?" A voice I recognize as Bobby's, one of Arthur's friends, asks.

"In her room?" my stepdad questions. "You like the frilly comforter and shit?"

Frilly comforter?

Are they in my room?

I freeze in place.

Why would they be in my room?

"Yeah." Bobby laughs. "It really gives off that virgin vibe."

Nausea crawls up my throat.

Why are they talking about virgins? In my room?

"Look, you're paying for her first time, but if you want to do it here, that's another hundred. And you'll have to do it when my old lady is at work. She won't say shit to me once I show her the money, but she might throw a fit if I tell her beforehand."

"Deal." I hear a jostling sound of slapping hands. "Six hundred and I get the first go at plucking that teenage pussy."

Arthur laughs at his friend. "Not 'til this weekend. In case she tries to go crying to someone about this, I don't want issues with statutory rape or any of that shit. Once she's eighteen, it's just a he-said-she-said. And with the reputation her mom has, no one is gonna believe her."

My body recoils, and my foot slips off the step.

I let go of the newspaper with one hand to grip at the banister.

The railing shakes, but holds. Moving as quickly as my shaking legs will go, I back down the steps and run to the front door.

Their voices are growing behind me, and I know I have to get out of sight. If they see me now, and find out that I heard... What they said...

Chest heaving, I turn the door handle as slow as I dare, to keep it quiet, then pull the door open.

One foot outside.

The voices are louder.

Second foot outside.

I can hear their footsteps.

I'm pulling the door shut, and I see their feet on the stairs.

My whole body freezes.

I can't shut the door while they can see it. If I close it and run, I'm as good as dead--no money. No clothes. And even though it's not what I want to do, I know what I have to do.

I push the door back open, pretending like I just got home.

They're halfway down the stairs, but I don't look up. I just wrap my arms around my middle.

"What the fuck are you doing home?" Arthur snaps.

"I'm s-sick," I stammer through the first excuse I can think of. And with the way my stomach is rolling, it's not even a lie.

"Gross," he sneers.

I hear Bobby snicker as they both walk straight to the kitchen.

Not needing an invitation to leave, I dart up the stairs and into my room. And even though I want to spend my time sanitizing every inch of the room they might have touched. I don't have time.

I need to pack.

Now.
Because I'm leaving tonight.

NERO'S CHEST IS RISING AND FALLING AGAINST MY back. It's the only sign he heard my words as they scraped their way out of my throat.

"I was so scared for so long after I left. And the thought of someone touching me…" I press back into him, and his arm tightens around me even more. "I wasn't ready. Then I wasn't sure how."

The mattress jostles as Nero shifts onto his back. "Come here."

Twisting around, I turn and lay against him while he readjusts the blankets around my shoulders. My head goes to that spot between his shoulder and chest. My leg hooking up over his.

Nero's arms encircle me in a hug.

"But then I met you." I say the words into his chest. Hoping he understands how much he's meant to me already. "And it finally felt like it was time."

"I should've made him suffer." Nero's words are gravel over sandpaper.

"What?"

He hugs me tighter. "I'm so sorry."

"It's over now," I tell him, reassuring him. "It took me longer than I'd planned but I got to control the experience. And no matter what happens once you *figure things out*, I don't regret giving it to you."

"I'll make sure you never do."

A large hand strokes over my damp hair.

"Go to sleep, Baby."

My breath leaves me on a sigh. "Goodnight, Nero."

CHAPTER 43

Nero

IT TAKES EVERY OUNCE OF SELF-CONTROL TO KEEP STILL as Payton falls asleep against me.

There's so much rage flowing through me.

Rage and regret, because I regret Arthur's quick death more than I regret any other sin I've ever committed.

I should've let her watch. Should've let her spit in his face as he gasped for his last breath.

The file King got me on Arthur showed most of his friends as deceased. And that piece of shit Bobby, better hope he's fucking dead already.

Pressing my nose to her hair, I do feel a slight sense of achievement over burning the house down, wiping it from existence.

Payton shifts in her sleep, burrowing further into my side.

I need to do right by her.

But that means keeping her away from my world, and away from me.

It's what she deserves.

CHAPTER 44

Payton

I KNOW I'M ALONE BEFORE I OPEN MY EYES.

There's a particular feeling a room has when it's empty. And now that I've experienced Nero in my apartment a few times, I can hardly believe I didn't feel his presence that night I left the door open for him.

Rolling onto my stomach, I press my nose into the mattress, inhaling. But all I can smell is the leftover scent of my rose body wash. *If he's gonna shower here on a regular basis, I need him to bring his own soap.* There's something about the way Nero leaves no trace of himself behind that makes me feel a little crazy. Makes that tiny voice in my head question whether he does really exist. That maybe I'm still a virgin, and I'm losing my mind, not falling in love.

I scoff out loud and shove myself up and out of bed.

Falling in love.

No, *that* would be insanity.

I can't possibly be falling in love with him already.

Rubbing sleep from my eyes, I shuffle a path to the coffee maker, only half paying attention as I measure out the water and grounds.

It's all just so weird. Because I feel like I understand Nero, even if I don't understand the details of his life. I mean, he basically admitted to being a mobster last night. But does that mean the same thing to everyone? Like is he a part of the actual mob? Like the stuff in movies. With guns and rivals and cops.

Considering he talked about his *enemies* and there were cop cars searching for him the night we met...

While the coffee trickles into the pot, I unlock my phone, open my browser, and type *Nero Security* into the search. He said it was the name of his company, and sure enough my screen populates with results for *Nero's Security Company*.

The second link from the top is the company's official website, so I click on it.

I've never looked at a security website before, but this seems pretty standard. And I'm not surprised that the color scheme is black with shades of gray. But when I click on the *About Us* tab, there are no photos of any of the personnel, and no details about the owner. It just talks about the basics. Founded fifteen years ago. Offices in eight states. Top awards for industry stuff I don't understand.

I go back to the browser and type in *Owner of Nero's Security Company Minneapolis* and some new results pop up on my screen. I click on one that sounds like a news site and see my first photo of Nero. He's in a suit, a serious expression on his face, standing in front of a brick building, shaking hands with... the mayor.

Intrigued, I quickly scan the article.

Finalized a contract with The City of Minneapolis to use Nero's Security Company on all new government building projects, over the next five years... Some speculation on the relationship between Minneapolis Mayor Oscar Devon and Nero, the owner of Nero's...

My eyes fly across the rest of the words, but there's never any mention of Nero's last name.

I search more variations, but nothing I type in gets me any more information on Nero the man.

When the aroma of coffee finally permeates my brain, I look

down to see that the pot is finished brewing and wonder just how long I've been standing here.

Tucking my phone into the shallow pocket of my pajama pants, I open the cupboard above the coffee maker and grab my favorite mug. It's a heavy ceramic, painted yellow, and from Grand Canyon National Park.

I've never been. I've never even left the Midwest. But I found it at a Goodwill a few years ago and it brings me a strange amount of joy. Because someone went there, and even if the mug is mine now, I feel like it holds the memories of the original owner. Like if I close my eyes real tight, I can pretend that I'm the type of person that takes vacations too.

Some day.

You will never worry about money. Not for me. And not for you.

Nero's words from last night skitter around my thoughts.

I might be naïve, but I'm not so foolish as to think he really meant that.

The steam from my mug makes my gaze hazy as I take my first sip.

Nero said a lot of things last night, and I believe he told me the truth––about him, about his life–– but I could feel his hesitation. And whether that hesitancy was really for my safety, or for some other reason, the fact remains, he's not here this morning.

Sighing, I turn toward the living room and decide to spend my day off as I usually would––on the couch, binge watching baking shows.

I've made it two steps, to the edge of the little island, when a rectangle of black catches my attention.

Sitting halfway between the counter and the front door is an envelope.

"How?"

Setting my mug down, I crouch and pick it up.

It's heavy. And the texture tells me it's made of a thick card stock. It's not the size of a normal envelope. It's shorter and fatter.

I glance around, like maybe someone will pop up and say *hey, that's mine.*

There's nothing written on the front, and flipping it over, I see it's not sealed.

My teeth bite down on my lip as I debate opening it. But it's in my apartment, and I can't picture Nero dropping it on accident.

My eyes dart back to the countertop. Maybe he left it for me, but when he shut the door, it slid off.

Maybe?

Exasperated with myself, I groan, "Oh my god, just open it!"

My fingers open the flap and pull out a single piece of paper, made of the same heavy black stock.

There's a small symbol embossed in gold at the bottom of the page that looks sorta like the letter A inside of the sun.

I blink at it, not understanding, then my fingers register raised letters on the other side of the paper.

When I turn it over, my mouth slips open.

It's an invitation. A fancy as hell invitation to a birthday party. For Nero. Tonight.

CHAPTER 45

Nero

"LOOKING RESPECTABLE, BOSS." ROCCO TIPS HIS HEAD to me.

I arch a brow. "Is that supposed to be a compliment?"

He smirks. "That's kinda the point of this whole thing, right?"

Sighing, I adjust my cufflinks and climb into the back seat of the armored SUV.

I couldn't bring myself to wear a full tux tonight. I feel old enough, turning 40, I don't need to wear a monkey suit on top of it. Instead, I opted for full black. Black shoes, black pants, black leather belt, black long sleeve button up, a black vest tailored to fit perfectly, with the black onyx cufflinks I stole off the corpse of my old boss.

So, it might not be the customary black-tie outfit, but for those that matter, I send the message I need to. And that message is *power*.

Rocco pulls away from my house, and I settle into the seat, preparing myself for an evening of schmoozing and irritation.

I hate this shit. Pretending I'm someone I'm not. Pretending I'm someone *respectable*. But it's all a part of the cover. And I know it needs to be done.

A sigh threatens to leave my body, but I lock it down. I can't be soft. From now until the end of the night, I can't show a single sign of weakness. I can't let them see the exhaustion I feel in my bones. The tiredness that only seems to ease when I'm with Payton.

Payton.

Watching the scenery as we exit my neighborhood and near the city, I think of Payton.

My little virgin.

The innocent girl 13 years younger than me.

I should feel like a piece of shit for what I'm doing to her, to her life.

But greed outweighs my guilt every time. And when it comes to Payton, I'm greedy all the way through.

There's just a few more things I need to sort out, before I drag her all the way into the dark with me.

CHAPTER 46
Payton

"THIS THE PLACE?" THE WOMAN DRIVING THE CAR ASKS as she slows to a stop behind a line of fancy-looking cars.

I look up at the massive stone building. "I think so." Then I look again at all the expensive vehicles ahead of us. "It must be."

I've never been to the Minnesota Historical Center before. I guess I was expecting an old house, or something like that. But this isn't a house. It's a whole freaking museum.

Trepidation fills my belly, and for the millionth time I debate if I should've texted Nero today.

But text him what?

Did you really mean to invite me?

He wouldn't have given me an invitation if he didn't want me to come.

Why didn't you just tell me about this last night when we were talking?

Nero hands out information like it pains him, so bringing up a birthday party would probably be torture for him.

"Want to wait? Or want me to let you out here?" the driver asks, her own hesitation obvious in her tone.

Her car is nice, by my standards, but the car in front of us is a Maserati.

"Umm..." I'm not sure how to answer. On one hand, yes I want to get out now, so I can pretend I also drove here in a luxury vehicle worth more than my entire existence. On the other hand, I don't want to walk all the way to the front door from here in my new shoes.

I wiggle my toes inside my high heels, already feeling the pinch since they're too narrow.

Weighing the options, I decide that my feet are going to be killing me no matter what, so I might as well save myself the humiliation of arriving in an Uber.

"I'll get out here."

"Alright!" She doesn't even ask if I'm sure, clearly happy to be rid of me and go pick up a new rider.

The second I open the door, my bare legs are greeted with chilled air.

Hunching my shoulders against the cold, I add a tip for my driver on the app, then stick my phone in my little clutch, pointedly ignoring the amount of money I've dropped on today. But this is the last expense, because hopefully Nero will give me a ride home. And hopefully this party has an open bar.

Starting up the long stretch of sidewalk, I keep my gaze ahead of me, not looking at the tinted windows of the vehicles as I walk past.

I can't spare the energy to worry about what they might think of me, I'm nervous enough as it is, walking into Nero's party.

I really wish he'd just talked to me about it, so we could arrive together. But maybe he was... *embarrassed?* Although it doesn't seem like the right word. I can't picture Nero embarrassed. But this might all be as new for him as it is for me. Obviously not the sex part, but maybe the relationship part.

As I near the steps leading up to the front of the building, I fall in step behind a glamourous couple.

The man is dressed in a tuxedo, but the woman is in a short red dress, giving me a sense of relief.

After finding the invite this morning, I caught the bus and

went back to Marshall's. When I was there yesterday, an amazing black sequined dress caught my eye. It was shorter than I'd usually dare to wear, had a deep-V neckline, and long sleeves. Just for fun I tried it on, when I was looking for my concert outfit. And even though it was tighter than I'd thought, the fitted material was flattering––the nonstop sequins worked to hide the lumps of my hips and belly. But I had zero reason to buy it, so I hung it back up and walked away.

Luckily, it was still there today. So I bought it. Just like I bought these god-awful ice blue pumps. They're super pretty, and they perfectly match the little clutch purse I found, but I swear my feet are already bleeding.

Climbing the steps, I resist the urge to wince as much as I resist the urge to tug on my hem. I can't think about how short the dress is, or I'll break out into a nervous sweat.

On the ride over, I started to worry that maybe I should've gone with something long, like a gown––not that I would've known where to look for one of those––but the dress on the woman in front of me is even shorter than mine.

I still have plenty to worry about this evening, but at least I don't have to worry about my hemline.

At the top of the steps, there are six men dressed in matching jackets with *Nero's* embroidered on the front. This must be part of the security team. Makes sense that Nero would use his own company for his party, but six guys? That seems like overkill.

Mobsters.

I swallow, my throat suddenly dry.

Is this party going to be full of men like Nero? Dangerous ones?

"Invitation?" A deep voice snaps my attention to the right.

A man the size of a house holds his hand out for me.

"Oh, yes. One second." I try to smile, but I'm suddenly terrified. I just want to get inside and find Nero. I know I'll feel better when I'm at his side.

I tip my head down as I open my clutch, and my hair slides over my shoulder, falling into my face.

I opted to leave it down in waves tonight, and I'll be happy to use it as a shield later, but my shaky fingers are having trouble enough with pulling the invitation out of my bag without the obstruction to my view.

Shaking my hair out of the way, I push aside my phone and lip gloss and pull the invitation free.

A slight embarrassment warms my cheeks when I have to unfold the invite, since it was too big to fit in my little purse. I hated bending it, but I'm glad I did. Because I almost left it at home and being turned away now might kill me.

He takes it from me, scanning it for a second before giving me the same treatment and furrowing his brows. "You here alone?"

"Um, yes." I sound unsure since I wasn't expecting the question.

"Most of the women are here as a plus one."

"Oh." That seems like a weird thing to say. "Well, I'm here with Nero."

The man narrows his eyes, scrutinizing me, and I don't know what he sees, but he stands a little straighter and motions for me to walk ahead.

I'm about to hold my hand out to take the invite back, but he slides it into a slotted box at his side. *Well crap, I wanted to keep that.*

I'm only mildly surprised when, a few steps later, I have to hand my purse over for inspection and pass through a metal detector, before I can finally enter the building.

The warm air of the interior is a welcome friend and I force some deep inhales to help my muscles relax.

There are several people walking in at the same time as me, so I follow their lead as they follow the signs directing us to the event space. As we get closer, the signs are hardly necessary, since the din of voices easily carries across the marble floors.

My steps slow to a stop, and I gawk.

Nothing could have prepared me for the grandeur.

The room is packed with people. Some mingling, others standing around those round high-tables in deeper conversation. There's a bar just to the side of where I'm standing, and another I can see across the room.

Music filters through the voices, and if I'm not mistaken, there's a five-piece band set up in the corner.

Just when I think I couldn't feel more awed, I look up.

The ceilings are soaring, so high up, there's a life-sized model airplane suspended above the crowd.

Wow.

I'm so out of my element. And the only way I'm making it through tonight is with alcohol.

Aiming straight for the bar, I watch the people in line ahead of me and notice they don't pay for their drinks. And there's not even a tip jar out. Huh.

"What can I get for you?" the bartender asks me, and I realize I hadn't spent any of that time thinking about what I'd want.

"Oh, um..." I trail off, my eyes trying to catalog all the bottles displayed behind her.

The side of her mouth lifts into a smirk. "I can help you decide if you want."

My shoulders sag in relief. "Yes, please."

She chuckles. "First question, do you want a little booze or a lot of booze?"

"A lot," I admit with a smile.

"Sweet or not sweet?"

"Sweet." I answer immediately.

She nods. "I have just the thing."

Watching her pour from bottles I don't recognize into a shaker, I give up trying to keep track of what she's making and turn a little so I can scan the room for Nero.

He's tall, so I feel like I should be able to find him. But I'm not tall, and there are so many freaking people here.

For Nero's birthday.

Once again, my stomach twists into a knot.

I've never been to a party like this, or around this many people. It's incredibly intimidating.

"Here you are."

I feel my eyes widen when I see the pretty blue martini sitting on the bar top. There's salt along the rim and the thinnest circle of lime floating across the surface.

"I'm gonna call it a margarita-martini baby." The bartender grins. "And I was admiring your shoes when you got in line, so I decided to make a drink to match."

"It's brilliant." I shake my head a little, amazed at her attention to detail.

When I start to open my purse, preparing to give her the last of my cash, she lays her hand on the bar. "We can't accept tips tonight."

"Oh, but––"

"Don't worry, this gig pays more than my last two combined, so we're good."

"If you're sure...?"

She smiles. "Positive. Enjoy."

I thank her as I carefully lift the drink and take a sip. Then I take another, larger sip.

The bartender has already started on her next drink, but she winks at me when I mouth the word *wow*.

I don't know why she was being so friendly to me, maybe she can tell I'm completely out of place and off the rack; regardless of the reason, I'm glad for her kindness.

Sipping on my drink, I work my way in and out of the crowd, but see no sign of Nero.

This is his party. You'd think he'd be easy to find. Or at the very least there'd be one congregation larger than the others, with him at the center. But there's nothing like that. So I scope out a random path, moving slowly, aiming for casual as I turn my head left and right looking for the birthday boy.

My body sways on my next step, as I teeter on my heels; I look down, alarmed, to find that my drink is mostly gone.

Remembering that the only thing I've eaten today was a cup of ramen, I vow to intercept one of the waiters I've seen walking around with trays of finger food soon and stuff my face. If the food is even half as good as this drink, it'll be the best thing I've ever had.

And it's then, as my mind is fully focused on food, that I spot the profile I could recognize by touch.

Dark hair styled back from his face, perfectly-thick beard framing his strong jaw, and a stance that comes from leadership. There's no question who's in charge here. And now that I've found him, I wonder how it took me so long. His energy is palpable. It's like I can feel him. Even with a dozen people still separating us.

As the crowd shifts, my view of him comes and goes, but I keep moving forward, side-stepping a man who shifts into my path.

Nero hasn't seen me yet, but my mouth is already pulled into a smile.

I can't wait to wish him a happy birthday.

All of these people are here for him, to celebrate with him. And he can say whatever he wants about what type of man he is but if I threw a birthday party for myself, inviting every person I've ever known, it wouldn't fill half of this space. Hell, it wouldn't even fill my living room. And that counts for something. Or it should.

His mouth is moving as he talks to the man in front of him, so I slow my progress.

I don't want to interrupt him. That would be rude, and awkward.

Thinking it would be best not to sneak up behind him, I circle out a bit until I'm approaching him from straight on, giving him a chance to spot me before I reach him.

My heart is beating so fast, my nerves rocketing into the stratosphere.

I take another sip of my drink to try and calm myself.

It's gonna be good.

Blowing out a breath, I move closer.

The crowd shifts again, and this time I'm rewarded with a sliver of Nero's full body. Wrapped neck to toe in black, he looks wickedly handsome. His chest looks sculpted, the way it's wrapped in that vest.

A bolt of red draws my attention.

Red nails.

Long, bright red nails, attached to slim fingers that are pressing against his vest. Right over his heart.

My feet stop.

My heart racing for a whole new reason.

The crowd shifts again, and a rock forms in the base of my throat.

Snug against Nero's side is a woman. A shockingly gorgeous woman. Whose slender legs, hips and waist are flaunted in a skin-tight red dress. Her giant breasts test the physics of her strapless neckline, and her raven hair is pulled up into a slick bun. She looks like she walked straight off a movie set.

And she's touching Nero.

I shift closer, trying to understand what I'm seeing.

Maybe they're just talking to each other.

Maybe she's one of those people who's really touchy with her friends.

Not that I'd want him to be friends with another woman.

Maybe it's not what it looks like.

I repeat that last sentence in my head, over and over, while my eyes move back to Nero's face. Hoping against hope for some sign that this is all a misunderstanding.

As I watch, I can see that Nero isn't paying her any attention. But he's also not pushing her away. He's preoccupied talking to that other guy.

Old words batter against the back of my mind, telling me I'm stupid. Worthless... And it's like Nero hears them.

His focus shifts over the other man's shoulder, and our eyes lock.

The feeling of it is like a physical weight. And not a comfortable one.

As he stares back at me, his expression doesn't change. He doesn't smile at me. Doesn't wince at getting caught. He doesn't do anything to even acknowledge that he recognizes me.

I take a step closer, wanting to talk to him. Wanting him to explain why everything will be alright. But he looks away, focusing back on the man in front of him.

My body stills, my jaw tensing, my walls wrapping tight around my heart, and something inside of me cracks when I realize it's the same reaction I have when I'm about to get hit.

The shame and fear and sadness bind together inside of me.

And when movement catches my eye, I slide my gaze down to watch Nero's hand curling around the woman's hip.

This time when I sway, I have to put my hand out, balancing myself on the arm of someone standing beside me.

I mumble an apology, even as my mind starts to slip into survival mode.

Nero's hand stays in place, and at his touch, the woman turns herself further into his body.

My eyes are already brimming with unshed tears, but I drag them back up. Hoping that maybe there's an explanation. That he'll be smiling, and wave me over, and tell me this is all a joke.

But he's not looking at me.

He doesn't even flick a glance my way.

My heart sinks deeper into my chest, squeezing in on itself to seem smaller, to feel less.

And all the while, Nero just stands there, pretending I don't even exist.

CHAPTER 47

Nero

AN AWARENESS SLIDES OVER MY SENSES.

It's that feeling I get when something has changed.

Mr. Gintley keeps talking, but I stopped listening.

My instincts have kept me alive this long. And I've learned the hard way to trust those instincts. To trust myself.

And only myself.

But those instincts weren't strong enough, not tonight. Because the last thing I expect to see when I move my gaze is Payton.

My Payton.

Decades of practice keep the surprise off my face, but my brain can't compute what I'm seeing.

Payton is here.

Payton is *here*.

At my birthday party.

In public.

Anger bubbles beneath my shock.

Wasn't she listening to anything I said?

Did I not make it clear that knowing me was dangerous?

My teeth clench together.

I need to get her out of here.

Nikki drags her claws over my chest, and I watch as Payton's wide eyes drop to track the movement.

Goddamn it.

I let my gaze lower too.

To Payton's cleavage on display, and the tight sparkly fabric clinging to every one of her fucking curves.

I settle on the short-as-fuck dress, showing way too much thigh.

That outfit is going to earn her ass a tanning.

I want to go to her. I want to shout at everyone to leave, so I can fuck some sense into her right here, in the middle of the room.

I can't do any of that though. Because I can't afford to bring a single ounce of attention to her.

And I can't let her bring any attention to *us*.

I need to force her hand. Make her turn away, walk away from me, without a word.

A thick sort of darkness fills my chest because I know what to do. I know what will work.

Another woman might storm over and throw a drink in my face, or confront me right here, in front of all the guests. But Payton isn't like that, she's been hurt too many times. She's too fragile. She won't stand up for herself.

Which is why she needs me. Because *I'll* defend her. I'll do any-fucking-thing for her. But right now, I need to break her heart. And it makes me furious.

With Payton's eyes on Nikki, I slide my hand across my date's back and curl my fingers around her hip. The feeling of her skinny body under my palm makes my skin itch. It's not the body I want to touch. Not the body my hands have imprinted to memory.

Even from several feet away, I can see Payton's face blanch.

I'm so fucking sorry, Baby.

She saw it, just like I needed her to. And Mr. Gintley saw it, just like I needed him to.

He never stopped talking, but I know he saw my attention

shift. And now, instead of wondering what I was looking at, he's looking at my hand on Nikki's body, and getting distracted by staring at her tits.

Nikki is so desperate, she reacts like a sow in heat, pawing at me even more.

You'd think she'd understand the deal by now. Clearly it's time for me to move on from our arrangement.

I pull my gaze away from Payton before she can catch me staring. And I watch as she stands in my periphery, the hurt rolling off her in waves.

But I don't move. Or react. I barely breathe, until I see her form spin and leave. And I hate myself more than I ever have before.

CHAPTER 48

Payton

I SWALLOW DOWN THE REST OF MY DRINK IN TWO gulps, as I stumble away from the scene behind me.

This can't be happening.

This can't be happening.

I'm a little unsteady when I set the empty glass on a table. Letting it tip over while I keep moving.

I just need to get out of here.

Like right now. Before I break down into sobs in the center of this party.

My heart lurches.

He's...

I blink against the tears that keep collecting in my eyes.

He's a bad man. Just like he said he was.

CHAPTER 49

Nero

I LET HER DRIFT OUT OF VIEW, THEN PULL MY PHONE out of my pocket.

"Excuse me, I need to take this." I cut Mr. Gintley off mid-sentence.

Pressing my palm into Nikki's back, she takes the hint and steps forward to cozy up to her new mark.

No one had actually called me, but they don't know that. And in a few quick taps, the line is ringing.

I nod at a person I recognize from City Hall, then angle away from them as King answers.

"What's up?"

He knows I wouldn't be calling him unless it was something important.

"Find me," is all I say.

King hangs up the call on his end, but I keep the phone pressed to my ear, giving the illusion that I'm talking to someone.

A few more people tip their glasses to me in acknowledgement, but none try to talk to me while it looks like I'm on a call.

Watching the glances, I realize it's quite the mix of people. Sure, it's my party. But the people here are either distant work or society acquaintances, and don't know me well enough to feel comfortable around me, or they're people that actually know me well enough to know they should be scared of me.

"Yes. Take care of it." I say to no one, before lowering my phone into my pocket, just as King reaches me, drink in hand.

"Nero," his greeting is formal, keeping up our front of only being friendly but not friends. "Happy birthday."

He extends his free hand, and I take it.

"Appreciate it."

We automatically adjust our footing, so the wall is at our sides and we're watching each other's backs.

"How's the party?" King keeps his volume low, and I know no one can overhear us above the music and droning voices.

"I need you to grab an artifact for me and put it in storage. Gently."

King swirls the amber liquid in his glass before taking a sip. "One I'll recognize?" he finally asks.

"Yes." My fingers itch to curl into a fist, but I keep them loose. "The coconut honey."

King's brows raise, the smallest amount, revealing just how surprised he is by my request.

"Here?" he clarifies and I nod.

Even if no one can hear us, I'm not taking the chance of saying her name out loud in this room. I know he'll understand what I'm getting at, since the only time either of us have used the words *coconut* and *honey* together was that one morning outside of Twin's Café.

"You sure?" he asks.

And I know he's not asking if I'm sure Payton's here. He's asking if I'm sure that I want him to go lock her in a storage room until I can get my hands on her.

"Positive." Then I reiterate, "Gently." Because this isn't one of our usual snatch and stores. The only torture she'll feel is the sting of my hand on her bare ass. And maybe my cock back inside her ass as well.

King whistles low but doesn't say more.

As he starts to leave his eyes flick over my shoulder then back to me. In a warning.

Turning to see who's approaching, I thank god I got Payton to leave when I did. This man is the exact reason I don't want her in my world.

The blond man with the sharp eyes and an exaggerated swagger stops before me.

"Mikhail." I say his name but keep my hands at my sides when he holds his out. "What are you doing here?"

He grins, turning his palm up before dropping his hand. "Can't I come wish a fellow businessman a happy birthday?"

"No." My tone is bland, but we both know I'm not joking.

Nikki, who'd walked over with him, moves back to my side. And even though she's doing exactly what I paid her to do, I hate her for it.

Mikhail lifts a shoulder. "Pity, I was starting to enjoy myself." His eyes trail down the length of Nikki.

I don't know if he's trying to imply something, or get me riled up, but I don't give two fucks if he sleeps with her. Now, if he so much as glances in Payton's direction, I'll rip off more than his finger.

"Sorry to hear that." I raise my right hand to eye level and gesture with two fingers.

Mikhail watches, weariness finally landing on his features. Features eerily similar to those of a man I killed fifteen years ago.

Four of my men materialize around us, their dark suits blending in with the crowd.

"This is hardly necessary." Mikhail tries to keep a smile on his face, but I can see his anger. Hell, I can feel it.

And I love it.

"Get the fuck out of my party."

CHAPTER 50

Payton

FOR THE FIFTH TIME IN AS MANY SECONDS, MY fingertips swipe under my eyes.

Keeping my head down, I make my way through the crowd. I just want to get out.

I want to go home and pretend none of this happened. Pretend I never met Nero.

The bodies start to thin, so I finally look up, expecting to see the wide entrance to the event space. But instead, I see a wall.

What...

Confused, I spin around.

You have got to be kidding me.

The plane hanging from the vaulted ceiling is on the wrong side of the room. *I* went to the wrong side of the room. The giant arched entryway I came in through is on the complete opposite side of the massive room.

No no no.

"Champagne?"

I blink at the waiter who materialized next to me.

"No, thank you," I respond automatically, before noticing the tray of flutes he's holding. "Actually, yes, please."

He gives me a polite smile, nodding to the tray.

I hesitate for one second before I tuck my purse under my arm and use both hands, grabbing a drink in each.

The waiter doesn't bat an eye at my behavior, moving away and on to the next guest without another word.

If I was a normal person, who had alcohol in her apartment, I wouldn't need to double fist it now. But I don't like wasting money on booze, and tonight calls for getting drunk, so the least Nero can do is supply me with drinks.

Nero.

My heart nearly stops at the thought of his name. And in response, I raise one of the glasses of champagne, and gulp it down like a frat boy. The bubbles rioting in my throat.

A woman walks out of the wall ahead of me, and I narrow my eyes.

It's then I realize I'm already drunker than I thought, because she just came out of a door.

Relief swamps me, and as I hurry toward it, I see the sign designating it as a ladies' room. On my way, I find another little table to set my empty glass on, then use my free hand to push into the bathroom.

The noise level drops when the door swings shut behind me, and I'm greeted with a large, dimly lit restroom fancier than any I've ever seen.

The marble floor continues throughout, the walls are covered in a dark floral wallpaper, and the stalls are all their own individual little rooms with floor-to-ceiling wooden doors.

Not needing an embossed invitation for this little party, my heels click across the floor as I make my way to an open stall door, locking it behind me.

Keep it together, Payton.

I press my butt to the door and bend forward, careful not to spill my full glass.

In my newly found privacy, I let my breath hitch.

Just once.

Get home. Get home, then you can lose it as much as you want.

You can cry until you throw up if you want. But not until you get home.

The bathroom is so fancy the stall has a shelf attached to the wall, rather than a hook on the door, for your purse or jacket. I set my drink on the shelf, then slip my phone out of my purse and open the Uber app.

It only takes me a few seconds to request a ride, and luckily, it's a busy time of night so lots of cars are available. I select one that's only five minutes away, then hit confirm.

Taking a breath, I pick up the second glass of bubbly and down it as fast as the first.

CHAPTER 51

Payton

OKAY, SO THAT SECOND GLASS MAY HAVE BEEN A mistake. My steps are even more unsteady as I push out of the ladies' room and back into the main party. Although the blisters on my feet are throbbing just a tiny bit less, and even though my vision is slightly blurry from the tears that are still sitting in my eyes, I think I might be able to pull this off and get out of here without having a complete meltdown.

I take a second to catch my bearings, and look around the packed space, deciding it might be best to just circle around the edge of the massive room. Cutting through the middle will require a lot of weaving, and my wobbly ankles aren't up for that.

I purposefully don't look in the direction where I saw Nero, or where I think I saw him, since I got all turned around, because I can't witness seeing him a second time. Or more specifically, I can't witness him with his arm around another woman a second time and keep my sanity.

A group of people off to my left shift and converge around one of the food waiters.

My stomach is empty––besides the booze––but just the idea of trying to chew and swallow something makes my insides roil.

Turning away from the food, I blow a breath out between pursed lips. I don't even want to see it.

Guess I'll go the other way.

Looking up, so I don't unwittingly bump into a tray of something, a large figure catches my attention.

He's not doing anything spectacular, just walking toward me, along the back wall. He's probably twenty feet away, but there's something about him...

He kinda reminds me of Nero. The way he stands up straight, the energy he exudes, the fact that he's handsome.

When his eyes catch mine, I look down, a reflex I can't seem to shake.

But then it hits me, and my eyes snap back up.

I recognize him, and tendrils of ice wrap around my limbs.

I recognize him.

He came into the café that morning. He was all nice, asking me what my favorite drink was and leaving me a huge tip.

I take one step back.

I told this man what drink I liked, and then Nero showed up and ordered that same latte.

They have to know each other.

It can't be a coincidence that this man is here.

He knows Nero. Nero knows him.

They know each other.

I take another step back, my foot tilting in the high heels.

Ever since that very first night, when Nero walked into my apartment, I always felt him watching. Felt him nearby. And even when I doubted that any of it was real, it comforted me to feel like someone cared. Twisted or not.

But sending someone else to check on me... having this big intimidating man come to my place of work...

Panic and sadness press in on me, making it hard to breathe.

Sending someone else makes it all so different. So bad.

How could he do that?

How could he trick me like that?

It's so stupid. So freaking stupid that it hurts my feelings. But so few people are nice to me. When this stranger asked what my favorite drink was, it... I don't know. It was weird, but it was still someone else in this world asking a question about me. Making me feel interesting.

But that was another lie. This man, like everyone else, doesn't care about me.

A tear breaks loose, slipping down my cheek.

Seeing my emotion, the man slows, and holds his hands up. It's probably meant to be a disarming gesture, but displaying his large palms like that only reminds me how much stronger he is than me.

How much stronger Arthur is than me.

And Nero...

A sound of sorrow pops out of my mouth.

Why did he have to make me feel so safe?

Why did he have to shatter the illusion I lived in?

I hadn't realized... I hadn't realized how unsafe I'd felt for my entire, pathetic existence, until Nero barged into my life. Then he wrapped me in his arms, holding my broken pieces together, and I felt safe. *Safe!*

I wish I'd never known that feeling.

The man takes a step closer, and I blink, sending a whole cascade of tears tumbling free.

There are a dozen steps between us, but I keep inching back at his approach.

Something about his manner says he's not just here to ask me to leave.

Which is when it clicks.

Nero is a mobster. And I bet this man is too.

My heart starts to pound even faster as fear surges up to match my sorrow.

I don't know anything. Not really. But what if it's still too much? What if I know too much?

The man takes one more step closer and my instincts take hold.

Without thinking past the *right now* I turn so my back is to the wall, and dart straight into the throng of bodies.

I bump a few shoulders as I go, but no one seems to notice, as they are too engrossed in laughing conversations.

I dare a glance over my shoulder. Hoping he'll be by the back wall, watching me leave.

But the split second it takes me to look, is all the time I need to confirm he's following me.

And he's close.

Oh god.

I pick up my pace. The alcohol helping me block out the way my shoes are pinching my toes.

"Excuse me." I shuffle past another group, taking a few quick strides across a small open section of floor. "Pardon me." I place my hand on the shoulder of a shorter gentleman causing him to turn left as I sneak around the other side of him.

I don't want to draw attention to my flight. Causing a scene wouldn't be good for me, I'm sure of it.

It's tempting to look back to check for my pursuer again, but I don't dare. I need to focus on getting out.

A stretch of space opens up before me, but the feeling of fingers brushing against my shoulders kills the small amount of relief I'd felt.

"King!" A voice booms out beside me, and the fingers drop away.

CHAPTER 52
King

Fuck.

Plastering a neutral expression on my face, I stop my pursuit and greet the asshole who shouted my name.

"Brenton." I shake his hand. "Nice to see you," I lie.

Most everyone in this room already knows who I am, but I don't exactly want Payton flying around with my name on her lips. Not that I think she'd do anything with it, but you never know.

"I didn't know you'd be here!" Brenton nudges the man next to him. "This is King Vass, the guy I was telling you about. With all the money."

Classy.

"Nice to meet you." I bob my head as I take a step back. "Save a drink for me. I gotta take care of something real quick."

I'm full of shit, but Brenton's smile is bigger than ever and his head won't stop nodding.

He's probably a decent guy. Owns a winery just south of the cities. But that's the problem, he's a decent guy. And I don't need any extra dead weight in my life.

Forcing my own smile to stay in place, I keep walking the direction I was headed, my eyes scanning the crowd for Payton.

I was *so close*.

I could've had her. My fingers brushed the fabric of her long sleeves, but I hesitated. And I hesitated because Nero wasn't specific.

To be fair, he wasn't in a position to give me a full briefing, but as soon as I felt the fabric under my touch, I faltered. Because what the fuck am I actually supposed to do?

The woman was already crying when I spotted her. Even though she was moving quickly and quietly, people were bound to have noticed her. And a crying woman in a party is memorable. Add on a well-known figure, myself, accosting said crying woman in the middle of a party, now that would be unforgettable. Exactly what Nero is trying to avoid.

Not to mention the fact that Nero is more unhinged than usual when it comes to Payton, and he might not react well to me manhandling her. Hell, he probably wouldn't react well to me touching any part of her. Which begs the question, how exactly am I supposed to get her to go with me, a stranger, to a private room, after Nero already did something to upset her?

Still searching, my eyes finally catch the sparkle of her dress and I curse to myself when I see she's already past the entrance to the party room, waiting for the fucking elevator.

If those doors close before I get there, she's as good as gone.

But if I can get the two of us alone in the elevator... that might do it.

CHAPTER 53

Payton

THE TIP OF MY THUMB TURNS WHITE AS I PRESS THE button harder to call the elevator.

"Come on. Come on." I urge the cab to hurry its climb.

It's early to be leaving, so there's no one else waiting with me, which I'm thankful for. Because if someone tried to engage me in small talk right now, I'd probably dissolve into sobs.

The need to look back for *King* prickles the back of my neck. But it's this elevator or nothing. There's no way I can outrun that man, and no way I'm trying for the stairs. His stride has to be twice as long as mine, he'd catch me in no time. Alone.

I shift my weight, the motion dulling the throb in one foot, but increasing it in the other.

The chime announcing the elevator startles me so bad I let out a small scream.

Cool, we'll add embarrassment to the list of emotions I'm already dealing with.

As soon as the doors are wide enough for me to squeeze through, I start to step inside, but nearly colliding with another body has me letting out another scream.

The girl facing me screams a little too, me scaring her over her scaring me.

"Jesus, Krissy." The older man standing next to her is shaking his head.

The girl giggles and swats at his chest. "She startled me."

The girl is beautiful, looks barely old enough to drink, and is wearing a dress that makes mine look matronly in comparison.

"Sorry," I mumble, and we shuffle around, letting each other pass.

The interaction almost makes me forget I'm being pursued. But after I press the button for the ground floor, I look up and lock eyes with King.

The bottom of my stomach drops, and I look away just long enough to press the button for the lobby level. Then I shakily push the *door close* button.

When I glance back up, King is striding straight toward me.

I hit the button again. Over and over, I press it as fast as I can.

King is halfway to me, jaw tight, fists clenched.

The doors start to slide shut.

"Please, please, please," I beg the doors, pressing the button.

King is four strides away.

Then three.

Two strides, his hand is reaching out.

And the doors close.

I slump against the side wall of the elevator, my breath coming in choppy gasps. But as the elevator starts to lower, I realize that the wall I'm leaning on is glass; and the man, apparently named King, is standing there at the railing, staring at me. But a moment before I drop out of sight, I see him curse and stride toward the stairs.

PANIC HAS FULLY CONSUMED ME BY THE TIME THE doors slide open so, I don't waste a second, squeezing out the door and hurrying toward the exit, hoping not to run into anyone this time.

I checked the progress of my Uber on the way down, and it should be pulling up outside right now. They'll only wait a few minutes, but that's more than enough time. If I'm not out those front doors in the next sixty seconds, I might never make it out.

The lobby is a grand affair, and there's a short flight of four steps to get down from the main open area to the front doors, where the security guards are standing around.

I'm too worried about King chasing me to notice that it started raining outside, and that enough people have come and gone, leaving tracks of water on the sleek stone steps.

On the second step, my stupid high-heeled shoe hits the slippery surface just right and slides out from underneath me.

Flinging my arms wide, I get my hand on the railing, but not soon enough. My momentum sends me landing, ass first, onto the solid edge of the step. Pain immediately shoots up my spine.

It hurts.

A lot.

But that's not the reason more tears stream down my face.

I'm done.

I'm just so fucking done with... all of it. My entire life.

Two of the guards are headed toward me, probably to help. But I don't want their help.

I don't want anyone's help.

Sitting on the step for another moment, I reach down and shove one shoe off, then the other. I never want to see these damn things again.

Loud footsteps echo across the lobby from behind me, and I'm out of time.

Wincing, I use the handrail to pull myself up.

Then I do the one thing I'm good at.

I run.

CHAPTER 54

Nero

MY EYES SNAP TO KING'S THE SECOND HE STEPS BACK into the party. And when he shakes his head, my temper flashes into a bright fury.

I checked my watch every minute King was gone, so I know exactly what time it is. And I know I have ninety-four minutes until I can leave.

And the second I can, there's only one place I'm going––to teach Payton a lesson.

CHAPTER 55

Payton

I can't stop crying.

I feel so stupid.

So goddamn foolish.

My palm roughly wipes at my neck, the tears trickling all the way down past my cheeks, before I pull my largest duffel bag out of the closet.

He told me. He freaking *told me* that he wasn't a good man. And like an idiot, I believed everything out of his mouth, except for that.

Brushing away more tears, I start with the essentials by emptying the contents of my underwear drawer into the duffel.

He told me he'd lie and cheat to keep me safe. He said it, just like that, but I didn't put it together. Not really. Because, to me, being with another woman doesn't keep me safe. It breaks my heart.

I take a second to press my fist against my chest, like it might lessen the ache inside my ribs.

It doesn't.

My eyes won't cooperate, the tears keep coming, but I keep packing.

I can't stay here.

I don't want to go. But I can't stay.

Life is hard enough without constantly looking over your shoulder.

I should know. I did it for years. Hell, I still break into a sweat when I see someone that looks like Arthur. The thought of him showing up on my doorstep is no less terrifying today than it was ten years ago.

I don't really believe that Nero would kill me. Not himself. But if he decides I'm a loose end... Or if one of his enemies saw me tonight... It won't matter to them that Nero doesn't care about me. They'll just kill me themselves when they find out I'm worthless.

No. I won't just sit around and wait.

At least this time I'm an actual adult and I have a little more money saved. Not a lot—hardly anything really—but it's enough to buy a bus ticket out of the state and stay in a cheap rent-by-the-week hotel for a month while I find another job and start collecting a paycheck.

My hands pause in the act of opening my pajama drawer. Maybe I can see the Grand Canyon after all. Arizona is about as far away as you can get from Minnesota without going to a coast. Plus, coasts are expensive; some small town in the southwest, with a diner that needs help, would be as perfect as my version of perfect can get.

With any luck, I'll never see Nero or Arthur again in my life.

My lips tremble, and I press them together.

I keep telling myself that *not* seeing Nero is what I want. And that the thought of never seeing him again doesn't make me feel like I'm going to die.

I pull the drawer open and start plucking out my pajamas. I buried the silk pair at the bottom of the drawer—the ones I was wearing the night Nero took my virginity—and as I pull the layers above away, I wonder if I should throw them in the garbage. Seeing them will only cause me pain.

But when I get to the bottom of the drawer, I don't find the shorts and top. Instead, I find two crisp hundred-dollar bills.

The sobs come in earnest now.

This feels dirty.

Feels like he's paying me off, like I'm some sort of prostitute, and nothing more.

It only takes thinking the word, before snippets of the night start to melt together.

The ultra-short dresses. The security guard's comment "most women are here as a plus one". The noticeable age difference, and attractiveness difference, of so many couples.

Could they be...?

But then there was Nero. He was perfectly matched by that woman. Both stunning. Both extremely well dressed. Poised. *Fit.*

I take a step back, until I can feel the bed behind me, and slump down to sit on the mattress. The sore spot on my butt––where I hit it on those stone steps––makes itself known. But it's nothing compared to the pain I feel on the inside.

Feeling more defeated than I have in a long time, I lay on the bed and curl up on my side.

I'm still in this ridiculous dress, the one I felt so proud of only hours ago. But now it feels as fake as Nero's promises.

I clasp my hands together in front of my mouth, the sequins around the neckline and sleeves scratching against my skin, but I don't have the energy to take it off.

Instead, I let my eyes slide closed.

I made sure the doors were locked when I got home. I even dragged the couch across the living room, positioning it against the front door. But I'm not really that worried about Nero coming to me tonight, it's his birthday and he's celebrating.

No, it won't be tonight, but it'll be soon. Which is why I'll leave before morning.

I just need to rest my eyes for a few minutes.

CHAPTER 56

Nero

MY TIRES SCREECH AS I SLAM ON THE BRAKES, STOPPING right in front of Payton's apartment.

I'm done hiding in the shadows.

And she's done living here.

The anger coursing through my blood has only grown in its intensity since I locked eyes with my girl tonight. Anger at her. Anger at Mikhail. Anger at myself.

I climb out of my car, striding straight for the front door, using my key to enter the building.

My footsteps pound up the steps to the second floor, her apartment key already in my hand.

It's not yet midnight, and the sounds of life and tv sets filter into the hallway from other apartments.

Good, background noise to drown out what's to come.

Twisting the key, I feel the click, then turn the knob.

There's some resistance as I push the door open, making my lip curl into a sinister grin.

If Payton wants to play in my world, then we'll fucking play.

CHAPTER 57

Payton

"WHA––" MY QUESTION TURNS INTO A SCREAM WHEN my body is harshly dragged down the mattress.

There's a large hand gripping my ankle, pulling me to the end of the bed. Causing my sequined covered back to catch on the sheets.

When I try to kick out with my free leg, another large hand grips that ankle, holding me still.

Even without seeing him, I know it's Nero, but that doesn't stop the fear from coming.

"Don't!" I cry, struggling against his grip.

I blink rapidly against the brightness, I don't know how long it's been since I laid down; I fell asleep with the lights on, and now they're blinding me as I try to make sense of what's happening.

"Please!" I sob. "I'm sorry."

My vision is blurry, but I can see the outline of Nero standing at the foot of the bed, imposing in his all-black, while he drags me toward him.

His dark laugh ripples over my skin. "Not yet, you're not. But you will be."

My lungs struggle to pull in air.

This is it.

214

This is how I die.

At the hands of the man who took my virginity. The fear I've had for a decade finally comes true. Only it's a different man than I've always dreaded. It's a new one.

I try to pull my legs free of his grip. "P-please! Just let me leave!" My hands flail to the sides, searching for a weapon that I know isn't there.

"Leave?" Nero scoffs. "You're never leaving my sight again."

I choke on my next breath.

Wait. What?

I repeat his words in my mind. "You're not...?"

His grip on my ankles tightens, even though I'm laying still. "I'm not what, Payton?"

I swallow. "You're not going to kill me?"

I know it's the wrong thing to say when pure rage covers his features.

In one motion, he pulls my legs straight, then twists his hands, flipping me over onto my stomach.

Disorientated, I don't have time to fight, before he's trapped my legs between his thighs.

He grunts when I buck my body against the hold, but it doesn't do anything to free my legs.

In response, the hem of my dress is jerked up, revealing my new lacy pair of boy shorts to his view. And my face flames red, because they're light blue, to match the shoes and purse I bought for tonight. An outfit I bought for him.

"Nero," I beg. Not sure what I'm begging for.

Forgiveness? Freedom? My life?

There's a click, and my body goes rigid.

I know that sound.

It's the distinct sound of a switchblade locking open.

My brief hope is dashed. He must've meant never leave his sight alive.

"I won't tell anyone," I sob. "I promise. I won't say anything to anyone."

Cool metal slides across my skin, just below my panties, on the curve of my cheek.

"What won't you tell them, Payton?"

Black dread tinges the edge of my vision. "Anything," I choke. "I won't tell anybody anything."

The metal moves, the blade slipping underneath the lace, the tip pointed up toward my back.

"I'm not worried about what you might say." There's pressure, then the fabric gives way, the elastic band at the top sliced through. Then another flick, and he's cut through my panties on both sides. "I'm more worried about what you might do."

One of his palms presses into the center of my back, pinning me to the mattress. But it's not necessary. The fear and confusion has me frozen in place.

The lace is lifted off my ass, and I picture him gripping the fabric, as he slowly pulls it straight up. The now loose material follows his movement, bunching up in my slit and dragging over my clit.

The surge of pleasure is so strong, so unexpected, I moan.

He grunts in response but says nothing. Instead, a single fingertip draws a line across my tender flesh, and I know he's tracing the bruise that's already forming from my fall.

The sigh he lets out is full of disappointment, and I feel it in my stomach.

"I'm sorry," I feel compelled to whisper.

"Not yet," Nero whispers back, then his hand cracks down on my ass.

The dull ache flairs to a bright flash of pain, and I suck in a shocked gasp. But then his hand is back, softly soothing the sting, pressing just hard enough to remind me of the bruise. Somehow it's also stoking a fire in my core.

A whimper leaves me, my senses warring between pain and pleasure. Warring between fighting and giving in.

"Don't touch me," I try to shout it, but it comes out weak.

The hand on my back slides down to my ass, the hilt of the

knife still there, pressed between me and his palm. The flat side of the blade against my plump skin.

His body steps back, so my knees are between his thighs, keeping me trapped.

With a grip on both globes of my ass, he spreads me.

I have half a second to feel his warm breath before his tongue swipes up the length of me.

My body jolts at the contact and he releases his grip on my bruised cheek only to slap his hand back down. "Hold still," he growls. "If you cut yourself on this knife, you will not like the consequences."

I freeze again, feeling the edge of the blade graze across my lower back.

My hands ball in the fabric beneath me. "Get away from me."

"No." Nero buries his face into me again, this time flattening his tongue over my asshole.

My pussy clenches so hard, I'm afraid I might come from that act alone.

"Stop!" I cry, with actual tears in my eyes, even as he licks me again.

I don't want him to stop. I want him to make love to me. I want him to touch me in *that* way that makes me feel special. I want to be the only woman he sees.

But I'm not.

Tonight proved that.

"I told you," Nero grits out, as he straightens up, his hands grabbing hold of my dress. "You had one chance to tell me no. But you didn't. You gave me that sweet virginity instead." The fabric at my shoulders is pulled tight before he slices up the length of my dress, with my bra suffering the same fate. "Now you're mine." Cool air flows over my back as the torn fabric is folded open. "Until the day we die."

We?

"But--" My body is vibrating, and I can't keep hold of my thoughts.

"But nothing." Nero snaps the words, dragging my body back toward him until my hips are right at the edge of the bed. With legs hanging off, my knees bump into the bed frame while my toes try to find purchase. His hand is back to holding me down, so I can't get my feet on the floor.

"But you were with her!" I shout the accusation. The memory of his hand on her hip seared into my brain.

"She's nothing!" he shouts back.

"Then what am I?" I cry the question.

"I already told you," Nero growls, dropping his weight onto my back. "You're mine."

Then, with one hard push, he sinks his cock all the way inside me.

CHAPTER 58

Nero

PAYTON'S DRIPPING-FUCKING-WET, AND MY DICK SLIDES deep into her pussy without resistance.

She tenses beneath me, her body and mind at war--wanting to hate me while also wanting to pull me in deeper.

"Get off me!" she cries, even as her pussy pulses around my dick.

She wants to hate me. But she doesn't. She can't.

And I'll prove it to her.

Because she's close.

She's so close.

And I'm not here to play fair.

I shove a hand between her and the mattress, not stopping until I feel her firm little clit against my fingers.

Her body arches under me, legs pressed together, and the more she squirms the tighter her pussy grips my dick.

"S-stop it!" Payton moans.

I grab her hair with my free hand, pulling her head back until our cheeks are next to each other's.

"Why?" I grate against her ear.

"Because, I-I'm going to--"

"Do it. Come for me." I rub the pads of my fingers over her clit in a rough pattern, and she explodes.

Her juices slick my fingers, and her convulsing walls try to pull the cum straight from my balls.

I clench my teeth and resist the draw to follow her over the edge.

We're only getting started.

CHAPTER 59
Payton

My whole body is shaking, the orgasm rocking me to the bone.

"That's right." Nero licks up my cheek, his grip in my hair as unrelenting as the hard dick buried inside me. "Feel me." He pushes his hips harder against my ass. "Know that it's me inside of you." His teeth drag down my neck. "Me that lights you on fire."

I pull against his hold in my hair, the harsh tug at the roots a welcome distraction from what's happening between my legs.

"You told me you'd cheat." I hate how pitiful I sound. "But I didn't think you meant like that."

A low rumble vibrates from his chest, through my back. "It's *not* like that." His grip leaves my hair, and I drop my forehead to the bed. But of course, his hands follow, his fingers rubbing soft circles against my scalp. "I wasn't with her like that."

I try to ignore the way his touch comforts me. And I try to ignore the fullness of his cock filling me. Just filling me.

"You let her touch you." My throat aches.

"Never again." The hand on my pussy is motionless, but he's still pressing against my clit and it's making it hard to think.

"You were touching her." My voice struggles, but it comes out as the loud accusation I feel.

"You haven't been listening." I can feel his frustration, even as his cock throbs. "She was there to distract the crowd. She was the fucking hired help, to keep people looking at her, and not wondering where I'd be spending the night."

Hired help.

I was right. He paid her.

"Have you slept with her?"

"That's not important."

"Have you?!" I'm back to shouting. My anger edging out my hurt.

Nero's upper body pulls away from me, and it's the missing pressure that makes me notice the way his shirt buttons were digging into my back. He's still dressed.

"You want to know if I've fucked that whore, Payton? Is my Sweet Girl really asking me that?"

His hands clamp around my hips, and I'm suddenly lifted off the mattress. My hands automatically push against the blankets and I barely catch myself when Nero pushes me forward, with his hips.

His cock is even deeper now, and with him buried to the hilt, I walk my hands up the mattress. The soft texture of his pants on the back of my thighs conflicts with the hard muscles beneath. And something thuds to the floor, that can only be the knife.

"Yeah, Baby. I have." He spits the words, and the admission slices through me. "I've fucked her."

Nero follows me up onto the bed. Kneeling behind me.

"Leave me alone."

His hands tighten on my hips.

"You want to know what it was like?" His tone is so full of anger it scares me.

I shake my head, because no, I don't want to know any more.

With both of us on our knees, Nero wraps his arms around my chest and pulls me up until we're both kneeling upright, our bodies flush.

With my arms free, he yanks the ruined dress and bra away. Leaving me fully naked, to his fully dressed.

"It was forgettable," he whispers into my ear.

Then, for the first time since he entered me, he pulls his hips back, until only the head of his cock is in me. My pussy lips spread around his girth, clinging to him.

"It was nothing."

His cock twitches, causing my clit to throb in response.

"Anyone I've ever been with, is nothing. Because they aren't you."

He thrusts forward on the last word.

My mouth drops open in a silent scream. And my hands claw behind me, trying to find something to hold on to. Trying to find him.

Catching the sides of his shirt, I twist my fingers into the fabric.

One of his hands slides up to hold me around the throat, the other presses hard against my belly, making him feel even bigger inside me.

Nero's loud groan of pleasure almost sends me into another orgasm.

"I've fucked other women." He pulls out and slams back in. "But not since I met you." His hips pull away. "And the ones before, they meant nothing." Another pounding thrust forward. "I never made love to them." The hand on my stomach drops away. "And I never killed for them."

Killed for them?

The hand on my throat slides up, so his thumb and fingers are framing the underside of my jaw, holding my head still.

"I'll only ever make love to you." His hips roll up, the tip of him hitting the end of me. "And I'll gladly kill for you. As many times as it takes."

A flash of light breaks through the haze of lust filling my brain, and I blink.

It can't be.

The gold ring...

My throat tightens.

It can't be.

Stupid girl.

Worthless cow.

Waste of space.

Fucking pathetic.

That ring digging into my neck.

That man terrorizing me.

Threatening me.

That ring representing the reason I was forced to leave.

The reason I've been all alone.

Terrified for years.

I gasp for breath and stare at Arthur's ring.

Arthur's ring between Nero's fingers.

"He's gone, Baby." Nero nuzzles his cheek against mine.

My eyes burn. "You... You killed him?"

Nero turns his hand up, letting the ring roll into his palm.

"I killed him."

Relief, greater than any emotion I've ever felt, consumes me.

Nero's grip on my throat grounds me. And changes everything. Erasing so much history in that one moment.

"He's gone?" Tears are rolling from my eyes.

"He's gone." Nero kisses my shoulder and I sag into his grip, my body losing its ability to hold me up.

Arthur is gone.

Nero wraps his arm back around my waist, holding me against him, letting me cry.

"He'll never hurt you again." Nero presses his lips to my temple, his tongue darting out to catch more tears.

CHAPTER 60

Nero

THE TASTE OF HER TEARS MAKES MY COCK THROB inside her.

"I told you, you're mine to protect." I lick another tear, savoring it. "Anyone who hurts you will cease to exist."

Her body trembles and I hold her tighter.

My dick shouldn't be so hard over this. But the small spasms around my length are too much to ignore, and I pull out, just a little, then rock my hips in.

Out, then in.

Again and again, with shallow thrusts as Payton cries in my arms.

There's a hiccup, before the last thing I ever expected to hear hits my ears.

"Thank you." Payton sucks in another breath and says it stronger. "Thank you."

My cock swells, and I jerk my hips back, pulling all the way out.

I grab her shoulders, twisting her around to face me, I frame her face in my hands. "Say that again."

Her gaze is wide, and bright, when she looks me in the eye. "Thank you for killing him."

With my grip holding her steady, I crash our mouths together. The taste of her truth filling me.

She doesn't fight me or resist. She opens to me.

With her tongue tangling with mine, her fingers are frantic as she pulls at my clothes.

But there's no time for that. She can have me naked next time.

Pushing her hands away, I shove her onto her back and follow her down. Our mouths fused together.

Payton lifts her legs, circling them around my waist. "Get inside me." Payton pants against my lips. "I need you inside me." She claws at my shoulders, keeping me close.

Warmth like I've never known swells inside my chest.

"Now, Nero. Please!" She tugs me closer. "I need you now."

There are still tears on her cheeks, her skin flushed to a deep pink, and she's never looked more fucking powerful.

I lift my hips enough to get the space I need, then, when my tip is greeted by her wet, greedy heat, I slam into her.

Our bodies connect on a groan. And the slow part is over.

My hips pump. My cock pushing in and out. My pants sliding down my hips with each thrust until my balls are slapping against her ass.

"You're mine." I circle my arms underneath her shoulders, hugging her against my body, as she hugs me back.

"I'm yours," she pants.

"Tell me you understand."

She nods her head against me. "No more other women."

"There are no other women."

Her hand reaches up, sliding into my hair before she grips it, hard. Like I just did to her.

I follow her pull and lift my head enough to look at her.

Her tits are rubbing against my chest, bouncing with each slam of my cock, but she looks as serious as I've ever seen her when she says, "No more women. No touching them and no letting them touch you. At all."

I grin. "There's my girl."

She yanks my hair. "Say it."

My balls squeeze. Fuck she's hot when she's worked up.

"No one touches me but you. And you're the only woman I'll ever touch again." Her pussy squeezes me with each promise, and I can't resist swiping a lick across her lips. "Now you."

"You're the only man I've ever touched." She stares into my eyes as she says it, and my cock starts to spurt. "The only man who will ever know what my pussy feels like." I piston my hips into her. "The only man who will ever fill me with his seed."

My cock erupts. Emptying my load deep inside her.

Crushing my full weight into her, the base of my dick grinds against Payton's clit, and that's all it takes for her to explode around me.

CHAPTER 61

Payton

I CAN HARDLY BREATHE, NERO'S WEIGHT CRUSHING ME into the mattress, but I don't care. I relish in the feeling of being trapped under him. Entwined with him.

My fingers are digging into his bunched shoulder muscles. Rising and falling as his back heaves under my touch. Apparently, he's having just as much trouble catching his breath as I am.

Nero groans as he shifts his body. I expect him to climb off me. But I should've known better.

Nero's hips pull back, his cock sliding almost all the way out, then he pushes back in.

My back arches with the reinvasion, everything too sensitive.

"My Sweet Girl." His mouth is on my shoulder, and he punctuates his statement by sinking his teeth into my skin. "Gonna have to give it a minute before I'm ready for round two. But I'm fucking you again when we get home."

I'm half delirious, so it takes a moment for me to process. "Home?"

He ignores me, tracing his tongue up the side of my neck. "I want to mark you. Let people know you're mine."

What is he talking about?

"You just bit me," I tell him.

"It needs to be permanent." I don't even know if he's talking to me, or himself. "A tattoo." My eyes widen. "But it would need to be somewhere people can see." Nero rocks his hips against me, his cock slowly softening inside me. "Maybe your hand." He adjusts his arms so his weight is on his elbows, and he can look down at me.

With his weight off me, I fill my lungs and shake my head. "I'm not getting a tattoo."

He grunts. "We'll see."

When he finally pulls all the way out, I can feel the mess of us, just like the first time.

The first time. Also the *only other time.*

I can't believe this is the second time I've ever had sex. Well, and whatever you call what we did at that concert.

Nero sits back so he can drag a finger down my slit, making my body twitch.

"So pretty," he murmurs.

The way he says it is so genuine, it heats my cheeks.

How a sweet compliment can make me blush after what we just did, I'll never know.

He lets out a huge sigh, then climbs off the bed. "Get dressed. We can shower at home."

Still naked, I press my knees together. "Why do you keep saying that? This is my home."

He shakes his head, as he tucks his dick back into his pants. And just like that, he's fully clothed.

"It is," I say slowly, like he doesn't understand.

His skilled fingers secure his belt. "Not anymore."

I drag my eyes away from his hands and up to his face. "What do you mean?"

"You're moving into my house."

Nothing this man says should shock me anymore, but here we are.

"No, I'm not."

He lifts his eyes to meet mine, and there's zero compromise in them. "Yes, you are. Tonight. Now." He tips his head toward the half-filled duffel in the corner of the room. "You're already packed."

I gape at him. "I can't."

"You can."

"Nero, you can't be serious."

"I am."

I stare at him. He really is. He's totally serious.

"You're crazy," I breathe.

His hands dart out, gripping my ankles, and he yanks me down the bed. Again.

Nero bends over me, putting our faces an inch apart. "For you, I'm fucking certifiable."

His lips press to mine, and I must be just as insane, because I feel nothing but comfort at his words. "Now get dressed."

Nero grabs my hands as he steps back, helping me to sit up.

The change to vertical makes my head spin a little, and I remember that I was well on my way to being drunk when I left the party. Though it seems like waking up scared half-to-death has some sobering qualities.

Nero's tucking his shirt in, and part of my brain tells me to grab a blanket and cover myself.

Sitting, naked––squishy belly on full display in the bright lights––in front of the hottest man I've ever met in person... it's a lot.

But the other half of my brain registers Nero's hooded gaze. And there's nothing but heat in his eyes. Heat and lust and need.

"I can't just move in with you," I sigh. Even if I've never wanted anything more, this is ridiculous.

His jaw works like he's chewing on his next words. "You will. You made that decision for me when you walked into my party tonight."

"But—"

He shakes his head. "The second you stepped foot in that building, you sealed your fate." Nero moves to my dresser and pulls open the top drawer. Finding it already empty he moves to the next, then scoops the t-shirts out in a pile and drops them into my duffel bag. "I wasn't ready. I didn't want to do it, Payton." He growls the words.

Nero sounds so hurt. Acting on instinct, I wrap the blanket around myself and go to him. "You didn't want to do what?"

His back is to me, so it's easy for me to see his shoulders bunch, and his head fall forward. It's a stance I know well. It's shame.

"I didn't want to touch her. Putting my hand on her hip like that, so you'd see it..." He takes a deep breath. "I knew how much it would hurt you."

The feelings of that moment float back into my chest, and I clutch the blanket tighter. "Then why did you?"

He takes his time to turn and face me.

When he finally does, he cups my face with his warm hands, keeping my eyes on his. "Because I needed time. I needed you to walk away from me before anyone knew who you were to me." His forehead drops to mine. "I keep telling you, Sweet Girl, I'm a bad man. I have enemies that will kill you, or worse, to torture me. And when they find out how much I love you, they'll battle each other, just to be the first to get to you. And if something ever happened to you..." He sucks in a breath. "I'll burn this entire city to the ground."

My heart is galloping behind my ribs. "You love me?"

Nero nods. "I must. There's no other explanation for how you make me feel."

My eyes well, and I'm so sick of crying, but this is the first time...

"No one..." I swallow against the tightness in my throat. "No one has ever told me they loved me before."

The look in his eyes softens, just the smallest amount. "Me either."

Mimicking his stance, I reach my hands up and press my palms to his cheeks. "I love you, Nero."

"Good." His chest expands on a deep inhale. "Good." I sniffle, but he shakes his head. "No more crying. Not tonight."

I nod, sniffing some more.

He brushes a kiss against the corner of my mouth. "And we'll talk later about you packing up on your own. Like you were gonna try and leave me."

"Okay," I whisper, our lips so close.

His exhale blows across my cheek. "And we'll never talk about you asking if I was going to kill you." His hands slip around my neck, and he pulls me into a hug. "I would dig my own heart out of my chest before I'd hurt you."

My arms circle his waist, and I hold him tight. "I'm sorry, I--"

He shushes me. "Not talking about it." His arms squeeze me, before loosening. "Now get fucking dressed, Baby."

Moving quickly, I grab up a pair of leggings, underwear from my duffel and a worn-to-threads oversized sweater.

In the bathroom, I do my best to clean myself up before getting dressed. Then I remember the whole conversation a moment ago, before the *I love yous,* and put all of my toiletries into a little bag.

I can't believe I'm just going to move in with him.

It's crazy. A terrible idea. Probably the worst. But... What do I have to lose?

Nero seems as head-over-heels for me as I am for him. And he's offering me everything I've ever wanted. A home. Security. Safety. *Love.*

It might be the wrong choice, but I'm taking it. If I don't, if I fight this and win, I'll only regret it every day of my life.

He killed Arthur.

An unhinged smile stretches across my face, and I turn away from the mirror.

There's probably something wrong with being happy about a man's death. But, wow, I'm so happy.

Composing myself, I open the door, Nero standing in the kitchen, my bag at his feet, and the couch pushed back into place.

"Ready," I tell him, but he's not looking at me.

"What's this?" he asks the question in a flat, almost scary, voice.

Following his gaze, I see the empty black envelope where I left it sitting on the counter.

I shove my small bag inside the duffel. Is he mad that it reminds him of the party?

"I'll throw it away if you want." I shrug.

Nero's eyes lift to mine, narrowed, like he's trying to figure something out.

Feeling defensive, I cross my arms. "You know, if you didn't want me to come tonight, you shouldn't have left me a freaking invite. Which, I might add, was an annoying way to find out it was your birthday." I lose steam as I go, my arms dropping back to my sides. "Happy birthday, by the way."

Nero grabs the bag with one hand and grips my elbow with the other. "We're going."

He starts to drag me to the front door.

"Wait!" I strain against his hold reaching back to grab my little purse off the counter.

He doesn't wait, but I manage to snag it. It's not my usual bag, but I moved all my important stuff into it before the party.

I use the time Nero takes to open the front door to jam my feet into a pair of black tennis shoes.

I'm still trying to get my heels into the shoes when Nero drags me out the door.

"What's the hurry?!" I stumble but his hold on my arm keeps me upright.

"I didn't leave that invitation."

CHAPTER 62

Nero

"WHAT DO YOU MEAN?" PAYTON ASKS, TRYING TO KEEP up with my long strides.

I don't answer, keeping my attention on our surroundings.

I shouldn't've fucked her. I should've dragged her all the way out of bed, thrown her over my shoulder, and carried her to my car. But *no*. Her thick, pale thighs just had to be on display. Her messy hair and tear-stained face forcing my dick from hard to steel.

"Nero?" She's jogging now, but I pull her to a stop at the top of the stairwell.

Letting go of her arm, I press my hand to her chest, pushing her back to the wall. "Don't move."

She nods, and I keep my eyes up as I crouch. In a matter of seconds, I tug up my pant leg, exposing my ankle holster, and pull my backup gun free.

Payton lets out a small gasp behind me, and I expect to find her eyes wide on my weapon; but when I stand, I find her gaze darting around, like she's helping me look for threats.

I have a moment of surprised pride before I remember her life has been haunted by demons too.

Thank you for killing him.

More pride swells my chest, but I push it down because now is not the time. I'll tell her how fucking amazing she is later.

"Grab the back of my shirt and stay close," I command, and she does.

With one hand holding the bag, and the other holding my gun, I can't hold her hand like I want to. But I need her touching me, so this will have to do.

There are no sounds below us, but I keep my gun up as we move down the flight of stairs.

When we hit the bottom, it's one turn and a handful of strides to get out of the building.

"I parked right outside the door," I turn my head enough to say over my shoulder. Payton's knuckles push into my back as she shuffles closer to me. "You'll get in first and shut the door."

"Okay."

I turn out of the stairwell, and with no one in sight, we move together.

We're nearly to the exit when a door in the hallway behind us opens.

I spin while dropping the bag, using that hand to hook Payton's side and keep her behind me.

A middle-aged man steps out into the hallway, and I bark, "Back in your apartment!"

My voice startles him, and he staggers back a step before he even lays eyes on me. When he does, his eyes widen even more.

It's obvious this man just lives here, but I'm not having him at my back as I walk out of here.

Payton tugs at my shirt. "That's just Fletcher."

I raise my gun from center mass to the man's forehead. I don't like that she knows his name.

"Now," I grit out.

The man, *Fletcher*, practically falls into his apartment, slamming the door as he does.

Scooping up the bag, I get us out of the building and to the car without seeing another person.

Pulling open the passenger door, I hustle Payton into the seat then slam it closed.

The entire car is bulletproof. If someone drops me right now, all she has to do is lock the doors and wait out the attack.

Probably should've told her that.

Striding to the driver's side, I slide into the seat, and toss the duffel over my shoulder into the small back seat.

"Seat belt."

As Payton buckles in, I start the car and tap the screen in my dashboard, initiating a call to Rocco.

The ringtone sounds through the car speakers, and I'm pulling away from the curb when he picks up.

"Boss?"

"I want you to bring in a full perimeter on the house tonight." Seeing no other traffic, I blow through the stop sign at the end of her street. "Or no. Plan on it for the foreseeable future."

"You got it." Rocco doesn't panic, or ask me why, which is the reason he's my Second.

"And I need a separate crew to pull everything out of an apartment." I recite Payton's address from memory.

"Clean up crew?"

"No." I slow the car just enough to make a sharp right turn onto one of the main streets that runs through downtown. "I need the personal items collected." My fingers tighten around the wheel. I want to tell him to send some women, the ones we employ for undercover work, but that would take more coordination than I have time for. "Make sure they're careful. Anything broken will be paid back tenfold."

I can feel Payton's eyes on me. But she doesn't get a say in this.

And she's really gonna hate this next part.

"I also need you to track down the owner of Twin's Café." Payton makes a squeak of protest, so I place my palm on her thigh, forestalling her. "Give her a roll and tell her Payton won't be working for her anymore."

"N--" Payton starts.

I flex my fingers on her leg and she falls silent.

"Got all that?" I ask.

"Got it," Rocco confirms.

"Good. You at the house?"

"Yeah."

"Stay there." I accelerate through a yellow light. "I'm headed back now."

I hang up, and Payton wastes no time speaking up. "You can't just quit for me. Or..." She waves her hands around. "Or, threaten Jean and Tamara, or whatever that was." She huffs. "I need that job."

"No you don't."

"Nero--"

I tap the screen, causing the car to fill with a ringtone again. "A roll is money, Baby."

That effectively stops her tirade. I'm not threatening her old bosses, I'm paying them off.

The ringing stops as the call clicks through.

"Fuck, man, you might not like sex anymore, but some of us do," is King's greeting.

I feel Payton's body stiffen, and I don't know if it's from what King said, or if she recognizes his voice. But to prove I still like sex, I slide my hand up her thigh, until the side of my palm is pressed against the seam between her legs. Her pussy heating the leggings so they're nearly hot to the touch.

My cock twitches and I have to force myself to remember why I called. "I need a favor."

"Of-fucking-course you do," King groans. "But if you ask me to try and detain your girlfriend again, I'm going to have to respectfully decline. Chasing her around me feel like a fucking monster."

Payton's leg shifts under my hand, as she turns toward me in her seat.

"No need. She's in the car with me."

There's a beat of silence before Payton breaks it. "Uh, hi." She lifts her hand in a little wave before catching herself and clutching it to her chest, probably embarrassed that she waved for a phone call. It was cute as fuck.

"Hey." King waits a beat. "You know Nero's a prick, right?"

Payton snorts out a laugh, and my head whips to the side to look at her.

Her hands slap over her mouth, her eyes wide.

"I'll take that as a yes." The bite of King's words are dulled by a yawn. "What did you need? Some of us are trying to sleep."

"I thought you were having sex?"

"Yeah, in my dreams, and I was fucking an iridescent mermaid."

"How would you even--" I shake my head, this isn't the time to get distracted. "I need you to pull the footage from outside Payton's door."

"Timeframe?" King's tone is all business now.

I glance over at Payton. "When did you find the invite?"

"Oh, um, it was this morning after I made coffee." She bites her lip, looking unsure.

"Close counts," I reassure her, stroking my thumb over her thigh.

"Maybe around ten? It was laying on the floor. I thought you maybe left it on the counter and it blew off when you shut the door. Or something like that." I hate how I can hear her confidence slip as she goes. Like she did something wrong.

I flex my hand on her thigh. I'm not well versed in comforting someone, but I feel her relax every time we're touching. "It wasn't there when I left around five. And the doors were locked; no sign of any tampering, so they must've shoved it under the door."

"Got it." I can hear King tapping on his laptop, meaning he was probably working in bed before he nodded off into his underwater fantasy.

"Send me what you find."

"You bringing her to your place?" he asks.

"We're on the way."

The car falls silent when the call ends, but it's not long before Payton turns her attention back to me.

"You said you did that *crap* to make me leave the party." She says *crap* like seeing me with that hooker didn't break her heart. "But then why would you want him to, um, detain me?" She uses King's word.

"Because I didn't want you near me, but I also couldn't have you wandering around that crowd alone. King wasn't going to hurt you, he was going to tuck you into a room until I could talk to you."

Remembering the shock I felt at seeing her there, my grip on the steering wheel tightens to the point of pain.

Payton blows out a breath. "So, if I'd've just gone with him..." She trails off, the rest unspoken.

We could have talked sooner. She wouldn't have had to cry herself to sleep. I wouldn't have had to break into her apartment.

The light ahead of me turns red. Slowing to a stop, I turn my head to face her. "It's good your reaction isn't to just go with a stranger. King is one of the few people I trust, but you didn't know that."

"But if I had..."

"No point in thinking on the *buts*. In hindsight, I'd probably have gotten extra pissed at one of you if my idea had worked." I can feel her look at me, so I lift a shoulder. "He was doing what I asked, but if he'd have touched you, I'd have to break his hand. And if you'd gone with him willingly... I'd've tanned your ass for putting yourself in danger." I flex my fingers. "Which would be on top of you putting yourself in danger by showing up."

"I'm sorry," she whispers.

"I know, Baby. I'm not mad at you anymore. Whoever slipped you that invitation is at fault. And I won't let it go unanswered."

Glancing over, I see her biting her lip, sure she has more questions about how that happened. I just don't have the answers yet.

My lungs expand on a deep inhale.

I've already admitted I fucking love her, what's a little more honesty.

"I'm not sorry about dragging you into this life with me. I should be. It's hard and cruel and unforgiving, but you're just as much mine as the dark is. And that means you belong here. With me." My gaze slides away from the road, to meet hers. And the understanding shining back at me buries itself in my chest. "It's not going to be a quiet white picket life, but it'll be ours. And no matter what I do to other people, I'll never hurt you. Not ever, Payton."

"I know."

Warmth fills me. "And I'll give you anything you want. Anything at all. But it'll still be nothing compared to what you'll give me."

"What will I give you?" she whispers.

"Peace."

Payton's small palm lands on the back of my hand, and I let her pull it away from her leg so she can intertwine our fingers. "You've already given me that."

Her words are so quiet, I squeeze her hand to let her know I understand, assuming she's talking about Arthur.

Her reaction to that ring was not what I expected. I hadn't really planned to whip it out while I was in the middle of fucking her. But I was too far gone to do anything else. Though a sobbing thank you would not have been on my list of possible reactions.

I'm sure she'll have more questions about him. Now's just not the time.

A low grumble fills the car and she lifts her free hand to press against her stomach.

I narrow my eyes on her. "Are you hungry?"

"A little," she admits. "I left the party before I got a chance to eat anything."

I've never been concerned with someone else's hunger before, until now. And now I know I need to feed my girl.

"Burgers or tacos?"

"What?"

"Do you want a burger or some tacos?" I repeat. "I could eat too, and there's not much at the house."

"I like any--" She starts but I flex my fingers around hers, making her sigh. "Tacos."

Confident that no one has been following us, I take the next turn and we make a short detour.

When I turn into the parking lot, aiming for the drive-thru, Payton snickers.

"What?" I ask.

She shakes her head. "I don't know why it's funny. I just wouldn't't've pictured you eating here."

I hit the button to roll down my window. "If I decide I'm *too good* for Taco Bell, put a bullet in my brain and end my misery."

A twinge of pain on my wrist has me jerking my arm away from Payton. "What the--"

She's glaring at me.

"Did you just pull out one of my arm hairs?" I ask in disbelief.

"Don't joke about dying." She sounds so serious; I know I shouldn't smile.

But I can't help it.

When she reaches for my wrist again, I lean away. "Alright, alright!" I put my hands up then gesture to the menu board ahead of us. "You know what you want?"

CHAPTER 63

Payton

WITH A WARM BAG OF FAST-FOOD TACOS ON MY LAP, I watch, mouth agape, as Nero pulls through a gate that looks like it belongs in front of a castle.

We're only about ten minutes outside of the city, but it might as well be a whole different world.

I've only gotten glimpses of the gigantic houses as we pass, since it's dark out and the driveways look like they're all a mile long, Nero's being no exception.

The gate rolls closed behind us automatically, but I don't miss the two men standing nearby.

On the first phone call Nero made when we left my apartment, he said something about "a full perimeter". I assumed this had something to do with security, so I'm not surprised to see more men walking around the property as we approach the house.

Not house. *Mansion.*

Nero's home looms out of the dark before us. It's two stories, approximately the width of my entire apartment building, with a front door that looks wide enough to drive through. The entire thing is surrounded with meticulous landscaping, illuminated by those ground lights that dramatically shadow the impressive architecture.

It's beautiful.

I open my mouth to say as much when a man walks past the front door, with a large four-legged beast next to him.

"You have a dog?!" I practically shout with my excitement.

Nero slides his gaze to me, as he turns the car toward the opening garage door. "Not really."

"But..." I shift to keep an eye on the dog, but then we enter the garage, effectively cutting off my view.

"The dogs are here to work."

"Oh." My shoulders sag.

While Nero turns off the car, I let my eyes skip over the other vehicles already parked inside the garage.

"You like dogs?"

I bite my lip and nod. "I've always wanted one."

"I thought your building allowed them?"

I don't bother asking why he knows the rental rules for my place. "No. I mean, they do, but dogs are expensive, and I didn't... I'd want to spoil it. And I knew I couldn't."

"What kind did you want?"

"I would've been happy with any kind," I sorta laugh. It sounds sadder than I meant it to, so I wave a hand. "I didn't mean that like a *woe is me* thing. I just meant that I'm not picky. I always assumed, whenever I could, I'd go to the shelter and get a small dog, since I had a small apartment, but the big ones are fun too."

Nero grunts in reply, and I'm thankful the conversation is over. I'm intimidated just from his driveway, I don't need any extra reminders of my poorness.

We open our doors at the same time, and I climb out of the car, food in hand.

He'd told me he was rich. Said it just like that. *I'm rich.* But I guess I hadn't really thought about what that meant. I'd just assumed he lived in a really nice condo. Which still would've been intimidating. This place though--I try not to gawk at the size of the garage--this place is next-level rich. This place is *movie star* rich--*I have a cook*--rich.

Nero's door finally shuts, and when he circles around the car to meet me, I see he has my duffel and the pretty blue heels I abandoned in the lobby of the Historical Society.

"You know," he says, when he sees where I'm looking. "Cinderella only left one shoe behind."

I fight my embarrassment by rolling my eyes. "Yeah, and Prince Charming didn't break into her home to find her."

Nero grins. "The villains always have more fun."

Jesus Christ, he's handsome when he does that.

"Come on, Princess." He tucks the shoes under his arm, then takes the bag of tacos from me, shifting it to the same hand as the duffel. This leaves me holding nothing and him with an open hand.

He holds his hand out between us, and I take it.

Side-by-side, we walk through the open garage door and back out into the night.

I saw a door that I was sure led from the garage into the house, but my curiosity over the route is answered when a man approaches to talk to Nero.

Listening to their conversation, I learn the man's name is Rocco, although Nero doesn't introduce us.

My first instinct is to be offended. But then I remember that, like the dogs, this guy is here to work.

Another man comes over, and the three of them talk about positions and timing and other stuff my brain is too tired to understand.

Nero is gruff with them. His words are clipped and every inch of him is taut with tension. The man, who grinned at me moments ago, completely replaced by this harder, scarier version of himself. Even holding high heels, a bag of cheap fast food, and a beat-up duffel, he looks intimidating.

With my eyes on the dark bristly hair of his beard, I think I finally understand.

Understand him. The danger. The situation.

What happened with that invite today is just the beginning.

A chill rolls up my spine and I tighten my grip on Nero's hand.

He doesn't outwardly react, except to squeeze my fingers back. But it's enough to remind me that I'm safe, that Nero can protect me.

He made it look so easy earlier when he pulled that gun out of nowhere and walked me out of my building like a soldier on a rescue mission.

He slipped into the role like it was nothing out of the ordinary. And looking at the men he's talking to--with their not-very-concealed guns, alert body language, and eyes that seem to be purposefully avoiding me--I realize that this is normal. For them. For Nero.

I don't hear what Nero says, but I know he's done talking because he's leading me across the sidewalk and to the front door while I'm back to gaping.

The door gets opened by someone on the inside, and I nearly gasp.

My movie star comparison was right. I feel like I'm on a set.

The ceilings go *all* the way up, making room for a giant chandelier. The glow of a thousand sparkling crystals bouncing off the grand stairway straight ahead of us.

"Wow." It's a dumb thing to say, but it's the best I can come up with.

My head turns on a swivel as he leads me through the house.

"I'll give you a proper tour later," Nero tells me, as we enter a gleaming kitchen.

I think he's gonna set the food down, but instead he goes to the refrigerator and takes out two tall bottles of water.

"We'll eat in our room, then you can go to bed," he explains.

"Just me?" I try not to pout.

"Unfortunately. I'll need to stay up while we sort this out." He hands me the waters, then holds his hand out for me again.

Shifting the bottles, so I'm hugging them to my body with one arm, I slip my palm against his.

I look up at him. "I like this."

He glances around. "The kitchen?"

A smile tugs at my lips. "That's nice too, but I was talking about holding hands."

"I'm glad," Nero says it so seriously that I snicker.

He glances at me, as he leads us to another, more hidden stairway behind the kitchen. "What?"

"It's just funny, how you said it."

"How I said *I'm glad*?"

He's truly confused, and that only makes it funnier. "Yeah, because you sounded like the least glad person ever."

The edge of his mouth lifts into a smirk. "You're kind of a smart ass, aren't you?"

I narrow my eyes, choosing not to answer, and Nero lets go of my hand to swat me on the ass.

"Get upstairs."

CHAPTER 64

Nero

PAYTON CONTINUED TO TAKE EVERYTHING IN AS WE made our way to our room--no questions, no stopping to look at anything, just silently observing. And it's starting to stress me out.

When I open the door to our bedroom, and she steps inside ahead of me, still not speaking, I finally break. "Do you like it?"

She looks over her shoulder and nods. "It's a really nice room."

"And the rest of the house, do you like it?" When she doesn't answer right away, I continue. "You can change anything you want. Furniture. Paint," I shrug. "We can gut the whole place or just buy something new."

Her eyes widen. "Why would I want to gut it?"

I don't need to look around to know what it's like in here. It's dark. Black everything. Huge four-poster bed. Modern with no frills, including the nightstands and lamps. A long table and a single chair sit against the wall; I occasionally use it as a desk, but it mostly sits unused. A walk-in closet too large for any one person to fill. And an equally dark and impersonal bathroom.

"We can add some yellow," I suggest lamely, remembering the touches of sunshine she had in her little apartment.

Funny how just a little color can make that small, shitty place feel like more of a home than this mansion I've lived in for more than a decade. I've never had a problem with this house--until right now.

"It's really nice." Payton trails her fingers across the bedding.

Knowing she's too nice to say anything bad about it, I drop the subject, already deciding what I'll do about it.

"Here." I put the bag of food on the empty table, then set her things in front of the closet. "Let me go grab a second chair, then we can eat."

Moving quickly, I find an ugly antique chair in one of the never-been-used guest rooms down the hall and carry it back into our room, where I find Payton carefully laying the tacos out in a row. She balked at the number I ordered, but fucking her into submission took a lot of energy and I'm starving.

A comfortable silence descends as we work our way through the tortilla wrapped meat and cheese. Payton looked at me out of the corner of her eye during the first few bites she took, like she was nervous about eating in front of me, but soon fell into her meal, same as me.

After finishing her second one, with me four and a half in, she wipes her mouth with the scratchy paper napkin and turns in her seat. "What did you mean when you told King to check the footage?"

I was wondering when she'd ask about that.

"After I met you, I had cameras installed in the hallway outside your door." I say it without one shred of remorse.

"Oh." She doesn't sound surprised. Or upset. "Did you know that I've met King before?"

I nod, chewing.

"He came to the cafe one morning," she elaborates. "Did he tell you?"

Swallowing my final bite, I shift so we're facing each other. "I was in the car."

"You were?" Her brows arch behind her bangs.

I nod. "He gave me that latte you made. The one you said was your favorite."

Payton gets a pensive look on her face. "Is that why you ordered it... that day?"

"It was good."

This gets me a small laugh. "Somehow you strike me as more of a black coffee person, not a frilly latte person."

My lips quirk into a smile, but my reply is halted by my phone ringing. It's King.

I hit answer and put it on speaker. There won't be any secrets between Payton and me.

"Did you get him?" I ask.

"I got *her*."

"Her?" I hate that I never even considered it would be a woman. Stupid assumptions can get people killed.

King grunts. "Yeah. The bitch tried to cover her face with a hoodie and sunglasses, but I got ID."

Payton's eyes are traveling over my face, watching the anger take over my features.

"Who?" I grit between clenched teeth.

King tells me.

"What're you gonna do?" he asks, knowing I won't be violent toward a woman.

I unclench my fists and roll out my shoulders. "I'm gonna call your sister."

CHAPTER 65

Nero

My knuckles knock three times against the painted wood.

This apartment building, in the middle of downtown Minneapolis, isn't that far from Payton's old place, but it's a world apart. There's a security guard in the lobby. Nice carpet on the floors. An elevator that works.

However, that security guard can be bribed. The elevator cameras can turn off. And the soft flooring means that the other residents didn't hear us walking down the hall. The icing on the cake is the person two doors down hosting a party, their music loud enough to muffle the sound of what's about to happen.

I rap my knuckles against the wood, then stand patiently while I listen to the deadbolt unlock and the handle turn.

Eyes I used to be indifferent to widen when they meet mine. And I watch a range of emotions flit across her face.

Surprise. Alarm. Caution.

It's never a good thing when the leader of the underworld shows up at your door unannounced, in the middle of the night. Unless, maybe, you're a prostitute looking to make some cash.

Nikki––in leggings and a crop top, hair in a high ponytail,

clearly not yet in bed—cocks her hip, placing one hand into the dip of her waist and the other against the doorframe.

"Nero, to what do I owe the pleasure?" Her mouth pulls up into what I'm sure is supposed to be a seductive smile. "Looking for a little birthday treat?"

I'd planned to flirt with her. To let her think I was here to fuck her. Get her to invite me in.

But when I look at her, all I see is the devastated look on Payton's face and the way the color drained out of her pretty features.

I see the security footage of Payton running away from my party and slipping on the stairs, bruising her perfect skin.

The tear stains on her cheeks.

The packed duffel on her floor.

I see her curled up on her little bed, passed out from too much crying.

And I decide to change my plan.

Darting my arm out, I grip her by the wrist. And when she stumbles back, I shove the door the rest of the way open.

"Ne—" she starts.

"Shut the fuck up!" I snap, moving forward into her space, forcing her to stagger back.

Nikki's lips move but she doesn't say anything.

"Really, Nero?" A new voice follows me into the apartment. "She even looks like a bitch."

Aspen, King's fiery little sister, kicks the door shut after she enters and flips the deadbolt.

"It's not like I was fucking dating her," I defend myself, sparing a glance at the shorter woman. Her hair and eyes the same shade of golden brown as King's.

"Hey!" Nikki forgets my command of silence. "Who the hell is this?" Her tone is filled with undeserved indignance, and it makes me wish she was a man just so I could punch her.

"This is the only chance you're gonna get," I snarl at her.

Keeping my grip on her wrist, I lead her to the dining table that's set in front of a large window. She backs into a chair that was left pulled out from the table, and I keep her momentum going, until she's seated in it, sideways.

"Stay." Sick of touching her, I let go and take a step back.

"What's going on?" Nikki whines, making Aspen snort.

"What's going on"—Aspen steps up to my side—"is *you* fucked up."

"I didn't--" she starts to deny.

I lean forward. "That one chance you have will disappear if you so much as try to lie to me."

Normally I don't let my rage show. Normally I maintain a mask of complete indifference, even if I'm slicing a man's tongue out of his mouth. But right now, I let it show. I let all my fury show.

Nikki bends back over the table, trying to get as far away from me as she can. Fear written all over her face.

Good.

"Ch-chance for what?" Nikki stutters through the question.

"A chance to live through the night."

The sound of her gasp bounces through the apartment.

I can see she wants to argue, deny that there's any reason I should want to kill her.

But I'm already here. Because I already know.

And she's smart enough to know that you don't cross me and live. By giving her this one chance, I'm giving her a gift that I don't often offer. And I'm doing it because I don't kill women. But if she pushes me, I'll find someone who does.

"Who told you to put the invitation under the door?" I don't specify what door. We both know what door, and I'm not saying Payton's name here. She's too good for this place.

Nikki's mouth opens then closes, her eyes flicking between me and Aspen, probably wondering who she is and why I brought her.

"Tell me now," I growl.

Nikki straightens her back. "No one told me to do it."

My eyes narrow. "What do you mean?"

I'm confused but Aspen isn't.

"Oh wow, that's sad." Aspen clicks her tongue with a laugh. "This bimbo was trying to break you and your girl up for *personal* reasons." The emphasis on personal makes my stomach twist.

The thought of putting my dick into anyone other than Payton makes my balls shrivel, no matter our history.

When Nikki doesn't deny it, I shake my head.

"Jesus Christ, how fucking delusional are you?" I'm even more pissed now. Thinking it was an enemy trying to attack me is easier to swallow than some clingy prostitute trying to fuck up my relationship by making it look like I was cheating on Payton. "How'd you find out about her?"

"The Mayor." Nikki has the nerve to lift a shoulder, like it's no big deal.

"The Mayor?" Every piece of information stuns me more than the last.

How the fuck did he know?

"We *had a date* the other afternoon." Nikki straightens in her seat, trying to appear composed. "He said he ran into you that morning at some little café. Mentioned that you were acting all obsessive over *the waitress*." She says the occupation like it's dirt, and like she doesn't spread her legs for a living. "Didn't take much to get the name of the place and the girl."

I'm gonna have to kill the mayor.

"How did you get her address?" Every word tastes like death on my tongue.

Nikki presses her lips together before answering. "I know a guy who works for the IRS. A phone call and a promise got me what I needed."

My chest expands as I take a large breath, attempting, and failing, to calm my rage.

"Did you bring the scissors?" I ask Aspen, keeping my eyes on Nikki.

Aspen produces a pair from somewhere inside her jacket. "Sure did."

"Cut it all off."

"Cut what off?!" Nikki tries to push the chair away from me but I hook one of the legs with my foot.

"Your hair, Nikki." Finally, the calm I usually achieve settles over me. "She's going to cut off all your hair. And if you struggle, she might slip and cut more than that. So, I suggest you act smart for the first time in your life, and sit fucking still."

Aspen circles around until she's behind Nikki, keeping her out of the kicking and scratching range.

"Don't!" Nikki cries when Aspen grips her long shiny ponytail. "Nero," she reaches for my hand. "Why can't you see how perfect we are for each other."

I stay out of her reach. "We aren't anything for each other." Aspen hacks through the thick handful of hair and Nikki starts crying. "You purposefully hurt the woman I love. If you were a man, I'd slit your throat where you sit. But instead, you're going to become invisible." The ponytail, elastic and all, falls to the floor. "I don't care where you go, but I never want to see you again." Aspen grabs clumps of the longer pieces and cuts them off, close to the root. "And if you so much as look at my woman, ever again, I will make you disappear for real."

Aspen cuts off another handful as Nikki breaks down into loud sobs.

"Grow up!" Aspen hisses, slicing through another clump.

"Nero!" Nikki hiccups, "I love you!"

"No, you don't. You don't love anything but yourself. And your appearance. Which is why I'm taking your hair."

Aspen makes a few final snips before stepping back to survey her handiwork. "Done."

I nod, pleased, and take a step back. "I'll send my men by in twelve hours. You don't want to be here when they arrive."

Nikki is too busy clawing at her bare skull to respond, but I know she heard me.

I let Aspen get a few paces past me before I turn and follow her back out the front door.

There's no one in the hallway, and no signs that anyone heard anything, so we keep our strides casual and make our way outside.

"So," Aspen raises a brow at me once we're on the sidewalk. "The mighty Nero has fallen in love."

"You'll like her."

"I hope so," she huffs. "You don't seem to have the best taste in women though."

I ignore her comment. "Where's your car?"

"Down at the corner," she answers, already walking that way, and I follow.

Aspen isn't soft, but she's here because I asked her to be, so I'm not letting her out of my sight until she's back in her car.

A rustling sound comes from an alley as we move past, causing Aspen to sigh. "Poor guy is still here."

I turn my head, expecting to see a homeless man, so I'm not prepared to see a scruffy dog sniffing through a pile of garbage.

Aspen keeps walking but I stop. "What do you mean still?"

She halts, coming back to look at the dog with me. "He was digging through the trash when I got here. Must be hungry."

"Do you think he's a stray?"

Aspen shrugs. "Probably. I wish I could bring him, or her, home. But my husband would kill me." My head snaps over in her direction and she waves me off. "God, you're just as bad as King. It's an *expression*."

"Better be." King, and therefore Aspen, are the closest thing I have to a family. I know King hates her husband but if he's violent toward her, I'll end him myself.

Aspen rolls her eyes at me. "My idiot husband might be an idiot, but he doesn't have a death wish. Pretty sure even *he* knows hurting me would get him a one-way ticket to the afterlife."

I grunt, then turn my attention back to the dog.

CHAPTER 66
Payton

THE PILLOWCASE AGAINST MY CHEEK IS SOFT AND cool, and my body snuggles into the feeling.

A girl could get used to this.

My eyes slide open, squinting against the sunlight creeping past the heavy floor-length drapes covering the windows.

It's Nero's room. In Nero's gigantic house.

Or as he calls it, *our house.*

I can't believe how casually he said it last night. Like it's actually mine, too. Like this is totally normal and something people do every day.

Meet a guy.

Have sex twice.

Fall in love.

Move from your tiny crummy apartment to this multi-million-dollar house and claim partial ownership.

Then live happily ever after. With the minor detail of people trying to sabotage us.

Or something like that.

I stretch my arm out in front of me, smoothing it across the unruffled bedding on the other side of the mattress.

My chest gives a funny clench, thinking of Nero out all night. But it's not from jealousy, it's from worry.

After King called while we were eating tacos, and after Nero made a comment about *inviting King's sister*, Nero told me about the woman, Nikki. He told me that the same beautiful woman who had her hands all over him, was the one who slid the envelope under my door.

A wave of possessiveness made me grip Nero's arm. I didn't care that we'd worked out what happened at the party. It didn't matter that we were stronger than ever. I just didn't want him to go to her. I didn't want *her* laying her eyes on my man ever again. Because even though Nero didn't say anything about her motivation, I knew it was personal.

But before I could object Nero gripped the back of my neck and dragged my mouth to his.

"What's mine is off limits. You're mine. And people need to understand the consequences of what that means."

With no way to argue, I did as he told me to do, by finishing my tacos and going to bed.

My fingers tap on the comforter.

I want to call him, or text him, or do something to find out if he's okay. Talking to that bitch shouldn't have taken all night. My teeth bite down on my lip. I have to trust that doesn't mean anything bad happened.

Getting up, I decide to be patient. For all I know, he could be somewhere in this house, working on his laptop, or doing whatever it is a mobster with a security company does.

My feet barely make a sound on the thick rug that extends out from under the bed, as I pad over to my bag, still sitting in front of the closet.

I was too tired last night to unpack my things, or take a shower, so I have to dig through the unorganized contents of the duffel until I've found my nice leggings and an oversized long sleeve tee.

I found the shirt years ago--and being a pastel purple, it's not my usual neutral colors, but I thought it made my eyes look bluer--and it's become my favorite item of clothing.

Carrying my bundle into the massive bathroom, I instantly second-guess the outfit I just choose.

This house is so fancy, so grand, I'm not sure how to act. Do people wear leggings in houses like this? Or do they wear pencil skirts and blouses?

Dropping everything onto the ten-foot-long vanity, I blow out a breath. It's not like I own a pencil skirt. Or anything that would be referred to as a blouse... Nero is pretty much always in a suit, but maybe at home he'll be more relaxed. And if not, there's not really anything to do about it now anyways.

Resigned to my poorly dressed fate, I reach into the shower to turn on the water. Then I pause because there are several levers and knobs.

The marble shower stall is big enough for half a dozen people, and more showerheads for twice that many people sticking out of the walls.

"Okay." The word comes out slowly.

First challenge of the day, figure out how to take a shower.

Picking a handle, I twist it, then jump back when my arm gets doused in a spray from above. So, a dozen and one showerheads, since I didn't see the giant round one hanging down from the ceiling.

After too many tries, I finally have a normal amount of water jetting out of the front wall and at a temperature just below scalding.

Stripping my clothes off, I leave them on the floor and step into the steam.

And groan.

It's not like I didn't have hot water at my apartment, but it never got quite hot enough and never lasted long enough to take the long languid showers I craved.

So, with no shame at all, I stand under the water, not scrubbing or lathering or rinsing. Not doing anything at all except enjoying the water pressure.

The heat melts the aches in my muscles, and as my hair gets soaked through, the constant stress pressing against my temples begins to fade.

I know this shouldn't be so easy. And I'm not delusional enough to think that there won't be any more hard days in my life. But for once--*for-fucking-once*--fate has decided to gift me with something, rather than take something away. And I'm going to hold onto it with both hands.

Nero loves me.

My lungs squeeze.

Someone loves me.

My heart swells.

Someone chased me.

My knees buckle, and I brace a hand on the wall as I lower myself, until I'm sitting on the warm wet tile.

My greatest fear, since I ran away from home, was Arthur or my mother finding me. I checked every dark doorway. I slept with a knife next to my bed for years. I'd wake up crying, begging them not to take me back. I didn't want them to come after me. I dreaded the possibility. But...

I tip my face down and suck in a breath, the water streaming over me.

But as bad as it would be for them to find me, it hurt that they never even seemed to try. It left me with a vast emptiness in my chest.

I would've taken my own life before I went back into that house. But to be so unwanted. So... *disposable.*

A true sob tears out of my chest.

Nero came for me.

Nero wouldn't let me go.

He'll never let me go.

The relief of not having to spend the rest of my life alone is so consuming I feel like I might drown in it.

Nero might be crazy. But he's mine. And he loves me. And even if it's wrong, I love him too.

I tip my head back, letting the water chase the tears off my face.

I'll never be alone again.

Nero standing in my doorway.

Nero walking into the café.

Nero pulling my body against his at a concert.

Nero washing my body in my small, cramped shower.

Nero breaking into my apartment to make sure I don't leave.

Nero telling me he loves me. Holding my hand in front of his men. Calling it our home.

I allow one more shuddering breath. One more moment of indulgence. Before I shake my head.

No more crying.

Using my feet, I scoot back until my face is out of the direct spray.

Crying is exhausting, and even though that was a quick little bout, I'm ready to crawl back into that big comfortable bed.

I need to collect myself and do the showering part of taking a shower.

I'm shifting my weight, getting into a kneeling position, when I see it. The recessed shelves built into the wall.

One is above my position, but the other is right at eye level. And a sound between a laugh and a choked cry tumbles out of me when I reach out and pick up the bottle of rose scented body wash. Next to it are three sets of very expensive looking shampoo and conditioner. All the bottles are shades of pink and they're all rose scented. And next to all of that is a fancy looking rose hips face wash and two big jars of body scrub, also rose.

I bet when I get out and dig through the cabinets, I'll find lotion to match the body wash.

Arching my neck, I look at the contents of the shelf above

mine. No surprise that the bottles are all men's products, except for a small, mostly empty bottle of red liquid tucked into the corner.

And I smile, because I know it was fuller than that when he stole it from me.

CHAPTER 67

Nero

THE SCENT OF ROSES HITS MY NOSE, BEFORE I EVEN reach the door to our room, and that's all it takes for my dick to get hard.

Shifting the mugs into the same hand as the coffee pot, I adjust my half-sprung cock before turning the door handle.

My eyes immediately look across the room and find the bathroom door open, but the room beyond is dark and silent. I feel a tinge of disappointment at missing Payton in the shower.

Then I see her, and a sense of rightness fills my chest.

She's standing in the doorway to the walk-in closet, damp hair twisted into a pair of braids, her bangs half-dry and a little wild. And her eyes...

I use my foot to kick the bedroom door shut behind me.

Her eyes are filled with a sparkle that's half excitement and half nervousness, and looking at them is like main-lining pleasure straight into my veins.

Her soft purple shirt...

I swallow.

She's so pretty. So fucking beautiful.

And I know I've done nothing to deserve her. But I'm keeping her all the same.

"Hi." Payton raises her hand in an awkward little wave, and I smile.

I honest-to-god smile.

Not a grin. Not a smirk or a sneer. A smile.

Her lips pull up to match my expression. "That coffee?" She tips her head toward my hands.

"Yeah." My feet unfreeze from the floor, and I cut the distance between us and hold up the mugs for her to take one.

Her nose crinkles in displeasure when she slides the handle off my finger.

"What's wrong?" I ask.

Her brows shoot up. "What? Oh, nothing."

"Payton." It's just her name, but she knows what it means. It means *tell me the truth*.

"It's really nothing, I promise. It's just..." Her cheeks pinken. "These cups are boring."

My eyes drop to the mug in her hand and then to the one in mine. "They're coffee mugs."

She huffs. "Exactly. Plain, boring, white mugs."

"As opposed to...?" It's been a long time since someone has dared to look at me like I'm an idiot, but that's exactly the look Payton is giving me. "What?"

"You're sending people to get all my stuff, right?"

I nod.

"Good, then I'll have something to contribute to the household." When I open my mouth to chastise her, wanting to tell her that she adds more than enough by just being here, Payton shakes her head. "I know what you're going to say, but just let me have this one. I'll feel good about sharing them with you."

"Fine." I lift the pot to chest level. "Still want some coffee, or do my boring mugs ruin it?"

Payton smirks. "I guess I'll survive."

Carefully, so I don't splash any hot liquid on her hands, I fill our cups then set the pot on the side table. "I thought you might be sleeping and would like coffee in bed."

"I was thinking about going back to bed after my shower, but then I got sidetracked putting my clothes away." She cups her hands around the bottom of the mug, holding it close to her face. "I hope that's alright."

"Baby, you can do whatever you want here. It's your home now."

She chews on her lower lip for a second, and just when I think she might say something infuriating, like *we're moving too fast*, she surprises me by not arguing at all. "I'm excited to see the rest of it. It's a pretty great home. Especially the shower." She lifts one of her braids to her nose. "I don't know when you had time to buy all that shampoo and stuff, but they smell amazing."

Shampoo is a stupid thing to feel pride over, but I feel it anyway. "I've been collecting them since the night you gave me your virginity. I figured you'd eventually be here to use it. And I was right."

"Oh." Payton's earlier blush intensifies. "I thought about you a lot, too."

Every time this woman speaks, she sparks new emotions to life inside me.

"Come on." I take her coffee and gesture to the mattress. "I wanna have that coffee in bed."

Obliging, Payton climbs up. When she's sitting cross-legged in the middle of the bed I hand her back her mug, then seat myself with my back against the headboard, so we're mostly facing each other.

We both take sips.

"Sorry, I didn't have any creamer," I apologize, thinking this is nothing like her favorite latte.

"It's okay. I like coffee in all its forms."

I hum, not sure if I really believe that. "Make a list of all the things you'd like to have in the house."

Payton's shaking her head before I even finish. "You don't need to do that. Black coffee is seriously fine. I drink it like that at home all the time."

"At your old home," I correct her. "And I don't just mean creamers. You need food. Things to eat when you don't want to order something. And whatever you need to make your coconut honey lattes."

"Well, to make it right, I'd need an espresso machine. And those are crazy expen—"

"Already have one," I cut her off.

Her mouth drops. "Really?"

"Really."

"You know how to use one?"

I find myself smiling again. "Not a clue."

She looks even more stunned. "Then why do you have one?"

"It was a housewarming gift from King. He said it made me look smarter."

She laughs, and the sound lodges itself behind my ribs. "That might be true if you'd actually used it." She takes another sip before asking, "I take it you've known each other awhile?"

I nod as I think about how to start. "I was fifteen the first time we met, which would've put him around nineteen."

"So, a long time ago, Mr. I-Just-Turned-Forty."

I give her a fake glare and she gives me a sweet smile.

"Okay so you were fifteen...?"

"I was fifteen and working for the Russians."

"The Russians?"

"Russian mafia. Bratva," I explain. No secrets. "I started as a runner, carrying money for them when I was just a kid. I think I was like eight."

"So young," she says sadly and I shrug.

"Typical story. Bad home life. Bad attitude. Lured in by the money and power of the brotherhood. Wanting someplace to belong." I can see the sympathy forming in Payton's eyes, and for the first time ever, it doesn't bother me. "When I met King, I was a soldier, and he was working for the Irish, doing pretty much the same thing. Except he wasn't the usual *mobster* type." I use

Payton's term from the other day. "He came from a well-off family, wasn't a stray with no last name like me."

"No last name?" Payton stops me.

"Must've had one at some point. But I was dumped at the church doors before I knew it." When she looks like she might cry I reach out and squeeze her knee. "It's not something to dwell on, Baby. It is what it is."

She lays a hand over mine. "Still sucks."

My lips pull up on one side. "And look what I've become."

Payton rolls her eyes. "Uh-huh."

"Anyway, neither of us were the norm. Used to be you had to be a blood relative to join, but as the years passed, and the families spread out, they were forced to relax their rules. Hence how a kid like me got in. But King wasn't some orphan. His family was well off, parents still married, at the time. But he was bored and brash and found himself joining, same as me. So even though we were supposed to be enemies, we"—I lift a shoulder—"connected. Became friendly. I was always a little jealous of him. Having that cushy life to fall back on. But over the next ten years I watched his grandparents die, his father die, his mother abandon him."

"That's awful."

"Yeah," I agree. "My life was hard from the start, but I was used to it. Didn't have a rug under me to be pulled out." I squeeze Payton's knee again, because I know she gets it.

"You guys were kinda like Romeo and Juliet," she teases.

I bark out a laugh. "Please tell King that next time you see him."

"You were star-crossed friends."

"We would've, and did, deny it. But yeah, we never really fit in under the old rank. So, the few times a year the families would play nice, we'd end up gravitating to each other."

"I heard once that soulmates aren't just for romantic relationships. You can have friend soulmates."

"I don't know anything about soulmates. And King might be

my brother. But you are my life." I rub my palm up her thigh. "No comparison."

She presses her lips together, and rather than making her respond, I keep going.

"It didn't take us long to realize there were rats in both families. Only the idiots thought they could use us to pass some secret code bullshit. Except King and I aren't idiots, so we cracked the codes and decided to make it work in our favor."

"This sounds like a movie." Payton cradles the mug to her chest.

"Except in movies everyone is beautiful. You should've seen these old guys. They were hideous, inside and out. The leaders of both families were corrupt, vile people, who stood for nothing. They'd never had to work for what they had. Never had to claw their way out of the gutter. Never even killed a man unless he was already being held down by three others. But when we figured out what else they were doing..." My anger bubbles back to life, thinking about it so many years later. "They were bringing in women from their home countries. Stealing them. Selling them."

"Human trafficking," Payton whispers.

"They hid it well. Only certain members were even aware of it, which is where the rats came in. Two guys thought maybe they could break off, join forces and build an empire on the backs of women. That's when King and I got dragged into the mess." I take a breath. "I wasn't lying when I said I did bad things. I do. But we don't do that. We don't sell women."

"I know." Payton doesn't flinch. "You wouldn't."

"I wouldn't," I repeat. "And we wouldn't let them either. So, we planned. We brought in only the men we trusted, recruited some more from the streets, and when everything was ready... we slaughtered them. As many as we could get our hands on. In both families." Payton dips her chin, and I swear it's approval. "We hit the same night, at the same time, with no warning. Most of them died. Some of them ran. And some joined us. And then together, we became The Alliance."

"So, the Russians and the Irish are gone, and now you and King run everything?"

"Except most people think it's just me. An organization like this is most effective when it looks like one man runs it all. People can't think it's a democracy. You can't give them the chance to try and turn you against each other. So, it had to be one of us, and King didn't want it to be him. By then, his dad was dead, but he still had sisters and a mom around. It was safer for them if King sank into the shadows. And considering any of the Irish guys who might've tried to out him died that night, it was easy for him to slip into the shadows."

"What about the people he'd recruited? Wouldn't they know he was kinda in charge too?"

I flip my hand over, and she laces her fingers with mine. "Most of those guys are dead now too." She grips my hand. "In the months that followed there were a lot of people coming for us-- me-- wanting to take the throne I'd created."

"But you kept it."

I grin. "I kept it."

"And now King is like a silent partner that no one knows about."

"Basically."

She seems to think it over before accepting it. "And he's close to his sister? The one that went with you last night."

"If, by close, you mean is she constantly bugging him and making him do shit he doesn't want to do, then yes."

This gets me another, more subdued, laugh. "That's good to know. I'll admit I don't really understand all the other stuff, but it's clear King is important to you. And I feel bad for feeling so scared of him." I open my mouth, but she squeezes my hand. "But, knowing he's close with his sister makes him seem more... normal."

"King is far from normal," I deadpan. "But he's one of the few people I would trust your safety to. So please don't be scared of him."

"I won't. And if you say I should trust him, then I will."

"Thank you."

I'm used to people doing what I want. But they do it because I pay them, or because they fear the consequences of disobeying me. To have this sort of compliance based solely off of trust... It's a different feeling altogether.

Payton's thumb brushes against my palm. "Thank you for telling me. I'm sure there are a lot of men in your position that wouldn't, but I'm glad you did."

I lean forward. "There'll be no secrets between us, Payton. No lies. No half-truths. If you ask me, I'll tell you. And if I ask you, you tell me."

I watch as she accepts this. "How did Arthur die?"

I should've expected that. But I'm not about to go back on my word. "Badly. But not badly enough."

"What do you mean?"

I let my memory replay the details of that night.

The fear in his eyes.

His screams when I started to rip his finger off. The number of yanks it took me.

The pain he must've felt.

The way his eyes bulged while he choked on his own appendage.

"I did it before you told me--" My chest expands as I inhale, trying to calm my rising rage. "If I would've known that he was planning to sell you, I would've made him suffer for weeks. Not mere minutes. I would've--" I think of all the things I would torture him with. All the vicious ways I could prolong his torment. But I don't need to put those thoughts in Payton's mind. "I would've made him beg me for death, rather than surprising him with it."

"You did it before I told you...?" She doesn't look shocked, just pensive. "I guess you would've had to, unless you went and did it right after I told you, before your party. Does that mean you went to North Dakota?"

Great time for me to implement the no secrets rule.

"The first night we slept together, I woke up in the middle of the night and flew straight there. I have a plane. That I fly," I clarify.

"But if I hadn't told you everything..."

"I knew enough from your nightmare on the couch. The night we met." Her mouth opens and closes. "I knew he'd hurt you. And that's all I needed to know."

She nods, and I watch her throat bob as she swallows hard. "Was my mom there?"

"No. She was working. We left her alone and torched the house. But if you want her gone too, just say the word."

"No," she whispers. "She never did anything to hurt me, but she never stepped in to help me either. So she can stay right where she is. It's what she deserves."

Payton keeps nodding, her breaths on the verge of ragged, so I take the mug from her hands, and set both of ours on the nightstand.

"Come here." I move down the bed until I'm lying on my back, arms open.

Payton crawls into my side. "Thank you, Nero."

My arm tightens around her. "You never have to thank me, Payton."

She snuggles further into my side. "But I always will."

I let my eyes slide closed. "I'd give everything for you."

Her palm presses over my heart. "But I'll never ask you to."

CHAPTER 68

Payton

My pillow shifts, causing me to release a grunt of dissatisfaction, before I register the faint sound of a vibrating phone.

"Shh, Baby." A big hand strokes down my back, and I keep my eyes closed while I burrow my face further into Nero's warmth.

"What?" Nero's voice is quiet as he answers, and I hear it in stereo through his chest. "Yeah." His hand doesn't stop moving as he listens. "He's here now?" Another pause. "Alright. We'll be down."

My eyes crack open when he uses the word *we*.

Nero's chest expands as he yawns.

"Did you get any sleep?" I ask, wiggling my fingers and toes to start waking myself up.

His arm raises from behind me, and I imagine him checking his watch. "Two solid hours."

"Two? I can't remember the last time I took a nap, let alone a two hour one." I tap my fingertips against his sternum. "Well, I guess yours doesn't really count as a nap if you were up all night. It's more like *finally going to bed*. Fully dressed," I add on, remembering he's wearing everything but the suit coat and shoes. His black socks are in my line of sight, and I wonder for one second if he's ticklish.

He yawns again. "Some shit came up when I was heading home last night."

"Bad shit?" I instantly realize it's a stupid question. Any sort of *shit* that comes up in the middle of the night is bound to be bad.

Nero settles his hand over mine, stilling my dancing fingers. "There have been rumors about some assholes trying to move in, and now that two of my men have been found dead in Chicago I need to go take care of it."

I press my hand firmer against his chest. "I'm sorry about your guys."

"Thanks, Baby." The hand at my back strokes down one of my braids.

"Why were they in Chicago? I thought all of your, um, business, was here in the Twin Cities."

"Most of it is. I don't run Chicago, that's someone else's, but we do business with him. And it was on one of those shipments that shit got fucked."

"So, you have to go there?"

I can feel his body shift as he nods his head. "I'll fly down in the morning. Should only be for a couple of days."

A blanket of sadness drapes over my mood. "I'll miss you."

"I'll miss you, too." Lips press against the top of my head. "But I have something that might help pass the time while I'm gone."

"Really?" I tip my head back so I can look up into his handsome face.

"Really. But we need to go downstairs."

Recalling his phone conversation about someone *being here now* I scrunch up my nose. "It better not be a bodyguard. That's not exactly *company*."

Nero tugs my braid. "That's not what I have to show you. But you will have bodyguards. Plural. And when I'm not home, you don't go anywhere without them." He gives it another tug. "I'm serious, Payton. You don't even wander around the yard without telling someone first. Okay?"

"Okay." The yard thing sounds ridiculous, but I can hear in his voice that there's no point in arguing. "Is it because of that woman giving me the invite, or because of Chicago?"

"Neither. Both," Nero sighs. "It's just how it's gonna be from now on. But you'll get used to it, and when you do, you won't even notice the guys anymore."

The concept feels foreign to me, once again feeling like a movie, but he warned me from the beginning that being with him would be dangerous. I guess this is just a part of that.

"Alright," I accept.

"Alright," Nero repeats.

And I'm left wondering how I'll pass the time. "It's gonna be weird not working. I've had a job since I was fourteen."

Nero grunts. "I'll get credit cards with your name on them, but anything you need, just tell me."

I bite my lip. Living here is one thing. Being handed a credit card, with a limit I'm sure I can't even imagine... that's something else.

Nero slaps me on the ass, before rolling away from me and out of bed. "I'm sure you'll stay busy."

I follow him off the comfortable mattress, thinking about what I'll do all day while he's gone. "Will I need to feed them?"

"Them?"

"The bodyguards," I clarify.

"No. You just ignore them."

I frown but take the hand Nero holds out to me. "Seems rude."

"They're here to work, not drop their guard over sandwiches." He opens the door, leading me out into the hall. "And they'll be outside."

"All day?" It's nearing winter, leaving them in the elements feels ruder than ignoring them.

"Trust me, Sweet Girl, walking the perimeter of our yard is the best gig they've ever had. I pay better than the mercenary companies most of them came from, and there aren't a bunch of fucking terrorists trying to blow them up everyday."

"That's something, I guess," I concede. "But don't they get cold?" I can't help but ask, even as my eyes dart around as we walk through the house.

I'm pretty sure this is a different stairway than the one we took last night.

"I'll give you a tour of the property when I get back, so you can see that they have their own, whole ass house, on the far side of the garage, with plenty of heat and food."

"Seriously?" I glance at him before focusing back on the steps.

"Most places with round the clock security do. The number will change when we need to bump it up, like right now, but there's always at least four guys working on staggered ten-day shifts. So it's easier, and more secure, for them to live here." He pulls me to a stop when we reach the bottom of the steps. "And if you need them, all you have to do is open a door and scream. Their most important job now is protecting you, and they know it." He uses his free hand to tip my chin up. "Understand?"

"I understand."

Nero presses his lips to mine. Just once. But I'm nearly panting when he pulls away. "Now, for your surprise."

I blink. I'd completely forgotten about the surprise.

"What...?"

A jangle. A little metallic jangle sounds from somewhere in the house. And my heart stops.

Nero whistles, and the jangling gets louder. Accompanied by the unmistakable sound of doggie claws on hard floors.

"You didn't?" I gasp, and my eyes are already filling with tears before the most beautiful creature rounds the corner.

"Oh my god, Nero," I sink to my knees. "You didn't."

The dog's wide chestnut eyes dart between Nero and myself as he approaches. He's covered in a wiry light brown coat and the cutest white paws. He's somewhere between the size of a lap dog and a Labrador, his thinness making him seem a little smaller than he really is.

"Hi, little guy. Or girl," I whisper, holding one of my hands out for him to sniff.

"He's a he."

His tail, covered in the same brown fur, gives a tentative wag, and I nearly choke on a sob.

"What's his name?" I can't stop myself from whispering, worried that talking too loudly will scare him away.

"Doesn't have one." Nero lowers himself to a crouch beside me. "But I was thinking he might look like a Toto."

I sniff as I nod my head. "He does," I laugh-cry. "If Toto was on stilts."

"If you don't like him––"

I snap my head over to look at Nero with an affronted gaze. Though the sternness is surely muted as my emotions continue to drip down my cheeks. "I love him."

Nero's face breaks into one of those far-too-cute smiles. "Just like that?"

A damp nose nudges against my hand, and I turn my head back to look at Toto. "Just like that."

"You love him as much as you love me?"

The dog shoves his way between us, circling around me, his tail in a full wag, his lithe body bending with every swish.

I grin. "More."

CHAPTER 69

Nero

MY EYES STAY FIRMLY ON PAYTON'S ASS WHILE SHE
bends at the waist, her front half out through the back patio door,
her back half in the kitchen.

"Toto! Come on, boy!" she calls out into the fading light.

Giving up my view, I move to stand next to her and look out
the French doors. "Not that I'm complaining, but what are you
doing?"

Payton startles. "Oh!" Straightening, she puts her hands on
her chest, over her heart. "I didn't hear you come up."

"Course not. You were too preoccupied waving that fine ass in
the air."

She rolls her eyes at me, then claps her hands together when
the mangy mutt comes sprinting toward the door.

After coaxing *Toto* into my car last night, I brought him over
to King's and asked him to have his vet look the dog over. King
has always had dogs, and taken good care of them, so rather than
source a fucking vet, I just used his.

I needed to make sure this dog had a clean bill of health, and
no tracker showing he belonged to someone else, before I gave
him to Payton. Because if I gave her a dog that keeled over dead
the next day, she'd probably kill me herself. And if she found out

some family was missing him, she'd of course want to *do the right thing* and return him. Which would break her poor heart and I'd have to punch my own face.

But other than being filthy and hungry, the doc said Toto was fine. Thinks he's around three or four years old. And he probably belonged to someone at some point, since he's house-trained and knows basic commands, but his malnourished frame, cracked nails and matted hair suggested he'd been on his own for a while.

Thankfully, King also had his groomer come over and clean the dog up, to the point where I barely recognized Toto when he came cautiously down the hall toward us.

I had a moment of doubt when he turned the corner, thinking maybe Payton would've wanted to pick out her own dog, but her instant tears and declaration of love made it obvious I did the right thing. And after, when I told her how Aspen and I had found him digging through trash, Payton burst into tears all over again. And I fell even more in love with her.

I'd never put much thought into finding a wife. Didn't really want one, but figured I'd end up with one anyway. And the few times I did think on it, I always assumed it would be with a hard woman. One that rarely smiled. One that was in it for the money and status. One that wouldn't shed tears for anything other than self-serving manipulation.

I couldn't have been further from reality. Because I wasn't meant for anyone *but* Payton.

This woman who wears her heart on her sleeve.

Who worries if the paid guards will be hungry or cold.

Who's shown more emotion in the last twenty-four hours than I've shown in the last twenty-four years.

She doesn't smooth out my rough edges. She fits into them.

The soft to my hard.

My better half, in every way.

Together, we step back as the dog skids across the threshold and Payton retrieves a treat from the new container decorating our kitchen island.

It was a gift from King, along with a dog bed, collar, leashes, toys, and a copy of *Dogs For Dummies* which I'm sure was meant to be a dig at me and not Payton.

"You told me not to go outside," Payton continues our conversation, and it takes me a second to remember what we were talking about.

Her fine ass bent through the doorway.

"Not exactly following the spirit of the law," I mumble but let it go. I don't want her standing in open doorways either, but I am the one who just gave her a dog that will need to piss in the yard several times a day. "How do you feel about dinner and a movie?"

Payton bites her lip and glances down at Toto who is now lying flat on his side on the cool floor, panting from his recent adventure outdoors.

Reading her reticence, I explain. "We won't leave the house."

"Wow!" Payton drags her hand across the back of the large leather sofa. "I thought we were gonna watch a movie in the living room."

I press a button on the wall and the curtains covering the front wall part to reveal a large screen, causing Payton to gasp.

Unfortunately, I had to spend most of the day in my office, getting things ready for my unplanned trip to Chicago. The Alliance shit is easy because I'm the boss no matter where I am, but there were a few meetings at my security company I had to reschedule. I've hired good people to fill every role, so I don't have to spend much time at the office, but of course this would be the week I was actually needed. Which means I wasn't able to give Payton the full tour of the house I'd promised. And it might've been practical to do it tonight but eating takeout pasta then watching a movie with her plastered to my side seemed like a better idea.

"This is quite impressive." Payton stops at the far side of the room, taking in the rows of sofas and large recliner chairs.

"You can come watch movies in here anytime you want."

"I wouldn't know how to turn anything on." She's looking up at the projector on the ceiling.

"If I'm not home, all you need to do is call me and I'll walk you through it. Same as anything else in the house you need help with. Except that espresso machine."

She grins. "How about I teach you how to use that when you teach me how to use this?"

"Deal." I see another question churning behind her eyes. "What is it?"

"Is there anywhere you don't want me to go?"

"In the house?" She nods, but I'm already shaking my head. I can tell she's asking because she doesn't want to overstep, not because she intends to defy me. "You go wherever you want. Open drawers, use whatever you find. The only place you can't go is the armory, but that's because it's locked."

"There's an armory?"

"More than one," I answer. "Rocco, my Second, is the only other one with access. But I'll get your biometrics added to the system once you're trained."

"Trained?" Her voice pitches up and I know I'm overwhelming her.

"Yes, trained." I close the distance between us and place my palm against her cheek. "I'm your weapon. If you ever need to scare anyone, you tell them you're mine." I brush my thumb across her soft skin. "I will keep you safe, Payton." I touch my lips to her forehead. "But you'll still learn how to shoot a gun."

Payton blows out a breath, giving me a tiny nod.

"And I bet you'll be a crack shot."

She snorts a little laugh as I successfully lighten the mood. "Guess, I'll be learning all sorts of new things."

"That you will. And speaking of new, I have a new phone and laptop for you up in our bedroom."

"But I have a phone."

"Baby, your phone sucked." Her mouth pops open at my insult, but she knows I'm right. "If you really want to keep your old number, I'll get it switched. But I already transferred your data into the new one, so it's all set up and ready to go. Same with the laptop."

"You," she stops herself and sighs. "I was going to say you didn't have to do that, but you already did. So, thank you." Payton gives me that soft appreciative smile that warms my insides.

"You're welcome," I tell her. "And tomorrow at noon you have a virtual meeting with an interior designer."

Her smile drops. "What?"

"You can set your laptop up in the bedroom, or kitchen, or wherever you like. But I also had a second desk brought into my office. We can share it until you get your own office designed. Or we can expand that one and share it all the time."

"What--Share?" She blinks like that will help her understand. "Why do I have to meet with a designer?"

"Because you need to remodel this place."

"I don't--Nero, that's..." She looks around at the extravagant movie room. "That's ridiculous."

"It's not." I take her elbow, guiding her to one of the plush loveseats. "I didn't build this house, I bought it. I had a designer come through and furnish it. I'm not attached to any of it."

"But I like it," she insists as she lowers herself onto the cushion.

I shake my head, following her down. "Start with the bedroom."

"But--"

"Sorry, Baby, you're not gonna win this one." I haul her into my side. "The bedroom is me. It's not us." I kiss her forehead. "It needs your color."

CHAPTER 70

Payton

TOTO'S SOFT SNORES, FROM WHERE HE MADE HIMSELF comfortable on a pile of blankets, is the perfect backdrop to the end of a perfect day.

And I have a feeling there's going to be a lot of perfect days from here on out.

Spending the day with Toto, getting to know each other, was better than I'd ever imagined. Of course, even in my daydreams I was still scraping by in an outdated little house, not living in a mansion, with a mafia boss.

My mafia boss.

I cuddle further into Nero's side, relaxing, as the familiar scene of Dorothy falling asleep in a field of poppies plays across the screen.

The arm around my shoulders tightens and Nero growls, "That's it."

My head lifts at his gruff words. "What is it?"

He's already dislodging himself from me. "I can't wait anymore."

"Wait for what?"

Nero doesn't answer, he just slides off the couch, and kneels in front of me. "Come here."

I don't have time to comply before he's gripping me by the hips and pulling me across the buttery leather until my butt is on the edge of the couch. My legs parting so my knees go to either side of his hips.

"Everything okay?" Humor and lust fill my voice, because he looks like a man on a mission.

"I'll be okay when I get a taste."

He hooks an arm around my waist, pulling me closer, until our bodies collide and his mouth slams into mine.

Heat explodes in my core as Nero leans into the kiss. His tongue demanding entry as his hard cock rubs against the seam of my leggings.

My hips rock, following the pressure, as my lips part to allow his tongue to sweep across mine.

We moan at the same time, and the vibrations weave together, trapping us in a cage of desire.

My breasts feel heavy. Achy. And I want to rip the bra from my body. I need the layers gone so I can feel his bristly chest hair against my nipples.

Just thinking about it sends a throb from my spine to my toes.

Nero's fingers crawl down my sides until they're hooked in the top of my leggings.

"Up," he demands, breaking the kiss only long enough for the one word.

And then his fingers start to tug.

I use his body to steady mine as I lift my butt off the sofa, and he tugs the leggings down my hips, leaving my thong in place.

It takes some wiggling, but Nero yanks them off and tosses them aside. Then he reaches for the hem of my shirt, pulling it up and over my head.

His eyes bore into mine. "Tell me again."

"Um..." My breath is coming in pants. I don't remember what we were talking about. *Were* we talking about something?

Nero shoves my bra straps off my shoulders, pulling the cups down.

My tits are fully exposed, and the thin layer of my panties is the only thing left to cover me. And that is already soaked through.

"Tell me you love me." He bends forward, taking one of my nipples in his mouth.

God, I love him.

Teeth clamp down on my nipple, making me cry out.

"Tell me, Sweet Girl." He licks across my other peak.

"Nero!" My fingers dig into his hair, needing something to hold on to as he sucks the tip into his mouth.

"I love you." I slide my hands down until they're framing his face. And I feel his jaw muscles move under my palms as he sucks. "I love you so much."

Growling low in his throat, Nero releases my nipple from his mouth to kiss me.

His lips are demanding, and I happily submit.

"Lay back." He snags a pillow from the other end of the couch and places it behind my back. So when he presses my chest, I recline onto the pillow, with my head propped against the backrest.

I'm so exposed. The small slip of fabric between my legs, and the bra around my waist like an avant-garde belt, should feel absurd, but instead I feel sexy. And desired.

Nero drags his large hands down my sides, my hips, my legs... until he's sitting back on his heels, drinking me in.

"So fucking perfect."

I try to sit up, wanting to touch him back, but he presses a hand to my stomach, pushing me back down.

Nero spears me with blazing eyes. "Stay."

His hands go to the buttons of his shirt, and I forget to fill my lungs with air.

This man. This man I love, the man whose hands I blindly dropped my life into, is something to behold.

As he shrugs his shirt off, his shoulders round with the action, muscles straining under the skin--I decide that the next time we're together, I'm going to kiss each and every one of his scars. I'm going to memorize them and learn their stories. I'm going to soothe over the memories with my lips.

Instead of undoing his pants, like I expect him to, Nero leans down.

Oh god.

I jolt upright again. "What are you doing?!"

He presses his palm between my breasts, shoving me back down.

"You know what I'm doing, Payton. I said I wanted to taste you." He uses one hand on my thigh to hold me open, then drags his hand down from my chest, over my belly until he's pressing his whole hand over my mound.

"I should've done this the first time." His tongue drags across his lower lip as he drags his middle finger down my seam. "I should've done this with your virgin blood dripping off my chin."

"I-I've never."

Except for last night when he licked your asshole, A little voice reminds me, and my core flutters at the memory.

Nero slides his fingers to the edge of my panties, pulling them aside, exposing my slickness. "That's good." His forehead drops to the soft spot just above my pussy. "You're such a good girl." I watch his back expand as he takes a deep inhale, moaning when he releases it. "Such a sweet girl." He shifts my legs until my thighs are over his shoulders. "And I'm going to eat this pretty little pussy until you're begging me to fuck you."

I'm so nervous and so turned on, my entire body feels like it's vibrating.

"Please!" I'm already begging, and he hasn't even started. "Please I want you to fu--" My plea turns into a strangled moan when his tongue roughly laves at my clit.

He didn't start gentle.

There was no teasing.

Just feasting.

Nero's fingers dig into the soft flesh of my thighs, his grip tightening as my body squirms, holding me firmly against his face.

Then his licks get longer. His tongue presses down harder. Running from my entrance up over my throbbing bundle of nerves.

It's so much better than I thought it would be. It feels so good. So intimate. So dirty.

One finger presses inside me, making my arms reach out. My fingers just twisting into the ends of his hair, and I hold on tight. Needing him to ground me.

"Nero!"

My skin feels too tight.

His finger slips out of me and I stare down as he straightens his tongue and does his best to shove it inside me.

"Oh god!"

His eyes look up in a hooded gaze, meeting mine, and I can't wait any longer. I can't take anymore.

"Please, Nero," I choke. "Please fuck me!"

Instead of stopping, his mouth clamps down over my pussy and he sucks on my clit. The pressure sending lightning bolts through my core.

His hands slide away from me, and I can see his shoulders moving, accompanied by the sound of a zipper lowering.

I'm so close to coming. My orgasm is right there.

"Hurry!" I cry.

Nero releases his mouth from me, his body instantly moving up to cover mine. "You want to come on this cock, Baby?"

"Y-yes!"

He opens his mouth, but instead of saying more, he groans, open-mouthed, as he shoves his hips forward.

His cock stretches me, and my body only waits until he's halfway in before waves of sensation crash over me.

My pussy constricts around his length and he drops his hand between us, his fingers pinching my clit, as I scream. And he shoves the rest of the way in.

CHAPTER 71

Nero

HAVING PAYTON'S SLIPPERY CUNT PULSE AROUND MY cock as she orgasms below me is the best sight I've ever seen.

I'm as deep as I can go.

Keeping one hand on her clit, I put my other hand on her shoulder, pulling her down onto my cock, as I rock my hips. Seating myself even deeper.

"That's it." Her pussy squeezes me. "That's it, Baby. Come all over me. Cover my dick in your sweet cream."

My thumb and forefinger roll around her clit.

"Too much!" Payton moans, but her back is arched, searching for more.

"Not enough, Baby." I lean in and press my mouth to hers. The taste of her transferring between us. "Never enough."

She's trembling. "I've already..."

I pull my hips back, slowly pushing them back forward. "You've already what?"

She blinks at me. Eyes going wide with each impale.

"Say it." I thrust my hips forward harder this time.

Payton wets her lips and my balls constrict.

"I-I've already come."

Hearing the word *come* in her breathy sex-voice is nearly enough for me to do the same.

"You're gonna do it again." I release my grip on her so I can shove my pants all the way off.

It takes some shifting, but I manage to kick one leg free without leaving Payton's warmth.

"I can't." She pants.

But I know it's not true.

I know she's close again.

I lift my freed leg so my foot is flat on the floor. Then I drag her further off the edge of the couch.

A moan drags its way out of my chest. "Fuck, Payton," I keep a grip on her, ramming my hips forward. "You feel so good."

Her hands claw at my shoulders, and I fall forward into her hold.

With Payton's arms around my neck and her legs around my back, I breathe in the scent of her as I force my hips to slow. To drag out our pleasure.

She's so wet. And I tell her.

"You're so fucking wet, Baby. Your pussy is so fucking wet for me."

She groans, grinding her hips up, and I know what she needs.

"You want my fingers on your pussy again? Is that what you need, Baby? You need to come?"

Payton nods against my shoulder, her whimper sweet and pleading.

"Alright, Sweet Girl." I slide a hand between us. My own breathing out of control. "I'll make you come, Pretty Baby." My fingers, so slippery with her slickness, glide over her clit. Back and forth. Faster and faster. Pressing down firmer and firmer. "I want to feel it," I growl. My own release so dangerously close. "I want to feel your juices seeping out of you." I lick across her temple. The memory of her tears dancing across my tongue. "Now, Baby." I grind into her then pull nearly all the way out. "Come for me now."

Obediently, Payton's slit contracts. Gripping me as she bows her neck back in a wail.

And the feeling of it all... The sight of it all... The idea that the next time I come it's going to be buried down that pretty throat... That's what sends me over the edge with her.

My muscles tense, and keeping just the tip inside her pussy, my dick starts to release ropes of cum into my girl.

After three pulses, I slam my hips forward. Shoving my release deeper into her channel. More pulsing out of my cock.

"Fuck," I rasp against her throat. "Jesus, woman. That..." I trail off, trying to catch my breath.

"That was intense." I can hear the smile in Payton's voice and my own lips pull into a matching expression.

"That was supposed to be slow and tender." I huff into the side of her head. "I was planning to be gentle."

Payton chuckles, making her tits bounce against my chest. "I don't love you because you're gentle."

I pull back to look at her. "Why do you love me?"

"Because you're mine."

The feelings that swell in my chest... Fuck.

I have to swallow.

I have to do it a second time.

There's not a single moment in my life where I've felt the stirring of happy tears. I've heard them described. I've seen it in movies, read it in books, but it always seemed like nonsense.

Except it's not.

I've had tears ripped from my body through pain and fear and rage. But not since I was a kid. Not since I was vulnerable. Not since I hardened into who I am today.

Payton reaches up and gently, so gently, brushes her thumb under my eye.

I watch, fascinated, as the pad of her thumb comes back damp. A tiny drop of my heart right there for both of us to see.

I'm not embarrassed. Payton claimed me. She claimed me like

I've claimed her. So, we're one now. And I'll never show her any doubt or embarrassment over my feelings for her.

She raises her thumb, and I stare, breath catching, as she slides it between her lips. Her tongue slipping out to lick the tear away.

I feel the urge to cry again, at the beauty of it, at the rightness of it.

Then the vixen below me grins around her thumb. "I can see why you like this."

Her voice is light. Happy. Full of love.

And it's all for me.

CHAPTER 72

Payton

A QUIET BEEPING PULLS ME INTO CONSCIOUSNESS before it's stopped.

"Sorry," Nero whispers, pressing a kiss to my hair. "Go back to sleep."

I slide the hand that's resting on his chest around to his side, and I squeeze him in a partial hug. "Just another minute."

His chest rumbles under my ear. "How swiftly you've stopped being a morning person."

Eyes closed, I smile at his tease. "I was never a morning person."

A big hand rubs circles on my back. "Then why were you working at a place like Twin's?"

"I don't know if it's the time of day or what, but breakfast places seem to have less harassment from customers." I yawn. "Or maybe it's just the fact that they aren't drunk. But the few times I've worked in bars, it wasn't fun."

Nero's heavy exhale ruffles through my hair. "I'm sorry I asked."

I try to look up at him, but he moves his palm to the side of my head, holding me in place.

"It wasn't that bad." I settle into his chest.

"No one will ever touch you again. Anyone tries and they die."

I probably shouldn't grin at that, especially since I know he means it, but I still do.

"Now go back to sleep."

Something bumps into the back of my leg, followed by a metallic jangle as Toto shakes his head.

Nero's chest shifts under me, and I know he's arching his neck to look at the dog who apparently snuck his way onto the bed last night.

"Little shit." Nero's tone holds no real censure, then he settles back down onto his pillow.

"Do you have to get up?"

"Yeah. Just let me hold you a while longer."

"Okay." My lids lower, and I let the warmth and scent of Nero lull me back toward sleep. "I'm going to miss you."

"I'll miss you, too," is the last thing I hear before I drift off.

SOMETHING COLD PRESSES AGAINST MY CHEEK.

I bat at it, squeezing my eyes shut against the bright light filling the room.

A tongue laps across the back of my hand.

"Gross!" I laugh, squinting up at Toto's furry face looming over me.

His mouth is open, and it looks like he's grinning at me.

"Morning, buddy." He bumps his head against my hand. "You want some scratches?" I ask, as I use my fingertips to scratch that good spot behind a dog's ears.

Toto leans his full weight into my touch and gratefulness for Nero fills my entire being.

I really do love that crazy man.

The sentiment is quickly followed by the all-consuming need to pee.

Moving slowly, I appreciate the soreness between my legs.

Toto follows me into the bathroom, sniffing his way inside the shower, while I relieve myself.

"I'll take you out in just a minute," I assure him, not wanting him to pee on the floor.

The dog wags his tail at my voice, as he carries on with the exploration.

Hurrying, I finish and shuffle over to the sink.

A sheet of paper catches my attention as I wash my hands.

It's a note from Nero, of course. And the perfect lettering in pure dark ink is exactly how I'd expect his handwriting to be.

> MORNING, SWEET GIRL.
> I SHOULD ONLY BE GONE A COUPLE OF NIGHTS, BUT I'LL COME BACK HOME TO YOU AS SOON AS I CAN.
> ROBERT IS DOWNSTAIRS. HE'S YOUR PERSONAL SHADOW AND HE'LL BE IN THE HOUSE. YOU CAN TRUST HIM WHILE I'M GONE.
> DON'T SPOIL TOTO TOO MUCH. AND DON'T TAKE THAT NECKLACE OFF.
> UNTIL I GET MY NAME INKED ON YOUR SKIN, IT STAYS WHERE IT IS.
> AND DON'T FORGET YOUR MEETING AT NOON WITH THE DESIGNER. START WITH THE BEDROOM.
> LOVE YOU.
> N.

Butterflies fill my stomach and I absently reach up to my throat, my fingers connecting with a small charm.

Dragging my eyes away from the paper, I look at my reflection in the mirror.

Sleepy eyes.

Messy hair.

Wrinkled tank top.

And a shiny gold necklace.

My fingers run over the surface of the pendant, feeling the embossed ridges.

I can't believe I slept through him putting this on me. Then again, you probably learn to be pretty sneaky when you're in his line of business.

Leaning toward the mirror, it takes me a moment to recognize what I'm looking at. The gold charm is circular, but not a circle. One half is an anatomically correct heart, the other half is a bloomed rose. The two halves meld perfectly with each other, and I press my hand over the metal, letting my skin warm it.

He's my heart. I'm his rose.

Toto barks and it makes me jump. "Alright, alright, I'm going."

I move as quickly as I can to brush my teeth and get dressed in something comfortable that covers me. Nero said I can trust Robert, but that doesn't mean I'm not leery of being alone with another man.

Nero: Landed. I'll call you tonight.

Nero: Morning, Baby.

Payton: Good morning. I hope you slept well.

Nero: You aren't here. So that's impossible.

Payton: I miss you, too.

Nero: Send me a picture of your breakfast.

Payton: Good morning to you, too. (Photo of coffee and a bagel.)

Nero: Good girl.

Payton: You want a pic of Toto's breakfast too?

Nero: I'll pass. Wanted to make sure you were eating. I have no doubt that dog is getting plenty of food.

Payton: (Photo of Toto next to his dish, food bits scattered all over the floor.) You're not wrong.

Nero: I should've brought you with me.

Payton: Does that mean you're not coming home tonight?

Nero: No. I'm sorry. This has turned into a fucking mess.

Payton: Just do what you have to do and don't worry about us. We'll be okay here.

Nero: I love you.

Payton: Good.

Nero: Payton…

Payton: I love you, more.

Nero: Payton…

Payton: Geez, fine, I love you exactly the same.

Payton: Toto just rolled over!

Nero: On purpose?

Payton: Yes, on purpose. I said it as a joke, and he just did it! Someone must've taught him some tricks.

Nero: I knew he was smart.

Payton: Do you think someone's looking for him? I don't think I could give him up if…

Nero: No one is taking that dog from you.

Nero: If he belonged to someone before, they lost that privilege when they left him on the streets.

Nero: I'll never let anyone take him.

Payton: I love you.

Nero: Next time you're coming with.

Payton: Could Toto come too? Are dogs allowed in the building?

Nero: I own the building. So yes, Toto can come. Hopefully he doesn't mind the plane ride.

Payton: We can have our first flight together. It will be mother-son bonding.

Nero: I'll teach you how to fly.

Payton: Uh… no thank you.

Nero: Non-negotiable.

Payton: You want me to be a gunslinging pilot?

Nero: I want you alive.

Payton: How about we start with you teaching me how to drive.

Nero: Consider it done.

Toto drops his bright blue tennis ball where he stands, then circles four times and promptly drops onto the rug.

"At least one of us is tired," I grumble, flopping back across the couch.

I shouldn't be bored. This house is humungous, and it has everything I could possibly want, but it's been a week since Nero left and I can only watch so many movies by myself.

And I'm just not used to this much downtime. Even with the e-book subscription he set up on my phone, and every streaming service on my laptop, and constantly answering emails about colors and patterns from the designer, I'm still bored. I can't even remember the last time I wasn't working full-time, or more than full-time. Even before I was eighteen, I had more than one part-time job. Looking back, it's a miracle I managed to graduate high school.

Graduate...

Chewing my lip, I wonder if Nero would be okay with me going to college.

That's a stupid question. Of course he'd be okay with it. He'd probably pay to have me admitted to some Ivy League school if I asked him to. But that's not what I want. A local community college would be nice, I think. Or maybe on-line schooling if we have to worry about safety.

I chew my lip some more.

What would I study?

My mind spins, but it can't land on an answer. It can't even come up with a list of options. I don't even know what my interests are.

Dogs?

I shake my head at myself, happy no one can read my thoughts.

Payton, what do you want to go to school for? Hmm, I dunno, dogs?

Rolling onto my side, I look at Toto.

I don't want to be a veterinarian. I don't have the stomach for that.

In all honesty, Nero will probably encourage me getting an education, but I don't think he'd let me work.

Speaking of hearing thoughts, my Women's Studies teacher from high school would be scratching the A's off all my old assignments if she heard that one.

But I really don't mind.

It's nice to be provided for.

It's nice to be taken care of.

It's nice to relax. To *truly relax* for the first time in my life.

My fingers drum against the couch.

So, if I don't need the money, and I won't use a degree for a full-time job, what does that leave me with?

Toto's paws twitch, already chasing something through dreamland.

What if... I bite my lip again.

What if I could do some sort of charity work? Whatever that means.

"Why is this so hard?" I whine out loud.

"What's wrong?" Robert's voice scares a scream out of me, which sends a no-longer-sleeping Toto into a barking fit.

I'm struggling to sit up. Toto's sprinting the perimeter of the room looking for danger. And Robert is standing in the entryway to the den, looking amused.

I slap a hand over my heart. "You scared me."

"And your little dog, too."

I roll my eyes at what has become his favorite line.

Deciding the threat has been neutralized, Toto picks a new spot on the rug, circles, then drops.

"What has you thinking so hard?" Robert asks, as he lowers his large frame into a chair across the room from me.

Robert is mid-thirties, looks like a cross between a Marine and a grizzly bear, and after the first afternoon together, when we realized he's just as awkward with women as I am with men, all the weirdness just kinda canceled out.

He's cool, but he takes his job very seriously, so even though I'd love to spend the day talking to him, I know he'll only allow himself to sit for five minutes, then it's back on patrol.

"I'm just trying to figure out what to do with my life." I grimace as soon as I say it, hearing how lame it sounds.

Robert raises one bushy brow. "A good looking, crazy rich, overly protective man isn't enough?"

I give him the side eye. "You can't have him."

Robert laughs. "*Terrifying* isn't on my list of fantasy husband attributes."

"Nero isn't terrifying."

"Uh-huh, whatever you say."

"What did you want to be growing up? Was it always... military? Or whatever you call this profession?" It's probably too personal of a question, but I'm starved for conversation.

"Mostly. Too many GI Joes probably." He shrugs. "What about you? There had to have been something you wanted to do."

"Sure. But I think the odds of me becoming a professional ballerina are pretty slim at this point." My outlandish dreams stopped around the time I turned nine. After that I only dreamed of getting away from home. There were no delusions that I'd become something grand.

Reading my mood, Robert pushes up out of his chair. "Well, existential crises seem like best friend territory, so I'll head back to work."

My smile is shaky, and as soon as Robert leaves the room, I let it drop.

Too bad I don't have a best friend.

Toto lets out a loud doggie snore.

"Sorry buddy, you don't count."

Staring at the wall, I decide that I do have a best friend. Nero.

I dig my phone out of my pocket, wanting to feel connected.

But then I hesitate.

What I really want is for him to come home. And in order to do that, he needs to finish what he's doing there. If I'm bothering him every time I want to talk, it's gonna take him that much longer.

But I want to talk with someone.

"Sure you can't speak?" I ask Toto.

He doesn't answer.

Blowing out a breath, I open the contacts list on my new phone.

As he'd promised, Nero had all my old info transferred over. Not that there was much.

My contacts are almost only coworkers and my bosses, specifically for when I'd get sick and need to call in or find a replacement for my shift.

I don't have anything as far as social media goes. When you

run away from home to avoid abusive parents, you can't exactly create profiles to stay in touch with high school friends. Not that I had any.

It's not like people were mean to me. I wasn't bullied much. There just wasn't anyone to miss me, so no one to stay in touch with.

I snuck out in the middle of the night, and I doubt there was a single person beyond my mom and Arthur that even knew I was gone. Well, except maybe my boss at the time. I feel bad about bailing on work without a word. But it wasn't worth the risk of a phone call. And she was kind of a bitch anyways.

Focusing on the names in my phone, I see that Nero added a bunch of new ones. Rocco, who I have yet to officially meet. Robert. Giles, Robert's backup. A number just labeled as Vet, and I assume that's who looked at Toto.

It's King's name that makes me pause. That man still kinda scares me, so having his contact info at my fingertips feels a little weird. He was friendly enough when he came into that café, the morning when Nero was apparently sitting out in the car.

Trying my latte for the first time.

But having King chase me through that fancy party... It felt like my heart was going to dissolve because it was beating so hard.

God, that was an awful night.

Until it wasn't...

Scrolling back up to the top of the names, I wonder what I'm even doing. Looking through my phone for a friend to call is like standing in front of an open fridge hoping for pizza, when you know damn well you only have expired milk, jelly and a bottle of ranch.

My thumb pauses, then swipes back the other way.

Betsy, waitress.
Branden, line cook.
Cole, dish boy.
Darlene...

I stare at the alphabetical list.

Where's Carlton?

I try to think what his last name is, like maybe it's listed backwards. But no. I don't know his last name now any more than I did when he gave me his number.

We've texted. He sent me that concert ticket. I have to have his number.

I type Carlton's name into the search bar.

Nothing.

How could it––

Nero.

Obviously, it was Nero.

My phone starts to ring in my hands, and I nearly scream again, catching myself before I wake the dog again.

At this rate Nero won't have to worry about how dangerous his world is, because I'll surely die of a heart attack within the next three months.

"Hi!" I answer, my voice too bright.

"What's wrong?" Nero's voice is immediately on edge, and I sigh.

"Nothing. I was just startled by the ringtone."

"Hmm," he hums. "What are you up to today?"

"Not much." I try my best to not sound ungrateful. "Played with Toto, who's currently dead to the world. Read some. Picked out fabric to replace the perfectly good drapes in our bedroom."

"That's good." Nero doesn't ask me detailed questions about the fabric and I wonder if he's having a bad day too.

"Everything okay with you?" I ask.

"Yeah."

Oookay. Clearly, he doesn't want to elaborate, which is fine. We talk every night, so I have a pretty good idea that he's cranky because he's not home yet.

"Can we find me a hobby when you get back?" The question sorta blurts out.

"A hobby?" His voice sounds a little more engaged, the idea of a hobby attracting his attention. "What were you thinking?"

"That's the problem!" I slouch back into the couch, letting my head tip back until I'm blinking at the ceiling. "I don't even know what my options are."

"It'll be okay, Payton. We can talk it through."

"Well, that's the thing too, I need someone to talk to. Because when you're not here, I don't have any friends."

"I'm not your *friend*, Payton." Nero uses his serious voice.

"I know, I know." I wave him off even though he can't see me. "You're my best friend. But what I mean is, I don't have any *other* friends. And now that I'm not at work all day, I don't have any human interaction. I mean Robert's great. But he won't ever just stay and talk to me. Because he's *working*." I deflate a little more. "Sorry, I'm whining."

"When I said I wasn't your friend," Nero's voice is suddenly full of what can only be described as smugness. "I meant that we're more than friends."

"Oh. Well." My cheeks start to heat and I'm glad he can't see me. "You're still my best friend."

Nero lets out that rumble that vibrates in his chest when he's feeling pleased. And it annoys me, because he didn't tell me I'm his best friend back.

"Speaking of friends," I snip. "I noticed you deleted Carlton's number from my phone."

There's a beat of silence, and it suddenly feels as if Nero is here, in the room with me. His roiling, male energy so thick I can almost feel it. "You're not seeing that prick again."

"He's pretty much my only friend!" I argue, not even sure why. I didn't mind Carlton, but it's not like I would actually have pursued a friendship with him.

"He's not your friend. And you won't ever see him again."

"Why!"

"Because he wants to fuck you!" Nero snaps.

I scoff. The idea, nonsense.

"That's one." Nero's voice is a growl.

"One what?!"

"One inch, Baby. Keep talking about other men and by the end of this conversation, you'll owe me every last inch of my dick buried deep inside your ass."

My pussy tingles at his unreasonable words, making it hard to speak. "I-He doesn't want to––"

"That's two. Keep it up and I'll have to fly home right now."

"Well... I..." My breath catches.

Before meeting Nero, I'd never had a single thought about doing *that*. But after what he did at the concert...

My chest feels hot.

Remembering the feeling of just the tip of his cock, going *there*, has me breathing faster.

"Jesus Christ." His words are thick. "You want that? You want me to take that ass, Baby. Do you want me to fuck your tight little hole?"

"I-I don't know."

"Fuck," he curses again. "Fucking hell, Payton. I'm hard as a rock."

I try to laugh, but I'm too turned on for that. "My panties feel wet."

A deep groan reverberates through the phone. "Don't touch it."

"What? But..."

"No, you did this to us, you have to suffer with me." He moans again and I instinctively know he's adjusting his cock. "Tonight, if I'm not home, you're going to go up to our bed, face-time me from your laptop, and come all over those fingers while I watch. Okay?"

"Okay." He must not be in a position where he can jerk off right now, so I guess it's fair for me to wait too.

"And if you need someone to talk to when I'm gone," he continues, "I can send Aspen over."

"Nero," I sigh. "I don't know her."

"You'd get along fine."

"Maybe, but you can't just send someone over and tell them to be my friend."

"Sure I can," the cocky man says. "But what do you need her for anyways? I'm your best friend, remember?"

"I remember you not saying it back," I grumble, seeing no point in denying my annoyance.

No secrets.

"Payton, you're my everything. My love. My Sweet Girl. My best friend." I melt at his words. "And when I get home, if you want to have more people around, we can make some friends."

That makes me laugh. "How?"

"No fucking clue. Take out an ad or something."

"Oh my god, Nero. You're hopeless."

"Love you too." He says it so easily. "I've gotta go. But have one of the guys go get you a coffee or something."

"Alright." I flex my fingers around the phone, wishing it was his hand I was holding. "I love you."

Hanging up gets harder every day.

It's ridiculous how sorry I'm feeling for myself. My situation has literally never been better. Not even close.

Even with Nero gone, I talk to him every night. We text all day. I send him photos of Toto and he sends me texts bossing me around, making sure I'm eating, asking what I'm doing. It's the most attention I've ever had. But now that I know what it's like to share a bed with him, I don't want to sleep alone. I don't want simple phone calls.

I want him.

Shoving up from the couch, Toto rouses with my movement, and we both go off to find Robert.

Lucky for us, he walks across the rear patio right as we approach the door.

I swing it open, and Toto trots chasing a falling leaf, before relieving himself in the grass.

When Robert notices me lingering halfway out the door he stops. "Need something?"

A plan forms...

"Uh, yeah, actually." I feel a little bad for what I'm about to do, but I need a field trip away from this house before I lose my mind. "Nero said it was okay if you took me to get a coffee."

Robert looks past me, into the kitchen. "Don't you make your own? All the time?"

"It's not the same. There's something *better* about it when someone else makes it. Kinda like when you get free food. Always tastes better than when you have to pay for it."

Robert doesn't move. "I'll just send someone out to get it."

I shake my head. "I'm going with. I gotta get out for a bit."

"Nero said you could go?" His doubt is written all over his face.

And he should be doubtful. I know full well that Nero didn't mean for me to go with. But I also know I'm nearing a mental breakdown if I don't get a change of scenery.

"We can do a drive thru. I'll get in the car in the garage and not get out until we're home again." It's the most over-the-top thing I can think of, but Nero's an over-the-top kind of guy.

"No offense, but I gotta ask him." The way Robert says *no offense* tells me he doesn't actually care if I'm offended.

While Robert texts Nero, I call Toto back in, and I pretend I'm not crossing my fingers for Robert to word the question in a way that will let me go.

Then I cross everything all over again, because when Nero finds out, he's gonna be pissed.

IT TOOK TWENTY MINUTES TO GET READY TO GO, AND I spent three of those minutes trying to convince Robert to let me bring Toto, but he refused.

Deciding to take the loss with the win, I used the time Robert needed to organize the men to run up to my room and change.

I know I'm not getting out of the vehicle. And I know all the windows are tinted. And I know it's stupid. But standing here in the garage, wearing tennis shoes, my good pair of jeans, a bra, a plain white tank top, and a black hooded sweatshirt I found in one of Nero's drawers, I feel ready for public.

I pull the fabric of the hoodie up to my nose. It doesn't smell like Nero. But it does smell like his laundry detergent, which is better than nothing.

Then, I keep the fabric pressed over my mouth, because I'm suddenly hit with the memory of digging around in the closet the other day, looking for boxers to wear to bed, and instead finding the stash of underwear he's stolen from me.

And if he gets to keep my undies, then I get to keep this sweatshirt. Except when he gets home, I'm going to make him wear it for a few days so the next time he leaves I have something that smells like him.

"Alright, Payton," Robert calls from his place next to one of the big black SUVs. "You're back here." He opens the rear driver's side door.

I follow his direction and climb up, buckling myself in after he shuts the door.

I have my phone tucked into my hoodie pocket, along with a twenty-dollar bill I still had stashed in my wallet. I doubt they'll let me pay for my drink, but I didn't want to just assume that someone else would pay for it.

Robert opens the front passenger door the same time as a man I only know as Giles, climbs into the driver's seat. I say hello, but he just grunts a reply.

When I see another pair of security guys getting into a second SUV, I start to feel a little bad. I didn't mean for this to become a whole two-vehicle, four-man ordeal. I just wanted some fresh air. Figuratively speaking, because I doubt they'll let me roll my window down. Robert probably has the kid locks on.

The engines rumble to life as the garage door starts to roll up, and my time for second guessing is over, because we're leaving.

It's no real surprise that we drive in silence. But it doesn't bother me. I watch the landscape go by, taking it all in.

When I first got here, it was late, dark, and I was exhausted from the birthday party disaster and subsequent *physical activities* in my apartment. So, I didn't get to appreciate the neighborhood.

The trees are large, the leaves that are left are fiery shades of red and orange, and from standing in the doorway whenever Toto goes out, I know it's cold. Right at that tipping point of freezing. But the bright blue skies and shining sun trick you into thinking it's warm past the windows.

We wind our way out of the vast development, gliding past estate after estate, each one as stunning as the last. Feels so surreal that this is where I live now.

Eventually we end up on a street that I recognize as one that will take us into the city.

I expect Giles to turn toward Minneapolis, the skyline sparkling off to the right, but he turns the other way, following the other SUV and taking us toward the closest suburb.

Makes sense when I think about it. It's probably the smart choice for security reasons, rather than going to the crowded downtown area.

My fingers absently trace a pattern on my thigh. This might be one of the weirdest moments of my life, riding in an armed two-car caravan just to go get coffee. But even with the weird, I'm actually feeling like myself again.

I love Nero. And I love the life we're creating together. It's just a lot of change. And, in my personal experience, change has always been bad. Usually awful. Definitely hard. So even though I'm happy with these new changes, it's a lot to take in. And being out here, I feel a little bit normal. A little like my old self.

"Copy." Giles's voice startles me.

When I look up front, I see the vehicle ahead of us pull into the drive-thru lane, rounding the back corner of the brick building and moving out of sight. But we don't follow. Instead, we stay stopped at the entrance to the drive-thru.

Robert turns in his seat to look at me. "Do you know what you want?"

I nod, having recognized the coffee bean and crescent moon logo on the front of the coffeeshop. "Are the other guys ordering it?"

He shakes his head. "They'll drive past the pick-up window and wait at the far end. That way we can't get blocked in."

My mouth opens in a silent O as guilt swamps me. "I'm sorry. I didn't know this was gonna be such a big deal."

At least it's late afternoon and I don't see any other cars trying to get in line.

"This is the job." Robert shrugs off my apology. "And it's good to keep the guys in practice."

Giles grunts again, this time in agreement. But instead of feeling better, I feel a little bit worse.

"Taking some lady to coffee probably wasn't what you had in mind when you did all your training."

Robert chuckles. "You're not just *some lady*. You're the boss's lady."

"Doesn't make it any less boring."

"It's not boring at all," he argues. "It's the nature of the job. You're either doing nothing or you're fighting for your life."

I grimace. "Sounds awful."

"We all gotta go somehow. I'd rather go down swinging than rotting away in a nursing home until all the dumb shit I've done to my body over the years finally catches up to me," Robert says it matter of fact, and I know he means it.

"Amen," Giles grumbles.

It's the first time I've heard his voice, and it's so scratchy he's almost hard to understand. Makes me wonder if one of the *dumb things* he's done to his body involves cigarettes.

I've seen those commercials. Maybe *going down swinging* wouldn't be so bad.

Giles takes his foot off the brake, and we roll ahead.

We make the turn to drive parallel with the back of the

building and I see that, indeed the vehicle ahead of us is at the far end of the little drive-thru lane, half-in half-out, waiting for us. And I can't help but wonder if they ordered anything, or if they just drove right through.

I hope they got something. Everyone deserves a treat.

Giles rolls down his window and I lean forward. "Can I have a large roasted chestnut mocha please?" I see Robert make a face. "And a bean pup?" His face contorts even more.

"The fuck is a bean pup?"

"It's a tiny cup of whipped cream. For Toto." I whisper the last part when the voice starts to talk through the speaker.

Sitting back, I smile a little to myself listening to Giles place the order in his gruff voice. I'm a little bummed the guys didn't get something, but not surprised.

When we stop at the pick-up window, I can smell the glorious scents of a coffee shop and it fills me with comfort.

I don't miss having every item of clothing I own smell like a café, but I do miss the scent of being surrounded by coffee and food. As crappy as some of my jobs have been, Twin's was a good place to work. No one treated me poorly. I was never told to smile. And I never went hungry while I worked there.

I place a hand on my stomach, feeling the softness, and for the first time when thinking about my body, I smile.

This is the body of someone who didn't starve.

This is the body that walked me out of hell to forge a life from nothing.

This is the body that left the patio door open so we could enjoy the stormy fall air while watching our favorite movie.

This is the body that led me to Nero.

And it's the body that attracted him to me.

This body is loved.

Overcome with gratitude, I pull my phone out of my pocket and type a quick message to Nero.

"Here." Robert's taken my drink from Giles and is holding it out for me.

Hitting send, I shove my phone back in my pocket and take it. The paper collar on the cup keeps it just the right temperature, so it's not burning my hands.

"And... Toto's drink." Robert says it like it's the most absurd sentence he's ever muttered.

Taking the tiny cup filled to the top with whipped cream, I grin. "He's gonna love it."

"You know we have some of that whipped cream shit at home, right?"

"Not the same."

"Yeah, yeah. Free food." He shakes his head, facing back forward.

The first SUV pulls out, and we follow, heading back home.

I bring the mocha up to my mouth, wanting so bad to try it. But I know it'll be too hot, and I don't want to burn the tip of my tongue and ruin the whole experience. So, I gently blow into the small opening on the lid and watch out the window as we leave the suburb behind us.

I'm thinking about how cute Toto will be with bits of fluffy cream stuck to his chin when my phone chimes with a text.

We're almost to our neighborhood, but I know it's Nero replying, and I want to respond.

I try to shuffle both cups into one hand. But spilling either in this pristine and expensive vehicle seems like a bad idea. So, I lean forward to put my drink into the cupholder near my knees. And bent over, face between the front seats, is when the whole car rocks.

A blinding light explodes in front of us, the noise earsplitting.

My eyes squint against the brightness, not understanding what just happened.

Then, seemingly all at once, Giles slams on the brakes and I jerk against my seat belt.

My hands tighten around the paper cups on reflex, and they both give way.

The pain lancing across my shoulder where the seat belt

snapped tight, is echoed in the burning heat covering my right hand.

And then it clicks.

I stare out the windshield, as the ball of flames contracts to show the burnt shell of the first SUV.

Robert is shouting something.

His gun is in his hands.

Giles turns the wheel and the vehicle lurches forward when he steps on the gas.

Robert yells something else.

At me.

But my ears are ringing, and I can't hear him.

"What?" I try to ask, but my throat doesn't work.

He starts to yell something about getting down, but a popping sound drowns out his words. And I watch in horror as the windshield turns white in front of Giles.

Robert reaches a hand back and shoves my head down.

The seat belt is stuck, so I bend as far as I can go.

I blink at the floor, watching my mocha soak into the carpet.

Another crack. This time it's louder. And red splatters across the upholstery around me.

Some lands on my hands. It's warm. And nausea swirls with my growing terror.

"Fuck!"

At Robert's voice, I look up.

And wish I hadn't.

Giles...

His head...

Tears stream from my eyes.

There's so much blood.

"Nero," I cry his name.

But he's too far away to help.

Gunfire fills the car.

I force my eyes away from Giles's unmoving form.

But Robert isn't shooting through the hole in the windshield. He's shooting across at the driver's window.

The bulletproof glass finally gives way. One shot escaping the car. A second before a pair of large vehicles slam into us. Crumpling the door at my side.

Silence.

Pure silence fills my brain as darkness swallows my vision.

Flourishes of anguish pierce my awareness as my world rotates.

As the seat below me lifts.

As the entire vehicle rolls.

CHAPTER 73

Nero

"You'll stay here," I tell Rocco, rubbing a hand over my face. "Watch the warehouse tonight and if it stays quiet, pull back and come home."

"Got it."

"And call the airstrip. Tell them I'll be there in a couple of hours."

He nods and turns away to make that call.

I felt my phone vibrate a couple of minutes ago, so I pull it out now to look at the text.

It's from my girl. Of course, it is.

> Payton: I love the way you love me.

That emotion, the one I only associate with her, slams into me.

"Tell them I'm headed there now," I call out to Rocco. I'm not waiting anymore.

My thumbs fly across the screen.

> Nero: It's as easy as breathing.

CHAPTER 74

Payton

AGONY.

My head. My hand. My shoulder. Hip. My entire body. It all hurts.

I try to blink my eyes open. Try to remember what happened.

Oh god, why does my head hurt so bad? My limbs feel like they weigh a thousand pounds.

There's a loud sound.

Or at least I think it's loud. My ears feel like they're filled with mud.

I try to blink my eyes open as something wet trails across my face.

Willing my hands to wipe it away, but I can't. My hands aren't working.

I blink again, my eyesight blurry, and try to make sense of what I'm seeing.

I'm in the back seat. But--my stomach lurches. Giles is slumped from the ceiling, dripping blood onto Robert's still body.

Another muffled crash vibrates my seat.

Not the ceiling.

We're sideways. The whole vehicle is on its side. Giles and I stuck on the top side, dangling in the air.

I try to look at Robert, lying against the window that's shattered against the ground. But I can't tell if he's alive.

Panic claws into my chest.

Someone did this because of me.

These men are dead because of me.

Another thud. Impact? And light streams into the hazy interior from behind me.

Voices, new ones I've never heard before, follow the light.

I try to call out. Try to beg Robert for help. But the words won't form. My brain won't cooperate.

But when hands grab at me, I scream.

I scream as loud as I can.

And it hurts so bad.

The new voices hiss at me.

They cut me free, and I crash into their arms.

More pain. More fear.

And when the voices grip my arms and drag me through the debris, out of the caved-in rear window, I fight.

I kick. And I twist. And I reach my burned hand out to claw at the faces in front of me.

I've always run. But this time I fight.

Because now I have things to lose. Someone to lose.

Because now I have someone to miss me.

The sound of my ringtone trickles through the blur of fear.

And I fight harder.

My lungs fill with agony at the force of my screams.

My muscles ache with every movement.

But then an arm circles my throat from behind.

And I can't scream anymore.

Because my body is failing.

And I can't breathe.

CHAPTER 75

Nero

I wait for Payton's response.

She always texts back. Always right away. Making me feel like she's just waiting for me. Waiting for any reason to talk to me.

Anxious to see her, I walk to the front door of the penthouse condo, with Rocco following so he can drop me off at the airfield.

The heavy door clicks shut behind him, and I'm still staring at my phone when the elevator doors slide open, and we step in.

We're just starting our descent when my phone sounds with a notification.

Except it's not a text.

It's an alert. The bright red notification sitting at the top of my screen.

Dread fills my stomach as I open it.

"What vehicles do we have out today?" I ask, my voice flat.

Rocco's at my side, looking at the same thing I am.

The app I have open fills the screen with little squares representing all my vehicles, letting me know their status and positions.

And one of them is gone.

There are no signs of an accident, not a stalled engine, nothing. It's just fucking gone.

The text I got earlier from Robert flashes in my mind. ***Okay to go get coffee?***

He couldn't possibly have meant...

My phone vibrates, and I watch as another square goes gray.

Ice fills my lungs, and I tap on the vehicle.

A reading scrolls across my screen. Showing the alerts as they happen.

Windshield penetrated.

It can't be. That would mean––

Driver's window penetrated.

Impact detected.

Roll detected.

Rear window penetrated.

I click on the GPS function.

Jesus Christ.

My chest hurts. I have to remind my body to breathe.

It's close to the house.

It's too close to the house.

On the map, there's a red dot where the other vehicle used to be. *Used to be.* Right next to the current location of the damaged vehicle.

Did someone blow up my fucking car?

I think about the first sensor notification on the second vehicle.

Windshield penetrated.

The *bulletproof glass* was penetrated.

The walls of the elevator close around me.

And my hands start shaking.

I don't remember the last time my hands were shaking.

With jerky movements, I swipe to my contacts and dial Payton.

I should call someone else.

Call my men.

I should tell Rocco to call someone.

But something... something deep inside of me is twisting.

The phone rings.

And rings.

And rings.

My free hand is clenched so tightly into a fist my fingers ache.

Another ring.

And as I'm stepping off the elevator, the call is answered.

"Pay--"

But I'm answered with her screams.

Screams that slice through my chest.

Screams that tear apart my soul.

"They got her." Robert's choked words mix with the sound of Payton's terror.

And I feel something I haven't felt in twenty years.

Fear.

All-consuming fear.

"Who?" I demand.

Robert coughs.

"WHO?" My shout reverberates through the lobby.

"Mik--" He coughs again. "It was Mikhail's men."

Then I hear something worse than Payton's screams for help.

I don't hear them.

I don't hear anything.

And I start sprinting.

Tires screech through the line, the same time I hear Robert drop the phone as he gasps for breath.

Crashing onto the street, I hang up and dial another number.

Hang on, Baby.

I'll get you.

King answers. "Hey."

"Get everyone."

"What hap--"

"EVERYONE!"

CHAPTER 76

Payton

MY HEAD THUDS AGAINST SOMETHING, AND I SQUEEZE my eyes against the pain.

There's laughter, male laughter, nearby.

"Did you see the way that thing lit up?" one voice asks excitedly.

"We all saw it, dumbass."

"Direct fucking hit!" The first man isn't deterred.

I slowly open my eyes, the floor beneath me rocking slightly, and I think I'm lying on the floor, in the way back, of some large vehicle. My knees are bent, and the rough carpet scratches against my cheek.

My hands are taped together, a thick band of duct tape encircling my wrists, and a new wave of panic fills me.

I'm being taken.

I press my lips together to suppress a whimper. I don't want to make a sound. I don't want them to know I'm awake.

At least I'm on my right side. My whole-body hurts, but my left side feels extra bad. Probably since that's the side where their trucks hit us.

I force my eyes to focus on the rear door in front of me, needing to stay awake.

But awake means thinking.

Giles is dead.

The two men in the first SUV... I don't even know their names, and they're dead.

And Robert.

My throat tightens even further.

Robert might be dead too.

And it's all my fault.

All because I wanted to leave the house.

Because I didn't understand.

Tears track from my stinging eyes.

I'd been told. Nero told me over and over again that it was dangerous. But I didn't understand. Not truly. And now I'm responsible for the deaths of so many.

The driver takes a turn too fast, causing me to bump my head again, sending black spots across my vision.

Breathing through the pain, I stare at the handle on the inside of the door.

Maybe I could grab it? Yank the handle and have the back door pop open.

But what if it doesn't work and I just alert them that I'm awake?

Defeat presses in on me, more tears filling my eyes.

Even if it did open the door, what am I gonna do? Roll out the back like a stuntman? Roll away from my captors, straight onto the pavement, only to be run over by whatever car is right behind us.

No.

Nero will come for me.

He will find me.

"I hope Boss knows what he's doing," a different man grumbles.

Someone else blows out a breath. "Better not let anyone else hear you say that."

"What're you talking about?" the first voice asks.

"Nero's not gonna take this lying down," the grumbly man responds.

There's silence for a long moment before the first man speaks again, only he's not chuckling anymore. "Who the fuck did we just grab?"

"His woman."

No one replies as a thick energy fills the interior of the car.

It's fear.

And it's not just mine.

CHAPTER 77

Nero

MY PHONE IS IN ONE HAND AS I OPEN THE THROTTLE ON my newly acquired plane. I needed something faster, and by the time this one is missed, it'll all be over.

Rocco is on a call next to me, executing his orders, the shit in Chicago forgotten about.

King would've gotten the ball rolling, using a codename to activate local assets, but I need Rocco to arrange the final details.

My eyes go back and forth between my flight speed and the dot on my phone screen. The dot showing me Payton's location.

I'm not sure how she'd feel about the tracker I put in the pendant on her necklace, but when it leads me right to her, I'm confident she'll thank me.

I haven't decided if I'll tell her I had it made from Arthur's melted down ring, she might balk at that. But the trophy of his death belongs to her.

And she belongs to me.

After today, when I get her back home, I'm putting a tracker under her fucking skin.

And if Robert doesn't die on his own, I'm going to rip him apart myself. Feeding the pieces to Toto.

Every second that goes by, I feel sicker and sicker.

My worst nightmare is playing out in front of me. The dot moving further and further away from our home. And closer to Mikhail's.

Fucking Mikhail.

The idiot forgets that I know that house, that I've done this before.

And this time I'm going to kill him. Like I should've done in the first place. Then I'm going to burn the whole thing to the ground.

With quick fingers, I swipe away from the tracking screen for one second to make another call.

As soon as it starts ringing, I put it on speaker and switch back to watching Payton.

The fed answers. "This oughtta be good."

"I need a favor."

"Yeah? And I need to keep my job."

"We both know that's a lie."

"Fair. But I would like to stay out of prison."

Being a fed in prison would be rough. But being one of the best underground MMA fighters I've ever seen, I doubt he'd have too much trouble.

He sighs. "What is it?"

"I need to keep a road clear."

"For how long?"

I glance down at the dot, seeing it slow. "Twenty minutes."

"Where?"

I tell him the name of the street and the name of the cross streets, designating the length I'll need.

The neighborhood is a lot like mine. The blocks, if they can be called that, are long. And mercifully straight. So my plan should work.

"What'll you do for me?" he asks.

"How about I kill Mikhail?" I keep my voice even.

The fed laughs. "Considering the address you just gave me, I have a feeling you're gonna do that anyway."

"Then I'll owe you one."

He sighs. "I don't want a war in my backyard, Nero. I can't brush that off."

"There isn't going to be a war."

"No?"

"This is an extermination."

He's quiet for a moment. "What happened?"

My mouth opens, and I have to swallow before I can get the words out. "He has my woman."

"Fuck," the fed curses. "Alright, fine. I'll jam shit on my end, keep my boys off your back. But twenty is all I can buy you." I can hear him typing on a keyboard. "When is this starting?"

I look at my GPS and the now stationary dot of Payton's tracker. "I'll land in thirty."

"Land? What the fuck are--"

I hang up.

Hang on, Baby. I'm almost there.

CHAPTER 78

Payton

THE REST OF THE RIDE WAS SPENT IN SILENT TORTURE.

I tried to figure out a way to free my hands, but there was no way to do it quietly. Possibly no way to do it at all. At least not for me.

We've been driving slower for the last few minutes, and when the car comes to a near stop to make a sharp right turn that has to be a driveway, I close my eyes.

We're here.

Wherever here is.

The car rolls to a stop and when the doors up front start opening, I work on slowing my breath.

I don't have any weapons. I don't have any idea how to defend myself, not against men like this. So, my big plan is to pretend I'm still knocked out. Maybe if they think I'm unconscious, they'll just set me down somewhere and leave me alone.

I have no grand delusions of escape. But I'd rather wait for Nero by myself, playing possum, then have to talk to, or interact with, whoever is responsible for this.

They don't want me dead. If that was the goal, they'd have just blown up both vehicles.

No, they want me as bait. They're trying to lure Nero in.

And it's going to work.

I only hope it goes epically bad for them.

The door swings open and I try to relax my features. I have no idea what a knocked-out person is supposed to look like, or how long someone is supposed to be unconscious after being choked out. But based on the action movies I've seen, which is probably all nonsense, people can be out for minutes or hours.

Cold air blows over me, stinging across the cuts that mar every inch of my exposed skin.

A man heaves out an annoyed sigh. "Alright, let's get her in."

Hands that are becoming unfortunately familiar grab at me roughly.

"Wait," another voice interrupts, accompanied by a quiet smacking sound, like the man just used the back of his hand to smack someone else on the chest. "This one can carry her."

The hands leave me. "Be my guest."

I almost jump when a new hand shoves its way between my side and the floor underneath me.

Staying dead weight is so much harder than I expected, but somehow I manage as the man hoists me up and over his shoulder. With my butt in the air and my head and arms dangling toward the ground, it's harder to breathe, but fighting would make everything hurt more, so I stay as limp as I can.

He jostles me with each step. And I feel tears track from the corners of my eyes up my forehead and into my hair.

I'm tempted to blink them away, to try and see my surroundings, but I don't dare open my eyes, unsure if anyone is close enough to see.

It doesn't really matter anyway. Even if I track a path out of the house and find a way to break out of an unoccupied room, I'll never be able to run. That car crash messed me up.

And the throbbing in my skull warns me that I might have a concussion. The upside-down blood rush only exacerbating the headache.

Doors open, then slam.

I'm taken up a few steps. Down a few steps. And I'm on the verge of full-out crying over the throbbing inside my skull when the man stops.

There's a knock, and another door opens, and we start to move forward again.

Someone does a slow clap, and I instantly hate them.

"So, this is her, huh?" The voice is smarmy and I'm assuming he's the one in charge. "Nice ass, I guess."

A sound I'm not expecting clicks across the room.

High heels.

Something inside me starts to uncoil. Women help women. This might--

A hand fists in my hair, yanking my head up, my neck screaming at me in protest.

I start to yell out in shock, but my outburst is silenced when something hard strikes my face. The blow connecting with my cheek and the corner of my mouth.

The hand lets go before I have time to focus on the person that struck me and my face drops back down, my nose colliding with the man's back.

"The bitch was just faking it." The female voice is full of so much hate I don't understand it. "She's awake."

"Now, now. That's no way to treat our esteemed guest, Nikki."

The name niggles at a memory in my brain, but then the man holding me bends forward, and I slide off his shoulder, crashing down onto an uncomfortable couch.

A pathetic cry escapes me.

Inside and out, everything feels like an exposed nerve.

How much pain can one person feel?

My head aches so bad. And out of all the abuse I've suffered at the hands of others, this is the worst.

The heels click their way toward me again, and I flinch.

Feminine laugher, dripping with menace, responds.

"That's enough," the man says, with a creak that must've been him sitting in a chair.

"This whore cost me my hair!" she snarls, her footsteps coming closer.

"I said enough!" His tone flips from casual to psychotic so smoothly, I finally lose that last grip I had on my self-control.

Tremors roll through my body, and with no reason to pretend to be strong, I curl up onto my side. The fear and agony too much.

From my angled view, I work to clear my vision.

We're in an over-the-top masculine office. There's a huge carved wooden desk across the room from me, probably twenty feet away.

I want to flick my eyes around, take in the rest of the room, look for exits, but my brain is too fuzzy. So, I keep my gaze steady on bodies behind the desk. One is sitting. One is standing at his side.

I've never seen the man before. His oily blond hair and rat-like features would make him look like a villain in any setting.

The woman who hit me rests her hand on the back of his chair, along with the name, snaps into place.

I can't believe I ever thought she and Nero looked good together. Seeing her here, standing next to the unfamiliar creepy man, I know that this is where she belongs. With the bad guy. The *actual* bad guy.

Disgust grows inside me. Any woman who willingly brings harm to another woman deserves the worst kind of punishment.

I don't know what she meant by saying I cost her her hair. But her head has been shaved nearly bald and it makes her look even more ferocious.

She narrows her eyes when she sees me looking. "Something to say?"

"Just f-funny." I have to clear my throat. "*You* calling *me* a whore."

The man burst out into laughter. And the woman, Nikki, takes one step in my direction before he grips her by the arm.

"It's not funny, Mikhail!"

"It's hilarious." He grins at me, and it chills whatever satisfaction I got from the insult. "I can see why Nero likes her." His grin morphs into something that I'm guessing is supposed to be a softer smile. "I'm sorry we had to meet like this, Payton Vawdrey. You've done nothing to me. And I apologize that you've been hurt." He lifts a shoulder, ruining his apology. "But needs must. And it's Nero's time to die."

I shake my head as best I can. "He's going to destroy you."

CHAPTER 79

Nero

MY TIRES SCREECH AS THEY TOUCH DOWN ON THE pavement. And I fight the controls, coming in faster and steeper than usual.

But I'm in a fucking hurry.

Rocco braces his hands on the instrument panel as we're jerked against our seat belts.

As promised, there are no cars in sight. Not on the road ahead of me. Not visible in the long driveways as we skid past them.

The street is empty.

Quiet.

Waiting.

I'm unbuckling before the plane comes to a stop. And a wicked grin pulls across my lips when I see I got it perfect, parked right in front of Mikhail's driveway.

"Want me to get it turned around?" Rocco asks.

The stretch of road ahead of us curves, there's no way I can take back off aiming this way.

I shake my head. "We'll leave it. A little gift for Tye to deal with."

Striding to the exit, we're both ready.

During the flight, we geared up. Bulletproof vests, mine over

330

my usual all-black with my suit jacket discarded along the way, one Glock on my left hip, one in my hand, and extra magazines in every pocket.

Rocco pulls the lever to lower the steps from the side of the plane, facing away from the target.

And as I climb down, movement blurs the tree line ahead of me, as dozens and dozens of men--dressed head to toe in black, armed to the fucking teeth--walk through the yards, toward me.

This. This is my element.

I wait in the center of the street while my men fill in around me.

"No one touches her." I project my voice, reaching everyone's ears. "Everyone else dies."

All heads nod.

Then another form, a man a little taller than the rest, strolls down the street toward us.

Sixty automatic weapons turn to aim at him.

King ignores the guns pointed at his chest, lifting his chin in my direction.

My men, glance at me, some with brows raised, obviously wondering what the fuck this Wall Street douchebag is doing here.

My nerves settle a little more. "Didn't expect a personal visit on this one."

King grins. "Wouldn't miss it." Then he hoists a heavy metal tube onto his shoulder. "And you forgot your key."

Without missing a beat, he turns, aims the surface-to-air launcher at the reinforced gate blocking Mikhail's driveway, and sets the missile free.

CHAPTER 80

Payton

"UH... BOSS!" AN ALARMED VOICE CATCHES MIKHAIL'S attention.

Using all my strength, I push up to a sitting position, just in time to see a pale-faced man run through the open doorway.

"Is he here?" Mikhail asks in an excited voice.

An explosion answers his question.

CHAPTER 81
Nero

My men pour through the smoke. Filing through the open gate and fanning out to the sides.

I signal to my three best shooters. "Up."

They nod and rush around the plane, climbing up the stairs, and onto the wing, before laying themselves out on top of the fuselage.

This isn't their first time. They know to shoot anything that moves.

The front door, approximately one hundred yards from the plane, opens. But before Mikhail's men can squeeze off even one shot, they drop.

Sharpshooter headshots.

The pace of the swarm increases, and we close on the house.

My gun is at my side.

This part isn't for me. This is when my men get their payback for the three we lost.

They want their pound of flesh, and they're gonna take it. Tenfold.

King enters the building just ahead of me. His motherfucking rocket launcher discarded somewhere in the yard; his pistol held at the ready.

He breaks off with the men as they part into teams. They might not know him, but they don't need to. He just proved he's one of us now.

A trio of men walk ahead of me. One takes a bullet to the leg but stays standing as they mow down the opposition.

The carnage is satisfying. The pools of blood reminding me that I'm in control. That this is my operation. And that I'm going to be successful.

Inhaling a lungful of gunpowder smoke, I tip my head back and roar, "MIKHAIL!"

CHAPTER 82
Payton

NERO'S VOICE ECHOES DOWN THE HALL, THE background of gunfire making it all the more ominous.

The guy who came running in right before the explosion, takes this opportunity to sprint back out the open door, running in the opposite direction of Nero's bellow.

"Pussy!" Mikhail spits.

I'm looking toward the door, waiting for Nero to appear, so I don't notice Mikhail approaching until he's almost on me.

I try to get away, but I'm too slow, and he gets a handful of my hair.

"No you don't." He doesn't give me time to stand, just pulls me off the couch.

I cry out. The extreme pain of being dragged by my hair fills my eyes with tears.

I thought I was done with crying. Figured a person can only have so many teardrops inside them. But I think I've proven that number does not exist.

My feet struggle to stay underneath me, and I get just enough purchase to stumble along.

This seems like the perfect moment for that woman, *Nikki*, to strike at me, but when Mikhail stops in front of his desk, spinning us to face the door, I see her inching along the far wall, sneaking toward the exit.

"And where do you think you're going?" Mikhail sneers at Nikki.

She stops, caught, but keeps the bitchy expression on her face. "I'm leaving! You said you'd kill the cow and make Nero pay!"

"That's what I'm doing!" Mikhail screeches, that polished insanity bouncing against the surface.

Nikki flings an arm toward the open door. "Don't you hear that? He's killing everyone! And he's going to kill you--"

A loud crack, so close to my ear it rattles my brain, fills the room.

I stare, uncomprehending, as blood blooms across Nikki's chest. Her fancy silk shirt soaking through in half a second. The pretty cream turning a deep red.

She stumbles, falling against the wall, then just sort of crumples to the ground, disappearing behind the couch, like she was never there at all.

My body starts to shake.

Every muscle. Every tendon. Every cell vibrates with dread.

I'm going to die.

My lungs start to contract. Not releasing. Not sucking in air.

I'm going to die.

A sob lodges against the oxygen trapped in my throat.

I don't want to die.

I'm not ready.

A ragged sound claws out of my chest.

I'm not ready.

I can't-

And then Nero is there.

Standing in the doorway. Surrounded by a haze of gun smoke.

He's just standing there.

Here.

With me.

Relief releases my lungs, and I suck in a breath.

He's here.

More tears roll down my cheeks.

The hot barrel of a gun presses against my temple.

Okay.

I focus on taking a breath.

Okay.

He's here.

With his eyes on mine, Nero tosses his gun to the ground.

He's with me.

He came for me.

The edges of my mouth pull up into a small smile.

I figured we'd have more time.

But if this is it, if we're going to do this together, then I'll be okay.

We can go now.

CHAPTER 83

Nero

I can see it in her eyes. She thinks this is it. That this is the day we die.

But it's not.

I step into the office, keeping my palms exposed, and kick the door shut behind me.

"You don't want her." I do nothing to hide the fury rolling through my veins. There's no point in playing it calm. "You want me."

Mikhail uses his grip in Payton's hair to pull her further in front of him. "That's the thing though. I think I might want you both." He leans in closer to Payton, putting his nose against the back of her head, inhaling.

I take a step forward and he shoves the gun harder against her temple.

"Throw the second gun."

I can feel my pulse as it thuds through my body, but I do what he says.

Keeping my eyes on Payton, I carefully check to make sure the safety is off before I toss the gun to the floor, a few feet in front of her.

She's tear-streaked. Hurt. Covered in scrapes. Her lip split.

There's dried blood on her hairline. Her hands are bound, and her stance is full of pain.

But she's alive.

And she's never looked more beautiful.

I take a slow breath.

Mikhail was already going to die. But now that he's put his filthy hands on her. Now that he's tried to smell her roses. He's all the way done.

"Your father was standing right where you are when I slit his throat," I tell him, fully disarmed. "We were standing there, face-to-face, and he was too fucking stupid to suspect a thing. But you." I dip my chin. "You know you're about to die. And that's enough for me." I take one step forward. "Except I won't just end your life. I'm going to end your existence." I take another step. "Your men are dead. Your money will be mine. No one will ever say your name again. Not ever. Because the memory of you will disappear with your last breath. So today, right now, you're going to suffer both deaths at once. And I'm going to deliver them."

I take one more step and the gun barrel pulls away from Payton, aiming at me.

"You better kill me with your first shot," I tell him.

Then I lunge.

And he shoots.

CHAPTER 84
Payton

THE SOUND IS DEAFENING.

The shot so close to my ear.

A red tear rips through Nero's sleeve, but it doesn't stop him.

The hand in my hair releases me with a shove, and I lose sight of Nero when my exhausted limbs give out and I fall to the floor, landing on my hands and knees.

There's a second shot.

And a third.

I glance up from the ground. And a part of my soul slips away when I see one of the bullets slam into Nero's chest.

He staggers a step.

I try to crawl toward him when my fingers connect with something hard.

I glance down, and find the gun that Nero tossed.

Without thinking further, I grip the heavy weapon between my hands. The tape around my wrists making it impossible to mimic the way I've seen Nero do it.

"Why won't you just die!" Mikhail screams.

Nearly blind with tears, I twist and drop my butt to the ground, raising the gun.

I don't blink. Or aim. I just pull the trigger.

And a split second later, dark red arterial blood sprays from Mikhail's neck.

He drops his own gun, both of his hands reaching up to slap at the hole in his throat. But blood pours from between his fingers.

He drops to his knees, and I uncurl my fingers.

Before the gun can fall in my lap, Nero is there. Catching it in one hand, the other pressing gently against my cheek.

"I'm here." Nero's voice is soft.

"Nero." My voice shakes. "I killed him. I k-killed him."

His thumb brushes over my cheek, then he stands, turns around, and squeezes the trigger. Over and over, he fires the gun until he's emptied the clip into Mikhail's slumped form.

Nero slides the gun into the holster at his side, then crouches back at my side. "I killed him."

I shake my head, but he cups my face with his large hands, holding my gaze on him.

"I killed him," he repeats. "I did that. Not you." He kisses me so, *so* gently. "Not my Sweet Girl."

Love fills my eyes.

Nero kisses me once more, before his hands drop from my face.

I feel a tug at my wrists, before they flop free at my sides, the tape torn away.

"Come on, Baby." He brushes back my hair. "My courageous girl." He touches my lips with his. "We gotta go." Nero's words are soft, but urgent.

I try to get up, but my body won't cooperate. It's done. So done with everything.

"Shh," Nero shushes me. I hadn't even realized I was crying. But at this point, it feels like I'm crying as often as I'm not, so I don't even try to stop. "I'm going to pick you up now."

He slides his arms under me.

I struggle but manage to wrap my arms around his neck, doing my best to hold on.

As he lifts, I try to stop my whimper of pain, but it still escapes.

"I'm sorry. I'm so sorry." Nero whispers it, again and again, as he clutches me to his chest and carries me out of the room.

My eyelids are so heavy.

I try to keep them open, but they keep closing.

"You're okay." Nero kisses my forehead. "You're okay, Baby." He hugs me tighter. "I see you're wearing my sweatshirt. Just couldn't stay away from my things, could you." He kisses me again. "If I could fit in your clothes, I'd wear them too. Wouldn't care if it was covered in yellow flowers, I'd sleep in it every night I was away from you."

There are other voices now. All male. And I try to look around, try to understand what's happened, but the first thing I see is a large splatter of blood marking a wall.

Squeezing my eyes back shut, I decide I don't need to see.

"It's all my fault." I nearly choke on the words, needing to get them out.

"No." Nero hugs me tighter. "It's not. This whole household was living on borrowed time. The world will be better without them."

Nero shifts, stepping through a doorway sideways.

"Keys in?" He calls the question to someone I can't see.

"Yeah, Boss."

"Good, open the passenger door. I'm driving her home in this one." I hear a car door open. "Tell everyone to leave."

"You got it."

Nero sets me on the seat, taking the time to buckle me in.

Before he closes the door, I hear him give one last command.

"Torch it."

CHAPTER 85
Nero

THE MEN ARE ALREADY FILING DOWN THE DRIVEWAY when I pull Mikhail's car out of his garage. We've used our twenty minutes, and it's time to clear out.

My rearview mirror shows dark plumes of smoke already billowing from windows of the mansion. And even though I'd love for this bright red, my-dick-is-small sports car to be a part of that burning mess, knowing I'll send it to the chop shop as a final *fuck you* to Mikhail makes me feel better about taking it.

Payton groans a little as she settles further into the seat, and I make sure to take the corner slowly as I turn out onto the street.

"We'll be home soon, Sweetness." I rest my hand gently on her thigh, not sure where she's hurting, not wanting to do more damage.

Her small palm covers my hand, so I flip mine over and lace our fingers together.

Her fingers squeeze mine. "Is that a plane?"

She mumbles the question a moment before her head lulls back.

THE DOC AND HER ASSISTANT WERE WAITING AT THE front door when we got home.

I called her from the air, knowing Payton would be hurting from the car wreck. But no amount of preparation or experience could prepare me for seeing my girl like this. Laid out on our bed in her underwear, bruises covering most of her body.

Payton woke up while we undressed her, but didn't ask any questions, just nodded when I told her the doctor was going to look her over. And I'm glad the doc was smart enough to bring her female assistant. Because if another man tried to even get a fucking glimpse of Payton right now, I'd likely rip his head from his shoulders, medical professional or not.

"I'm going to use an ultrasound to check for fractures, but that's just a precaution. I don't think anything is broken," Doc tells us as she sets a laptop up on the nightstand before nodding to me. "While we're doing this, you'll get stitched up."

If it wasn't for the constant glances Payton kept taking at my torn sleeve, I'd've forgotten I was even shot. It's just a tap. Barely a flesh wound, in and out of the bicep, but I'm not going to give Payton one more thing to worry about. So, I sit at the foot of the bed, my injured arm facing away from Payton, out of her sight, and I let the assistant do what she needs to.

Payton continues to stay quiet, answering questions about pain levels, moving body parts as requested, and I ignore the fact that the assistant doc just stabbed my arm full of Lidocaine without asking. It's probably for the best, because simple gunshots are still a bitch to clean, and I have better things to focus on than suppressing my own pain.

Like Payton's expression.

It's so full of guilt and sadness, it makes my chest hurt.

Pain will pass. But those emotions...

What is she thinking?

Is she regretting ever meeting me?

Does she blame me? Hate me?

What if she asks to leave?

What if she demands to go back to her old life?

My teeth clench.

I won't let her.

That's what'll happen. I won't let her. I'll make her stay, and I'll make her remember that she loves me.

When my arm is bandaged, I turn more toward Payton, and place her feet in my lap.

The desolate look is still on Payton's face when the doctor finally stands.

"I know it doesn't feel like it, but you're a very lucky girl Miss Vawdrey," the doc tells Payton, patting her hand, and I hate that I don't have a last name to give her. "I don't see any signs of fractures and the skin abrasions should all heal well." My eyes move to the gauzy bandages around Payton's wrists where the tape dug into her smooth flesh. "The concussion is the most serious matter, but all you need to do is rest." The doctor moves her gaze to mine. "Keep her in bed. And keep her hydrated. Bright lights might bother her, so keep them low. The headache is normal. I'm leaving painkillers for her to take, that you can start in a couple hours, since I gave her a dose when you got here." I nod. "Above all, keep her calm, and she'll be fine."

"Alright." My voice comes out gritty, having not used it in so long. "Will you help me get her dressed before you leave?"

Payton shakes her head.

"Baby." I kneel beside the bed. "There's less of a chance of me hurting you if they help."

Payton just shakes her head again, so I sigh and let the doctors leave.

I keep Payton in sight as I collect a small stack of clothing–– clean underwear, a pair of sweatpants and one of my t-shirts. We work slowly, but together get her dressed in fresh clothes.

When I try to get her to lie back down, Payton shuffles up the bed so she's sitting against the headboard.

"You need to lay down."

She shakes her head, clutching at my hand.

I let her take it, hoping it's a good sign. If she wanted to leave me, she wouldn't want to touch me.

"I-I'm so sorry." Her voice bursts out of her on a sob, and I'm instantly on the bed with her, pulling her to sit crosswise on my lap.

"Shh, Baby, no. You have nothing to feel sorry for."

"It's all my fault!" she hiccups, fat tears rolling down her cheeks.

I keep one arm around her back, holding her to me, and use the other to lightly grip her chin, making her look up at me. "Payton, Baby." I kiss the corner of her mouth. "You did not start this feud. I did. I started it fifteen years ago when I slaughtered Mikhail's family. He was just a fucking kid, so I let him live." I shake my head. "I told him what a piece of shit his father was and I trusted him to grow up and do better. That's on me. I should've ended his life with the rest of them, but I didn't." I kiss the other corner of her mouth, tasting her sadness. "And I have to live with that. I have to live with knowing that every mark on this beautiful body is my fault."

She shakes her head. "It's not."

I press my forehead to hers. "It is. And I'm sorry."

"But..." Her breath hitches. "The bodyguards. G-Giles. And the other car." Her fingers dig into the front of my shirt. "And--"

"Not your fault." I sway the smallest amount, rocking her with me. "I know this sounds callous, but the men that work for me don't expect long lives. They know what they're getting. And they know what dying on the job will get their families." *Money. Lots and lots of money.*

"But if I hadn't tricked Rob--" Her voice catches and for the first time in what feels like forever, I tell her something good.

"Robert's fine."

She tips her head back to look into my eyes, trying to see the truth in my words.

"He's fine," I repeat. "Or he will be. Until I fucking kill him myself for putting you in danger."

"He's really okay?" she asks, ignoring my threat.

If it wouldn't upset her more, I'd absolutely put a bullet in the idiot's brain. But now he owes me. He owes me a fucking life debt, and he'll pay that back by being her shadow for the rest of his borrowed life.

Digging my phone out of my pocket, I send a quick text. "He's fine, you'll see."

Setting my phone down, I cup her cheek. "Tell me what you need me to do."

Payton blinks those teary midnight eyes at me. "What do you mean?"

"Tell me what you need," I plead with her. "Tell me how to make this up to you. Tell me what you want, Sweet Girl. Tell me, and I'll do it. I'll do whatever it takes to keep you."

My heart is pounding in my chest, that underlying current of fear continues to plague me.

Payton raises a hand, placing it over mine on her cheek. "I want a big wedding."

My mouth opens, but no sound follows.

Beneath my palm, her cheek plumps in a small smile.

"Say that again," I rasp out.

"You already saved me. In so many ways." Her pained expression softens. "You don't need to do anything else, except keep loving me." My heart clenches so hard it feels like it might crumble. "And I'd like a big wedding dress. One of those puffy skirt ones from the reality shows. And flowers. Lots of flowers."

"So many flowers," I agree, closing my eyes, seeing it all exactly as she describes. "With Toto as a ring bearer."

As if on cue, there's a soft knock on the bedroom door.

"Come." I open my eyes and keep my arms around Payton, holding her in place.

The door cracks open and Payton gasps, seeing Robert's face in the doorway, banged up, but fine, as promised.

He inclines his head, then steps back, allowing an overexcited Toto to shove his way through the door before Robert pulls the door closed, leaving the three of us alone.

Toto's nails scratch across the floor before he launches himself onto the bed, wiggling against Payton's side.

"And a live band," I supply.

Payton nods, scratching Toto behind the ears when he drapes himself over my legs, his head at her hip. "And the best food. Too much of it."

"Of course." I kiss her forehead.

"Now let me ask you." I inhale her scent, the essence of her beauty filling me. "Payton Vawdrey, will you marry me?"

"Let me answer." She leans back, staring up into my love-filled gaze. "It was always going to be you."

Epilogue One
PAYTON

"WELL, I'D SAY HE'S LIKELY TO SWALLOW HIS TONGUE."
Aspen grins, sliding the delicate jeweled headband into my hair.
"And if he doesn't, I'll have my brother beat him up after the
ceremony."

I take her hand, my manicured nails shining a pale pink.
"Thank you." She rolls her eyes, but I don't let go. "Seriously,
thank you. For all of it."

In the six months since *the incident,* Aspen has become my
first true girlfriend.

It wasn't always smooth. At times I thought she might want
to shove me out a window. Or drop a house on me. But we spend
nearly every weekend together, now, either shopping and eating,
or coordinating the next large fundraiser she's a part of. And with
her help, and Nero's money, we've expanded two of the local
animal shelters, supplying them with quality food and installing
air conditioning to the kennel rooms.

"Quit thanking me and go get married." Aspen gives my hand
the quickest squeeze, which is basically a hug from her, before she
hurries out of the room.

Stepping back from the gilded full-length mirror, I do a final
twirl then head out of the bedroom.

As promised, I worked with our interior designer to *freshen up* the house, starting in our master suite.

We kept the chunky black four-poster bed but draped it in sheer gray fabric, giving it an ethereal feeling. That mixed with the yellow and white bedding, makes it the perfect place to curl up together. We covered the walls in a soft gray and gold wallpaper and replaced the chairs with high-back emerald-green velvet chairs so when the mood strikes for a late-night snack we can sit in comfort.

It's perfect. And we're slowly working our way through the rest of the house.

My heels clack on the steps as I head down the main staircase.

Robert's eyes widen and he lets out a whistle. "Well, I'll be."

As my personal bodyguard, he's also become one of my best friends. I know his constant nearness started under a threat to his life, but I like to think he's fond of me too. And I'm happy to have someone to walk me down the aisle.

When I reach the bottom, I stick my foot out from under the white skirt to show my sparkly red shoes.

They're a bit over the top paired with my princess ballgown, which is covered in hundreds of tiny silk flowers. But over the top is exactly what I wanted. Exactly what I never thought I'd have.

And even though our guest list is small, the most important people in our lives are here, and we get to share our love amongst friends.

Friends.

Robert hands me my bouquet and I squeeze the stems with shaky fingers. The red, yellow, and orange roses were Nero's only request. Said I should always smell like roses. And that I should always be surrounded by color. Because I'm his bright spot in every day.

When I sniffle, Robert shakes his head. "Don't start crying yet. At least wait until the boss has had a chance to look at you."

I blow out a breath and nod my head. "Okay. I'm ready."

NERO

I WASN'T READY.

I'll never be ready.

My chest expands with pride and love, and so much joy, as Payton walks down the petal-strewn aisle toward me.

I knew this would be one of my favorite memories of her, which is why I insisted on having it here, in our gardens. Because I'll walk out here every single day, for the rest of my life just to relive this moment.

Her dress. Her hair. The sparkles shining off every inch of her have nothing on the look in her eyes.

Pure adoration.

A love I don't deserve.

When she reaches me, I place my hand on her cheek. "You look fucking beautiful."

One tear drips from the corner of her eye even as I feel her smile under my touch.

"You look pretty handsome yourself," she whispers.

The preacher clears his throat, and Toto lets out a bark, but I've never been big on following the rules, so, while I have her, I press my mouth to hers. Sealing our promises with a kiss.

Epilogue Two

PAYTON

"This is, hands down, my favorite vacation we've been on," I tell Nero as we look across at the sunset.

With my head on his shoulder, I can feel him chuckle. "Really, Mrs. Nero? The Grand Canyon is better than our honeymoon in Belize?"

I still get flutters whenever someone calls me that, *Mrs. Nero*. Especially when it's him.

"Ornate beach vacations are so last year," I joke. "This"—I extend my arm out—"this is true magic."

One of the sun's rays catches on my wedding band, sending a riot of reflections off the thick circle of rubies. And I think of the engraving inside. *There's no place like home.*

Sliding off the bench, I lower myself to my knees in the grass in front of Nero.

"What are you doing?" He asks the question but his lids are lowered because he knows exactly what I'm doing.

Instead of answering, I press my palm over his rapidly hardening cock, the thin material of his athletic shorts hiding nothing.

"Park is still open, Baby. We might get caught."

I bat my lashes up at him, tugging down the band of his shorts until I'm able to grip his cock and pull it free. "We should probably be quick then, huh?"

Nero's jaw is working. He wants this. I know he does. But he does not want any of his men to see me with a dick in my mouth, even if it's his.

And I know he's going to say just that --bring up the security detail that's waiting just on the other side of the scruffy pines--so I stop his complaint by wrapping my lips around him.

"Jesus Christ," Nero hisses, his hand snapping out to grip the base of my ponytail.

I smile and his hips jerk.

"You think a blow job at one of the seven wonders of the world will make this my favorite vacation too?"

I nod my head, taking him deeper with the movement.

"Fuck." His cock pulses in my mouth. "Fuck, you're totally right."

Without warning me, Nero applies pressure to the back of my head. But I knew it was coming because I know what he likes, so I'd already relaxed my throat and released the tension on my neck.

When he presses down, I go all the way, taking him deep into my throat until my nose bumps against his abs.

"Shit!" He drags my head back up, his cock slipping free from my lips. "You okay--"

The expression on my face shows him just how okay I am.

"Goddamnit, I love you." Nero uses his hold on my hair to haul me up, slamming his mouth against mine for a clit-tingling kiss. His grip tightens and my entire body lights up as he guides me back down. "Time for you to swallow this dick, Baby. Let me have that throat, and then when we get back to the hotel, I'll fuck you til you pass out."

"Promise?" I grin, licking up his length.

"I'd never lie to you," Nero groans as he shoves my head back down, and I swallow him greedily while the sky explodes with color around us.

KING

About the Author

Like all her books, S.J. Tilly resides in the glorious state of Minnesota, where she was born and raised. To avoid the freezing cold winters, S.J. enjoys burying her head in books, whether to read them or write them or listen to them.

When she's not busy writing her contemporary smut, she can be found

lounging with her husband and their herd of rescue boxers. And when the weather

permits she loves putting her compost to use in the garden, pretending to know

what she's doing. The neighbors may not like the flowery mayhem of her yard,

but the bees sure do. And really, that's more important.

To stay up to date on all things Tilly, make sure to follow her on her

socials, and interact whenever you feel like it!

Don't forget to sign up for the newsletter https://sjtilly.com/newsletter

Links to everything on her website www.sjtilly.com

Acknowledgments

If you've made it this far, thank you from the bottom of my twisted heart.

I knew I wanted to venture into the dark, and Nero was the perfect guide. I hope you enjoyed the adventure, and I hope you were as grossed out during the "finger scene" as I was writing it.

Huge thank you to my mom, Karen. You gave me my first romance book. You helped me edit my first romance book. And here we are TEN books later, perfecting our routine. So thank you for the hours and hours of reading. And the hours of listening to me babble about plots. And for embracing some of the fucked up ideas that went into this book.

Thank you, Kerissa, for being such a good girl. xoxo Truly, you're the best. And I don't know where I'd be without your help and feedback and friendship.

Thank you, Brittni Van, for being you. And for being such a great editor. I'm so incredibly happy to know you.

Thank you, Ellie, for joining the Tilly bandwagon. We're a mess, but we're a hot mess, and I'm happy to have you aboard.

Thank you, Lori Jackson, for bringing Nero to life via hot guy covers and discreet covers, and for putting up with my chaotic brain.

Thank you, Mandi, for your constant support and phone calls.

Thank you, Mr. Tilly. I know you would probably rather do anything other than listen to me explain the plot of this book One More Time, but you sit through it anyway and I appreciate you.

Thank you to my sister, Lindsay - Goofhead, for always being excited about everything I write.

Thank you, G. Marie, Elaine Reed, and S.L. Astor for being such a great support group. We started with writing sprints, and we've become so much more.

Thank you, Cat Wynn, for listening to every voice memo I send you. And for letting me co-host the Tall Dark & Fictional podcast with you. (Subtle plug.)

Thank you, Mikayla, for being such a bright spot in my days and for reading Nero early, giving me all your reactions. If anyone wants to send her book mail, check out her Wishlist @lovemikaylaeve

Thank you, Stephanie and Liz, for being my eagle-eyed early arc readers. You take so much stress off my shoulders.

Thank you to my entire ARC team. I cannot thank you enough. Your energy, your encouragement, it's one of a kind, and I love you.

Thank you, Jen, for your work in promoting Nero, and over-all, in putting up with me.

Thank you to my agent, Katie, for working to get this book into the hands of foreign readers before it was even published.

Thank you, Dad, for telling your friends I write dirty books. You asked me if I put you in my acknowledgments, and here you are. Let's see when you find it. And thank you Roxie for surely reading this first!

Thank you, Ali, for reading Nero early and for just being an amazing human being.

Thank you to the rest of my family. I truly come from the best people. And that's why I'm able to be me. To write like me. And to be confident.

And, as always, my life wouldn't be what it is today if not for all of my amazing supporters.

Thank you, Banshees.

Thank you, Ginger and Kanani, Vegas was better because of you both.

Thank you, Annie--my OG--and Cici, for all your sweet words.

Thank you, Nikki, for your awesome videos and for letting me use your name for *this bitch*.

Thank you, Payton, for letting me steal your name for this book. It was perfect.

Thank you, Sam and Ashley, and Rachel, and B.J. and Suga dicks, I mean Dominique.

Thank you, Melinda and Chula and Karen, for your constant support.

Thank you, Other Karen and Anna and Betsy, for always cheering everything I do.

And thank you to all of the people I haven't named. I only have so much brain power left right now, and I know I'm missing so many special people. But please, trust me when I say, I appreciate you too. It's such a fucking honor to be able to write stories for you. And I'll keep doing it for as long as I can.

Until next time, in the words of my grandma, be good. But if you can't be good, have fun.

Also by S. J. Tilly

Alliance Series
Dark Mafia Romance

NERO

Payton

Running away from home at 17 wasn't easy. Let's face it though, nothing before, or in the ten years since, has ever been easy for me.

And I'm doing okay. Sorta. I just need to keep scraping by, living under the radar. Staying out of people's way, off people's minds.

So when a man walks through my open patio door, stepping boldly into my home and my life, I should be scared. Frightened. Terrified.

But I must be more broken than I realized, because I'm none of those things.

I'm intrigued.

And I'm wondering if the way to take control of my life is by giving in to him.

Nero

The first time I took a man's life, I knew there'd be no going back. No normal existence in the cards for me.

So instead of walking away, I climbed a mountain of bodies and created my own destiny. By forming The Alliance.

And I was fine with that. Content enough to carry on.

Until I stepped through those open doors and into her life.

I should've walked away. Should've gone right back out the door I came through. But I didn't.

And now her life is in danger.

But that's the thing about being a bad man. I'll happily paint the streets red to protect what's mine.

And Payton is mine. Whether she knows it or not.

KING

Okay, so, my bad for assuming the guy I was going on a date with *wasn't* married. And my bad for taking him to a friend's house for dinner, only to find out my friend is also friends with *his* wife. Because, in fact, he *is* married. And she happens to be at my friend's house because her husband was *busy working*.

Confused? So am I.

Unsurprisingly, my date's

wife is super angry about finding out that her husband is a cheating asshole.

Girl, I get it.

Then, to make matters

more convoluted, there is the man sitting next to my date's wife. A man named

King, who is apparently her brother, and who lives up to his name.

And since my *date*

is a two-timing prick, I'm not going to feel bad about drooling over King,

especially since I'll never see him again.

Or at least I don't plan to.

I plan to take an Uber to

the cheater's apartment to get my car keys.

I plan for it to be quick.

And if I had to list a

thousand possible outcomes... witnessing my date's murder, being kidnapped by his

killer, and then being forced to marry the super attractive but clearly

deranged crime lord, would not have been on my Bingo card.

But alas, here I am.

DOM

VAL

When I was nine, I went to my first funeral. Along with accepting my father's death, I had to accept new and awful truths I wasn't prepared for.

When I was nineteen, I went to my mother's funeral. We weren't close, but with her gone, I became more alone than ever before.

Sure, I have a half brother who runs The Alliance. And yeah, he's given me his protection — in the form of a bodyguard and chauffeur. But I don't have anyone that really knows me. No one to really love me.

Until I meet him. The man in the airport.

And when one chance meeting turns into something hotter, something more serious, I let myself believe that maybe he's the one. Maybe this man is the one who will finally save me from my loneliness. The one to give me the family I've always craved.

DOM

The Mafia is in my blood. It's what I do.

So when that blood is spilled and one funeral turns into three, drastic measures need to be taken.

And when this battle turns into a war, I'm going to need more men. More power.

I'm going to need The Alliance.

And I'll become a member. By any means necessary.

Sin Series
Romantic Suspense

Mr. Sin

I should have run the other way. Paid my tab and gone back to my room. But he was there. And he was... everything. I figured what's the harm in letting passion rule my decisions for one night? So what if he looks like the Devil in a suit. I'd be leaving in the morning. Flying home, back to my pleasant but predictable life. I'd never see him again.

Except I do. In the last place I expected. And now everything I've worked so hard for is in jeopardy.

We can't stop what we've started, but this is bigger than the two of us.

And when his past comes back to haunt him, love might not be enough to save me.

Sin Too

Beth

It started with tragedy.

And secrets.

Hidden truths that refused to stay buried have come out to chase me. Now I'm on the run, living under a blanket of constant fear, pretending to be someone I'm not. And if I'm not really me, how am I supposed to know what's real?

Angelo

Watch the girl.

It was supposed to be a simple assignment. But like everything else in this family, there's nothing simple about it. Not my task. Not her fake name. And not my feelings for her.

But Beth is mine now.

So when the monsters from her past come out to play, they'll have to get through me first.

Miss Sin

I'm so sick of watching the world spin by. Of letting people think I'm plain and boring, too afraid to just be myself.

Then I see *him*.

John.

He's strength and fury, and unapologetic.

He's everything I want. And everything I wish I was.

He won't want me, but that doesn't matter. The sight of him is all the inspiration I need to finally shatter this glass house I've built around myself.

Only he does want me. And when our worlds collide, details we can't see become tangled, twisting together, ensnaring us in an invisible trap.

When it all goes wrong, I don't know if I'll be able to break free of the chains binding us, or if I'll suffocate in the process.

Sleet Series
Sports Romantic Comedy

Sleet Kitten

There are a few things that life doesn't prepare you for. Like what to do when a super-hot guy catches you sneaking around in his basement. Or what to do when a mysterious package shows up with tickets to a hockey game, because apparently, he's a professional athlete. Or how to handle it when you get to the game and realize he's freaking famous since half of the 20,000 people in the stands are wearing his jersey.

I thought I was a well-adjusted adult, reasonably prepared for life. But one date with Jackson Wilder, a viral video, and a "I didn't know she was your mom" incident, and I'm suddenly questioning everything I thought I knew.

But he's fun. And great. And I think I might be falling for him. But I don't know if he's falling for me too, or if he's as much of a player off the ice as on.

Sleet Sugar

My friends have convinced me. No more hockey players.

With a dad who is the head coach for the Minnesota Sleet, it seemed like an easy decision.

My friends have also convinced me that the best way to boost my fragile self-esteem is through a one-night stand.

A dating app. A hotel bar. A sexy-as-hell man, who's sweet, and funny, and did I mention, sexy-as-hell... I fortified my courage and invited myself up to his room.

Assumptions. There's a rule about them.

I assumed he was passing through town. I assumed he was a businessman, or maybe an investor, or accountant, or literally anything other than a professional hockey player. I assumed I'd never see him again.

I assumed wrong.

Sleet Banshee

Mother-freaking hockey players. My friends found their happily-ever-afters with a couple of sweet, doting, over-the-top in-love athletes. They got nicknames like *Kitten* and *Sugar*. But me? I got stuck with a dickhead who riles me up on purpose and calls me *Banshee*. Yeah, he might have a voice made specifically for wet dreams. And he might have a body and face carved by the gods. And he might have a level of Alpha-hole that gets me all hot and bothered.

But when he presses my buttons, he presses ALL of my buttons. And I'm not the type of girl who takes things sitting down. And I only got caught on my knees that one time. In the museum.

But when one of my decisions gets one of my friends hurt... I can't stop blaming myself. And him.

Except he can't take a hint. And I can't keep my panties on.

Darling Series

Contemporary Small Town Romance

Smoky Darling

Elouise

I fell in love with Beckett when I was seven.

He broke my heart when I was fifteen.

When I was eighteen, I promised myself I'd forget about him.

And I did. For a dozen years.

But now he's back home. Here. In Darling Lake. And I don't know if I should give in to the temptation swirling between us or run the other way.

Beckett

She had a crush on me when she was a kid. But she was my brother's best friend's little sister. I didn't see her like that. And even if I had, she was too young. Our age difference was too great.

But now I'm back home. And she's here. And she's all the way grown up.

It wouldn't have worked back then. But I'll be damned if I won't get a taste of her now.

Latte Darling

I have a nice life—living in my hometown, owning the coffee shop I've worked at since I was 16.

It's comfortable.

On paper.

But I'm tired of doing everything by myself. Tired of being in charge of every decision in my life.

I want someone to lean on. Someone to spend time with. Sit with. Hug.

And I really don't want to go to my best friend's wedding alone.

So, I signed up for a dating app and agreed to meet with the first guy that messaged me.

And now here I am, at the bar.

Only it's not my date that just sat down in the chair across from me. It's his dad.

And holy hell, he's the definition of Silver Fox. If a Silver Fox can be thick as a house, have piercing blue eyes and tattoos from his neck down to his fingertips.

He's giving me Big Bad Wolf vibes. Only instead of running, I'm blushing. And he looks like he might just want to eat me whole.

Tilly World Holiday Novellas

Second Bite

When a holiday baking competition goes incredibly wrong. Or right...

Michael -

I'm starting to think I've been doing this for too long. The screaming fans. The constant media attention. The fat paychecks. None of it brings me the happiness I yearn for.

Yet here I am. Another year. Another holiday special. Another Christmas spent alone in a hotel room.

But then the lights go up. And I see *her*.

Alice -

It's an honor to be a contestant, I know that. But right now, it feels a little like punishment. Because any second, Chef Michael Kesso, the man I've been in love with for years, the man who doesn't even know I exist, is going to walk onto the set, and it will be a miracle if I don't pass out at the sight of him.

But the time for doubts is over. Because Second Bite is about to start - "in three... two... one..."

Made in the USA
Middletown, DE
16 March 2025

72751761R00210